SPARKS FLYING

Also by Kim Lakin:

Cyber Circus (2011)
Rise (2019)

SPARKS FLYING

The Collected Short Fiction of

Kim Lakin

NewCon Press
England

First edition, published in the UK April 2023
by NewCon Press
41 Wheatsheaf Road, Alconbury Weston, Cambs, PE28 4LF

NCP 299 (hardback)
NCP 300 (softback)

10 9 8 7 6 5 4 3 2 1

ISBN: 978-1-914953-44-6 (hardback)
978-1-914953-45-3 (softback)

Text layout by Ian Whates
Cover by Ian Whates and Kim Lakin,
utilising an image by Yabadene Belkacem

Contents:

Johnny and Emmie-Lou Get Married	7
Rotten Things	17
The Island of Peter Pandora	35
Field of the Dead	57
The Shadow Keeper	87
Deluge	103
The Wassailers Wedding	119
Divinity	123
Goblin	131
Asenath	153
The Harvest	189
Wanderlust	207
Before Hope	223
The Killing Fields	241
About the Author	253

For my family and friends. When I was all but ashes, you fanned the embers with love, patience, resilience and grace.

Thank you eternally.

Johnny And Emmie-Lou Get Married

First off we had to get to the church. Emmie-Lou in her Poodle skirt, tight sweater, bobby socks, and high tail. Me in thick-cuffed Levis, white vest, black hair – soaked and scooped in pomade – and a pair of devilish, twelve-inch creepers. Emmie-Lou's white dress was in the boot. *Don't get it creased, Johnny.* I wouldn't get it creased. Couldn't say the same for my shirt, crumpled up on the back seat of my Chevy Bel Air like a used pack of smokes. I never was one to waste energy on threads.

Billy revved his Daimler Dart, and, yeah, it had a dirty throat but that machine was wired. It might have been dark, but the gas lamps that lined the street lit up every inch. The engine had been cranked proud of the bonnet like a sprawling heart of chrome. Four silver pendulum arms rotated, appearing to drive a colossal tick tock movement connected to the drive shaft. Pipework wormed in amongst the gristle of the engine, or beanstalked over the roof. The boiler squatted up back in its studded metal jacket. Now and then, a rack of variegated piston valves let off bursts of steam.

I swallowed. Billy's Dart was one fat cat and Emmie-Lou was the cream.

Hell wasn't she! I eyeballed the dips, hips and lips of the Rocketeers' top doll, a paper shaker at Franklin High who wore team ribbons in her hair and was all but wed to Billy. Problem was Emmie-Lou didn't want what Billy was offering. She might've been born on the east side, which made her Rocketeer to the bone, but that didn't stop her from being real gone on a Fly. Real gone on me.

Except, in Dragsville, a Fly and a Rocketeer didn't go together. Each gang had its own part of town, way to fight, favoured machines and gene pool. Muddle the DNA and both sides took exception, the Flies by repossessing my glider wings and suckers, the Rocketeers by riding my thieving ass out of town. Or at least trying to. Truth was, I'd turn Jock before I'd abandon the blue-eyed baby riding beside me.

I shot Emmie-Lou a look made up of all the good stuff I felt inside. We'd been jacketed ever since we first spied each other in the school yard, her with a mouthful of Popsicle, me with a match hanging off my lip and a switchblade in my pocket. She'd flickered into view like the gasses streaming out of the open blower of my Chevy. Emmie-Lou; blackest hair, true-blue peepers, and a cupid's bow you could hook your mouth around and never let go of. For me, the deal was sealed there and then. As for Emmie-Lou, she'd stared right on back. I guess she must've liked what she saw.

Widening my nostrils, I sucked in the scent of her. Emmie-Lou had claws, curves, and a smell on her like cream doughnuts and summertime sweat – which was how she was two months gone, and why we were church bound. All I had to do was get us there, and whip Billy's ass in a race to Sinners' Square in the process.

Rocketeers caged us in on three sides. Behind us, the gang's elite were holed up in their Daimlers, Ac Aces, bullet-nosed Studebakers, and Nash-Healey's – coupés that gleamed with aluminium trim, rear-mounted water tanks, and every sort of billet. The remainder loitered on the sidewalk, or, to be exact, hovered above the concrete, mist shooting down from the twin pipes of their body-moulded backpacks. My one-time gang, the Flies, were nowhere to be seen. All that stood between me and oblivion was the girl riding shotgun at my side and the steel wings of my Chevy.

A doll in skin-tight pants and a cherry patterned halter sidled out to the middle of the strip. She peeled a red ribbon out of her high tail and raised her arm. The Dart worked up thick blowbacks of steam. I held the Chevy on a knife's edge.

The instant the doll let go of the ribbon, I mashed the loud pedal. Grit whipped off the Chevy's steelies despite its locker. Reflected in the rear view, flames splurged out of the exhaust. And then the torque had me, moulding my spine back into the seat. In those first few seconds, Billy was just a bad taste in an otherwise lip-smacking cocktail of speed and adrenalin. The strip ahead was deserted, could've stretched for miles for all I cared. Emmie-Lou was a sweet knot of breath at my side. The Chevy parted the air like silk.

Then Billy rumbled up to my left shoulder. Tucking in my chin, I glanced sideways to see Billy smiling back, his starched white collar angled like a fin.

My gaze flicked up to the rear view. Rocketeers buzzed at our back ends. That's when she spoke, my blue-eyed baby, my Emmie-Lou.

"Give 'em hell, Johnny." Leaning over, she touched her tongue's tip to my ear – just as Billy must've popped the seal on the steam feed to give his Dart a swollen belly. His vehicle shot ahead on a meaty belch of cooling air. Simultaneously, the Chevy lurched. Emmie-Lou's mouth ricocheted off my skull. She fell back into her seat as we were wrenched high at the bumper, the front two steelies screaming in futile rotation.

"Billy's got us on a leash." I bit down on the words as the chain connecting the two machines whipped taut. Billy snaked his Dart from one side of the strip to the other, and I'd a good idea why. Sooner or later, the momentum would build, allowing Billy to release the hook-up and send us slamming into any of the derelict warehouses that walled us in on either side. It was a dirty game, would've worked too if it hadn't been for the fresh hydraulics I'd installed two weeks earlier.

Glancing at Emmie-Lou, I registered the smear of blood where she'd hit her bottom lip on my hard head. My heart strings cramped.

"Fasten yourself in."

She did just that. I swiped a hand across the bank of switches in the dash.

Time folded as the front of the Chevy jackknifed, a 72 volt system working off the twelve batteries underpinning the lowrider's underbelly. The four corners of the vehicle shot up then dipped. I snapped more switches. The Chevy's entire body leapt skyward, pitched front then back, and juddered down on dumping cylinders. We left the ground every few seconds, our crazed bunny hop transforming that colossal machine into a thing of flesh and metal.

Somewhere along the line, Billy lost his hold on us. I dragged the Chevy's ass off a curb, showering the streets in sparks off the scrape plate.

"Okay, baby?"

Emmie-Lou was hot in the eyes. "You always were a wild ride, Johnny."

I pinned up a corner of my mouth. "About to get wilder." A swirling fish bowl of a water tank reflected in the rear view; I'd plumbed it into the stretched bumper to even out the weight. Cranking a lever, I drew on that reservoir now to power the twin guns at the Chevy's backend, flipped a switch and uncapped the cut-outs. The black shark roared.

Billy dove left then right. I aimed dead ahead. Billy's Dart had the pretty face of a pro street dragster but my Chevy had lungs on it. The black shell hunkered down on an open-wheel chassis, 34-inch skins bolted on either side while the rear wheels tucked in at the tail where the fibreglass had been tubbed to accommodate them. Downshifting, I yanked a steel handle in the roof, stoked the engine then floored it. We streaked past Billy's Daimler in an explosion of blue-black flames.

The street widened out into four lanes. No traffic, which was understandable; it was Rebel's Hour, those 60 minutes before dawn when the good folk snoozed like babies in their cradles and only cats and hobos inhabited the city. And the racers. I tucked in my shoulders as if to streamline everything that could create resistance. In Dragsville there was always some punk wanted to race you.

Right that second, it was a blonde flattop called Billy, who just happened to be one of the founding members of the Rocketeers. We'd never see eye to eye, Billy and me, and not just because his crew terrorised the neighbourhood, flying in at unlatched windows to steal a honey or a wallet, or dumping fistfuls of nails onto the streets below, a helluva slice of rain. No, the truth of it was that Billy and I were the bovver boys of our tribes, destined to clash skulls. But while we were renegades, I'd strayed that bit too far for the Flies. Now I was on my own.

Billy shifted in real close; if I hadn't got chrome nerf bars mounted wide either side of the Chevy's skirts, he'd have scuffed me up good. As it was, I kept my eyes on the cool grey slip of road and the clock tower of the church as it peeled into view.

"You ain't got Billy licked till we're wed, Johnny." Emmie-Lou stated, breathless and wide-eyed.

"I know, baby. He'll never stop hammering us 'til that band of gold's wrapped around your finger. But don't doubt me now, Emmie-Lou."

"Never could, never would," she smouldered, but I caught a glint of fear in her eyes.

She was right to be spooked. Billy had found his speed again, elbowing in as we turned off 99th Street and into Sinner's Square. The track narrowed, our machines swerving in to buddy up on the Inner Circular. In that same instant, something slam-dunked the Chevy's roof, prompting my best girl to throw up her hands like a scream queen. I pinched my eyes. A second clang reverberated, shaking my nerve; it sounded like the fist of an iron man. Then I heard the hiss of steam, not the piped flux that powered the stomach of my machine, but a rent in its mechanism… or, to be specific, a crack in the squat, rear-mounted boiler. I rapped the Speedo with my knuckles. Five miniature dials whirred and continued to lose momentum. One glance at the rear view confirmed the worst of it; the boiler was weeping hot green water onto the road, the misted tank starting to clear as it cooled to reveal one hell of a splinter.

It was the third strike which shook me back to my fighting best. I drew wide, sucking in the belly of the Chevy to ease up onto the sidewalk and narrowly avoid the stalks of the gas lights. Glancing over, I saw a hammer arm wielding a tremendous steel wrecking ball at the rear of the Dart. How the weight of the thing didn't roll that coupé was anyone's guess, but Billy had always been the physicist. Meanwhile, I was just a grease monkey… I was also the better driver. There was one chance and one chance only to end the thing well, at least for me and Emmie-Lou. I crushed the brake. Cranking the suicide knob hard to the right, I swung the Chevy between two gas lights and back out onto the track immediately in the shadow of the Dart. I caught Billy's face ghosting his rear view. No two eyes had ever shone as cold.

"Gonna ride your back, Billy," I shot beneath my breath. My fingers swept the bank of switches at the dash, closed around and depressed a lever by my thigh. A final blast of steam punched in to fire up the hydraulics. The front two corners of the Chevy dipped way low. Then we kicked off a full two metres clear of the strip, stomachs tumbling, blood roaring in our skulls.

The landing was sweet and tough by equal measure; sweet to feel the reverb as the Chevy hit the Dart hard across the shoulders, steelies revving off the wide-bottomed boiler to send us flying out over Billy's head to crash down out in front; tough because I heard the stunt take its toll on the ride that had cost me three years working the pumps at Mickey's Garage. I flicked the steering, then hit it hard to the left, the Chevy clawing its way into a bootlegger and coming to rest alongside the church door. The Dart slammed in hard to the black shark's trunk. Steam filled the air like a pea souper.

I leant across and unbucked Emmie-Lou's seat belt.

"Think you can run now, Emmie-Lou?"

"Sure thing, Johnny."

"Then grab that pretty frock of yours and let's get us to a preacher."

"Just one problem, Johnny." Emmie-Lou's face drained. "Billy's at the window and he's touting a blade."

Nothing to worry about, my blue-eyed baby. Let me deal with the bad dog at the door. Let me take the knife for you. Let me carry the weight. Out loud, I said, "So Billy's not gonna give it up till blood's spilt. Okay then."

Emmie-Lou's hand was a branding iron at my forearm. I smiled at her with my eyes, then cranked the door handle, slid out a boot, crunched down on a stone as I rose, and eased out. "Get dressed," I said last thing and shut Emmie-Lou in.

Billy was fired up. Spit escaped out a corner of his mouth as he breathed hard. His eyes stayed cold, though. He rocked side to side on spread feet, one hand out for balance, the other clenching the blade. I kept my silverware hid in my palm; I trusted the catch to spring open inside a second. It'd been tripped enough times to keep it fit for purpose.

"Least you didn't end up in the weeds, Billy." I fixed on him grimly. "What's more, I ain't hunting pink slips. Dart's yours, and to pay the necessary, it's a helluva blower. But my Chevy won the race fair and square. Time for you and me to part ways."

"And Emmie-Lou?" Billy tugged on his collar, its stiffness etched on his face.

"Knocked up. Part Fly, part Rocketeer, our rug rat's gonna be a mutant by both gang's standards, a kid who can't fit, no way no how." I eased back against the still-warm Chevy, cocked my head and squinted at Billy. I squeezed out a drop of true feeling. "I'd give up my pink slips for that runt, for its blue-eyed mamma too."

In those last few moments between end of Rebel's Hour and dawn, Billy squinted over, the smallest trace of understanding at his lips. The seed of a smile grew up at the edges, and I saw then that it was anything but friendly. I was suddenly aware of the dark shapes of a hundred or more Rocketeers' machines at my back, their engines idling. The occasional spurt of steam was a bleak reminder of the gang members hovering nearby. I tensed my hand around the blade. Billy kept on smiling.

Emmie-Lou startled the pair of us. The door handle clunked and she started to emerge, white silk frothing at her ankles. I glanced at her with a blaze of yearning, just as Billy stepped forward and slid in the knife.

For an instant, she was soft, doused in scent and yielding. Then the blood began to seep through her dress. My flesh felt as if it were scorched off my bones. Devil's mercy, the ache! So much gut wrenching pain as my girl stumbled backwards from both Billy and me, and up onto the church steps where a preacher stood, dressed head to toe in black and condemnation. He caught Emmie-Lou as she fell, manoeuvred the both of them down onto the steps and sat, cradling her head like a child's.

I turned towards the Chevy. Staring at my reflection in the driver side window, I contemplated who was real that instant, the torn man on the sidewalk or the two-dimensional figure in the glass. A second later, I spun around, blade unsheathed.

The slash to Billy's throat was deep and neat, designed to drain life quickly. He made a motion as if to come for me, but I was already striding away. Billy was done for. He just didn't realise it yet.

Dawn stripped the layers of night from the sky. I fell to my knees on the first step. It was more than I dared do to disturb Emmie-Lou, cradled safely as she was in the arms of a better man. Outta the corner of my eye, I registered Billy stagger in my direction before he fell face forward, his blood greasing the strip like a skid mark. The air was thick with noise as the Rocketeers flocked.

No matter. If there was no Emmie-Lou, I'd slip the blade between my own ribs.

"Johnny," she whispered.

I leant in, trembling.

"It's not over 'til we're wed."

Agony dug in at my forehead. "They're coming for me, Emmie-Lou. There ain't time."

"You promised, Johnny. You, me, and the babe. Said together we're gonna see this jacked up world reborn."

Her words were an adrenalin shot to the heart. I stood up. "Start reading, preacher."

The man glanced at me. My expression must've been crazed enough to convince him.

"Dearly beloved. We are gathered here today…" His voice was a dark scrape of sound.

I met Emmie-Lou's gaze. She seemed less substantial then, like a figure cut from burnout and reminding me of how she'd looked on the day that we first met.

"Do you take this woman…"

"Hell, yeah!" *I'd try my best, Emmie-Lou.* But there'd be no reaching the end of this marriage service for me. Scaring my mind with her fading image, I turned back around to face the street.

In their slim-cut suits, white and goolish green starched shirts, Chelsea boots, and steam-powered backpacks, the Rocketeers edged in, the gleam of hatred in their eyeballs. Blades flicked out from palms and pockets. Time bled away. I was breathing stolen air.

It was a stiff metallic crunch followed by the hiss of ebbing pressure in miniaturised hydraulics that alerted me to the swarm overhead. They came now, a thousand Flies, tumbling down from the bell tower in zigzagging, jagged motion. I watched them punch the long iron candy canes of their suckers hard against the brick, depress levers in each palm to release the gas, then freefall. I remembered that great rush of air and disconnection from the earth, and it flooded me with awe and sorrow.

Having pleated their suckers into half-a-metre long cylinders stored at their backs, other hundreds of Flies blackened the skies. Landing on the sidewalk in-between me and the hordes of Rocketeers, the gang members lowered their arms, concertinaed their canvas glider wings into the back pouch in their leather, and drew out their suckers from the sheaths at their spines. They whipped the skull-crushing iron canes out to their full extension; steam oozed from the tips.

I sat down as Emmie-Lou said, "I do." Retrieving the band of gold from a jeans' pocket, I slipped it onto her finger. Then I scooped her out of the preacher's arms and pressed her body hard to mine to stem her wound.

Flames of hazy sunlight filled the streets. All around us, two gangs slugged it out for control of the strips in Dragsville. Inside my best girl, a babe kept on growing in the muddied image of a Rocketeer and a Fly.

~*~

To me, there are few things more exhilarating than the smell of scorched tyres and petrol fumes. My love of hotrods – in particular, bashed up and bruised rat rods – was sparked by an interest in 1950s Americana and the rockabilly music scene. I've also always wanted to write my version of *Romeo and Juliet/Westside Story*. In "Johnny and Emmie-Lou Get Married", I found my star-crossed lovers, a pair of rival gangs in the Flies and the Rocketeers, and my take on a bitter-sweet ending. Really, though, the star of this story is a blistering hotrod race through deserted city streets at Rebel's Hour.

Rotten Things

"One minute there ain't nothing there but dirt, the next, there it is. A house! Painted yellow as a warbler bird. Got a skinny door up front, like one eye peeping out on the world. There's a porch too, with a red roof, and the whole thing's built long, each room bolted to the last. And that's about the size of it. I'm telling you, Uncle Joe, that house ain't like nothing else I ever did see."

Edmée's so busy describing a strange house that's materialised out of the swamp overnight that she misses the warning signs. Bellyful of whiskey, Uncle Joe pushes off the couch and towers over her before she's had time to take a breath.

"What're you doing wasting time out on Cemetery Road, Edmée Romero?" he slurs. "I told you to get them papers and tobacco and get back on home. Now I'm hearing how you got distracted by a whole lotta nothing and trying to shovel that shit as truth."

"I only got a glance while passing." Edmée knows it doesn't help to defend herself, but she can't help it. As her momma used to say, 'Someday all this backtalking will get you in hot water, Edmée Romero!'

Seems today's that day as Uncle Joe grabs her by the dress collar, yanking her up so high her toes skim the ground. He brings her in close to his bag-of-skin face. His eyes are urine-coloured. "You get on my last nerve." He cranes his head over a shoulder. "I'm done telling the girl to do as she's told!" he shouts as Edmée kicks and gurgles, trying to catch her breath.

"Toss her in the canal with the mudbugs and the gators!" calls back Aunt Hailey from the kitchen in that deadpan way which says she couldn't care less if her boyfriend Joe throttles the life from her niece, just as long as they're both quiet before she settles opposite the TV for her *Maury* reruns.

In the end, Uncle Joe lets go just before Edmée blacks out. He leaves her gasping on the stained carpet while Jackal, the Labrador retriever driven half-wild with beatings, fusses about and tries to lick her face. A new kick to the dog's backside sends it skittering through the fly-screen door leading to the backyard and down to the water.

Edmée goes to follow the dog on her hands and knees. But Uncle Joe hasn't finished with her. In fact, judging by the tightness of his jaw, he's only just warming up. Edmée knows she can't fight a grown man, especially not one who's built like a bull. Likewise, she can't appeal to her aunt, low on wits and high on oxy on account of an ulcered leg.

Lacking options, Edmée tries out the gappy smile that always prompts Mrs O'Lay, the preacher's wife, and her church ladies to fuss and pinch her cheeks and 'want to eat her up with cornbread and gravy'. Uncle Joe isn't so keen on smiling. He grabs Edmée by the wrist and shakes her like a sack of red beans.

'There ain't nothing good about a stranger rolling in from outta nowhere and thinking to take up residence. Reminds me of your dead momma, turning up like an ill wind, shaking you off her skirts and expecting others to raise you!"

"When she was pregnant, that no-good sister of mine got stared at by a handicap negress." Aunt Hailey comes in from the kitchen. She's got fresh highlights and the buttons done up wrong on her blouse like she's touting for business.

"Hear that, girl? You were cursed even before you were born!" Uncle Joe gives a loud hoot. "No wonder your momma didn't bother getting you baptised!"

Aunt Hailey drags on her cigarette. "A child that ain't been baptised and pokes mischief every which way it can? That child is a Lutin. My granddaddy used to tell tales of how them bad spirits would play up and cut the fishing line, break the crawfish baskets, and suck all the life outta the swamp so that dead things rise." She narrows her eyes through the exhaled smoke. "Is that what you are, Edmée? A Lutin? Goddamn devil spawn."

"'Aint my fault Momma went and died!" Edmée cries, but she's shushed with a backhander. The impact makes her brain rattle in her skull.

"Shut yer mouth, girl!" Uncle Joe looks ready to strike her a second time.

"Yeah, shut yer mouth!" Joe's daughter, Brandy, stands in the doorway, hands in the bib of her dirty dungarees, chewing a wad of gum like her jaw's spring-loaded. There's two years between her and nine-year-old Edmée, close enough in age to make her despise her younger kin.

"Gonna put her in the swamp then and stop her chattering? You've been threatening it long enough!" Aunt Hailey sinks into the couch. Her pencilled eyebrows dance as she drips ash.

"Make her eat maggots again, Pa!" Brandy runs to the kitchen. Pretty soon, she can be heard rooting through the garbage can.

Edmée drowns out the world around her. In place of the nutty rubber taste of maggots, she imagines a great tin bath set over BBQ coals, the salt scent of boiling crawfish and the sunshine flavours of buttered corn.

But Uncle Joe doesn't want to feed her maggots. He's after bigger thrills. "Say, Hailey. That big old alligator still hiding out beneath the house?"

"Yeah, Daddy." (Aunt Hailey's name for him when the bedroom door's shut and the trailer shudders.)

"Gonna feed her to the gator, Pa?" Brandy runs back in and holds her hands in the air like she's calling down the moon.

Edmée's scared to her bone marrow. "But I got your smokes!"

Uncle Joe isn't listening. He hoists Edmée over a shoulder and carries her out of the swing door. Aunt Hailey calls after them, "I'm watching my show now!" while Brandy pushes past on her way down the steps to where Jackal's whining with nervous excitement.

"Get!" Uncle Joe threatens a kick and sends the dog slinking away on its belly. He nods to a broom resting against the steps. "Poke that gator awake, Brandy."

Grinning, Brandy grabs hold of the bristle end and uses the pole of the broom to poke about under the trailer. All the while, Edmée's kicking and screaming until she hears a throaty hiss near the spot Brandy's worrying at.

"I'll be seeing you, Edmée Romero!" Uncle Joe bends down and sends her flying out under the trailer like unrolling a rug.

Tossed in amongst the pepperweed and the vines, Edmée can't breathe through terror. Stillness stretches, thin as a strand of

Brandy's gum. Then a huge, fanged shape rushes from the dark and envelopes her in the breath of rotten things.

Marie St Angel's washing the blood from her hands when the cry rings through her. A child's, she decides. Not an infant or an adolescent, but an age between. Holding her hands up in front of her face, she wriggles heavily ringed fingers and homes in on the sound.

"I hear yer," she tells the spirit, and quickly elbows aside the chopping board with its dead rooster. Opening the kitchen cupboards, she roots through her emporium of herbs and spices and bone bits. Taking down what she needs, she measures out handfuls, capfuls and pinches into a mortar bowl and grinds the ingredients with the pestle.

"Sin on skin. A slow rub of harm. Three of them to be hollowed out and fed to Papa Ghede."

She dips five fingers into the mortar bowl, strokes the herb rub across the hollow at the base of her throat and smears it into the hair clinging at her shoulders in thick serpentine coils. The smell fills her nostrils, fresh as grass, muddy as brine, taking her mind to the depths of the bayou.

"Rise up, child," she whispers. "Rise up and follow ma voice."

Out in the depths of the Louisiana swamp, Edmée opens her eyes to a surging depth of cold. *I'm blind,* she thinks as the world stays black. *The devil's sucked the sight right outta me!* But then she realises it's inky water she's swallowed up in.

I've gotta get free. I've gotta get free!

She kicks out with her feet and use her hands as paddles. Grasses weave around her shoulders and she battles to fight free. The darkness pales as she rises up, up, until all above is rippling silver.

She surfaces at last, spluttering and gasping.

The blue-black bayou ripples all around her. Overhead, the moon is a vast freshwater pearl.

Edmée's limbs are stiff as she fights her way to the canal bank. Under her feet, the marsh grasses are slippery as worms. The ground, when she finds it, sinks and clogs between her toes. She drags herself ashore and collapses in the dirt.

How did I end up in the water? Holding a slim, algaed arm up to the moonlight, Edmée tries to remember her own name. *I'm nameless*, she thinks, and rather than lost, she just feels empty, as if scooped out with a spoon. The sweltering night builds around her and she gets to her feet, which are the same greenish hue as her arms. Her clothes are threaded with swamp moss and tiny fish. She goes to flick one away at her neckline - and feels a ring of rough dips. Bitemarks? Before she can dwell on the thought further, she feels a voice rise up within her, filling her up on the inside until there is no emptiness left.

'Come to me,' says the voice.

Edmée turns towards inland and shuffles forward.

The only thing to do is take it real slow; Marie knows this from experience. Spirits aren't fond of being rushed, especially new-borns. They get twitchy and confused. Too prone to dwell in the 'was' instead of moving to the 'now.'

Marie sits in the old rocker on her porch, rifle resting across her knees. Beyond the steps, a field of grass stretches down to the glistening bayou. She listens as the sweet gum, elm, sycamore and cottonwood creak and moan, and the cypresses sway their medusa manes of Spanish moss. She hears the wild grapes, the trumpet creepers and all the ferns, lilies, irises and hyacinths whisper. She's lulled by the bark of frogs and hiss of alligators and the lone call of a night heron. And underneath the hullabaloo, she hears the spirits start to wake. They sense she is open to them; Marie knows that from experience. Her task now is to sift through the noise and find the one she wants.

Marie has always been happy to guide an uneasy spirit. She just wishes it didn't have to involve unearthing every other dead wanderer inside the locale! The spirit Marie's after is oozing suffering and rage, she's already plucked a thick ribbon of the stuff out the air and stored it in a mason jar.

She pats her rifle. The spirits are liable to manifest as zombies since she's baited them with the *Song of Solomon* read aloud from a

King James bible. There's also the herb rub at her throat and hair, and a bottle of perfumed Florida water – the latter for Papa Ghede, just in case that psychopomp decides to swoop in and take the newborn for himself. Marie catches the whites of his eyes out the corner of hers and rocks harder in her chair to keep him between the worlds of the living and the dead.

"I'll call yer later, Papa," she tells him. "First, I need la luna to shine down and the child to come. I need to even out the scales of balance, father, yer know this."

Moonlight fills the vista as they come from the marshland and the boggy shallows of the river – dripping skeletons that shudder and lurch, dusty corpses escaped the over-ground crypts, even a solitary infant in an unbuttoned romper which toddles out of the water in top-heavy rushes of movement. The spirts are eager to appeal to her – they want forgiveness, explanations, deliverance, even divinity. Marie senses all of their needs as the floorboards creak under her rocking chair.

Soon enough, she's forced to her feet. Some ghosts rest easy; others like to feast on the living and a soul raiser like Marie's bound to smell good.

Jaw flapping, eye on a thread, the nearest ghoul is beat up and hungry. Resting the butt of the rifle against a shoulder, Marie squeezes up an eye and pulls the trigger. The ghost catches a face full of rock salt and turns into grave sludge. Next up is the infant. Face puffed grey, eyes white and roaming, it toddles towards the porch steps at a rapid rate. Marie takes a shot and the body bursts like a blood blister.

"Where are you, child?" Griping the necklaces of bead and bone at her neck, Marie senses the newcomer very close now. A few more pot-shots from the porch and she finds her - a zombie girl, walking on peg legs and already ravaged by her short time in the canal.

"Welcome, child." Marie indicates the rocking chair. "Sit."

In stilting movements, the decaying young thing makes it to the rocker and collapses back into it. Meanwhile, having landed the fish she wants, Marie picks up the mortar bowl of herb rub and a flickering white candle in its tall jar. She climbs down to the bottom step of the porch, where the rest of the swamp crawlers are shuffling closer.

"Goodnight all. Rest awhile again." Marie holds up the candle and sprinkles the herb rub over the flame which blazes gold then dies back.

When she looks past the smoking wick, the ghosts are gone. All but the green-skinned girl sitting in Marie's rocker.

Edmée is ushered inside the kitchen of a strange house. She worries at a chip of memory like a sore. Words niggle. 'Painted yellow as a warbler bird!'... 'That house ain't like nothing I ever did see...'

"I'm Marie St Angel. Now drink." The woman puts down a glass of muddy water on the table. The water tastes bitter, but Edmée drains the glass and wipes the back of her hand across her mouth.

"It don't taste good, but that's the vinegar. Gotta have you thinking clearly, child. Gotta wash them swamp juices outta your brain." Marie grins, showing shiny black teeth. Gathering up her colourful skirts – a contrast to her white shirt and white mop cap – and chinking with all jewellery strung about her, she takes a seat on the opposite side of the table. "No surprise you're thirsty! Death'll do that to you, especially if you don't know how to move forward."

Edmée parts her lips. What comes out is a dribble of swamp water and a dry croak.

"So I'm gonna tell you what we do. First, you gotta reabsorb these memories as infected the air. Oh, I know they're nasty, but you gotta face them."

Marie has Edmée follow her out the kitchen, through the bedroom, and into a parlour – all the rooms leading into one another. There's not much to the room - a bald velvet couch, a dusty bureau, a rag-rug on dark floorboards and blackout curtains at the windows either side.

"Sit, child," she tells Edmée again, who sits stiffly on the smoke scented couch and watches as the witch woman roots around in the bureau and retrieves a black drawstring pouch the size of her palm. Into it, Marie feeds a stone which she declares was "fished out the swamp", a sliver of wood "from the belly of a 500-year-old cypress felled by a storm", a dried up, gnarly toe from a chicken foot, and something invisible she shakes from a mason jar and calls "the ribbon of rage I caught off you earlier, child." She pulls the drawstring tight.

Marie lights a yellow candle – "To reveal hidden truth," – and a black candle – "To shine a light on negativity." She turns around, gris-gris bag in one hand, hochet rattle in the other.

"Time to call on the Voodoo Loa and wake back up, child. And if Papa Ghede ask you to go with him before we is done, bind him with a bite of this." She tosses an apple to Edmée, who fails to catch it. As the fruit rolls across the floor, Marie shakes the gourd rattle and starts to dance in shuffling steps. Under candlelight, she roils her glistening brown stomach and pants and moans in appeal.

Suddenly, she darts forward and thrusts the gris-gris bag into Edmée's mouth.

The swamp girl swallows instinctively.

"Now you've got your mojo back!" Marie cries, eyes lurid as the mercurial moon.

The first thing Edmée does is scream. Loud and long as if the alligator's still got its jaws clamped at her throat. She remembers the pain – so much pain! – as the creature performed its death rolls and she was crushed.

Three more things Edmée recalls from her final moments. The first is Brandy making a *hoo-hoo* sound of delight while peeking under the trailer. The second is her aunt, yawping from above, "You went and did it then, Daddy?" The third is Uncle Joe bellowing, "How do you like that, Edmée Romero? Bet you don't feel like time wasting now, huh?"

After had come silence – scratchy and uncomfortable – until something brought her back around beneath the duckweed and cattails in the water.

"Edmée Romero," she says in a voice thickened by the marsh salts in which she's embalmed.

The witch's face looms in. "That your name, child? Edmée?"

"Are you Mami Wata?" Edmée has a sudden memory of her mother praying to the deity to deliver her from debt.

"Quite an imagination you got there, Edmée. I'm Marie St Angel, remember? I'm a conduit for the Loa, them sacred mystères as sit between the supreme creator and mankind. Sometimes I'm a soul raiser, bringing back the dead as need revenge. But tell me, child. Who else do you see in this room?"

"A man," says Edmée. Words felt like clay in her mouth. "Got a skull instead of a face." She narrows her eyes, which feel a-swim, and takes in the man standing by the bureau. "Hat, waistcoat, gold buttons, black coat down to his knees like he's playing trumpet at a funeral."

"Quick!" Marie's eyes flick off to the corners of the room. "Throw him the apple!"

It takes Edmée some scrambling about on her mildewey limbs, but she picks up the apple and tosses it to the man.

Papa Ghede snatches the fruit out of the air, grins and takes a bite.

"Candlelight will show us the way. And this smoke." Marie dances a burning bundle of herbs before the girl's face. "Tell me, child. Who's wronged you?"

"Aunt Hailey," says the girl, still zombie but with a speck of life thanks to the gris-gris bag in her stomach. "I did try to love her, but she gone and fed me to that man."

"Man?"

"Uncle Joe. Meanest son of a bitch I ever did meet."

"Any other?" Marie pushes her face through the smoke.

"Brandy. She's a bit more grown than me, but got a whole lotta rot where her heart ought to be, maybe on account of her daddy."

Marie shows her teeth, black lacquered where she paints them with vinegar, iron and vegetable tannins so spirits can't see her whispering magic. "So, you go pay them a visit, Edmée Romero. Get your spirit virgin-clean before Papa Ghede takes you to them crossroads we all visit in the end."

The way Edmée starts jerking suggests she's not keen on visiting her murderers.

Marie exhales noisily. "You need to make them pay, no matter how much it ails you. There's a balance to keep in check, you know that I'm certain. But I agree you might need a bit of help."

From the bureau, Marie fetches new tools – a generous pour of whiskey in a glass and a fistful of cotton wool. "Put this in your nose." She tears off scraps of cotton wool and offers them up. "Like we're laying out the dead."

Wordlessly, the girl takes the white scraps and plugs her nose.

Marie downs the whiskey, riding out the burn before she lights a cigar and drags on it heavily, enveloping them both in piquant smoke.

"Now Papa Ghede is busy chewing on his apple, we need to ask a favour of a second of his kin. Baron Samedi will guide your hand and get the job done." She shows her black teeth. "Just don't get seduced by his power. The Baron is fond of a young soul, specially them as have been murdered."

Edmée's listening, but most of all she is smiling at the laughing, dancing man who's appeared in the room. The Baron dances away and she follows, making her way to the front door. With heavy steps, she lets the Baron lead her along the bank of the bayou – through the tufted grass and flat weed, around the black willow and larch where the bull frogs and pig frogs and turtles belch and paddle – and then out through the wild sugar cane. It is a good hour before they arrive at the battered old trailer in the swamp's depths. As the Baron gestures she should take the lead, Edmée makes out the flickering lights of the television and, beneath the front steps to the trailer, a pair of gleaming golden eyes.

Brandy's sat cross-legged in her room. KSMB's on the radio and she's got an open bag of Zapp's potato chips between her legs. Every so often, she dives a hand into the bag and throws a handful of chips into her mouth.

She's feeling smug that Edmée's dead. When Brandy's Pa had started dating Hailey, there'd been a time when she and Edmée weren't far off being friends. For a while, she'd even let Edmée come frogging. While her father worked the power till, Edmée tracked any activity beyond the boat with the spotlight and Brandy leaned over the side and grabbed those floating bull frogs gone rigid on account of the light, shoving them into a wet burlap sack to keep them clean until morning.

It hadn't taken Brandy long to start wishing it was Edmée she was stuffing into that sack. One night, the light went out and Edmée fell forward, knocking Brandy over the side of the boat. For what had felt like the longest time, Brandy found herself kicking against the slimy water of the wetlands and the dead fear of a bite from an alligator or a water moccasin. Her father spent his time hollering at Edmée to sit still and Brandy to be quiet as his big hand reached over and pulled her back aboard, dripping and stinking like a bowl of road ditch crawfish. She'd gone for Edmée, punching and kicking while her father turned the light back on and watched a while before coming between them. Brandy had been left with a scar down one cheek where she'd sliced it open when dragged back aboard and a violent hatred for the scrawny girl crowbarred into her life.

Cramming in a fresh mouthful of chips, Brandy nods and thinks, *Yeah, I sure am glad to see the back of that fool!*

It's a strange sound that makes Brandy frown and get to her feet. There's an old air conditioning unit in the bottom half of her bedroom window, duct-taped to the trailer's outside wall. The unit rattles, but Brandy's grateful for it in the raw heat. Now she leans close and listening in. The noise is oddly familiar, and she gets a flashback – of Edmée's little dry breaths as the girl lay dying after the alligator decided she wasn't worth the trouble and retreated further under the trailer.

Brandy runs back as the unit shunts forward. Next moment, it crashes down onto the floor and something's crawling through the gap, rapid as a spider. Before Brandy gets a chance to cry out, the figure is across the room in a rush of jittering limbs. An icy hand covers Brandy's nose and mouth, stifling her attempt to cry out. In a long mirror tacked to her wardrobe door, Brandy sees the ghoul and almost chokes on her terror. Edmée's mouldered green arms have her gripped.

"Gator's awake," says the ghoul girl. Her jaw stretches unnaturally wide, exposing a mouth packed full of curled teeth.

Brandy's scream dies in her throat as Edmée bites down.

*

In the parlour of her cottage, Marie blows out the first of three candles. She senses Papa Ghede at her shoulder, still working his way through the apple.

Sprawled on the couch, Aunt Hailey hears some kind of noise. Only trouble is she can't bring herself to care. Her dealer Billy-O had stopped by earlier, leaving behind a vial of white rocks and taking with him almost all of her welfare. Toking off the pipe, Hailey holds the smoke in her lungs, longing for the butterfly flutter of her very first hit months earlier. The loss of that euphoria makes her cry a little – real tears that flow freely when she exhales and the beautiful wave hits. Joe's been warning her to lay off, driving home the message with a fist to the kidneys. Mostly though, he lets her be on account of her festering leg. What he doesn't see is a deeper pain that comes from finding her sister face down in a pool of her own vomit a year earlier while Edmée crouched nearby, wailing about her momma being dead. There'd been no choice but to take the girl in. After a while though, Edmée's natural cheer and resemblance to the dead sister who OD'd out of Hailey's own stash had made her hate the girl.

"Made it too easy on Joe to kill you!" she mutters, froth working up at the corners of her mouth. "Should have stayed quiet more often. Should have stopped all that yabbering."

Through the chemical haze, she sees Edmée standing in the doorway – a twisted daydream of the child as was. Thin watery strips of hair cling to Edmée's cheekbones, which are covered with the thinnest smear of green skin so that the skull pushes through.

So repulsive is the mirage that Hailey's own skin crawls. The thing looks horrifyingly real! Smells real too. Stench of opened bowels, brine and putrefying flesh.

"Edmée?" Hailey's mouth pop-pops. "I'm seeing monsters!" She dances the flame of her lighter over the bowl of the pipe and takes a fresh hit to stave off the nightmare. "You just never did know when to quit," she says when Edmée doesn't go anywhere.

When the ghoul smashes the pipe from her hand and pushes her down onto the couch, Hailey can't piece together what's happening.

How can she be mauled by a hallucination? Yet here she is, thrashing about like she's a cheerleader again, trying to fight off a horny jock. The dead girl's just so heavy and so strong, like there's lead in her bones!

"Get offa me! Get off!" Hailey's pinned down and the ghoul leans over, that awful face hovering above from hers. "We're kin, Edmée," she whimpers, and a final lie, "I told Joe to leave you be."

Edmée cocks her head, the misty gel of her eyes reflecting Hailey blubbering below. A wet hand reaches for Hailey's mouth and squeezes until the woman's tongue pokes out.

"Stop the yabbering," says the ghoul, baring bloody teeth.

After Hailey's tongue is torn out, Edmée starts in on the rest of her.

Marie blows out the second candle while, riding along with Edmée, the Baron's having a high old time. He's gleeful to play witness to the killing. Mankind's never been fond of behaving and the fact makes him jitterbug on the bones of the ancestors. And the best of the circumstance is Marie St Angel, that Voodoo queen with the drifting house and niggling need to help murdered souls right the scales, was the one to summon him.

Not that the girl needs his help any! She's doing just fine on her own, as if murder comes natural.

Joe's exiting the backwoods of his property. Over one shoulder, he's got a pair of dead armadillos caught in the wooden traps he'd set up specially for the vermin. He doesn't like to leave the carcasses out in the wild to rot on account of the stench and them being a draw for wild hogs. Equally, he doesn't like carting them around given how armadillos are disease-prone. "Leprosy, rabies, you name it them fuckers got it," he'd taught Brandy. Tried to teach Edmée too once upon a time, but the girl had a habit of getting under his skin. Just like Jackal, that stupid dog he'd fed to the alligator after Edmée. The girl had been too big for the reptile to eat in chunks. The dog had been an easier meal.

Tonight, the old lady in the sky is so bright he can see his way without a camping lantern and he bypasses the trailer to head down to the wooden pier where his jon boat's tied. At the end of the pier, he throws the dead armadillos out. They land in the water with a soft splash and he pictures the bones picked clean by alligators.

A snapshot fills his mind. Of dragging Edmée's body out from under the trailer alongside what was left of the dog, and carrying both sets of remains down to his boat. Half an hour later, in the dark of an overgrown inlet on an abandoned private property, he'd eased the dead overboard, first what was left of the dog, and, second, Edmée. Last thing he'd seen was the girl's glassy, bloodshot eyes, staring up at him as she slipped below the surface.

Joe shrugs off the memory and fishes out a beer from the cooler on his boat. He sits awhile on the bench nearest the engine, supping from his can and listening to the wild hullabaloo of the swamp. Every so often, something skitters over the surface of the water. All around him, trees rustle in a wind he can't sense.

Why did the girl get under his skin so much, he wonders? Was it that she'd looked more appealing with each passing day? Everything about that child had made him uncomfortable. The way she'd squirm up onto his lap and bounce around until he had to throw her off. The way she'd put on her little jean skirt and pumps and tie her t-shirt into a knot to show off her bellybutton. And the way she'd parade in front of him, looking so much like her dead momma as she wriggled her shoulders and shouted, "Watch me dance, Uncle Joe! Watch me!"

Joe slurps from his beer can. He stares over the side of the boat at the glittering black slick – and sees Edmée staring back just beneath the surface. His first thought is the beer's taken effect early and is making him see things. Except, the dead girl keeps on rising, her bloated white eyes staying fixed on him. She surfaces, inky water draining from her shoulders, and Joe drops his can and scrabbles back from his perch, making the boat rock.

Edmée keeps on rising, up and up until her whole body is suspended over the bayou. Toes skimming its surface, black hair writhing. Her skin is grey marble under moonlight. Moss clings to her like bark canker. Water spills from her parted lips.

"Sweet Jesus!" Joe backs up, knocks over his cooler and struggles to stay upright. Forcing himself to look away, he goes to climb ashore only to realise the boat has come unfastened from the pier and he's drifting into the dark. The only option is to jump overboard and wade back to land, hope he makes it before any critters take a bite! Except, when he turns his head back, the ghoul is not only on board but leaning over him.

"I'll be seeing you," says the swamp girl. Her skull flares up through her paper-thin green skin.

"Not if I see you first, you dead motherfucker!" Joe drives his hands around the girl's neck. The feel of her slimy flesh almost makes him let go, but he keeps on squeezing. Squeezing and squeezing until, any second, he expects the girl to turn to grease between his fingers.

"Goodnight, Daddy," says Edmée, and cranes her jaw wide.

Joe stares down into a deep black throat, its own lagoon, and he thinks how her last words are less a nickname than a fact. He tries to fight against the secret daughter he'd never asked for, but his hands slide right off her. He yanks his fists back, only to find there are strands of the demonic girl's hair suckering at his fingertips, pulling him closer. He's cursing up a storm, his heart choking on its own beat. The ghoul slides her icy arms around his waist, hugging him tight while her limp hair continues to crawl over him of its own accord and his nostrils baulk at her decay. As hard as he resists, Edmée holds tighter until, finally, she tosses back her head and her jaw snaps apart – stretching, stretching.

She clamps down on his chest, tearing through his t-shirt to the belly meat. Joe cries out, only to have his voice cut short by the agony. He wants to run, to fight, to murder his dead daughter all over again.

Instead, he shudders as Edmée burrows her head under his skin.

Later, having collected up all three heads, Edmée squats down beside the steps to the trailer. She peers under. Two rheumy amber eyes stare back.

"Here you go, Mister Alligator," she says, and tosses the heads under.

"Welcome back, child." Marie waves Edmée in through the front door. She leads the way across the parlour, the bedroom with its little bathroom poked into a corner, and back into the kitchen where she's mid-plucking the rooster free of its russet feathers. A plate of thyme and rosemary's burning on the windowsill, purifying the air against foul play.

"Come. Sit." She points to the chair alongside the table where the girl had sat two short hours back. "It takes strength to drain a life and you've done for three of them!"

As the girl takes a seat, the thread-veins across her face and throat are picked out in a pearlescent pink colour. If possible, she appears more monstrous than before, yet also more alive.

The witch leans in. "Is that you, Baron? Squatting in this child like a mean ole gator stuck in a drain? If I look closely, will I see them yellow eyes of yours amongst her reeds?" She plays with her necklaces. "Murders all done, Baron. So I'll be thanking' you, but it's time to pass on again."

Something flickers across the dead girl's face. The ghost of a skull, flaring beneath the skin. The manifestation vanishes.

"That's right, Father. I'll call on you again soon."

When the girl stays sitting opposite, Marie feels a new wave of discomfort. "The Baron. He's all about sin and the darkness, and he loves him some whiskey and a fat cigar. But your face ain't his. I've an idea I could swallow all the liquor in Louisiana and you'd be unmoved."

Oh, Marie has seen some sights in her time! But there's something new in the way Edmée stares across the table. Marie swears there's even the trace of a smile on the dead girl's lips.

"Have I had you wrong, child?" She gets to her feet and backs up slowly. Her hand closes around the handle to her broom cupboard. "I thought your spirit called out to me because it was murdered and needed help in healing. Papa Ghede would have led you to a place of rest by now if things were that easy. But, ah no! Here you stay, awash with the blood of thine enemy." Marie marks out the cross over her brow. "I see it now. You're having too much fun with murder, Edmée Romero. Like you're dancing a Mardi Gras Mambo."

Marie opens the cupboard at her back with a soft click. "There's only one kind of spirit has this much fun being wicked. Tell me, child. Were you baptised?"

Edmée – wicked, playful Edmée who overloaded her mother's pipe, and pushed Brandy into the swamp, and flirted with her own father in front of her Aunt Hailey and kicked Jackal more times than any other – bares her curved, flesh-feathered teeth.

"Only one kind of spirit likes to tease and torment its prey, afore and in death. *Lutin*!" Marie breathes the name of the devil's own children – those rotten things which come from having never been bathed in holy water and so beloved of the Baron. "Oh, you tricked me into raising your spirit, Lutin! You tricked meh well. And now you want a taste of Marie St Angel to go along with them three you've already murdered, yah?"

The devil child cranes her jaw unnaturally wide. Marie throws open the cupboard door, grabs her rifle and blasts the Lutin with rock salt.

The spirit flickers, like crackling static. But all of Marie's spells to give the dead girl substance now work against her and Edmée regains a hold on herself.

Tucking her gun underarm, Marie grabs her skirts in her fists and runs to the back door. She flings it open as the Lutin charges with ungodly speed, ensnarling her in slimy arms and whipping wet hair. Marie manages a whistle and a dark shape dashes in through the door. Matted with duckweed and lousy with tiny blue crabs, the dog, Jackal, launches at Edmée, wrestling her to the floor with its own whetted teeth.

"I told you murdered things come back!" shouts Marie. "That's why I live in a shotgun house, the sort that's built to deal with spirits, specially them as have outstayed their welcome!" She runs again, from the backdoor, all the way through her magic cottage to the front door, which she throws open.

"All murdered things come back," she repeats.

Waiting on the porch are the recently deceased – Brandy with her throat ripped out, Aunt Hailey missing her tongue and a good portion of her face, and Uncle Joe with a howling wound where his belly used to be.

"She's ready for you." Marie steps aside, opening up the line of sight to the back door.

The ghouls rush between the rooms in a tumble of jerking limbs. Gathering up Edmée as they go, the spirits of the murdered propel themselves towards the back door. As one snarled ball of teeth and skin, they tumble out into the void – all except Edmée, who clings on to the door jamb either side and snaps and snarls at the air with her alligator teeth.

Marie raises her shotgun, sights the Lutin and squeezes the trigger. The rock salt hits Edmée hard in her tiny chest at the exact moment the newly materialised Papa Ghede holds out his apple core and lets it fall. Edmée tumbles backwards into the long night.

After the dead are gone, Marie closes the doors at either end of her house. Papa Ghede's vanished but he's left a couple of gifts. On the bureau, she finds the gris-gris bag which helped the Lutin mix mischief from beyond a watery grave. And there, asleep on the kitchen floor, is the zombie dog.

Marie goes over to Jackal and kneels down. She pats the matted fur where the moss grows and the crabs scuttle, and the mutt rolls its big old dead eyes and sighs contentedly.

"Well, okay then, boy. You can stay and keep me company." She nods towards the rifle leaning up against the stove. "I'm warning you though. One false move..."

Straightening up, Marie goes back to the sink and sets to plucking the rooster again.

Out in the wilds, the Louisiana swamp settles into itself and a magic house winks out like the spattering flame of a candle stub.

~*~

I love American Gothics. Voodoo, jazz, Easy Rider-immortalised graveyards, Cyprus trees weeping shrouds of Spanish moss, the eerie fetidness of the swamps – all fuse into a syrupy elixir of dark tales and humid horror. *Rotten Things* is my ode to the peculiar history, rich folk lore and stranger-than-fiction goings on of the southern bayous and those who inhabit them.

The Island of Peter Pandora

Peter caught the fly between his palms. The insect buzzed and tickled.

"Aren't you the jolly little irritant!" Peter parted his hands slightly and tried to peep in. When the fly flew out, he snatched at it. A trace of gore stained his hand.

"Funny bug." Peter didn't bother to brush off the insect's remains, but picked up the wrench and plunged his hands into the Lost Boy's stomach.

"Those Rogues. They'll do for me one day," said Nibs in his chiming voice.

"Ha! They'd have to catch me first and Peter Pandora is not easy to tie down." Peter lifted his sharp chin a notch. Locating the flywheel under the leather heart, he adjusted the torque. A squeeze of oil from a can and the gears moved smoothly again.

"I am nothing if not exceptional." Peter slid the bolt plate back across Nibs' stomach. He cleaned his hands on a rag.

"You're the bravest and the best, Peter." Nibs craned in his legs, rocked onto his porthole backside and got up off the grass. Steam oozed from his joints.

Peter nodded sagely. "I am." When the Lost Boys failed to concur, he shot them a savage look. "What say my men?" He bit his bottom lip.

The animatronic band wheezed into life at the command.

"The finest mind in the French empire." Tootles cradled his fat bowl belly; Peter had fashioned it from a condenser casing and a girdle of steel ribs.

"Master of the fair isle of Tsarabanjina. We are loyal to the last." Curly nodded enthusiastically, exciting the frayed wires that poked out his skullcap.

"The last! The last!" echoed the twin tinies who Peter had not bothered to name. They were rather a nuisance with their rudder flippers which got stuck in the sand or left visible tracks up the banks like turtles come ashore to lay their eggs.

"Slightly?" Peter adopted a grown-up's tone.

"I have a headache," said Slightly as farts of steam escaped his back boiler. "And Mother on the gin and Father's run away with the fairies."

Peter crossed his arms. He considered Slightly's head which had been all but bashed off, with only a couple of wires attaching it to the body.

"The Rogues shall pay for their attack." Peter unhooked the wrench from his utility belt and wielded it. "What say my men?"

"The finest mind in the French empire."

"Master of the fair isle…"

"Enough!" cried Peter, and apart from the taps of water pipes and the crackle of wood inside their boilers, the Lost Boys fell silent.

Three hours later and Slightly's head sat back on his shoulders. The iridescent blue of day was giving way to the black and oranges of dusk. Peter led his robot band through the tall reeds, kicking up crickets and newborn mosquitoes. The air was full of flavours – cocoa, coffee and sea salt; Peter breathed them in. This was his favourite part of the day, when the stars his father had loved so much began to wink overhead, and when the rumble in his belly told him it was suppertime.

"Did any tuck survive the raid?" he called over a shoulder.

"Papaya, banana, sweet potato." Tootles sounded proud of their haul. Peter had hoped for a fish supper, but he let things slide. His men had survived being attacked by the Rogues when collecting provisions earlier that day. Plus, they could always go a-hunting again tomorrow.

"A banquet fit for kings," he managed. His spirits cheered at the sight of the raggedy tree house with its smoke stacks and the fat brass trunk of his father's telescope pointing skyward.

"Run on ahead, you and you," he told the twin tinies. "Get the water boiling under the supper pot. Light the lamps."

The pair set off, rudder feet swishing through the reeds. A minute later, Peter saw the glow of lamplight at the windows. Smoke trickled from one of the tall stacks.

Peter entered the clearing. Tootles, Slightly, Curly and Nibs arrived alongside, oozing steam and sweating oil. Moths danced in the twilight like fairy folk. The detritus of scrub and husk made a noisy carpet underfoot. 'No creeping up on me,' thought Peter smugly.

He stepped onto a wooden palette, grabbed hold of the ropes and heard the winch start up. The ground dropped away and he sailed up to the tree house, that great nest of palm leaves, reeds, flotsam and jetsam, turtle shell, coral chunks and ship wreck. Crawling in at the tarpaulin-covered entrance, he slammed a large iron lever forward and sent the palette back down to fetch the others.

Standing up and placing his hands on his hips, Peter took in the chaos of the room. The hairy trunks of seven coconut trees sprouted up through the living quarters. Golden Orb spiders nestled among the eaves, their sun-coloured silk forming a glittering canopy.

"Home sweet home." Peter rocked back onto his heels and separated his toes, planting them on the reed matting with a satisfying sense of grounding.

James and Wendy Darling had come to Tsarabanjina – a tropical island located northwest of Madagascar Main Island and forty nautical miles from Nosy-Be – in the year of our lord 1889. A twelve-man strong crew assisted them to offload the numerous tools of Mr Darling's trade – spy glasses, constellation maps housed in leather tubes, an oversized compass with gold and ivory inlay, easels and other drawing apparatus, and, of course, his pride and joy, a giant brass telescope. Mrs Darling, meanwhile, was content to haul ashore her own box of tricks – metal-working tools, saws, hammers, piping, sheet steel, and every conceivable nut, bolt and screw. And while many ladies would have protested at the steaming wilderness, Wendy embraced it. Befriending the tribe on the south side of the island, she enlisted those strong, cocoa-skinned men to help her build an observatory among the trees.

Peter had been four years old, his sister Bella, six months. Leaving behind the dreary greys of London for Tsarabanjina's endless blue sky and ocean, both children felt as if they had stumbled upon paradise.

Three years later came the Three Bad Events as Peter called them. First, a tremendous cyclone storm which sunk his parents' dhow offshore. Second and far more devastating, the death of both parents from Typhoid Fever and inside two weeks of one another. And third, the islanders muscling in on his and Bella's seclusion and insisting so kindly and so absolutely that the youngsters go with them. Peter had refused with every violent response he could muster. Bella, though, went with them. At the age of seven, Peter had found himself alone with only the sounds of the waves lapping the shore and the contents of his mother's workshop for company.

"Time to fill your cakehole." Slightly stood at the brink to the observatory. His insides turned over with a faint clanking sound.

Peter peered into the telescope's eyepiece. Venus, the morning star and his father's life's work, shone in the night sky. "Such an elegant turn of phrase, Slightly," he muttered.

"Want me to put on false airs like Rogues?" Slightly elevated a backside flap and let out a guff of steam.

Peter slid the cap across the eyepiece and made his way across the room, weaving in and out the map stands and tables full of paperwork. He slapped Slightly on the arm, producing a hollow rumble.

"I really did use up the odds and sods at the bottom of the drawer when I created you, Slightly."

The Lost Boy seemed pleased with the fact. His boiler bubbled softly as he led the way into the dinner den.

"Peter! So glad you can join us." Tootles tapped the space on the bench next to him. "Have a seat, there's a good chap."

Peter eased in besides Tootles even though the crueller part of him wanted to say, 'No, I won't. I shall sit opposite between the twin tinies just to show who is boss around here.' By way of compromise, he vowed to ignore Tootles for the evening.

"So what's the plan, Peter? How do we make those Rogues pay?" Nibs banged his fist against his stomach plate, a reminder of the torn internals he had suffered at their hands.

Peter spoke through a mouthful of turtle and sweet potato stew. "We lure them in from their hidey hole and then we garrotte them."

"Sounds marvellous," said Curly.

"Masterful," added Tootles.

"How'd we do it?" The twin tinies asked in unison.

Peter put his elbows on the table and lent in. The Lost Boys mimicked him.

"I am going back below and I'm going to raise the Ticktock."

His animatronic companions oohed then fell silent, the cicada song of the night punctuated by the whir and knocks from their steaming bellies.

It was Slightly who spoke up. "What's the Ticktock?"

"What's the Ticktock?" Peter leapt onto his seat. "What's the Ticktock?" He stepped onto the table, narrowly missing his bowl of fruit mush and the Lost Boys' flagons of oil and platefuls of grease. "Only the bringer of destruction. It is the hand of God, the great leveller." He knocked a fist off his breastbone. "It was my mother, Wendy Darling, who told me of its power. 'Be careful, son, the Ticktock is not a toy. It likes to buck and spit.'"

"But you'll tame it, won't you, Peter?" Tootles showed his metal tooth pegs.

"Naturally. First, though, I've got to commander the thing from the deep." Peter danced up and down the table, upsetting a jug of rainwater and splashing through it as if he was jumping in puddles at the park. "I do so love to go a-hunting!" he cried.

"Can we come too?" piped up the twin tinies.

"Onlyme." Peter puffed out his chest. "This quest requires cunning and lashings of cleverness. Besides..." He dropped to his haunches and ladled a mouthful of stew into his mouth. "I'm the only one who knows how to swim with the Mermaid," he said thickly.

Later, when the Lost Boys had completed their chores and joined in Peter's rousing rendition of *Jolly Rain Tar* – after which he had instructed them to stoke their boilers, wind innards and sup enough water to tide them over until the morning – companions and master had gone their separate ways. The Lost Boys took up patrol duty on the tree house's vined balcony while Peter climbed onto his parents' reed-stuffed mattress, beneath a canopy of mosquito netting. Besides the bed was the gramacorda which his father had used to archive his discoveries. A few times, his mother had thought it amusing to speak into the horn and record the bedtime stories she told Peter onto one of the foil scrolls. While the heat had warped the greater part of his father's recordings, three of his mother's tales still played. That night, Peter selected her rendition of *The Tin Soldier*. Lying back on the bed, he let his mother's spirited narration lull him to sleep.

He was woken once during the night by the sound of footfall on the ground below. Peter imagined he heard a chilling, all too familiar grunting, but sleep overtook him again.

The sun was high in the sky when Peter awoke. While the Lost Boys breakfasted on their oil and grease, their creator tucked into spiced fish baked in banana leaves. Soon the conversation turned to the night watch. The Lost Boys denied any sign of intruders. Peter remained haunted by the conviction they were wrong.

"Rogues have curdled my dreams long enough." Peter fastened his utility belt at his waist and slammed his hat down on his head. "Time to fetch up the Ticktock." He knocked a hand off his brow in salute. "See you later, alligators."

Half an hour later, having battled his way through the mosquito infested reeds, Peter arrived on the north shore. The sand was toasty between his toes. Waves foamed at the shoreline. The clear blue ocean stretched away to tiny islands known as the Four Friers. Two large rocks 'kissed' a little way out to his left. His mother's workshop burrowed into the cliff to his right.

At the entrance, Peter cocked his head and leant in, drinking from the fresh water which streamed down the rock. He stepped inside the workshop, blinded by the sudden transition from brilliant daylight to shadow. It was dry inside – precisely the reason his mother had selected the cave – and battened with wooden shelving.

Peter lit oil-filled dips in the rock. The makeshift sconces flickered whenever he walked by, causing his shadow to dance over the walls seemingly of its own accord.

Numerous engineering supplies had gone down with his parents' ship, but the workshop was still well stocked. Several shelves were dedicated to trays of nuts, bolts, screws and nails. Giant bobbins were wound with rubber pipe while smaller versions held various gauges of copper wire. Two workbenches stood on stilts on the uneven surface; one was stained with oil, the other with blood. Tools hung off nails between the shelves – hammers, bow saws, hand drills, chisels, scalpels, vices and tourniquets. One basket held clean bandaging. Another overflowed with soiled.

Standing in his workshop surrounded by the tools of his labour, Peter was glad he had come alone. As much as he enjoyed his elated status among the Lost Boys, there was a tendency for their restricted audio to grate. More than anything he longed for the stimuli of sentient conversation. But his efforts to create companions had birthed all manner of dark breed among the Rogues. His gaze lingering on the blood-stained bench. One worse than all the rest. Hookie, the ape-man. Had Wendy Darling known that in introducing new animal species to the island she would provide her son with the raw materials to investigate and reinterpret life, she might just have tipped her caged specimens overboard on route and drowned the lot. Instead, she was the enabler for Peter's experiments, having left behind science books, engineering diagrams, pencilled notes and a veritable operating theatre.

"Much good it does me!" Peter protested out loud.

Not that he had any intention of moping around and feeling sorry for himself, Oh no, Hookie and crew had played their final trick on him. It was time to deal with the Rogues like any other group of wayward children.

A long tarpaulin-covered object occupied the far end of the cave. Peter pulled off the cover. The Mermaid's polished wood shone in the greasy lamplight.

Pitched between the perfection of motherhood and the gutsiness of a Rogue, Wendy Darling had always demonstrated a soft spot for the underdog. In engineering terms, her pet favourite was an untutored Catalonian inventor called Narois Monturiol I Estarrol. To the young Peter, his mother's daytime stories were as engaging as her bedtime stories were soporific.

"Imagine it, Peter," she would say, a glint of passion in her eye. "While his competitors were busy developing submarines for military purposes, Monturiol was a communist, a revolutionary, a utopian. He saw his machine as a way of improving the lives of poor coral divers. Here, Peter." She would lay the open book before him and stab a finger grubby with oil at the illustrations. "Such a beautiful design. A wooden submarine supported by olive wood batons and lined with copper. Why copper?" She would shoot the question at him like a bullet.

"For structural support?"

"No, Peter, no. To stop shipworms from eating the hull."

Even as an intensely intelligent child, Peter had been haunted by images of giant worms chomping down on the wooden submarine. And while he was nonchalant about Monturiol's morality, he did appreciate the inventor's design ethic and had proceeded to apply it to a solo submersible he nicknamed the Mermaid.

A pair of polished wooden sleds allowed him to push the Mermaid out of the cave and through the sand to the water's edge. He paused for breath and mopped his forehead with a forearm. Seeing it in the sunlight, he was reminded just how perfect a machine the Mermaid really was. The 'head' was a wood-staved cabin with a broad strip of glass tied around its middle like a ribbon. This cabin housed the controls and a driver's seat which revolved to allow for a 360 degree view through the glass. The boiler was built into the torpedo-shaped 'body' and heated via a chemical furnace; the compounds potassium chlorate, zinc and magnesium dioxide were from his mother's dry store, and while their combination produced enough power to heat the boiler, it had the added bonus of generating oxygen to supplement the supply in the cabin. The true magic, though, was in the Mermaid's tail – five feet long, covered in wooden scales, and tapering to a brass-plated rudder.

Pushing the Mermaid offshore, Peter held his breath and ducked under the water. He swam beneath the submersible and emerged in a small moon pool to the rear of the cabin. Securing himself in the driver seat, he twisted a stopcock to flood the boiler and began to work his way through the operative checklist.

It was the 28th of February 1893 when the storm hit. Peter's family had been living on the island for eight months, and while numerable supplies had been brought ashore, some larger items were stored in the traditional dhow boat moored offshore. As Peter had learnt since, December to March saw violent cyclones assault the island and its neighbours, the usual tropical serenity giving way to torrential rain and clockwise circling winds. The dhow was well made, used to carrying heavy loads up and down the East African coast. But even with its lateen sail lowered, the dhow could never have weathered that assault. Sometime between dusk and dawn the ship tore loose of its anchor, drifted and sank near the second Freir. His parents had called it the devil's work. Peter had come to view the shipwreck as a treasure trove.

The water was fantastically clear as the Mermaid dipped below the surface. Peter moved the weight along the line by his right shoulder, adjusting the angle of the Mermaid's descent. The smooth action of the tail drove the submersible forward at a steady rate of four knots. All around him, shoals of fish danced, their brilliant colours transforming the ocean into a fairyland. Corals burgeoned below like giant fleshy roses. A solitary turtle drifted by, buoyed on an invisible current. The creature stirred the water with its front flippers then drifted once more – the nonchalant old man of the sea.

Lying beside a great crease of volcanic rock, the dhow's sharply curved keel reminded Peter of one half of an eel's open jaw and he felt the jolt of discomfort he always did at the sight. The feeling gave way to excitement; Peter wanted to fly out among the wreck and peel strips off it for no other reason than it might please him. The rational side of him argued that the wreck was best preserved for future foraging.

One thing he did intend to secure that day was the Ticktock. His mother's ledger listed it under 'Weaponry/24 pounds of copper.' He knew the Ticktock had been stored in a large chest with a skull and crossbones etched on top – his mother's idea of a joke, given the

Ticktock's practical application. That box now lay at the bottom of the ocean, wedged between the crease of rock and the ribs of the dhow. Up until that moment, he'd had no need for such an item, but Hookie and the rest of the Rogues had become a damnable pest. They needed swotting like sand flies.

The boiler to the rear of the cabin mumbled soothingly. It was hot inside the Mermaid, but Peter didn't mind. Yes, he risked drowning or being baked alive in his handmade submersible, but he'd always entertained the idea that to die would be an awfully big adventure! He pulled on a leather strap above his head to regulate the heat off the boiler and stabilise the craft. A small adjustment to the sliding counterweight and the submersible hovered alongside the large chest.

'Peter Pandora. You possess the cunning of a crow and you are as wise as the stars,' his father used to say. Peter sucked his bottom lip. "Indeed I am, Father," he whispered. Scooting his seat forward on a greased wooden rail, he took hold of a pair of iron handgrips. His fingers pressed down on ten sprung-levered valves. Arms unlocked on the front of the cabin; each metal limb was tipped with a grabber. Peter manipulated the handgrip valves to open and close the grabbers and secured a hold on the handle of the chest nearest the curl of rock. The other handle was trapped beneath the boat's mast, and while the arms siphoned off power from the boiler, magnifying his strength threefold, he still got slick with sweat as he tried and failed to pull the chest free.

"Move, you bloody thing!" he cried, irritated at the situation but pleased with his use of the swear word. The chest stayed wedged beneath the mast and he had to break off trying to move it and catch his breath. Water pressed all around, muffling the sounds of the boiler and the churn of the engine.

Peter stretched out his fingers and was about to work the handgrips again when something large crashed into the cabin's exterior wall. He spun around in his chair, staring out the window strip. Legs disappeared from his eye line, the soles of the feet like black leather. Peter whipped his head the other way and caught a glimpse of horns, thighs like fat hams, and a snout. When the Mermaid began to rock, water lapping at the moon pool and threatening to flood the cabin, Peter knew he had attracted company – and not that of a whale shark or a mantra ray. The hands rocking his craft were strong and animaltronic, with claws that scraped the hull.

"Rogues." Peter bared his teeth gleefully. "You're no match for Peter Pandora!" He concentrated on the handgrips and tried again for the Ticktock. Bodies hurled themselves against the submersible. Peter was grateful to have a grip on one trunk handle since it helped anchor the Mermaid.

"Wild things!" he called out to the creatures pestering him. "To catch a fellow unaware. But that's the nature of Rogues, isn't it?"

Faces appeared at the glass. Part mechanical, part animal, the Rogues stared in with colourful glass eyes which reminded Peter of Christmas baubles. One Rogue had goat horns grafted onto his iron-plate skull. He butted the glass and blew bubbles out his ear canals.

"All bluster and no backbone." Peter stuck out his tongue. By way of reply, one of the Rogue crew tried to come up through the moon pool; Peter stamped on the creature's skull-cap. The invader sank down and swam away, air escaping the steam-release vents at its knee joints.

He'd scared one off. The rest appeared perfectly happy to continue rocking the submersible. Meanwhile, a dark shape materialised through the dust cloud kicked up by the Rogues. The figure swam with broad, confident strokes, the scythes that served for hands sweeping out in glittering arcs.

Peter slammed one hand forward, driving the corresponding grabber hard at the mast, splintering the rotten wood. Hookie drew closer at speed, the sweep of those long, muscular arms matched by the frog-like pump of his huge legs. Underwater, Hookie's fur was dark and sleek. His silver teeth shone.

At last, Peter got a lock on the other handle and lent back in his chair, pulling the handgrips towards him. Secured in the Mermaid's arms, the chest lifted off the ocean floor. Peter pressed a foot peddle to lock the arms in place then released the handgrips. Adjusting the weight counterpoint to allow for the burden, he raked a hand across the bank of switches to release the sand ballast in the storage cylinders and unleash a fresh head of steam to drive the engine. He engaged the throttle and powered up, Rogues tumbling aside in the submersible's slipstream. In his mind's eye, he pictured Hookie slow up and, without expression, watch his craft disappear.

"You must stay with us now. My wife will care for you well. We are a good family and, together with the rest of the village, we will feed and clothe you." The islanders' representative had appeared kindly and concerned. He'd smiled and clapped a hand on Peter's shoulder.

Seven years old, Peter had surveyed the horseshoe of islanders. Bella's hand had gripped his – not because she was scared of the Malagasy with their open faces and choppy way of talking but because, even at three and a half years old, she'd known he wouldn't stay.

Over the years, Peter hiked to the south side of the island on occasion. Hidden at the forest's edge, he spied on the villagers and his sister. The malady Bella had been born with was as much a gift as a trial and one which suggested she was only capable of registering one emotion at a time. On occasion, she would kick and wail in blinding rage. But there were also calmer moments when she would concoct detailed puzzles from the rows of shells she painstakingly arranged. Sometimes her laughter was high and tinkling. Sometimes she sat and stared out at the sea for hours, as if her mind had flown far away. Then Peter would see one of Bella's Malagasy brothers come and take her hand and sit with her awhile. Perhaps her new family thought her enchanted. Peter was pleased that Bella was happy. He was also sick at heart and resentful.

For the most part, Peter had been left to his own devices on the north side of the island. He didn't interfere with the fishing trips or beach BBQs or Famadihanna ceremonies where the Malagasy would exhume the remains of their ancestors, wrap them in silk and entomb the bones once more. In return, the Malagasy left him to play puppet-master with his band of loyal Lost Boys and itinerant Rogues – the later steering clear of the islanders ever since one inquisitive specimen had been speared in the chest like a giant turtle.

There was one exception to the rule, though. Two days after his underwater expedition, Peter was holed up in his workshop with the

Ticktock when he caught a glimpse of movement at the mouth of the cave.

"Tigermaw. I can see you." He waited, staring out from the gloom. All he heard was the noise of the ocean.

Satisfied that his mind was playing tricks, Peter gave his attention back to the Ticktock. Dipping a small scrubbing brush into a coconut shell containing a solution of salt and vinegar, he set to work removing the patina from the brass.

A stone struck him on his left temple.

"Damnation!" His eyes flashed aside. This time he saw feathers of hair poking up from a crop of rocks at the cave's entrance.

"Go away before the Rogues get you, girl!" he called, slamming down the scrubbing brush.

As quick as Peter liked to think he was, his reactions didn't compare to Tigermaw's. She fired off two more stones from her slingshot. One struck Peter's thigh. The other nicked his ear.

"Enough, Tigermaw! Don't start what you can't finish." Using a ruler as a makeshift catapult, he sent two slugs of nails towards the rocks. Apparently, the scatter gun approach worked. He heard a gasp.

"Peter Pandora, you are a sorcerer. You deserve a hundred stones upon your head," came the cry from the rocks.

"And you are slow brained, and a savage to boot!"

"What are you cooking up today, evil boy?" demanded Tigermaw, standing up suddenly and striding inside the cave. She approached his workbench, hands on hips, lemur-large eyes blinking as they adjusted to the dark. *How fantastically fearsome she looked,* thought Peter. Face painted with white swirls. Dark hair spread high and wide like wings. The shift she wore was a faded rose pattern. Her feet were bare.

Tigermaw pointed at the copper barrel of the Ticktock. "Will that be a tail or a nose?"

"Neither. It is a method of upping the stakes against the Rogues."

"Ah, so it is a weapon." Tigermaw glared, daring Peter to deny it.

"It is *the* weapon, savage girl. I'm going to fill those Rogues with so much lead they won't have brains intact to bother my Lost Boys and me ever again."

"By Rogues, you mean the demons you yourself conjured? They are mischief makers, but nothing more serious than children in need of their father's affection. But instead you cast them out as failed experiments."

Tigermaw leant in close. Peter felt her breath on his lips. It made them tingle.

"Would you have us behave the same with your sister, Bella?" She stabbed a finger up at the roof of the cave. "Bella is angry with her maker for taking away her parents, making you a stranger, and giving her an unusual nature. Should she be destroyed too?"

Peter folded his arms across his chest. "What do you know about my inventions? You have no more right to apportion feelings to a Rogue than to a Jackfruit. As for Bella, she is a free spirit who must be allowed to fly. Your people should not try to contain her, else she might just rise up and bite you on the nose."

"Ah, Bella is a good soul," said Tigermaw with a dismissive flick of a hand. "The only bad around here is a little boy who plays with flesh and machinery over choosing a normal life lived alongside his sister." The girl's big black eyes softened. "My family will still take you in, Peter. You can have a home."

"And see my life drain away until I am old and wrinkled, just another bag of bones for your people to cherish. No thanks. I'd rather stay here with my Lost Boys."

Tigermaw sighed; to Peter, it was a sign of submission and he put his nose in the air.

"And what about the Rogues?" It was Tigermaw's turn to cross her arms. Under the lamplight, her war paint was luminescent.

Peter picked up the scrubbing brush and attacked the Ticktock's patina again. "I'll kiss each and every one goodnight with this then fashion myself a grandfather clock from their remains."

Tigermaw stared at him, and for a moment Peter saw himself through her eyes as the true monster. He started scrubbing again. When he next looked up, the girl had gone.

Lying in bed listening to his mother's bedtime stories on the gramacorda, Peter would occasionally feel the pinch of loneliness. At such times he would question the ethics of his companion machines. Life was his to give or take at the flick of a switch or the turn of a key. But where he had really strayed from the moral path was in his creation of the Rogues – in particular, Hookie. Most Rogues owed their origin to the livestock his parents had introduced to the island – pigs, goats, sheep. Hookie, though, was a rangy old orangutan his mother had rescued from a street performer in Borneo. Shot through with arthritis and pining for Wendy, Peter had decided to put the creature out of its misery. But had the family pet deserved vivisection and animaltronic rebirth? Had any of those poor dumb animals wanted the gifts he had bestowed – intelligence, conscious thought, and all the suffering that came with an awareness of one's own mortality.

That these moments of lucidity were rare testified to Peter's absolute self-belief. Secure in his divine right to mix, mess and mesh, he'd created monsters. Now it was his choice to destroy them.

Evening settled around the circumference of the camp. Tootles had done an excellent job of collecting dry wood. The fire pit roared, spitting sparks like shooting stars. Slightly had unfastened a little at the neck again. He walked to and fro, muttering, "Midnight feast, he says. Go cook it up, he says. What from, say I? Fairy dust?" In spite of his limited larder, Slightly had magicked up a decent spread of deep fried hissing cockroach with its greasy chicken taste, vegetable and coconut curry, a platter of bright orange jackfruit pieces – resembling dragon scales laid out on a knight's shield – spiced rice, and crab claws. In lieu of a table, Peter had instructed the Lost Boys to bring up a bench from the workshop. No one had bothered to clean it so they ate amongst sawdust and iron fillings.

The moon was fantastic – pocked and shimmering like a cherished half a crown. Everyone tucked into the feast, Peter crunching up cockroaches and greasing his chin with crab juices, the Lost Boys taking great mouthfuls, swilling the useless matter around their jaws and disgorging the lot into personal spittoons. Peter didn't mind. He had his feast. Now all he needed were a few extra guests.

Ten more minutes passed. The Lost Boys were in danger of mauling all the food.

"Leave some to attract the blighters," he shouted. His mechanical companions froze mid-grab. They brought their arms back down slowly and fell silent.

"They should be here by now." Peter bit his bottom lip, scowled and forced himself to drop the childish expression. "Fetch the gramacorda, Curly, and don't get your hair stuck in it this time when you wind it. Twin things, bring the music scrolls." He crossed his arms and stared out at the surrounding darkness. "Come out, come out, wherever you are."

Before long, Curly and the twin tinies descended from the tree house on the elevator platform. Curly set the gramacorda down on one end of the workbench. Each twin carried a number of cylinders.

"What song shall we have?" demanded Peter. "*Whist the Bogey Man? Jolly Little Polly On A Tin Gee Gee?*"

"*Daisy Day*!" cried Tootles, patting his tin-pot belly contently.

Peter ignored him. "*Maple Leaf Rag*, it is."

Curly saluted at the order. Locating the right cylinder, he slid out the foil sheet, fed it in then cranked the stylus into place. As he worked the handle, his wire hair bobbing, he became just another extension of the machine.

The ragtime tune plinked and plonked, cutting through the peace of the forest like swords through reeds. Peter tapped his feet to the music while watching the peculiar lurching dance of the twin tinies in the centre of the clearing. They made for pleasant little morsels of bait, he decided. Curly sent the crank round and round, keeping up the tempo. Tibs forgot his sentry duty and belched steam from his mouth as he tried to recreate the musical notes. Only Tootles remained seated, no doubt eyeing up the last dregs in the oil can.

Peter strained to listen past the music and the mechanical orchestra. Was that the drag of scythes across tree trunks? There was no wind, but something whistled out among the reeds.

"Hush now, Curly." He glared at the Lost Boy who let go of the crank and steeped away from the gramacorda as if it was nothing to do with him whatsoever. The rest of the gang fell still and the silence pressed in.

Yes, there it was – the distinctive yo-ho-ho of Rogues' pistons and the swish of their footfall. They came through the reeds, fifteen not-quite-anythings. Bred on steel skeletons with nerves of copper wire and clinking steam-driven insides, the Rogues were the monsters to his Frankenstein.

Stepping out from the reeds, the creatures spaced themselves out around the edges of the clearing. Each carried a makeshift weapon of a long wooden spike or a rock hammer. They showed their silver teeth and breathed heavily.

Lastly came Hookie, two pig Rogues moving aside to make way for him. The Lost Boys seemed to understand the point of the feast – that big shiny homing beacon – and stood up straight, chests plumped. Peter had not built it in them to know fear – which was not to suggest either the Lost Boys or the Rogues had turned out as pliable as he might have imagined. This was especially true in Hookie's case.

"Peter Pandora." The ape-man spoke slowly, feeling the weight of each syllable. His tremendous, muscular shoulders were matted in orange hair. His metal breastplate reflected in the moonlight. "What a wonderful feast. And music too. Are you holding a party for us?"

"A party for Rogues? What a notion! No, Hookie, I am throwing you a wake," hissed Peter.

Hookie's long arms swung by his sides. The huge scythes serving as hands glinted.

"In which case, I must apologise, for I have made the intolerable faux pas of attending my own wake while still alive. Which, I have to say, seems an idea worth prompting. After all, there ain't a man alive who wouldn't risk a breach of etiquette under those circumstances."

"Except you aren't a man, Hookie. So how could you know?"

"Ah, that old chestnut. So you can give an old ape a voice to speak but refuse him humanity on the grounds his nose is a little too bulbous." Hookie gestured to his hairless grey face. "Or his hands a little too extraordinary." He held up his scythes.

"You gave me a headache," said Slightly, lunging forward. He stopped short of the ape-man, his motoring whirring inside his chest.

"I did? At least your master was good enough to put you back together again. I wonder if he would do me the same kindness." Hookie's seven foot frame towered over Slightly's four. Peter had always liked to experiment with proportions.

"Poor Lost Boy. A windup doll without a soul."

"Don't go claiming a soul now, Hookie. You are an animal with a metal spine at best."

Peter was pleased not to flinch when Hookie knocked Slightly aside and ran at him, one scythe stopping an inch short of his throat.

"If that is all I am, it is of your making. I have begged to continue my education under your tutorage. But no, the second I show a mite of interest in your precious books, you banish me and my kind from the only home we've ever known." The sickle hand shook slightly. "Well, if you don't mind awfully, the Rogues and I are inclined to move back in and boot you and your Puffing Billies out."

"You can try, Hookie." Peter stepped back and grabbed hold of the ropes, activating the platform winch. He rose rapidly towards the tree house, leaving the ape-man behind. Looking out, he saw Hookie beat his scythes against his breastplate and let out a deep bellow. Peter responded in kind, beating his chest with his fists. It was invitation enough for the Rogues to attack. Two pigs took on Nibs and Slightly, their spears clattering off the Lost Boys' chest plates. Not that Rogues were discouraged that easily; they drove the spears at Slightly's skull and Nibs' tessellated arm panels. Slightly lost his head. Nibs shed scales, exposing his inner workings.

The twin tinies fared better against the reanimated goats. Forming tight little balls, the twins propelled themselves at the goats' legs. Horns battered off them, ineffectual against the rudder feet and steel bellies. While Tootles belly-flopped the sheep, Curly added his muscle to the assault, spiking the Rogues with his wiry hair and pulling their tails.

"Ah, my fine men. Show no mercy to the Rogues!" Peter smiled. It felt phenomenally good to witness the carnage below. He was a god ruling over a universe of his own making.

"Do we honour you with our split guts and flesh wounds?" Hookie called up from the base of the largest coconut tree supporting the tree house. Unlike the rest of Peter's creations with their colourful glass orbs, Hookie retained the deep brown eyes of the orangutan. Peter felt a pang of longing for the companionship of the wise old ape he had murdered.

"You are to leave the island and swim far far away," he told Hookie. "No more night raids, no more crying at the moon, no more effort to be what you are not."

"And what is that, Peter Pandora?" Hookie drove the scythes into the trunk of the tree and began to inch his way up. "I am not to be intelligent, and yet you built me so. I am not to behave like an animal and yet you insist I refrain from bettering myself." The scythes scraped up and in at the trunk. Hookie's grey muzzle moved closer.

"You are missing the point of servitude," spat Peter. "You want to question and learn and exceed your master." He danced off to the back of the platform and ripped down the tarpaulin. The sight of the Ticktock set him aglow. With its cooper barrel restored and polished up, the steam-canon looked like a piece of the sun. One end was enclosed in a chemical furnace chamber, the other loaded with gunshot.

Peter stood behind the canon, hand going to the firing valve just as the first of Hookie's great claws appeared over the platform's edge. The ape-man's shoulders rippled with muscle mass as he hauled himself up and got to his feet.

Hookie's deep brown eyes settled on the Ticktock, which clicked over in anticipation of being discharged.

"I ask for books and you give me bullets?"

Peter jutted his chin. "You should have towed the line, Hookie."

"And you should have left me an ignorant ape!" Hookie lunged forward, scythes whirring. Peter tripped the firing valve; water gushed into the trigger chamber, evaporated in an instant and discharged the canon. A starburst of gunshot escaped the barrel. As the ape-man fell, the tip of one of his scythes nicked Peter's cheek. He lay at his creator's feet, blood escaping his flesh parts. His metal guts wheezed and spluttered.

Peter rolled the ape-man over to the platform's edge. He rested a foot on the creature's blood-stained breastplate.

"Goodbye Hookie."

He pushed the body overboard.

Seeing their captain defeated, the Rogues took flight into the forest. Peter didn't mind. He could always pick them off another time. Below, his Lost Boys had suffered rather badly. Slightly's head lay a foot or so from the rest of him, mouth flapping like a fish out of water. Tootles wobbled about on one spot, belly skewered by a spear. Nibs had split open again, wires and cabling erupting from his chest plate. Curly appeared to have been scalped. Only the twin tinies looked well preserved as they circled the clearing, fists raised, rudder feet flapping.

Peter put his hands on his hips. He nodded in satisfaction. Victory was his. Letting his head fall back, he opened his throat and crowed.

It took Peter three days to repair his Lost Boys. Rather than drag their hefty machinery down to his workshop, he chose to bring his tools to the clearing where he worked beneath the glare of the sun and well into the night. He constructed a canopy from palm leaves which he strung together. In the evenings when the temperature was still intense, he stacked the fire pit high, more for company than any other purpose. Watching the flames, he would fancy he caught the gleam of eyes out among the reeds. Sometimes he thought they belonged to animals gone Rogue. Other times, he believed they were bright black – Tigermaw's. Once he fancied he saw a glimpse of yellow hair and he called out Bella's name urgently, like a lost sheep calling for its mother. When no answer came, he cursed his stupidity and returned to tinkering with his toys.

At last, his band of steam and clockwork men were put back together again. Slightly uttered those time immortal words, "I have a headache", before stalking off to the platform and setting the winch in motion. Soon he was installed in the safety of his kitchen, putting Curly to good use as his commis. Tootles broke out into an idiotic monologue on the mating habits of lemurs so that Peter was sorely tempted to smash him up again. Nibs and the twin tinies seemed unaware of any time lapse and spun round on the spot, fists wielded as if still engaged in brawling. Peter sent the three off into the forest to hunt, their clanging and hissing gradually receding until the night fell quiet again. Cicadas pulsed in the grasses. He could hear the ebb and flow of the ocean. It was all very beautiful, and all very dull. For not the first time since the great ape had fallen, Peter found his gaze returning to Hookie. Flies had bothered the remains all day. The creature's muzzle was mud grey, the jaw open, the protruding tongue still and mollusc-like.

Peter approached the body and gave it a firm prod with his toe. He crossed his arms and stared up at the blanket of stars overhead. For an instant, he felt the magnitude of his insignificance next to that heavenly expanse. Pointlessness threatened to crush him alive. He hated the thought and forced it aside. He needed more than the Lost Boys. He needed someone to truly show him the meaning of love and of hate.

His gaze returned to Hookie. Dare he attempt to reanimate the ape-man's decomposing corpse? It struck him as a dark art, but no more so than any of the other acts of a twelve year old boy who creates living creatures out of flesh and metal. And didn't all heroes need a foe to fight?

By the light of the moon over a faraway island, Peter Pandora set off to fetch his tools.

~*~

I have always been enchanted by the story of Peter Pan, or *Peter Pan and Wendy* as the original book was called and *Peter Pan, Or the Boy Who Wouldn't Grow Up* to use the title of J.M. Barrie's original play. Ever since I was a child, I've had a secret hankering to be both Peter and Wendy, each fearless in their way, and I always intended to marry the devilish, debonair Captain Hook when I grew up! When editor Scott Harris approached me to contribute a steampunk reimagining of a classic fiction tale to the anthology *Resurrection Engines,* I decided to combine H.G. Wells' *The Island of Doctor Moreau* with my favourite children's story. A dark animatronic take on Peter and his Lost Boys, I tried to retain Peter's impish humour while exploring the true 'lost' nature of a little boy who doesn't want to grow up.

Field of the Dead

Dean Bartholomew Richards saw three figures at the periphery of his vision. Sunlight filtered the stained glass and the Lady Chapel was transfigured. He tilted his chin to the blaze. Lichfield Cathedral was the Lord's House, he told himself. It was not to be slighted by spirits.

A cold wind blew in from the direction of the altar. Dean Richards turned around slowly, the three figures shifting so that they continued to flicker at the corner of his eye. He walked past Saint Chad's shrine and felt the temperature drop. Shadows lengthened. At his back, the sun went in.

Something wet touched the dean's nose. He dabbed it with a sleeve. Staring up at the distant vaulting, he saw snow dusting down. He had heard about the phenomena from the canons but hoped it just the fantasies of young men left alone in a dark cathedral. But in his heart he could not deny the haunting had become more substantial. The workforce retained by the cathedral architect, Mister George Gilbert Scott, had reported screams of the damned, shadows writhing over walls and spots of raging heat. Ice coated the Skidmore screen, a thousand tiny diamonds amongst the gilt. And then there were the children, their arrival always heralded by the inexplicable fall of snow. Dean Richard rubbed the bulb of his nose. Faith kept him stalwart.

"Come, children," he whispered, fearing the words.

Snow dusted the flagstones. Silence packed in around him.

He spotted them at the foot of The Sleeping Children; two girls in nightdresses – and exact replicas of the dead sisters depicted in the marble monument. The elder child made the shape of a bird with interlaced fingers. The younger smiled. Snow settled on his shoulders, and he forced himself to advance to within several feet short of the sisters. Kneeling on the cold flagstones, he clasped his hands.

"The Lord's my shepherd, I'll not want; he makes me down to lie." He heard the tremble in his voice but pressed on. The important thing was to focus on the appropriate passages. The beatitudes for these pitiful, not-quite children? Or a parable to lead them to the light? He fixated on his hands until curiosity got the better of him. Glancing up, he felt a jolt of fear. The girls had moved closer and knelt side by side, their insubstantial hands joined in prayer. But the longer he stared at the ghosts, the more solid they became.

"In pastures green, he leadeth me..."

The youngest girl's lip curled back into a snarl. "The quiet waters by..."

The older sister flinched, a blur of movement.

To the dean's horror, both underwent a metamorphosis. Eyes flickering shut, their skin turned silky white while their bodies stiffened and set.

The dean could not help himself. Forgetting the three spectres at the outer reaches of his vision, he stretched out a hand to comfort the poor dead children.

"Sleep now," he whispered, hand hovering above the youngest's exquisitely carved head. "In the arms of the Lord." He lowered his hand to bless the girl.

The ghost girl's eyes shot wide open, her sister's too – stone angels brought to life. Their mouths strained and the screams of hundreds of men issued forth.

Dean Richards leapt back onto his feet. The noise was ear-splitting and unnatural. Flames burst from the flagstoned floor and licked the walls. Shadows writhed. The snow changed to falling ash.

"Our Father who art in heaven." The heat was terrible. "Hallowed be Thy name." Dean Richard felt searing pain and stared at his palms to see the flesh bubbling. *Help me, my God*, he cried inside, and aloud, "Thy kingdom come, Thy will be done!"

He tried to run. The smell of burning bodies filled his nostrils and he tripped, his head pounding against the flagstones. His lips blistered around his prayer. The blackness set in.

Lichfield. City of philosophers. From the pig–in–a–poke cottages and elegant residences of Dam Street to the shady sanctuary of Minster Pool to the dung-and-fruit scented market place, Lichfield was glorious in its middle Englishness.

Nowhere was this more apparent than in The Close. While the city walls and its south and west gates were long gone, the elitist nature of the estate remained. Grand establishments housed the ecclesiastical and the educated in a square around the magnificent red-sandstone cathedral.

The exception was the new breed of specialist who had taken up residence. Stonemasons crawled about the western front of the cathedral like nibbling spiders. Hammers chinked. Chisels spilled red dust into the air.

On the afternoon of Monday October 22nd, 1855, the strangest figures for miles around should have been the craftsmen at work repairing the cathedral. But that changed the instant a troupe of five men came marching past the row of Tudor townhouses opposite the western front. In feathers and rags, they wore rings on their fingers and bells on their toes and carried patchwork packs like colourful hunchbacks.

The stonemasons would later tell their families it was a change in the air which first alerted them to the mummers. Hanging off precipices many feet up, the men detected a country aroma. Their minds turned to hay ricks, windfalls, smoking jam kettles and bonfires. A few even smiled before they craned their necks to look.

Sitting on the steps to one side of the courtyard, a set of plans across his knee, Canon Nicholas Russell detected the scent and was reminded of long summers at his grandmother's cottage in Alrewas. But then he squinted over at the mummers' troupe with their multi-hued ragged tunics and sooty faces, and he had visions of ungodly rituals enacted on chalk hills, of painted faces, and runes cast, and unfettered sensuality. Nicholas clutched the plans to his chest and got up.

The troupe arrived at the base of the steps. Each man wore a variation of the rags. One had fantastically blue eyes and an embroidered red cross around his neck. Nicholas shuddered at the sight; it had a blood and bandaged look. The next grinned like an imbecile, showing fat white teeth. The man wore a pair of stitched ass ears on his head and stood, running what appeared to be a pin on tail through his hands. A third wore a tall black hat and was exceptionally thin. These three were peculiar in their own right, but it was the two figures to the fore of the group who disturbed Nicholas most. One was a monster of a man with green skin and blackened eyes, who wore a necklace of dead, dried things. The second was a boy of ten or so, wearing red horns and a doublet of scarlet rags.

"Good afternoon, gentlemen." Nicholas hated the quiver in his voice.

The man in green nodded. "Isn't it?" He inhaled deeply. "Lichfield in Autumn. Reminds me of my childhood."

"You're a local man?" Nicholas eyed the weird fellow.

"Once upon a time. It probably takes a city as ghost-riddled as Lichfield to produce a man of my ilk." He glanced back at his men and they shrugged agreement.

Ghost-riddled? Nicholas tensed. Had the stonemasons been gossiping? Certainly he and his fellow cannons had done everything in their power to refute the rumours, but the apparitions would insist on appearing to clergy and layman alike.

The leader of the troupe leant in. That smell of mouldering fruit and damp straw… Nicholas almost choked against it.

"Word was put our way concerning Dean Richards' recent incapacity."

Nicholas tried to compose himself. The man's flippancy grated. But before he could respond, the boy with the horns butted in. "Want us to warm up them working folk, Mister Savage?" The boy produced a black velvet bag held by two sticks, almost identical to the collection purses used in the cathedral.

"Good idea, Thom. Go on now, fellas. Get us a crowd going."

The devil boy and the other three climbed the stairs between Nicholas and the man in green. Leaving their organic perfume in the air, the four strode over to the scaffolded west front.

Mister Savage, as the devil boy had referred to him, called after them. "Ask after the best ale house. One with lodgings." He arched a thick black eyebrow. "Some people need guidance. Without a strong hand we're as lost as lambs. And there are always wolves on the prowl, hey minister?" The man's shoulders shook in amusement. Tiny bells inside his clothing tinkled.

Nicholas folded the plans and slid them into a pocket of his cassock. "It is good to see a Lichfield son return to the fold. And now, you will excuse me." He glanced pointedly up at the late afternoon sky. "The weather sickens."

He prepared to hurry off when Mister Savage brought his huge green face close. The man's breath smelt of freshly dug soil. His eyes shone blue-white.

"Dean Richards sent word that he wishes to see me. Be a good fellow and lead the way." His heavy brow swelled. "That's a demand, Canon Nickolas."

The Deanery was a red-brick mansion with tall chimneys and a central roof pediment. Ailen imagined an interior dedicated to stoked fireplaces, plum pie and antique furnishings. Indeed, the house proved all of these things when a bustling housekeeper let them in – and in spite of her clear alarm at Ailen's costume. The comforts of the home did not extend to the dean's bedroom, however. Following the faintly sanctimonious young canon across the threshold, Ailen was disappointed to find the room in semi-darkness and the air perfumed with lavender. Disappointed because he had hoped a strong-willed man like Dean Richards would not have taken ill after his fright.

"The Shakes," Ailen muttered under his breath.

Canon Nickolas glanced back. "Excuse me?"

Ailen shook his head. "Nothing."

A lamp burnt low on the bedside cabinet. By its weak light he saw eiderdowns piled high on a large bed, wall-mounted crosses, dried lavender arrangements – to soothe the nerves – and long tapestry curtains drawn tight to keep the cold out. Or something other.

Sound issued from beneath the eiderdowns. Muttered prayer – or as Ailen understood it, just another form of incantation.

"Dean Richards?" said Nickolas.

The covers were thrown back. Dean Richards stared out, wild eyed, a halo of white hair about his head.

"Nickolas?" The dean scrubbed his fists into his eyes. He blinked at Ailen, mole-like. "And you, friend? Are you phantom or mortal man?" A shiver visibly passed through the invalid and he hugged himself.

"Mortal, if in the guise of a handsome devil." Ailen grinned – which prompted the dean to clutch the eiderdowns up to his chin. "Forgive my crass humour, Dean Richards. It comes of a good many years on tour with a mummers' troupe."

"Mummers?" The dean chewed the word over. "The archbishop's people mentioned a mummer. Pied Piper of the dead, they called him."

"Aye. That'd be on account of this." Reaching into his pack, Ailen pulled out a long metal pipe. Worked in silver and brass, the instrument appeared to be a cross between an oboe and a mechanical Chinese dragon. "I blow here." Ailen pointed to the reed-tipped tail. "Notes are produced here." He indicated a series of plated 'gills' along the tail pipe. "I change pitch with these." Two wing sections coruscated out where the pipe fattened at the body section. "And here is the mouth." He worked a series of nodules along the neck to exercise the metal jaw.

"So you are our Spirit Catcher?" Dean Richards relaxed his grip on the eiderdowns and sat up.

"What's a Spirit Catcher?" The canon's voice was laden with fear and judgement.

"The man who will cleanse our great cathedral of its unwelcome parishioners," said the dean, rifling through the drawer of the bedside cabinet. "Ah." He produced a purse and rested back against his pillows.

"Eight shillings and nine pence for the tall spirits. A crown apiece for the two girls." He arched an eyebrow. "Half up front." Loosening the string at the neck, he handed the purse to the canon. "Count it out please, Nickolas."

The canon faltered. Ailen knew it pained the pious young man to play any part in the transaction. After all, such talk of ghosts bore more in common with the earth spirits entertained in pagan rites than Christian doctrine. But Ailen could see many things others could not, including the canon's desire to please his seniors and progress through the church. He wasn't surprised when Nickolas kept his concerns private and dug around inside the purse. Dean Richards gestured to a chair off in the shadows. "Sit with me a while, Spirit Catcher. Let me tell you what I know."

An hour later, the dean slipped back into his muttered prayer and strange hugging of the eiderdowns. Ailen stood up. Coins belonging to the church jangled in his pocket. He slid the dragon pipe back inside his pack and retrieved an envelope which he presented to Nickolas.

"Arrow root, garlic, lilac, mint, and mercury. Sprinkle the powder at the windowsills, the threshold and at the foot of the bed." Nickolas looked as if Ailen had handed him the severed hand of a baby.

"I want nothing to do with your witchcraft!"

"Then the Shakes will continue to pollute the dean. Leave him be or use this." He held up the envelope pointedly then laid it down on top of the bedside cabinet. "Your choice."

The King's Head, Bird Street, reputedly opened its doors in 1495 and had since served as a coaching inn, birthed the Staffordshire regiment, and acquired its fair share of ghosts over the centuries. Approaching the building, Ailen saw a silver blue orb flicker at a window on the third floor. Voices came to him – men readying for battle, their muskets and pikes knocking against armour as they moved. He was struck by a thick bitumen stench, felt the dry heat of flames. A woman screamed inside the public house. But the voice did not belong to the living. Instead, the scream looped back on itself and then faded.

Unlike the activities in the cathedral which the Dean had described, these hauntings were moments in time caught in the King's Head's ancient footings. Even the kitchen maid who had perished in the fire was just a shade. He saw her as he stepped into the bar. Most would experience her movement as a brief sensation of cold. Closing the door at his back, Ailen watched her sweep the floor, mindless of the patrons in her path. He was brought back to the land of the living by a blackened face looming in.

"Cutting it close. But the crowd's nice and eager. Here." Willy Bones, part-time exorcist, full-time Fool, shoved a pint of ale into Ailen's hand. "Quaff it quick. Our Saint's about to announce us." Ailen sank a drought from the ale glass. The King's Head had a generous quota of patrons, all gathered around the edges of the room to allow for a makeshift stage. Thom's character, Little Devil, stood to the back alongside the anaemic Doctor, Naw Jones. Playing the part of Saint George, ex-clergyman, Popule Brick, faced the audience and bowed.

"Greetings good patrons and drunkards too. A merrysome Autumn eve to you. Our play today is fearsome bold, a tale of quandaries aeon's old. I am Saint George..." A patriotic cry went up from the crowd. "I like to fight."

Willy leapt in to deliver a verse. "He smites Man, wyrd worm and ass alike."

Saint George crowed over the laughter and pointed at Willy.

"Lo, the Fool who pulls a tinkers cart, brays eey ore, lifts his tail and f..."

Tom's Little Devil danced in.

"Far and wide doth search the godly saint, to fight the bad – or those that ain't.

"But no good deed goes quite right, when the devil watches from the night."

Tom withdrew. To the crowd's delight, the Saint lunged at the Fool wielding a squeezebox as a weapon. On the run, the Fool dashed over to Ailen, who offered up the mechanical dragon pipe. While the Saint played a jig on the squeezebox, the Fool brandished the dragon pipe. Steam oozed from its jaw. The audience oohed and aahed at the oddity. Willy, the Fool, made no attempt to play the pipe. Instead it was paraded as the wyrd worm mentioned in verse – a puppet with gleaming scales and tick tock inner workings.

Performing their ceremonial dance about the floor, the Saint succeeded in overpowering the dragon; Willy mimed the creature's death throws then tossed it back to Ailen, who caught the pipe and tucked it back into his pack.

Running back over to Popule, Willy announced, "Saint George has slain the worm fast and true, and now my sword will do for you."

Willy stabbed the man in the belly with a finger. Popule howled and made a great show of staggering about the stage, to the great amusement of the spectators. At last, he collapsed and lay on his back.

Willy tugged on his donkey ears.

"Oh lord, he's dead! Oh me! Oh my! Why'd that old windbag go and die?

"I'll have to face the Queen's cavaliers, and me not yet supped all my beers."

Ailen strode out onto the stage. He stopped opposite Willy, the crowd clearly enthralled by his bulk and appearance.

"Behold! The woodland son, the Jack o' the Green," exclaimed Willy, sinking to one knee. He clasped his hands, imploring, "Oh sacred son, do not judge me by this bloody scene. Indeed the knight deserved to die." Willy tugged on his donkey ears. "He was a greater ass than I."

Alien held out his arms, the feathered sleeves of his tunic fanning out like wings.

"I cannot save this Christian son, who slayed my worm for sport and fun,

"But to save thee gross palaver, I'll do away with the cadaver.

"In my wyld wood where fairies dwell, I'll make his death a living hell!"

He swooped towards the onlookers, saw a flash of fear in their eyes accompanied by nervous smiles. At his back, Naw stepped forward, tall black hat exaggerating his height.

"At peace, Green Man, you know as I, all return to your wyld wood once they die."

Naw switched his attention to Willy. "Doctor Sham. I alcamise stone into gold, heal the sick and lame,

"Help spirits rest, clear unwelcome guests and raise the dead again."

Willy, the Fool, butted in. "You raise the dead? Oh say it's so, and to the gallows I'll not go."

Naw knelt beside Popule, who rolled his eyes and stuck out his tongue. Holding his arms out in appeal to Willy, Naw said, "This holy knight I can revive at your behest,

"For one tenth your mortal soul – and the devil take the rest."

Thom jigged from one foot to the other at the back of the stage. He hissed in a loud aside, "I've use for a foolish man, spread on toast like gooseberry-jam."

The Doctor waved his fingers over the prone Saint.

"Wake up, wake up, our noble son, there's beer to sup now the play's done.

"Arise, Saint George, with magic black, so this young fool escapes the rack."

Popule staggered to his feet, reeling about the stage so that his audience lent away, laughing and clutching their ale glasses tight. The Fool, the Doctor and the Saint joined hands and bowed as one. Thom began to circulate the pub, holding out his black velvet purse by its twin sticks and requesting mummers' alms. Meanwhile, Ailen stepped forward and bowed. Sweeping out his feathered arms again, he delivered the final verse.

"It's story's end, night's drawn in and we must bid farewell,

"To saints and fools and wyrd worms beneath our mummers' spell.

"If we have cheered your Autumn eve, please spare a coin or two,

"And so we take our final bows and bid goodnight to you."

Ailen Savage knew it took a special breed of man to want to assist a Spirit Catcher. He had been born to it, his great grandfather having originated the role. In the year 1754, as a young man with a fascination for Elemental Folklore, Tam Savage had found a way to divine a restless spirit and capture it via a multi-metalled steam pipe. At a time when religion was in decline and science providing the answer to many of life's mysteries, Tam Savage had chosen to work alongside the local vicar as a Spirit Catcher. Perfecting his skills and instruments, he had passed the knowledge down to Ailen's father, who, in turn, had passed it on to Ailen. Some argued it was a brutal business to introduce a child to. Ailen considered it no less dangerous than a life spent in Birmingham's factories or down Leicestershire's coal mines or taking a chisel to the worn-out heights of Lichfield's cathedral.

Less obvious were the reasons why the others joined him. "I can see the science in your method," said the canon, Nickolas. He hugged himself against the cool air, or the awesome sight of the cathedral veiled in early morning mist, Ailen wasn't sure which. "That pipe contraption of yours. It has a heathen design but the science is no doubt godly." Nickolas lowered his voice. "You are a man of breeding. Why take up with a mummers' band?" He pointed ahead to the three men and the boy dressed in costume and makeup even at that hour.

"I'll set you straight, Canon, because you aren't a man to see past his own faith or social standing. Once, mind, and then no more said on it. Those men might be carved from God's arse-end, but they are still of his flesh. There's living and undead aplenty outside of your great and glorious cathedral and Willy, Thom, Naw and Pop have helped me separate the two more times than I care to remember. Take Willy there." Ailen nodded at the man wearing the donkey ears. "He's a product of Lancashire and Cajun blood. Look past the makeup and you'll see his features lean towards the exotic. Turns out Willy's mother couldn't take the Lancashire climate. Back home in her native Louisiana, she contracted Typhoid Fever – or became possessed as Willy tells it. In the third week, she started to cut the flesh from her own bones. Willy lent himself out to every witch around – drawing water, mending what was broken, giving up food meant for his own mouth, all in a bid to learn the way to cast the demon out."

Ailen's eyes softened. "Willy didn't learn enough in time to save her. After his mother's death, he returned to Britain and put his skills as an exorcist to good use." He placed a heavy hand on the canon's shoulder. "The others have similar tales. We sniffed out the fear in each other – not fear of personal attack by the supernatural elements we encounter, but fear that we would not save others from those same dangers."

Nickolas frowned. He took time over his words, as if adding to a stack of cards. "Please understand, Mister Savage. Dean Richards is in a vulnerable state and our cathedral... it houses some remarkable treasures."

"And you think we may find those too great a temptation to pass over, being the lowly vagabonds that we are?"

"Not you, Mister Savage. You are an honest Lichfield son, no doubt. But the men you travel with are a coarser breed. By your own admission, one is part-negro..."

Ailen drew himself up. In that instant, he appeared less man than something gnarled and grown tall over hundreds of years. "Do not judge a man by his skin!" he thundered. The canon flinched as the mummer moved in close. "The very fact that spirits have survived beyond death and haunt your cathedral should be enough to illustrate our worth beyond the boundaries of flesh."

A flicker of confusion crossed Nickolas's face.

They were interrupted by Naw, materialised through the mist. He smiled, an expression that exaggerated his skeletal appearance.

"Mister Savage does love a good debate on subjects of a spiritual and religious nature. But he don't always appreciate the force of his vigour." Naw's soft welsh lit instantly humanised him.

"Of course. It is good and right for a man to exercise his intellect. But my apologies, sir, we have not met properly. I am Canon Nickolas Russell."

Naw shook hands. "Naw Jones. Of Caediff. Mummer, spiritualist, historian." He laughed kindly. "Please do not hold the latter against me."

Nickolas looked newly flawed by Naw's generous spirit and education. Ailen almost felt sorry for the man. He consulted a small brass pocket watch hidden amongst his tunic rags. "What time do the stonemasons start work?"

"8.00am," replied Nickolas.

"We have an hour." Ailen pointed at the bunch of keys the canon carried. "Please accompany us. I will need to hear all the details you can offer on what has occurred inside." He slapped Naw on the back. "And hopefully our historian here can go some way to explaining why."

"...very little in the way of restoration until the architect James Wyatt undertook repairs late last century. Wyatt's idea was to create a church within the cathedral – a bullish idea to my mind which saw the interior whitewashed, the arches of the choir filled in, the High Altar removed and seating right through to the Lady Chapel." Nickolas held up his hands, indicating the magnificent restored interior. "Mister Scott has repaired this great building with flare and sensitivity."

"It is certainly soul-rich," murmured Naw, intent on the device he held in his palm.

The tan leather box housed a circular device with a flickering hand – not dissimilar to a compass, thought Nickolas, distracted from his efforts to show superior knowledge of the cathedral's architectural history.

"And that device suggests as much?" Nickolas stared quizzically at the box. The hand was a shard of purple crystal.

"Amethyst." Naw tapped the glass cover over the dial. "Wards off danger while protecting mental and psychic clarity." Circling slowly on the spot, he cast a long thin shadow.

"Have you located the source of the apparitions?" Nickolas felt the weight of the cathedral keys at his belt.

"The source?" Naw pointed down. "We're standing on it. One thousand Christians murdered on this spot during Roman occupation. And what about the three spires above us – coincidental or in homage to the three martyred kings buried at Borrowcop Hill?"

"Nothing but folklore!"

"So their prominence on the city seal is a misnomer?" Naw eyed his ghost compass intently.

Nickolas blustered, "I'm simply saying a town as rich in history as Lichfield is bound to have an abundance of pagan lore and country legends."

"And the shrine?" Naw pointed to the far end of the nave and the High Altar with its decorative apse. "Saint Chad died in 672. But while he was originally interred here in the cathedral, the Reformation saw the bones travel as far as France and return at last having acquired a third thigh bone. So legend has it." Naw inclined his head respectfully. "Yet still you believe, Canon Nickolas."

*

The boy stood to the fore of the south east aisle. A bird fluttered among the ceiling arches. Dawn lent the stained glass windows a subtle glow.

"Thom?" Ailen approached slowly. The lad was so still he could have passed for a statue. He appeared absorbed by a large white marble sculpture of two young girls at rest in one another's arms. "I'm not sure about this spot, Mister Savage. I think it might be colder here." Thom cocked his head. "Are the girls' bodies buried beneath?"

"Dean Richards said not. It's just a monument. Commissioned when the mother lost both girls and a husband who was a Reverend inside three years." Ailen laid a hand on the cool stone of the eldest girl's forehead. A shooting pain ripped up his arm and he pulled away.

"You all right, Mister Savage?"

"Yes... yes, Thom. Thank you." He cradled his arm. The pain subsided.

"I touched the stone before you came and wasn't hurt." Thom sucked his lower lip.

"Could be the children sense a kinship in you? Although..." Ailen stared at the monument, half-expecting the two sisters to open their eyes and stare back. "Objects can attract and house ghosts. I'm suspicious that the sympathetic rendering of the two dead girls has attracted a poltergeist. They are attracted to the young."

"Aye. And I remember how difficult it is to trap them buggers."

Ailen smiled and nodded. "Difficult, not impossible. But I may need to use you as bait."

Thom and Naw busied themselves salting the doorways; the windows were adequately protected by their ecclesiastical stained glass depicting Saint Chad and other holy entities. The sounds of stone being chiselled and idle banter filtered in from outside. The stonemasons had started work.

"If you are afraid of ghosts you might want to step outside so we can close the salt line behind you."

Nickolas found he was addressed by the mummer Knight – or Popule as the boy called him. The man had impossibly blue eyes.

"I'm not afraid," the canon lied.

"Should be." Popule dragged down his tunic at the neck, revealing a web of scar tissue across his collar bones. "Poltergeist pinned me to the floor of my church in Ashbourne. Poured blazing lamp oil all over my chest." He pushed up his left sleeve. His arm was marred by healed burns and bites. "Ghosts lash out when aggravated. They learn to throw a punch, grow teeth."

"You are a clergyman?" Nickolas wasn't sure whether to find the fact settling or disturbing.

"*Was.*" Popule put down his pack and undid the string at the neck. He talked as he retrieved a number of items. "Once the spirits had laid their marks on me I was lost to the Shakes. Know what that is?"

Nickolas thought about Dean Richards cocooned in eiderdowns. "I think I do."

"I pray you never experience it yourself and know for certain. Even if you can find a Spirit Catcher to doctor to you, the sickness never truly leaves your soul. It's always hovering, just below the surface." Popule glanced up. Surrounded by a weird cornucopia of objects, he looked like a warlock from a romantic painting. Nickolas recognised sticks of chalk, a small brass bowl, a bunch of lavender, smelling salts and a tinder box. Less familiar was a long belt fitted with cartridges of some white mineral and the gun which accompanied it.

Popule picked up the weapon and appeared to weigh the measure of it. It was a beautiful object, thought Nickolas, remembering the rusty flintlock his grandfather had used to shoot rabbits on the family estate. Popule's gun had a long silver barrel, at least a foot and a half in length, and spiralled like a hazel branch. The load mechanism was a traditional cylinder, just larger. The hammer and trigger were cast from an intensely black metal. The handle was an exotic deep red hardwood. Symbols were inlaid in brass wire along the handle; they struck Nickolas as Arabic. The ex-clergyman sensed his interest. "A revolver. A few years ago I was fortunate enough to be able to discuss my requirements with a visiting American, Mister Samuel Colt. He was able to adapt his brand new design to fit my specialist requirements. Here…" Popule picked up the gun and spun the barrel. "The cylinder revolves to align the next chamber and round with the hammer and barrel. Shoots cartridges of solid rock salt. I can fire the salt as a bullet. Or if I close this small grid across the muzzle, the salt splinters and scatters. See?"

Nikolas flinched as Popule pointed the gun at his face. He forced himself to stare down the capped barrel.

"Salting the doorways keeps the spirits where we want them. Inside." Popule's strange blue eyes twinkled. "And this revolver helps stun them if needs be. Ghosts like the sort you have here are not inclined to come quietly." He gave his weapon an affectionate pat and slid it into a holster at his waist, the long barrel running the length of his thigh. He slung the cartridge belt over his head and slid an arm through.

"If you are staying – and in these circumstances it's always good to have a man of God not as lapsed as I – then you better open your mind to things the church doesn't care for." He put a hand to the side of his mouth, shouting, "Seal the doors! The canon's staying put." Kneeling, he picked up the chalk, appeared to examine the patterns of light on the flagstones, and began to draw.

It started out this way. Men moved stones set in place for hundreds of years and with no mind to the consequences. Sometimes a structure was deplete of spiritual energy and alterations left the ground sleeping. But for one as entrenched in bloody history as Lichfield Cathedral, the ghosts' awakening was inevitable. Of course the disturbances could have been avoided with the right consecrations and herbal homages buried beneath the dirt at ten foot intervals around the building's exterior. Fortunately for a Spirit Catcher such as Ailen, these rudimentary ghost traps were not common knowledge – which meant there was profit to be made in tidying up after enthusiastic architects.

Two hours in and the chalked traps were set. The mid-morning sun shone in weakly at the high windows. Dust speckled the air. Stonemasons performed their noisy work on the Gothic facade.

Behind the scaffolds, row on row of ancient kings were being restored to their plinths.

Inside the cathedral, Ailen called his men to order and asked, "Canon. Would you say a prayer?"

The mummers formed a circle and bowed their heads. Nickolas started to speak; the shake in his voice betrayed his nervousness. Ailen kept his gaze on his surroundings. He caught flickers of motion out of the corners of his eyes. Three figures, all exceptionally tall and twisting up from the floor near the South Transept. Each wore something on their head – a crown? The figures disappeared when he tried to focus.

Smaller shadows danced about the walls – hundreds layering over one another. The floor was patterned with them. Ailen knew that, for all their numbers, these were harmless shades.

"See them, Mister Savage?" Despite his devil garb, there was still innocence in Thom's eyes.

"I see them, Thom." Ailen kept his voice low so as not to interrupt Nickolas. Prayer niggled restless spirits. Used in isolation, it was a slow, unreliable exorcism method. Combine prayer with psychic weaponry and the fight became quicker if potentially messier.

The boy swallowed and stared down the length of the nave. "We got to clear them all?"

"No, lad. Most are harmless. We've got three ghosts to parcel up. Powerful ones. And then there's the poltergeist." Ailen pointed a finger up. "I think we got its attention."

Twenty or so prayer books levitated overhead. Canon Nickolas's prayer petered out.

"Everyone back up slowly." Ailen led by example, his dragon pipe trained on the floating books.

The circle of men widened.

With a tremendous crack of leather spines, the books began spitting out their pages. A few stayed intact and careered down like black hail stones. Ailen saw Nickolas receive a cut to one eyebrow. The wound bled into the canon's eye; he dabbed at it with a handkerchief and mopped his glistening brow with a sleeve. Other books aimed for Popule and Thom. The ex-clergyman fired his revolver. Slugs of rock salt punched through the books, the blast holes giving off smoke.

"I take it your prayer woke the blighter." Willy winked at Nickolas. "You all right there, friend?"

Nickolas nodded. He looked deathly pale.

All the books had fallen. Except for the sounds of the men working outside, the cathedral was silent.

"Which direction next?" Ailen kept his pipe close.

Naw consulted his compass. He pointed south-east. "Originated at The Sleeping Children monument. But the reading is south-west now, vestibule most likely. Also..." The historian wheeled around, checking the coordinates. "I have a second reading from the South Transept."

Ailen nodded. He had a partial view of the South Transept, a shaded arm of the cathedral at that hour.

"Tell me, Canon. What do you see in those shadows?"

The canon forced his gaze in that direction. He cocked his head.

"I see nothing."

"Good. Then you won't mind assisting Popule and Naw investigating that quadrant."

"Oh. Oh, I see. Do I need to be armed?" asked the young man tensely.

Popule brought two fingers to his lips, kissed and pressed them to the cross around his neck. "Faith, Canon. All the weaponry you need."

Nickolas thought he knew the cathedral intimately, but the South Transept's atmosphere seemed queer while its shadows deepened. "See them now, Canon?" Popule pointed to the far end of the transept. "Blur your eyes and stare ahead. Don't try to look at them directly. They'll disappear."

Nickolas played with the keys at his belt. He wanted to call the mummers mad men and demand they leave that sacred house. But then he remembered the dean, all tucked in on himself against some unseen foe. Nickolas slit his eyes and focused ahead.

Three silhouettes came into focus, just as if they had moved to stand immediately behind him when he was looking in a mirror. The figures were wraith-thin and stooped. They wore long robes, cloaks, and spiky crowns.

"Still not scared?" Popule shot aside.

Heart drumming, Nickolas shifted his focus to the ex-clergyman. Popule rested his revolver against one shoulder. His strange blue eyes coruscated.

Willy led the way and Ailen let him, knowing that Willy's failure to save his possessed mother burdened him with a lifetime's worth of guilt. Sometimes Ailen wondered if all Willy's travelling pack contained was guilt – great sticky clumps of the stuff. Which was why the man had to lead the way now, face the demon first, and strive eternally for relief from that weight.

"What have we got, Willy?" Ailen brought up the rear, followed noiselessly by Thom. He liked to know the kid was with him. It gave him courage as the antechamber threatened to seal them in.

"Angry raggedy sprite. You see the shadows?"

Ailen looked. The shadows cast by the rippled stone of the numerous arches spiked out as they passed. Bone fingers stretching.

"Air too. You got a lungful of that sulphur?"

Ailen grimaced. "One of the least appealing aspects of our job." He glanced back at Thom.

"What do you see, lad?"

Colours danced in Thom's wide eyes. "It's a cross one, Mister Savage. I see red mist coming off the stones. Waves of it."

"Aye." Ailen watched the mist tendril out. "What's at the end there?"

"Chapter House," answered Willy over a shoulder.

"A dead end."

"Not literally I hope." Willy showed his teeth. He stepped aside. "You going to pipe the nasty inside?"

Ailen nodded. "Get ready to join in the song, Willy." Thom stuck close, twitchy and bright eyed. He clutched a handful of lavender stems from Naw's stock for protection. Ailen put the mouthpiece of the dragon pipe between his lips. A small sighting lens was mounted halfway down the body; Ailen squeezed up one eye and peered through. The mist transmogrified into clawing, fleshless arms. A hideous face loomed amongst the tangle of limbs. "Angry is an understatement." He concertinaed out the wing sections of the pipe and sounded his first note. Long and low, a musical whisper.

Something shifted in the atmosphere, in a manner that Ailen recognised. Where the poltergeist had only been playing with them before, now it began to understand the men posed a threat. The faces in the mist broke open, revealing spindly teeth. Ailen didn't falter. Playing a second note, he kept the mist inches from their faces. His grandfather had calibrated the pipe at a frequency too seductive for the spirit to ignore. The men moved through the narrow arched doorways into Chapter House and the mist followed.

"Is that the last of it?" Willy pushed back his sleeves. "All right then. I'm going to block us in." He stood between the narrow doorways, raised his arms sideways and touched the stone either side. He closed his eyes. "Nasty raging thing, this one. Don't leave me too long."

"I won't." Ailen flexed his large fingers around the winged extension of the pipe. Thom stared around the room, enthralled. Willy began to chant – weird, ancient, dangerous words in the language of the dead Ailen did not want to understand. Instead, he played the long, slow notes on his dragon pipe and walked in a circle around the sigil chalked onto the floor.

The mist altered, becoming more substantial and moving in ripples. As Ailen played, a fat tendril oozed out from the wall, drawn to him. It nosed at the mouth of the dragon pipe like a cat sniffing an offered morsel. Ailen continued to weave a circle around the sigil while Thom stayed quiet nearby and Willy kept up his peculiar chant. Slowly, doing his level best not to spook the spirit, Ailen moved the fingers of one hand onto the brass nodules along the neck of the pipe. Steam escaped the dragon pipe's opening jaws.

Ailen crushed his fingers around the neck of the pipe and the jaws slammed shut. The tendril lashed side to side, the tip of it suctioned. Willy's voice faltered, but he struggled on, his face crumpled in pain.

Running over, Thom produced Popule's smelling salts and waved them under Willy's nose. Willy showed the whites of his eyes, but managed to refocus.

Ailen touched the tip of his pipe to the floor sigil, attaching the tendril to it. He began to trace out the design with his footsteps, and the poltergeist was forced to follow, tethered to the embroidery of lines.

It was the cry of a wounded man from the other side of the cathedral which broke the spell. The misty poltergeist quivered and thwacked, tearing free of its tether to the sigil. A heat wave burst around the walls, prompting Willy to utter his own cry and collapse, knocking the smelling salts out of Thom's hand. The bottle shattered on impact with the flagstones.

Naw fell back into Nickolas's arms, leaving a ghost warrior's spear slick with blood. A tremendous crack sounded; Nickolas saw the slug of rock salt punch in at the back of the ghost's head. The apparition flickered and snuffed out.

More warriors solidified out of the walls. Their flesh was crisp and black, their weapons large and brutal. A few carried swords. Most wielded axes, spears and short blades.

"What are these devils?" cried Nickolas. Lowering Naw to the floor, the canon brushed the blood from his nicked eyebrow and tried to focus.

"Devil is the right word for them! Get Naw over to the sigil, haul up inside its circle and quote your bible." Popule flipped the grid over the muzzle of his revolver and fired. Plumes of salt exploded into the air; the warriors faded as it dusted down. Seconds later, they were whole again.

Fresh blood trickled from Nickolas's eyebrow. Fear threatened to liquefy his bones as he dragged Naw onto the sigil, leaving a glossy red trail behind. His conscience bucked as he thought about the occult symbols beneath his feet. But he remembered Popule's words about him having to open his mind. Seeing the ex-clergyman dodge a tremendous hammer blow from one warrior, he began to recite. "In you, oh Lord, I have taken refuge; let me never be put to shame."

Popule fired off cartridges. The warriors went up in flames, but still more kept materialising out of the walls.

"Deliver me in your righteousness. Turn your ear to me."

Spectres lunged in Nickolas's direction but backed away when they struck the circumference of the sigil. Death's stink was in the air.

"Why haven't the other three spirits moved?" he called between snippets of scripture, pointing at the colossal wraiths under the large stained glass window.

It was Naw who answered, gulping in great lungfuls of air. "The three Christian kings. Martyred in the time of the heathen Emperor Dioclesian. 288AD. Their burial ground is at Borrowcop."

"That's just a legend!"

"Yet here they are," panted Naw.

"But why are their spirits here and why do these demon warriors attack?"

Ghosts charged at the sigil. Nickolas gabbled a fresh section of psalm; the warriors' weapons struck the air overhead like hammers brought down upon an anvil. In an opposite corner of the South Transept, Popule shot a couple clean through with his salt revolver.

"The warriors protect the lords, who are linked to this site by their own spilt blood." Naw let out a sigh. "I'm blacking out, boyo. Help Popule fight the good fight." The Welsh man's eyed rolled and he slumped unconscious.

The spirit evaporated the instant Willy lost his hold on the archways. Ailen ran over to his friend, who collapsed into his arms. He lowered Willy to the floor. Thom worried at the man's tunic collar, loosening it.

Ailen stepped away. "Check his hands," he said.

Thom turned Willy's hands palm up. They were burnt red-raw.

"Stay here, Willy. Thom and I can see to the devil."

"Not in a month of Sundays." Willy sucked air through his teeth and fought his way to standing. "We've spooked the blighter now. You are going to need me to chant to help chain it. First, though, you're going to need to coax the flibbertigibbet out of its hiding place.

Ailen glanced at Thom. "The poltergeist likes you. I need you to lure it out." He placed a hand on the boy's shoulder. "Don't worry. It can't harm you."

"Someone has been harmed, though. We heard the cry." Thom looked pained. "It sounded like Naw."

Ailen pointed through the arched doorways. "Let's deal with the ghost. Then we can help our man, Naw."

They exited the vestibule to find the sun had set. The nave was cavernous and very dark. From the south side of the building came the crash of swords, canon fire from Popule's revolver and the young canon's quivering prayer.

"On second thoughts, I'm going to help Naw and the others first." He pointed in the direction of The Sleeping Children monument. "I know where to find you."

Ailen arrived in the South Transept to see Popule fire off salt spray and the five ghost warriors who had him cornered fade at their edges. He looked for the canon and found him muttering prayer and gone wild about the eye. Naw bled at the canon's feet. The sigil provided them with a circle of protection. But if Popule and he were to catch the spirits, they would need the trap to be empty.

"Canon!" he shouted, avoiding the slice of a ghost's axe by dipping low. "I need you to exit the sigil if we're going to tie the spirits down."

"But they'll destroy us the instant we step off," answered Nickolas, close to tears.

Ailen chuckled. "How soon you adopt our wicked pagan ways, Canon." Again, he avoided the fall of the axe and, seconds later, the huge sword plunged towards his throat. "Have faith in your own spells, Canon," he called. "Prayer will keep the ghosts at bay long enough."

The canon looked doubtful. Ailen had no choice but to trust the man would exist the sigil in time and hopefully drag Naw out too. Charging towards Popule like a bull elephant, Ailen cried, "I'm going to pipe them in. Salt ain't enough. These spirits are too ancient and justified."

Justified in misunderstanding the alterations to the building and wanting to keep their death bed intact, Ailen thought as he ran through the salt mist, tasting it on his lips. Figures came at him, their burnt flesh, whited eyes and flashing weapons seemingly birthed from Hell. Ailen fought their blows with bursts of notes off his dragon pipe. Ahead, the three kings flickered beneath the stained glass window. Their crowns were thorny, their bodies elongated like men put to the rack. Ailen didn't need them to speak to sense the tremendous anger issuing from them. He would have liked to reason with the three ancients – reassure them that the stonemasons were repairing not destroying. But he knew enough about ghosts to know they were capable of raw emotion but otherwise inflexible.

His tune quickened as he approached the kings. Images smoked his mind – hundreds slaughtered by Roman hands, crowns falling into pools of blood. The noise of battle tenderised his brain. Still he played, steam spilling off the mouth of the instrument. The images broke, spraying up pain and torn flesh and death – so much death. The faces of the kings distorted. Their bodies leant towards him, drawn to the pipe. Thinner and thinner they stretched, as if hypnotised. In rapid snaps, the dragon pipe's jaw got each by a thread.

Ailen walked backwards, towing the spirits in the direction of the sigil. He sensed shadows lunge for him, heard the pop of salt in the air and knew Popule was keeping the warriors at bay. The kings, meanwhile, became trailing ether. Ailen didn't look away for a moment but kept on stepping backwards until he saw the chalked line of the sigil underfoot. He heard the canon chanting his bible passages a few feet away; all he could do was trust in the man to have left the sigil's sanctuary and taken Naw with him. Stepping off the sigil, he twisted at the waist, cast out over the chalked circle and released the jaw of the pipe.

It took only seconds for the kings' spirits to interweave on top of the weird symbols, like stitches in time. The instant their masters were gone, the ghost warriors dissolved. Returned to history.

Ailen nodded at Popule, who returned the gesture. Nearby, Canon Nickolas hugged Naw. His young face streaked with blood and tears, the canon's eyes danced about the walls and he kept up his muttering. *The shakes*, thought Ailen.

He would tend to the young man later. First he had a poltergeist to catch.

From a distance a person would be forgiven for mistaking the two young girls in nightgowns and the boy in mummer's garb for best of friends. Ailen, though, knew the girls owed their manifestation to a malevolent spirit. Once upon a time he had been interested in the origins of such entities, had studied papers by the great spiritualists of the modern age. It was Willy who had convinced him that there was no reasoning with a poltergeist, no explanation which would aid his understanding or his empathy. There was only the squatting toad of a spirit inside its chosen object, ready to scare or taunt or main at whim.

Yet seeing Thom conversing with the ghost girls suggested a softer, human presence. Ailen knew it was a lie. He joined Willy in the shadows.

"The others alive?" Willy nodded sharply in the direction of the South Transept.

"Naw's wounded. Canon's got the Shakes. Popule is in one piece."

Willy glanced up. "Beautiful building this. Shame it's built on a field of the dead." He sucked his gums against the pain of his burnt hands and stared back over at Thom. "Seems almost a shame to interrupt them."

"Aye. If they were what they seem." Ailen slipped the macabre necklace from around his neck. It was one of Willy's voodoo creations, made up of dead beetles, lambs' wool, chicken claws and the dried remains of mice. He pointed at the apparitions of the two girls. "We both know poltergeists love dead things." He rattled the necklace. The girls moved onto all fours, shoulders hunching, cocking their heads one way then the other. Hanging the necklace off his belt, Ailen adjusted his grip on his dragon pipe. He muttered: "I could use a little salt in the atmosphere."

A hand patted his shoulder. Popule's. The man's eyes shone crystal blue, the soot covering his face streaked by sweat.

Popule fed a fresh cartridge into his revolver and spun the barrel shut. Ailen was glad of the backup as he stepped out of the shadows.

"You all right there, Thom?"

"They're very sad, Mister Savage," Thom replied. Ailen felt the familiar twinge of regret not to be recognised as so much more than the boy's employee. But his own feelings were secondary to the boy's safety.

"The real sisters were buried miles away, Thom. At peace, let's hope. Our poltergeist here likes the way their monument looks and has bedded down. Now I want you to tell your friend it has the choice to leave or we can exorcise it."

Thom bit his bottom lip. "All right." He turned back to the girls, who had crawled close, their opaque white eyes rolling.

As Thom spoke to them, Ailen felt the atmosphere still like the surface of a millpond. When the girls started to fade, he felt a tinge of relief. Had Thom really talked the poltergeist into leaving? *Wonderful, kind, accident-prone Thom.*

The wall of fire rolled around them in seconds, firing off a heat wave. Both girls opened their mouths unnaturally wide and the screams of Lichfield's martyred issued forth. Ailen steeled himself against the noise. Thom backed away.

The poltergeist had no intention of losing its new friend. The girls' heads morphed into a mess of silvery, mouth-tipped tentacles while the bodies remained separate. It crawled towards Thom, a crablike Medusa.

"Get away, Thom." Ailen stepped between the boy and the poltergeist, causing it to rear up on its back limbs, tentacles hissing. "Start chanting, Willy! Popule. Keep the air full of salt!" he demanded, and put his lips to the reed of the dragon pipe.

Rock salt burst overhead like fireworks and Ailen began to play. The poltergeist tried to sink back into its marble tomb. It tugged at itself as if attempting to prise free of thick mud. Ailen quickened his tune and bit out at the spirit with the steaming jaw of the dragon pipe. The poltergeist arched away, a serpentine movement at odds with its lower, crabbing limbs. Seconds later, it scrabbled around to the opposite side of the chalk sigil marked out on the flagstones.

Wind blew in – red hot and scented with decay. Willy's chant grew weaker; Ailen suspected the man's palms were freshly aflame. Blinking against the ash and snow whipped up by the vicious spirit alongside Popule's salt sprays, he fought to put one foot in front of the other. Blood trickled from his ears, his nose. Ailen pressed on against the tremendous volume of suffering and the searing heat of the funeral pyre from many centuries before. One thought gave him strength – some ghosts stay to ease the agonies of those left behind. Others stay to torment those who lived on. The poltergeist belonged to the latter and needed to be put back among the demons.

Ailen ran the last few steps, lungs baking against his ribs. He grasped the neck of his dragon pipe, burnt the tips of his fingers on the glowing nodules and clamped the steaming jaw around one misty tentacle. The poltergeist writhed, but Ailen held fast this time. Hearing Willy's voice harden, those ancient, occult words seeming to pepper the poltergeist's surface like hot coals, Ailen moved to the sigil's edge.

"I make you an offering. Scraps of death for peace inside this hallowed hall." Retrieving the voodoo necklace from his belt, he tossed it into the chalked circle. Arching at the spine, he cast out with the dragon pipe and released the jaw.

The poltergeist streamed into the sigil. Writhing and whipping against its bonds, it found itself dragged down over the symbols, one tentacle at a time. As the last thread of it tacked down onto the sigil, the screams of the martyred ceased. The wall of flame around the men brightened then went out.

A month passed before the large man came to call at The Deanery. Mrs Rook would later describe the pains it put her to trying to place the gentleman. His suit was cheap cloth but cut well enough while his starched shirt collar hugged the neck. But the face – a mask of steel with scars aplenty!

The man's voice betrayed him. Nickolas recognised its depth from his place before the fire and gripped the blanket across his legs on instinct. He forced himself to let go and call, "Mrs Rook! Show Mister Savage in. He and I have business."

Nickolas heard the housekeeper falter, perhaps afraid of the name. But then she must have ushered in their visitor because the front door closed and heavy footsteps sounded across the hallway.

A man like Ailen Savage didn't wait to be shown the way. He materialised in the doorway of the sitting room, blocking out what lay beyond.

"Canon Nickolas."

"Mister Savage. Come in, do. Get by the fire. Mrs Rook says the weather is unseasonably bitter."

"I won't stay long." The man approached the fire nonetheless and stood before it, arms crossed, his face more weathered for its illumination. "I didn't call earlier as I was helping Naw get back on his feet. I see that you too have been nursed back to health," he said after a few moments.

"Dean Richards has gone to the seaside to continue his recovery. Very kindly, he installed me in the house under the care of Mrs Rook until his return."

Ailen's lips curved. "Seems you and the dean had use for those herbs I gave you after all."

Nickolas shifted in his seat. "If you are asking if my mind has been opened to the supernatural and to magick worked outside of the power of prayer then the answer is yes, Mister Savage. Yes, the spirits have left their mark on me." Nickolas touched a finger to the fresh scar at one eyebrow, trying to control the shake of his hand. When the man opposite nodded gravely, Nickolas knew he understood that the true scar lay on the inside.

Keen to change the emphasis of their conversation, he asked, "How did you dispose the remains of the spirits?" Nickolas's own mind had corrupted in the aftershock of events. Glimpses of them came to him occasionally – the cathedral's fixtures sparkling with salt as if in an ice age, Naw collapsed at his feet, the air laced with the stench of burning.

Mister Savage kept up his unwavering stare. "We washed the sigils away with holy water. Helps to have an ex-man of the cloth in the form of Popule. He blessed a good few buckets worth and we baptised God's house anew."

"Oh. Oh, I see." Nikolas liked the sound of the cathedral being newly sanctified, even if at the hands of one of the mummers' troupe. He retrieved the package tucked in beside him for safe keeping.

"The second half of your fee, Mister Savage. And thank you."

Washed clean of rags and soot, the chief mummer looked even more intimidating. His large hand took the package and pocketed it.

"You aren't wearing your costume. Has the mummer season ended?" asked the canon, unsure how to close the conversation.

The man dipped his great head. When he glanced up, tears glistened in his eyes.

"Anniversary of my son's death. I like to clean up once a year to pay respects at his grave."

"I am sincerely sorry to hear of his passing. May the lord keep him." Nickolas felt a twist of sorrow in his gut for the strange giant of a man.

"He ain't ready for the Lord yet," said Mister Savage. He shook back his shoulders, shrugging off the mantle of mourning.

Nickolas peered quizzically at his guest. But the mummer seemed all talked out. He walked away and filled the doorway once more.

"Goodbye, Canon Nickolas."

"Goodbye, Mister Savage."

Heavy footsteps crossed the hallway floor again. The canon heard the front door open and felt a blast of cold across his exposed skin. Seconds later, the door slammed to.

Outside, the evening air was sharp and pure. The cathedral loomed before the Spirit Catcher like a rock of ages. Sculptures burgeoned. Stained glass burned like jewels, lit by internal light. Lichfield slumbered all around.

"Come now, Thom. Let's go meet the others," said Ailen to the ghost boy at his side.

"Yes, Mister Savage," Thom replied.

Together, father and son stepped off into the night.

~*~

For my contribution to *The Mammoth Book of Ghost Stories by Women*, I looked to one of my favourite cities, Lichfield, and the grand gothic cathedral which dominates its historical heart. I've always found Mummers both fascinating and terrifying in their ragged garb and face-paint, and my play within the story incorporates the traditional elements of Mummer storytelling. "The Field of the Dead" is a supernatural take on the Pied Piper fairy tale, and my version of a Victorian *Ghostbusters*.

The Shadow Keeper

For two days in late October every year, the town of Burton-on-Trent becomes home to *The Statutes*; a bustling bazaar of laughter, fun and fortune, with bright carousels, sugar mice and candies, Ferris wheels and fairy-lights, swing-boat rides and ghost trains, dark-skinned gypsies, strong men in pantaloons and The Great Hall of Mirrors – where we are all transformed into midgets, beasts and giants.

Welcoming in the first decade of the new century, this carnival atmosphere is somewhat recent, and much removed from the fair which I remember when, in 1871, I pushed my way through the jeering crowds of townsfolk and bought the life of a tortured child for a penny. I should have known then that I could never save her; that the real monsters hide beneath the semblance of skin. But there was such sorrow in the great sunflowers of her eyes, and I wanted to protect her. Little did I realise that the tormented stranger had her own angel of deliverance; the darkness inside.

October, 1871

Miss Mabel had been engaged in my family's service for nigh on twenty-five years. She was an industrious sort, who would polish the family silver until it shone like moulded moonbeams. But even Miss Mabel's hands began to tremble when she reached three score years and ten. Loath to replace the kindly maid, my parents decided to employ some young girl as a sort of helping hand. So it was that, one Saturday in late October, I found myself despatched to the local hiring fair with instructions to secure a 'good strong lass who would mind what she was told.'

It was early. The sun was newly risen and the sky had the delicate complexion of peaches and cream. Passing through the villages in the open gig, I breathed deeply, enjoying the country scents of the season – smouldering bonfires and windfalls in the orchards. Coming into Burton-on-Trent, these pleasant odours were soon superseded by the high stench of yeast for which the brewing town was famed.

But even the cooper seemed to have laid down his hammer and joined the crowds at the hiring fair that day. Whiskered farmers mingled side-by-side with the gentry while squealing pigs dodged the hands of their masters and kid goats shrieked like teething babes. The place resembled an overrun farmyard. There were horses led by a thief's nervous hand; there were bulls pulled along by the rings through their steaming nostrils; there were cows with mud-caked hides and rich men in top hats and poor men in flat caps and ragged children chasing chickens through the crowds.

Securing the horse and gig, I made my way into the fair. I saw pinch-faced gents arguing over this price and that, shepherds with twists of lambs' wool pinned against their smocks, and – whip in hand – a carter or two. But seldom a mop, and only then when it was held by an aged, toothless maid. At length, though, I saw the crowd thicken and the distant platform of the hiring stage. Forcing my way closer, I could just make out the spokesman's rustic banter.

"Betsy Dawkin. Four score years and not one day older. Milly Smith. Fifty six years in service. She's worth your penny, gentlemen. Fred Hancock. Sturdy farmhand. Knows how to sheaf and bale."

There would be a brief pause between the names as some gentleman secured the hiring hand with a coin. At least, that was how I guessed it to be, for I was still some way to the back and my view was somewhat poor. But as a new set of hiring hands climbed onto the platform, I spied a tall, broad – woman with a youthful face and a mop resting in her big, brown hand.

"Yes," I cried at the provision of her name and the spokesman gave me an odd little bow. Finding my way to the front with sudden ease, I held up my coin with a triumphant flourish.

The crowd was strangely silent. An inexplicable tension gripped me. In confusion, I looked across at my impromptu choice of maid – and was appalled by what I saw.

Not a natural woman, but a giant child I had hired. Towering above the adult 'statues', she was a weird, ungodly thing. Tears trembled on the coarse eyelashes, threatening to flood the land with a boundless salt-rich sea. I was speechless.

The first tear fell with a lumpish splash and the fragile silence shattered.

"Oi! Mister," bellowed a youth at my arm. "What you getting yourself a freak for? Starting a circus?"

"Not natural that, mister," came a second cry, and, "That's never the Lord's doing!" from another.

"My arse is prettier than that!" thundered a pork-bellied farmer, pushing past me. At that, the crowd erupted into laughter and the giant fled from the platform.

"Rot in hell for your cruelty!" I glowered, thrusting my elbows about me. But the townsfolk only laughed the more, or thumbed me in the back and called me 'Stupid boy'. Forcing my way through, I found her at last, huddled under the shadowed struts below the platform.

"I am Master William Ward," I offered, sounding more severe in my new position of authority than I actually intended. "You, I understand, are Miss Kitty Brooke."

"Aye," she sobbed, turning her thick-set face towards me. She struggled to speak through her tears. "Me mam. She called me it because it means 'pure of heart'. She didn't know for sure when I was a babe, of course, but reckoned if I were to turn out so big, I couldn't 'elp but have a big 'eart to go inside."

"So your full name is Catherine?" I asked gently, remembering the tale of her tortured namesake.

The girl nodded and shuffled awkwardly out into the daylight, where she straightened up to six feet tall or more. Her hair was pretty, capturing all the colours of the autumn sun. But nothing could disguise the awful truth; that she was a monster for every part of her was mammoth. I willed the muscles in my face to disguise my true alarm. "How old are you, child?" I stammered.

"Twelve year old, Master William."

"Then you would spend your hiring penny on what? For you know it is yours. It is customary for hired hands to drink to their new master's health. But I'm not sure that should be the case here."

"Well, I'll drink to yeah with a cup of water instead and save me penny for when I'm grown and 'ave an 'usband." The giant child smiled so broadly I feared she might eat me whole. Wearing a faded smock of bottle green, she seemed to me a potter's joke; body cast in clay, her primitive features dipped in garish glaze. The malformation was compounded because the bulk of her weight was held about the waist, so that even her great head and limbs seemed strangely out of proportion.

Dear God, I thought to myself, what of such a creature when she is fully grown? Even now, as I led the girl through the hiring fair, people pelted fruit at her unnatural frame and despised her for being something other, wrong and strange.

After their initial disbelief, my family saw Kitty in much the same way as I; a tragic creature betrayed by her own body. Only my father seemed somewhat reserved in his welcome, shaking his head and ignoring Kitty's presence for the most part. I put this behaviour down to his annoyance at my choice, for while the girl was indeed the most gentle of giants, she was slow of body and even more so in mind.

"Where do you come from, Kitty?" I asked one day, as the huge child stooped above the kitchen table, shattering eggs as she tried to break them over a bowl.

"I don't know that, Master William," she sighed. "Mam let me go when the vicar told her I were devil's work. But I don't care much for the remembering of me past. I like only now." Her mouth opened wide and she bellowed with laughter like some wild, forest thing.

"But you must have had a kind master before now," I continued, gesturing towards her swollen, outsized belly.

"Ah, Master William. Now that'd be my shadow," she answered strangely. "You see some of it without. But I keep most of it within."

Her words were foolish and I worried for her mind. "Have you ever attended school, Kitty?" I asked on sudden impulse.

"Course I haven't, Master William. I only just got your penny and it ain't enough to pay for schooling."

"But would you like to, Kitty?" I offered, overwhelmed with Christian spirit. "I am a school master in the village and I am sure I could arrange it."

Where I had expected joy, there was only a twisting of her thick, ugly brow. "But I would afear the little 'uns, Master William," she confided, "...and I would be afeared for meself. Even them that's small poke and point and call me names."

"Then I will make sure that you enrol in my class, Kitty Brooke, and I will watch over your shoulder wherever you go."

"You'd be 'ard pushed to reach me shoulder, let alone watch over it," she spluttered, and her gigantic laughter filled the room once again. I laughed awkwardly, feeling myself a small, mis-balanced master next to the giant at my side. My sense of inadequacy increased tenfold when Kitty turned and whispered like a great north wind against my ear, "I trust you, Master William. With your gold 'air and blue eyes, you looks like a guardian angel to me all right."

The classroom had that same unnatural sense of quiet which I had encountered at the fair. Every child stared at the giant as she knelt beside a desk, her frame being too cumbersome for an infant's chair. Occasionally, Kitty would meet their prying eyes, and then hide herself again in the vast sail of her shawl.

Determined to distract the cruel attention, I stood before my desk and instructed the children to: "Recite! Apple. A.P.P.L.E. Ball. B.A.L.L. Cow. C..."

"I see a cow," came a boy's unkind whisper.

"...O.W. Dog. D.O.G, Egg." (I thought it best to continue.) "Fish. F.I.S.H." (I had it in my mind that the girl had to learn for herself how to survive.) "Giant. G.I..." Appalled by my own stupidity, I froze as the familiar laughter erupted.

I was about to demand restraint when something remarkable happened. Kitty snorted and then roared with laughter, stamping her huge boots against the ground in excitement at my blunder.

It was enough. Within the week, she was carrying the other children about on her back like tiny birds. In place of disgust, the majority of the children became enthralled by her magnificence. In lessons, Kitty was quite overwhelmed by their attentions – so much so that one afternoon, I had to send her to stand the corner. The whole event was somewhat farcical though as the giant girl could only wear the Dunce Cap on her hand, where it fitted snug as a mitten.

Kitty found a particular friend in Sukie Potts, a child born dumb. Without language, they spoke with one another by chalking pictures on a slate. Here, the giant would draw a sun, and there, the mute might scribble a rainbow, so that the chalk became their common tongue, and imagination their sole means of communication.

One youth alone refused to let them be. Being a teacher, I knew little of the internal wranglings of the playground, but there were certain moments when I caught the truth of it. One such afternoon, I was walking past the school's outbuildings when I heard a small commotion.

"I see you, Kitty Brooke. You're even uglier when you pee. Look! 'er knees stick up by her 'ead as she'd doing *it.*"

The noises of a one-sided struggle followed, and I recognised the cruel nasal tones of a boy called Bernard Gregory.

"What's the matter, Stupid Sukie. Did Kitty get your tongue?"

"Oi, Bernard!" came the high pitched squeal of another boy. "Dip 'er in the lav. Go on, Bernard."

"All right. Come on, Stupid. Oh, hullo there, freak. Get out me way. I said out me way!"

I had heard enough. Turning about the corner, I prepared to box each boy's ears until they stung like their nasty tongues, when my breath stopped short.

Towering over the Gregory boy, Kitty seemed to be deflating to half her usual size as a great billow of… what was it… smoke, or some other form of darkness… poured forth from her angry, gaping mouth.

"Kitty!"

In an instant, the black vapour vanished; almost as though the girl sucked it back inside her mouth. Both boys had had their backs to Kitty, so they showed no sense of alarm. Instead, Bernard Gregory simply dropped the trembling mute from the nook of his arm and kicked his feet bashfully; his freckled face full of spite.

"Ten lashes for you, boy," I bellowed, and cuffed him about his ginger head. "And five for you, Jackson. Easily led. Do you hear me?

Easily led." The two boys skulked back towards the school, poking each other and whispering. I turned to Kitty.

"Is this bullying customary?" I demanded, furious that she should keep such secrets.

"Aye," she murmured. "But its Sukie I afear for. She don't 'ave the darkness, watching from inside."

As she spoke, a strange distance came into her eyes. It was as though she had lost sight of my presence. Then she hoisted the small girl onto her back and they lumbered away; the giant and the mute making a queer silhouette against the burnished autumn sun.

I could find no explanations for Kitty's weird words, knowing only that as the weeks passed by she seemed to lose that fighting spirit. Her time in the classroom was spent quietly now, without a trace of the joy she once brought with her laughter and her smile. Even Miss Mabel – who had embraced the giant as a misplaced daughter – noticed the alteration, and sighed morosely as she scrubbed the hearth alone. Perplexed, I took the unusual step of discussing the matter with my father.

Stroking his silver beard, and shifting his spectacles up and down his nose, my father fixed me with his stare.

"Forever the idealist, aye son? What good will come of schooling her anyway, that's what I want to know?"

"Well, Father," I began, adjusting my own spectacles so that they balanced on the tip of my nose. "I rather thought we might try to give this poor child a quality of life."

"So is that what I pay her good wages for?" My father scowled. "I had supposed she was here to assist that aged scullery maid of ours."

"Which she does of an evening, Father. But she will be more useful to society if she has an education."

"Society!" scoffed my father, and with such derision in his voice that I blushed at my stupidity. "What will society offer such a creature? Do you think anybody out there..." – he threw his arms towards the study window – "...will give a damn for her education? Paah, William. You are a young fool."

"I don't understand you, Father," I complained bitterly. "You are a doctor. Where is your compassion for this poor girl?"

"Oh, William." My father sighed, and his arms fell to his sides. He gestured to the patient's chair before his desk, and begrudgingly, I sat down. "The girl will be despised no matter how much she studies. And where is the need? In addition to her size, you recognise the thickening of the facial features, the disproportional head and extremities?"

"Yes, "I muttered, frustrated by his medical technicalities. "But does her humanity not teach us anything?"

"She is a victim of her own body, William, and of society's cruel regard. Look to your Bible where giants are the malevolent fruit of fallen angels, or to fairy-stories. When Jack floors the giant, do we not all cry 'Hurrah'? There is no welcome, no acceptance, no degree of understanding – there is only fear and the inherent desire to destroy."

My father's words left me silent. I pulled at a lock of my golden hair and felt the sweat come in beads across my young, perfect brow.

"Kitty suffers from *Acromegaly* – a malformation of the bones, most likely linked to pituitary tumours. Her condition is terminal, William. You do realise that. She will not live beyond her youth."

I glared at my father, resting back on the laurels of his orthodox existence, and at that moment, I hated him for his scientific apostasy. Then a sound came from the doorway.

My father had maintained my gaze throughout and I had my back to the door, so how long she had stood, listening to the bitter truth of her condition, I could not guess. I tried to read the giant's face as she entered, curtseyed clumsily and presented my father with the evening paper. Her expression was vague, the slashed mouth twisted up at one corner, but with no suggestion of anger. Then she swept past me and I saw the lips tremble as though her giant heart might break.

Dashing from the room, I found her in the stairwell. A storm of tears fell from her eyes, eyes which at that moment seemed to possess a crystalline beauty, like two glass balls; seeing all, yet knowing nothing.

"He speaks only from logic, Kitty, and God knows there are more wonders in this world than his science can ever account for." I faltered at her gaze.

"They always said I were of the devil. Seems the Bible says it too."

"The ancient Greeks believed giants the offspring of their Gods," I offered lamely, knowing no words could erase her suffering. "And not everyone will treat you poorly. What of Sukie? She is a kind and honest friend."

Kitty answered me with all the wisdom of her simple world: "Sukie is a mute, Master William. And 'er feathers match me own. So I have to watch over 'er, just like you watch over me."

She turned about and climbed away towards the landing. As she entered the glare of lamp light, her vast shadow enveloped me and for a second I felt an inexplicable sensation of warmth, reaching into the depths of me like a familiar, all-embracing darkness. Then the shadow passed over and the feeling was gone.

I stood alone in the hallway and noticed my own reflection in a mirror there. With my fingers, I stretched the skin unnaturally about my eyes and contorted my jaw at a peculiar angle. What if I too suffered such a mask? The prospect was horrifying and I loosed my fingers and realigned my jaw. Now I saw only the true image of my face, and a handsome one or so many would say. Yet, I could not help wondering – what would the mirror reflect if it could show the man within?

Winter's thin grey twilight filtered in at the high window, suffusing the classroom in its maudlin gloom. Beyond, the noise of children at play in the yard was a lilting constant, a sound that, for some reason, grated on me horribly that afternoon. I shuffled on the perch of my stool; worked the nail of a little finger into the wood grain of my desk; applied both palms to the sides of my head.

The next lesson was to be an entomological study of the pupa of the common Cabbage White. I, however, was preoccupied with a different type of cocooning, namely Kitty's. Over recent weeks, she had closed off to me and no amount of sunny words could entice her to resurface. Sore at the fact, I had buried myself in my father's books, sure that there had to be *some* way to disprove her bleak diagnosis. Every journal left me with the same surmise; the girl was cursed by man and nature.

Hooking my spectacles down off my nose, I eased a fingertip up and down the crease between my eyes, my teeth set on edge by the renewed drone from the school yard. Was there nothing of hope beyond those rigid, scientific annals, no scope for miracles even at the simplest level of showing kindness to a dying child? My head felt bruised, my heart sick at a world that knew nothing of compassion, only cold dead logic.

Twisting down off the stool, my fists knitted, I froze suddenly. The mute stood in the doorway, her tiny bird-boned hands wringing at her skirt. Tears greased each cheek. Her mouth formed frantic shapes and emitted a Ppp-Ppp of whispered breath.

"What is it, Sukie?" I asked hotly; and cruelly since she had no capacity to answer. Instead she performed a queer charade, scooping her arms out to give her shrivelled frame bulk while balancing on her tiptoes. At the same time I heard a god-awful hubbub break out above the natural noises of the school yard.

"Kitty!" Grasping the mute by one of her tiny hands, I fled the room.

"Get away!" I cried, fighting my way through the screaming children, "Step aside, now!" Amid the clamour and the wailing, I forced the taller ones aside and then I saw her; lying face down in a dark pool of blood. Her great limbs were splayed, the tangled mess of hair thickly patched with ruby.

"My god," I whispered. "The poor tortured child."

The mute girl ran from me and huddled close to Kitty's body, biting her littlest finger and staring wildly all about. Crouched close by, his hands clenched so that the knuckles bulged white below the skin, the Gregory boy rocked to and fro.

"I swear you will pay for this final act of cruelty, boy," I thundered, feeling my fingers twitch with the force of self-restraint.

But the boy showed no reaction, only cowered where he knelt while his wide eyes flitted first here, then there.

"Did you hear me, boy!" I bellowed, but still nothing; just the darting pupils and idiotic gibbering. "You, boy," I glared at one of the other children. "Find Constable Firth. And you had best fetch Doctor Ward," I added, glancing again at the lifeless giant, and the deranged boy near his victim's broken body.

Kitty Brooke died of a head injury sustained from a fall, or so the coroner's report would say. As the one who ordered the unusually large coffin, spoke with the vicar, paid for the choir, and supported the stricken Miss Mabel as the grave was filled with earth, I called it something other; death by sorrow in a heartless world. For me, the poor creature might have looked like a giant, but she had wept like an innocent babe in arms. And when I saw her laid out in the bare boxed coffin, she seemed so much smaller, so much more of a child than I remembered her to be.

"Well, do you know, Master William. I thought the very same," exclaimed Constable Firth when I relayed this observation to him, a week or so after Kitty's funeral. "But she was a kindly lass, aye? And you were good to her, as good as any natural father."

I shivered involuntarily. "And the Gregory boy? Any word on his *spontaneous* madness?" My tone was deliberately dry.

"Now, Master William," admonished the foolhardy Constable. "I know that you are sour, and understandably so. But he is a child – be it a blasted menace – and whether he pushed Kitty or somehow tripped her up, I'm sure he meant her no real harm. And his insanity is genuine for he will neither eat nor drink through fear."

"May he live a long and tortured life, then," I exclaimed bitterly, but the Constable's look of consternation made me leave the boy alone. "The mute. What of her?"

"Well there's an odd little thing. We all feared she might die of fright being a sickly sort, but she seems quite well. Uncommonly happy in fact, or so her mother told me when I met her in the butchers. Although, as her mother tells it, Sukie has adopted one queer game. She draws pictures on slates and the cobbles in the yard, and they are always the same."

"That is strange," I murmured, absorbed by my own thoughts. "I wonder, Constable Firth. Does the grocer still sell butterscotch?"

Sukie dug her tiny hand into the paper bag, snatched a cube of candy and popped it into her mouth.

"It's very kind of you to call on me and poor Sukie, Constable, and you also, Master Ward." Mrs Potts struggled with the ties of her apron; a streak of flour dashed across her chin. "She was very sad her friend had to go to meet the angels, weren't you, Sukie? But I told her that Jesus would take care of Kitty now, and Sukie thought that best, 'eh lovely?"

The wordless child continued with her drawing, her fingers dusted pale by the chalks she clasped in hand.

"Always the same pictures," sighed Mrs Potts. Smiling nervously, she suggested, "Draw a picture of a cow, Sukie. Or a portrait of the Constable. He'd like that, wouldn't you, Constable Firth?"

"Why yes, mam."

"But I think I like the pictures Sukie is drawing now," I intervened, stooping down so that I could examine the scenes upon the slates.

Certainly the animation was child-like. But the images told a sort of primitive story. In the first picture, Sukie had drawn what I supposed to be our giant, filling most of the slate like a great Humptydumpty. There was the stick hand of the bully, for his freckles were dotted across his face like the pox. In the next, the giant was tumbling, and by the third, had hit the ground. But it was the fourth and final picture which held my interest. Here the giant seemed a small deflated figure, with match-stick limbs and a button head. And the bully? His figure was lost beneath a cloud of scribbled chalk.

"What is this meant to be, Sukie?" I asked softly. The girl lifted her head and pointed at my feet. "I don't understand," I muttered. She pointed her littlest finger at the same spot once again and I stood up, looked about me, then behind me and understood at last.

As I stood in the path of the sunlight streaming through the window, my shadow extended out behind me like a ghostly doppelganger.

*

The door to the boy's bedroom was ajar. Faint noises came from inside and, with a degree of caution, I entered. The curtains were drawn and the place had the dank, close scent of the bedridden. In the half-light, I made out the huddled figure of the boy beneath a nest of sheets and blankets.

"Stop this nonsense, boy," I snapped, pulling angrily at the bedcovers.

"Master Ward?" The voice was weak.

"Yes, it is I. Show your face, Bernard Gregory."

With pale, trembling fingers, the boy pulled the blankets tentatively back from his face. I was stunned by his changed appearance. He had always been a thin scarecrow of a boy with a wild blaze of ginger hair. But the child I saw before me had a skull for a face and hair, white and wispy.

"By God, Bernard," I exclaimed. "Whatever has happened to you, boy?"

At my words, his scared eyes danced about the room. Then his face crumpled and he wept with fear. "It came to me, Master Ward, when the big 'un died. I didn't mean nothing, Master Ward, I promise. I didn't mean no 'arm." There he dissolved into a fresh flush of tears so that I knelt close by him, reminding myself that he was but a child. "The darkness, it is in me. Sometimes, it is thick and heavy, like an old river. Other times, I feel nothing till it pours out from me. Then it moves about the room like a monster!"

"Are you telling me this thing came from Kitty?" I asked, trying to fathom the route of such madness.

"Aye. Cause I done 'er wrong. I didn't mean it, Master Ward," the foolish boy wept. "Sometimes, the dark speaks to me and it tells me about 'er, shows me pictures from 'er life and I feel the fruit hitting me back as the people throws it, and they call me names and it makes me weep. But then the dark gets mighty again like a cold black wind and it scares me, Master Ward. Cause I know I done 'er wrong." At that, the child fell into such a rage of sobbing that I lost the edge from my anger and put my arms about him.

"Then why not make your peace, Bernard," I suggested. "Perhaps all Kitty needs is to hear just one cruel person say that they were wrong?"

I have never known why I said such a thing, but perhaps I sensed the presence of that darkness myself, for certainly, there were strange shadows looming high about the walls, and again, that deep sense of warmth.

The boy slipped his frail legs off the bed and began to climb into his boots. He stopped for a moment and looked at me, his pale face full of anguish.

"I thought I should go to 'er, Master Ward. I never meant such harm."

The Christmas air was cold and frosty as we stood at the graveside and I held the boy's withered hand in my own. There was no headstone as the ground had yet to harden, so there was only a small wooden cross to mark the grave. But there was a suggestion of remembrance in the flowering branches of Winter Jasmine, arranged in a jam jar by Miss Mabel. The yellow star-bursts of the opening petals reminded me so of the giant child's summer smile, and the brightness of her laughter, gone forever from our house.

"Should I make me peace now, Master William?" asked the poor cruel child at my side.

"It's not your peace which concerns me, Bernard," I answered in truth. "It is Kitty's, for she deserves that gift."

The boy wrapped his scarf about his neck and knelt close to the ground, and he whispered something there, of understanding and of sorrow. In that fantastical moment, forgiveness was received from the grave as I watched the fine outline of a diaphanous mist slip over his tongue and melt away into the ground.

"Shall we go home now, Master Ward?" asked the small boy tentatively, breathing warmth onto his frost-bitten hands.

"Yes," I answered slowly. I took the hand of that small broken boy once again and so we left Kitty Brooke to the silence of the grave.

The mirror in the hall shows a very different image now. The once golden hair is fine and silver, and the skin holds the lines written over a lifetime. It is the face of a frail old man which others now see when they overlook me as a fool, or say cruel things as though I simply were not there. And yet the man inside remains the same. He is still breaking eggs over a bowl for a smiling giant, or tending her grave wishing always he had saved her.

Even the shadow has changed, but its watchful presence reminds me that even the living have their ghosts and that these are the dark keepers of the inner self; the mirror-house reflections of the soul.

~*~

Every year, my home town of Burton-on-Trent plays host to the Statutes. These days it is a psychedelic riot of a funfair. But its origins lie in the hiring fairs of the late eighteenth century, where tradesfolk and domestic staff auctioned themselves off to the highest bidder – a process which struck me as one of the more peculiar in British history.

With a love for M. R. James and the Victorian Christmas ghost story, I wanted to capture the spirit of these comforting yet unsettling narratives. My protagonist, William Ward, represents the optimism of youth while his father is both pragmatist and cynic, with half an eye on the past and half an eye on the shifting tide of science, psychology and pathology which permeated the Victorian age. Kitty is an amalgam of victimhood and vengeance, a natural Frankenstein's monster with a swollen heart and inner darkness.

Deluge

Wakatire. Some call it the city of the dead, everywhere reduced to this ash bone bowl. The wanderers have learnt to inhabit the ancient coral beds, hollowing out a maze of tunnels and cave dwellings. Penthouses occupy the tallest stalks. Few things grow in Wakatire, except the biospore air plants that spider out from various crevices and the mulch engineered in the city's bowels, fresh crops grown off the decomposing lipids of the old. The smell never abates. It sticks inside your nostrils and you can never pick it free.

Which is how come I end up at Red Rim so often. The great clinker hole stinks from the ever-replenished furnaces which drive the city. Sweat melts off me as if I were made of wax not flesh. But I find comfort there amongst the salamanders and the east coasters who don't mind the task of chipping off the outer frills of coral and feeding the furnaces. 'A city needs its feeders as much as its philosophers,' my father used to say. I don't know what I think about that now he's long since added his dead bones to the flames. I only know the city is about to fall and I have nowhere else to go.

Funny then that now is the time I notice him. Dark, sweat-soaked skin. Mouth like a bow saw. Neck stretched by fat beadwork. Hair tied high and falling in a black rope down his back.

"Eloise Jinn," he says, quiet as a boy in prayer class. "The Thwumper says you should get on home now. We're about to scrape the bellows."

I glance over at the Thwumper, who stands alongside the bellows' cork and doffs his cap. The man smiles gingerly; west coast Thinkers like me are famous for our delicate temperaments and what if I kick up a fuss and refuse to let them beat the soot from those leather lungs? I have the support of a wealthy family and the police protection that affords.

Luckily for this particular Thwumper, I am not your average west coaster. Not any more.

My gaze returns to the one who spoke. "By your leave," I tell him. It feels as if feathers trace my belly as he stares. His pupils are so very black. Unfathomable. But I catch a sneer at a corner of his mouth. He thinks my west coast formality is sarcastic. "I mean it," I tell him, collecting my journals and cradling them.

"And why would you mean it?" he asks, eyes glittering.

And he's right to ask. But, to me, we are all wanderers, no matter which direction we swept in from.

Night falls. I brew tea from the mint hocks in my window box, sit in the curve of coral alongside my studio window and stare out at the stillness. He eases in next to me, skin like a furnace, and I remember the friction between us a short while ago.

His name is Lo Lim.

"I thought your home would be higher up the stacks." He nods towards the window. Beyond, the giant coral stalks are lit with the windows of the masses. Ours is a city composed of dead bodies – a weevilled necropolis. I live near the ground. My neighbours are weed stitchers, bone jewellers and other artisans mixed in with the richest east coasters. Below me lie the burgeoning cellar homes of the mulch farmers, furnace workers, shit cakers, tunnellers, beast butchers, tanners and fibre juicers. Above me are my kin, wealthy west coasters.

I imagine the smell of my father's bones inside the furnaces again. "Are you trying to suggest you don't know the gossip about me? I know furnace workers are busy men but even you have got to wonder why a Thinker like me hangs out at Red Rim."

Lo shrugs. His naked shoulders are broad, muscles well-defined. "Noise of the bellows is too great to talk over."

"Ah." I tuck myself up beneath his arm. "You know my name though. Eloise Jinn, as in the Jinn Delwah Dynasty. My father was hanged for piracy a year ago." I tip my beaker towards the city and Omini – the dead ocean bed which stretches beyond. "He captained an ironclad. You've heard of them, I'm sure. The pirate ships that terrorise travellers to and from the city."

I deliver the information cold. Lo responds rather nicely. He pinches my chin and brings my lips to his. After the kiss, he stares at me intently.

"A pirate's daughter. I like that."

"Before my father's darker sideline was uncovered, I knew him as a Thinker. I liked that more."

"Uhuh." Lo sits forward and gestures to the cluttered interior below our coral bough. "And have taken up the pirate's studies where he left off."

I'm suddenly self-conscious of the mess of instruments and implements. My observatory strikes me as an organic mass in an otherwise desiccated environment. The orrery dominates the floor, a petrified tree of woven weed with mulch ball planets set in constant motion. It creaks under the pressure. My thermometers are stacked in a corner like thin, slime-filled coffins. Journals gather dust in crevices. Mulch dregs sour in discarded bottles.

Housekeeping bores me. Only the science is sacrosanct.

"Thinker is just an academic title. I wear the robes because they give me licence to use the Thought Halls. The police guards never check my credentials. If they did, they'd know I was disbarred for my father's crimes. The rest of the Delwah Dynasty shipped out of Wakatire rather than face the shame. I wanted to finish my father's investigation." My face burns with enthusiasm. "See the Geo-Scales? The Aneroid Barometer? Those are my tools now I'm cast out. They let me see the future."

Lo nuzzles my neck, sparking the flesh. "And what do you see, weather witch?"

It was a month previously that I attempted to speak with the High Council. My father had known my Thinker skills were best suited to geology and meteorology – branches of science which had fallen out of favour in Wakatire, almost as if the city was bitter with the barren landscape it inhabited. Everyone knew the fame and fortune makers were Mulch Mechanics and Phosphor Synthesisers. So intent were the Thinkers of Wakatire on finding new ways to thrive in a dead ocean bed that no one cared to pay attention to the atmosphere creeping up.

All the same, I had tried to make them listen. Donning my fake robes, I signed up for a speaker spot at the appointed hour and took to the grand stand in the Council Tower. The craquelured dome loomed overhead, filtering the blaze of the sun so that the room became a green underworld. Council members hunched on the surrounding benches like wrinkleneck birds awaiting my death.

"Sukea Zae," called the speaker. I had assumed the identity of a bona fide Thinker and friend. I was the better student; I didn't think she'd mind owning my findings if they saved our world from annihilation.

Except, Wakatire is a tangled weed when it comes to its ruling dynasties. My father always said I had his bloodline imprinted on my bones but I had never seen the physical similarities. Someone did that day, though. A plump west coaster with a face nibbled by gum rot.

I was a minute into presenting my paper, 'The Impending Deluge on Wakatire and the Omini Basin,' warning of the low-porosity of the volcanogenic ancient seabed. I detailed the fossilisation of the millennia-old coral, and how the weather was in flux. Precipitation was imminent I told them in a whisper.

Looking back, I suspect they would have thrown me out for fear mongering and hocus-pocus even if the man hadn't leapt up out of his seat, poked a finger like I was a charred corpse in their midst, and declared me a member of the disgraced Jinn Delwar Dynasty. I lost a decent set of robes that day. A friend in the form of Sukea Zae too.

I tell Lo this, nice and calm as if it had happened to someone else. He listens, the creases intensifying at his forehead. I finish talking and he climbs down from our lovers' nook to walk between the instruments. I follow suit, lured in by the way his hand traces the thinned plant glass of the Aneroid Barometer, how his eye lingers on the clockwork guts of the Geo-Scales where I weigh my rock samples. Best of all he seems to like the milky vial suspended in the heart of the barometer case. The liquid has a life of its own and never tires.

"A witch's brew?" He smiles at me but keeps the creases at his brow.

"Shark's oil. From the liver of an ancient creature. Timeless technology." I bed down to peer at the small cyclone spiralling in the fluid.

"One of your father's plundered treasures?" Lo joins me, hip to hip, staring at the antique bile that confirms what I already know. The storm is on its way.

"So, Wakatire is to be lost to a watery grave?" He tries for humour but his voice catches.

"We are in a basin. The city's footings are not porous." I can't control my exasperation. "Wakatire is damned and so am I because not one fool will listen."

"I will." Lo's black eastern eyes bore into my western green. "I bet Cha Jinn Delwar would have to."

"You know my father's first name?" I'm not angry, more numbed by the knowledge he has known the truth about me all along.

But then Lo says the most surprising thing. "You'd do worse by his legacy than sideline the Thinker side to your heritage and channel the pirate instead."

An hour later, we're at the edge of the city known as The Skirts, a ground level hovel for those east coasters who can't even afford the safety of Below. Here, babes are picked off from their cradles by desert dogs, the coral has corroded like rotten teeth in a dead man's jaw, and pirates might be inclined to hole up a while, drink Mulch Mead and sing raucous songs.

At least that's how I've always imagined it. Except now I'm actually walking through these cursed alleys, the last thing I can imagine is a good time singsong… any form of a good time for that matter. It occurs to me that Wakatire might not be meant to survive. In a world built quite literally on poverty and prejudice, there had to come a time of retribution, didn't there? I sense the elements themselves demanding it.

"We need to walk out into the night some," says Lo, and I know he knows I am frightened. My father's rogue side has not filtered through yet. Instead I'm a lily-livered Thinker. The dead ocean beyond the city is as alien to me as the eastern man at my side.

"Do we need weapons?" I'm thinking of the west coasters' myth of the spirit Kraken which rises up from its rock bed to drain the living.

"It's not far," is all Lo says. He takes my hand as we step into the darkness.

Omini. The great seam of fossilised ocean crust where a sparse few air plants grow, and loneliness. But still men cross it, wagons burdened with wares to sell in Wakatire, or – when they decide to abandon the hot algae stench of Below and strike out for a new nirvana – piled high with meagre belongings. Either way, the pirates take advantage of the caravans.

But standing here in the aching stillness of Omini, it is hard to imagine ever encountering another living soul. The air tightens around me, the temperature runs black-hot, and for the first time I really feel the shift in the atmosphere. Everything's bunching on top of itself, amassing heat and promising a supernova of reaction when the pressure becomes too much.

"We don't have long," I tell Lo. I think of the children back at The Skirts who have survived the dessert dogs only to die anyway, and I have to force the thought aside just to keep on walking.

Lo stops abruptly, tugging me back by my hand. He folds me into his arms. I might have been held in the grip of the atmosphere.

He pulls away and stares. "Daughter of Cha Jinn Delwar." He smiles handsomely. "Weather witch." Then he whistles a long hard note.

Thunder reverberates off the boundless distance. For a moment I think the sky is splitting. But then I see the ground in front of us shift and a huge shelf of bedrock lift up on iron chains. Out from the lightless crevice emerges a vast metal ship – an ironclad. Its sides are bolted with solar scales. The wheels are three times the size of those belonging to the Mulch Tractors Below. Headlamps blaze either side of a great tarnished grill. I'm reminded of ink plates of the spirit Kraken in children's books. I squeeze up my eyes against the glare off the headlamps and look for the tentacles. But this is a manmade leviathan.

A hatch opens in one side and a rectangle of light floods the bedrock.

The engine sustains a low reverberating pulse. Warm, stale air feeds my lungs. Pipes weave about the walls like intestines. The mechanical mind of the ship lies before me – a huge bank of levers, dials, vine-leather pump grips, valve racks and a giant wheel moulded from mulch fibre. No windows, only the fat tube of the periscope feeding up into the ceiling like a femoral artery. The crew of the ship blend in.

The captain speaks. "Cha was a good man. Didn't deserve to dance at the end of a rope. But that's Wakatire for you. Police the poor, protect the rich."

"Eloise has read change in the skies." Lo nods at me. "Cha's daughter says Wakatire is going under and neither the police nor the High Council will listen to her. But I've assured her that pirates have keener hearing."

The crew move out from the walls, expressions pitched between fear and menace. I'm coated in sweat. For the first time since I interpreted the data and drew my bleak conclusion, I'm among folk who really want to hear what I've got to say. So I lay it out for these strange, savage men and women who knew the side of my father he hid so well. I borrow charcoal and papyrus and sketch the nature of the ocean bedrock, the colossal basin of Omini, the tunnelling city of Wakatire where even air struggles to pass through. And here comes the crux of it. The point at which the pirates knock elbows and laugh me out into the desert.

"It's going to rain. Rain hard. Rain like the world is going to end."

No one laughs, or even smiles. Instead all eyes stay on me.

The captain rounds on his crew. "Who has family in The Skirts or Below?"

Two east coasters stand forward of the rest.

"Romlin, Nigi. Go! Be back here within the hour. We'll sail over Omini and get as far as we can before the storm breaks.

Lo nudges me. "Is that action enough for you?"

"I can't begin to guess." I drag a hand over my face, feeling the familiar angles of a Delwar. In part, I desperately want to be right about the downpour over Wakatire – to be proven a true Thinker.

But another part of me is acutely aware that my being right condemns thousands to death by drowning. What can I do, though? Only this, I tell myself, watching the two men disappear out the hatch.

But even as they go, the room falls silent. A few dark drops spatter the gridded floor near the open hatch.

"We wait one hour," hollers the captain after the men.

Kai Kecko served on my father's ship for fifteen years, it turns out. Like Lo, the captain wears his hair in a high tail, a style not exclusive to but favoured by eastern mystic men. That the captain and his nature boys should be willing to accept my frantic science is eye-opening. I can't help wondering if these pirates are the true Thinkers and Spiritualists. Certainly Lo has me enchanted. He stands, shoulder to shoulder with me, and the heat radiating off him is volcanic. I'm amazed at how reassured I feel in his company, and again I question the morality of Wakatire's ruling elite versus the homely intelligence of the man at my side.

But this is not the time for soul searching. It is the time for action. Kai Kecko has his face to the periscope. His crew are rabid in their testing the integrity of the solar scales both inside and out. Whenever a crew member returns from outside, they're soaked through to the skin, eyes wild as the weather.

"What help can I be?" I ask Kai Kecko.

The captain pulls his face away from the periscope. "What help *can* you be?" He snorts before ordering Lo to "Leave off the mollycoddling. Cha's daughter isn't the sort to crumple. Any girl who can put herself before the self-same High Council responsible for hanging her father has guts as ironclad as this vessel. Now you take the wheel and get ready to steer my ship true. She's never been tested in water before so who knows if we'll keep afloat or sink like the sinners we are."

Lo pulls away from me, and it's tough on us both, like separating magnets.

As Lo takes the wheel, Kai Kecko stares at me expectantly.

"I can navigate by the stars. I can anticipate wind patterns…"

"She's a weather witch," interrupts Lo, this time without a trace of a smile.

Seemingly this information means something to the crew. They nod at me in acknowledgement and their anxiety softens.

"Every ship needs one," says the captain. "Maybe our instruments can do everything you can, but a storm as mighty as that you are predicting can play havoc with the manmade. Always best to have a navigator on board who feels the way of things in her bones."

I want to argue, insist that I am a scientist and my observations are reliant on manmade instruments too, not just hunches. But Lo looks at me and I see such genuine belief in his black eyes that I keep quiet.

The same whistle Lo had used earlier echoes around the bridge, piped in from the howling wilds outside.

"Romlin and Nigi. Open the hatch," demands the captain.

Lo revolves a spoked wheel to release the hatch. A window onto the night opens in the wall. The rain falls beyond like drops of mercury. The ship pitches sideways, the water collecting up under the wheels and making purchase difficult on the smooth rock face. The pirates gather at the hatch, hold out hands and whisk the families inside. Last come Romlin and Nigi, shouting something unintelligible about eyes in the desert. I catch a sense of dread among the crew. Theirs is a sudden call to action; Lo takes to the ship's wheel, Kai Kecko moulds his face to the periscope while shouting "Hi there! Draw anchor, dip the headlamps, man the coke canons!" and the crew slot into place about the deck, hands on lock-switches, eyes on dials. Romlin and Nigi's wives shoo their broods off into the quarters to the backend of the ship and I'm left alone in the centre of the deck, awkward and afraid.

When the bullets come, they slam against the scaled craft with force. I hear the great wheels revolve against the slick ground and the high keen of whirring gears.

"No good, Kai. The water's risen past the keel. Wheels are out of action," calls a ship mate.

"Keep them turning long as you can. Momentum's got to help some," I answer. The outburst takes me aback as much as the captain, but he put his face back to the periscope sight and mutters softly, "Aye."

Again, the bullets ricochet off the ironclad's exterior and I press my back into the wall, finding hollows fitted there for the purpose. The ship rocks, pitches, and is afloat.

"Police cruiser. A riot wagon, which may just stand a chance of weathering it out there," says Kai Kecko. "Eloise Jinn Delwar, help the gunmen with the coke cannons. I suspect you'll prove a natural shot."

Beyond the bridge, the hull is an echoing iron pit. The coke cannons are huge, rear ends steaming and giving off an unmistakable red hue. Pirates work the hand-cranks alongside a series of circular hatches in one wall; the hatches spiral open and each canon is shunted forward on greased tracks.

"Stoke her high," cries one operator to two others – coke shovellers, judging by how they don't stop to argue but take up the long handled dip spades and attack the overflowing coke hole at the far end of the hull. The operators drag back narrow flaps in the sides of the canons, revealing embers that crackle in readiness.

It strikes me suddenly that I've been so wrapped up in proving my science that I haven't stopped to think about how much danger I am in. But then I laugh hysterically, causing the crew manning the guns to turn and stare. I'm in an ironclad, being shot at by desert police, and it's all so irrelevant next to the cataclysmic storm.

The pirates eye each other. A red-tanned woman with rings in both nostrils strides over, her footing a little uneven as the ships rocks.

"Daughter of Cha. Let me tell you this much in case you're harbouring a few feathers of Thinker softness on you yet. You can fight a lifetime against the big men in their ivory towers, but when Mother Moon decides to unleash her deluge, it won't matter if you're highbrow western or eastern scum. All will go the same way." The woman holds up a thumb and directs it down. Her black eyes pinch. "But maybe we stand a chance in our iron box. First, though, we've got to take out the bastard police."

I see then how completely these dangerous men and women believe me. I'm Cha's daughter. The least I can do is apply my bookish intelligence and prove a quick study. I nod, and the woman rocks with the motion of the ship like a Scare Night bobbing thing. Finally she turns and strides back over to her canon.

The room shakes with the tremendous reverb off the glowing guns. I put my hands to my ears. Smoke gnaws at my lungs. I taste sweat on my upper lip.

Yanking open the coke flap of my canon, I take a face full of blow-back off the red hot coals.

"Fully stoked," shouts my neighbour before discharging his own canon in a great crush of noise.

A long thin telescope protrudes from the wall. I try to go with the rolling motion of the ship, lean in and look through the eyepiece.

My father once spent the night on the balustrade circumnavigating one of the highest academic institutions in Wakatire, highest by reputation and location. His story went that, as a young apprentice, he had been challenged by his mentor to sit outside in one of the worst dust storms to hit the city, the aim being to learn to tune out his surroundings, no matter how violent, and solve a series of geothematic posers. Tucked up in his robes on that roaring pinnacle, a mulch fibre sack worn over his head and shoulders, my father couldn't resist peeping out at the greyed whirlpool of Omini. The dust stung his eyes. The taste of it soured the corners of his mouth. But for some reason he couldn't stop looking at something way off in the distance. A wavering form with tentacular limbs that oozed and stretched.

Eye to the telescope, I find myself understanding how easy it would be to envision the spirit Kraken in the misty blue-black beyond the ship. But while my father had enjoyed the excuse of youth and taken flight back below, I can enjoy no such relief. And something is materialising through the storm – two vast silver wings arching out and down from the egg sack of a small cabin. The police cruiser has adapted to the aquatic conditions very well. Reflections off its huge questing headlamp dance in the sky like streaking bioluminescence. Gobs of flaming coke graze the wings now and then but mostly the pirates' aim is ineffectual. The cruiser, meanwhile, is equipped with state-of-the-art algoid-fuelled engines, the lightest, toughened mulch-fibre bodywork, and a magna-bond harpoon hooked up over one wing.

Apparently, I'm not the only one to spot the harpoon. A cry goes up from the woman with the ringed nose and the rush is on to stoke the canons.

"Take your shot!" the woman tells me, and she's right, I need to because I can see the cruiser manoeuvring in the water in order to aim the harpoon. I'm not sure how much engine power is required to pull clear of a magna-bond strike but I suspect the ironclad is too old and ugly to attempt it.

I put my hand on the canon trigger, a thick iron lever bandaged in mulch wool, and watch through the telescope. The ship around me bucks and dips; I tap into its rhythm, tunnel my gaze to the harpoon, and fire.

The canon kicks back, knocking me to the ground and winding me. Pain erupts at my breastbone, leaving me choking for breath. The pirates pay no attention to my war wounds. They come at me through the smog like ghosts in the gut of the ironclad. "She's got her father's aim," they tell one another, picking me up and dusting me down. I press my eye to the telescope sight.

It should pain me to see the harpoon rig in flames. Haven't I just attacked a police cruiser while in the company of a band of itinerant east coast savages? What has happened to the girl in love with rocks and solitude?

Washed away, I realise as the flaming mess of the harpoon seesaws at the cruiser's bough, prompting the craft to list.

The ironclad originally belonged to a spice merchant and had been acquired by Kai Kecko far east some fifteen years previously. So the captain informs me while staring into his periscope and barking instructions to his crew. Water played no part in the craft's design, only the safe transport of the fine spice powders in the hull now occupied by the sunset coloured coke canons.

"Will the ship hold up?" I ask stupidly, knowing this is the very question on everyone's lips.

"The ship will hold," shouts Kai Kecko. He glares at me. His black eyes demand the fact.

But Lo interrupts, "The engine is less resistant to waterlog."

I join the pirates in soaking up the water that feeds in at the ship's breast plates – small dribbles that form an ever growing pool at our feet. The sopping rags we use are passed down the line to where one man reaches out of a canon porthole and squeezes them off in the rain. I hear the engine choke and splutter in the bowels of the ironclad, and I see Lo working the vast bank of levers and switches in-between tugs on the ship's wheel.

"I'm losing her!" he cries.

All around us, we feel the ship shudder as the engine struggles against the flow of water. With one last pull of muscle, that heart organ fails. The interior of the ironclad dims; only two wall lamps pulse weakly. The ship moans and roils. Rain beats against the iron skin like thousands of hammering fists.

How many times did my father spy a police cruiser in the distance and power down, waiting out the minutes in the hot tin can of his ironclad? Did the silence roar in his ears, like the violence of the storm now assaulting Kai Kecko's vessel?

"I'll man her by hand," Lo tells the captain. It takes me a moment to process the weight of what he's saying. Another wheel exists up top inside a bolt-on cabin that is open to the elements. If Lo can hole up inside, he can attempt to steer us to safety.

"But how are you going to see anything out there?" asks a crewmember, voicing the thought we all share… which is when Lo's beautiful oceanic eyes turn on me.

"I need a weather witch."

If hands can betray a heavy heart, so it is with the captain's. He revolves the spoked wheel at one side of the roof hatch in slow, steady motions. The hatch unseals with a 'thssk' of releasing air. It is as if we've opened the lid of some ancient box, and in doing so, unleashed all of the abominations of the Underworld. The wind screams above us. Rain lashes in at the crack.

"Mother Moon keep you safe," says the captain, patting our shoulders. Then he thrusts the hatch aside and Lo and I climb out.

The weather hits me straight in the gut. My cheeks sting with the violence of the rain. As Kai Kecko's strong brown hand forces the hatch shut, I fight to stay upright. The tug on my wrist reminds me that Lo has insisted on tethering me to him by a length of mulch rope – long enough to give him free rein to work the new ship's wheel, short enough to keep us together if one or both get swept overboard.

The cabin is just big enough for the two of us. While it has a roof, all four sides are open to provide a panoramic view. The best thing about our environment is that the water drains straight out of the cabin and over the sides of the ironclad; unfortunately we face the constant danger of losing our footing and draining away with it.

I press my back into the moulded curve of one of the corner struts. Lo battles to hoist the lock levers and activate the wheel – a huge circle of iron with winged spokes that revolves every which way thanks to its reactive fixtures. The stalk on which it is mounted bends and twists. The winged spokes billow out or deflate, depending on which way Lo powers the wheel. And doesn't it take some force to guide the craft! Even through the maelstrom, I see the swell of Lo's muscles, as if he is as much a part of the movement of the storm as the wind and rain.

"Help me work our way clear of Wakatire!" he calls.

At first that doesn't make sense. Lo and I walked out into Omini in order to find the pirates, leaving the city behind. But I force myself to move and, holding tight to the strut, peer out past the ship. Then I see the truth of it; Kai Kecko's ironclad has been washed in close to the city – or at least where Wakatire once was.

"Bank right," I tell Lo, feeling the prickle of the north wind across my face and realising he can use the thrust to feed the wings of the wheel. The water has risen high over Red Rim and The Skirts. Steam billows off the roiling surface. I imagine the furnaces below gasping against the flood. Waves strike the corralled city walls like boulders. Bodies tumble in the froth – men, women, children. East coasters drowned in their own suffering.

The ironclad sails over the top of the hovels, now buried far below. I can't help thinking we're sailing over a mass grave. Overhead the sky is swollen with cloud; it scares me to watch the way it folds out from itself and amasses.

I force the fear below my ribs.

"Guide us between the westerners' towers," I tell Lo. "They'll shelter us from the worst of it."

"Can it get worse?" yells back Lo – and oh yes it can. I see countless tiny twisters spiralling overhead. I think about the shark oil's ancient weather-warning and I read the sky as clearly as the contents of that vial.

"Take us in as carefully as you can." It's a ridiculous request. The huge waves carry the ironclad in-between the coral towers on a violent current. I brace myself against the strut at my back as the ship impacts on the ancient walls. Lo curses, water pouring off him as he works. I read the currents, taste the changes in wind direction, and conjure up a route between those spindled rocks. The world is rising up to meet the sky and it's difficult to know where one begins and the other ends any more. Wave after wave smashes up against the vessel. Once I slip and go careering hard off the cabin's edge; Lo drags me back up, the black depths of his eyes fossilised. The terror of it chokes my lungs. My eyes feel full of silt.

I recover to see the first purples of dawn breaking over the new ocean. Sailing through the city's coral crown, I see towers threatening to collapse, their numerous windows fibrillating with life. It takes me a moment to realise I'm seeing people crammed into those tiny spaces. I catch their cries on the wind, the noise drifting in and out on its own tide. As Lo guides us through the steaming whirlpool, I stare up at the windows full of Thinkers in their expensive robes. Below will be flooded entirely by now, the violent flow banking up inside the sealed city and forcing its way inside the towers. Many windows are already transformed into waterfalls.

From beneath us comes the creak of splintering coral. Wakatire looms overhead, a thrashing beast in its death throes. It strikes me then that the spirit Kraken has always been the city. Gobs of flaming mulch weed float below like thousands of eyes. Dead muddy up the water. The towers of learning crumple in.

My father was considered one of the foremost Thinkers of his time. From what I've heard so far on board Kai Kecko's ironclad, Cha was an even finer pirate. His bones went into fuelling Wakatire, but his true legacy lies in the freethinkers who've outlived the city and who set sail now for a new nirvana. Wanderers we may be but isn't it better to live unanchored than sacrifice one's life to a city of the dead?

This much I understand as the waters finally settle. Lo gathers up the length of mulch rope and I go to him. The sky breaks free of cloud cover and the world turns gold.

~*~

The composition of our world with its geodes, precious metals, fossils, and ancient sea beds has always struck me as an Aladdin's cave of wonders. Likewise, the wild autonomy of atmosphere, precipitation, cloud formations, and all the other elements of weather fill me with awe.

In writing this story for Jurassic London's anthology, *Pandemonium: Stories of the Apocalypse*, I looked to the epic paintings of artist Francis Danby for inspiration, in particular "The Deluge". In this, Danby's last ever study, Noah's Ark is depicted amongst the raging torrent of the Flood, an angel weeps over the death of a child, and animals and people cling desperately to branches amongst swirling waters and beneath a blood red sun. My story grew from these roots, the city of Wakatire taking on a Sodom-and-Gomoraesque quality in its elevation of the rich. My ark is a pirates' Ironclad, my Noah, a renegade Weather Witch.

The Wassailers Wedding

For as long as the seasons have turned on Nature's Wheel and the sky's shone blue, gold and black, the Willetts and the Crumps have been at odds. So family legend has it. At nine years old, I was a Willetts and this much I knew to be God's honest truth. Over a hundred years ago, my great, great grandmother, Ivy Willetts, took umbrage to Nelly Crump, a fellow matriarch from Middle Street, winning first prize for her homemade cider at Stroud's county fair. Cider, the making and consuming of, being my family's business for as long as trees have grown apples, the idea of a Crump besting our fabled amber was nothing short of warmongering.

Which explains the mood in our cottage one Saturday in February in the year of 1891, as a case of impending wedlock threatens to unite the two families. Climbing off the bed I share with my brothers Frank, age six, and Thicket, age four – born with a headful of hair – I can already hear the arguing.

Flora, whose fault the whole thing is, has set to whining about a lack of roses in her bouquet – "…that I gotta 'ave fer me and Will to be 'appily wed."

Aunt Alice spits back, "Who says it?"

To which Flora hollers, "Tradition!" like it's the final say on everything.

If Flora's after comfort, she won't find it in Aunt Alice. "Wedding like this 'un don't need to last," grumbles the old maid. "Leave 'em Crumps to take care of their fool boy can't keep 'is trousers knotted."

There, Flora gets to wailing again about 'love' and 'entwinedness' and every other kind of sickness which makes me roar and wake the others with my cheek about how Flora and Will have done enough entwining. Soon, me and Frank and Thicket are bouncing on the bed and father's up and yelling, hair sticking on end like the orchard scarecrow.

*

'The Wassailers' Wedding' the folk of Stroud are calling it, news having travelled as far afield as Painswick to the north and Rodborough to the south. At least that's Uncle Elbert tale, and, for me, anything out of my favourite uncle's mouth is golden as a swig off the cider barrel. He helps us boys into collars that make us fuss and smooths our hair with a lick of spit. "There, fellas," he says at last. "Yer fit to wear the green." Then he helps us into our raggy jackets and soots our faces, just like every Willetts lad and lass before us. Uncle Elbert, he huddles us close and whispers, "It may be a wedding, but there's still a bowl to tilt and spirits to frighten. So don't forget to pull 'em faces, and pull 'em good!"

It's another hour before Pa's got our ma by the arm and she's kicking out her bad leg what got damaged at the mill. Ma's wearing her Sunday Best and pa's disappointed; I can tell so by how he keeps tugging his moustache, like it ought to have stuck up for him. In his rags and soot, Pa looks like a ragamuffin monster and Ma's his stolen faery queen.

It's still early when we get to church. Thicket has the ivy'd wassailer's bowl what my family's supped from every Twelfth Night. Flora has her roses – on account of a dried arrangement Aunt Alice found graveside and half-inched – and Ma's got a big old carpet bag that squeaks at the hinges and rattles now and then.

Since the law says they must wed before noon, Flora's keen to get on with it. So we squeeze into those pews opposite the Crumps and steal glances over at the vagabonds – Mister and Missus Crump, sniffy in their finery, and Will's three younger sisters too. Prig, Pea and Piggy me, Frank and Thicket call them – and soon enough, them three and we three are pulling faces across the aisle. As for the other Crumps, they're sneaking looks back at us, as if half-a-church of wassailers is something peculiar! Then Flora walks in, rosy bouquet in hand, Father's arm in the other, and they see her raggedy dress, long as the ground, pheasant feathers in her hair, and red clay at her eyes, and I swear every one of them Crumps leans away.

But I notice Will by the altar eying Flora, and he's got a grin wide as a greengage with a split skin and he's laughing like he's got the wild in him.

*

Through town, we take our procession, Crumps dragging their heels at the back. But even they must like how folk have turned out specially. Flora, she's out in front dancing like a firebird, and Will, he's taken Pa's role as the Broad – fat wooden face dancing on its stick above his shoulders, two great horns threatening the sky. The rest of us bring up the rear, Aunt Alice nestling the wassail bowl between the curd sacks of her breasts, ma on her walking stick, pa hooting and tooting on a pipe, and Uncle Elbert and us boys stomping out a jangly racket.

"Wassail!" we cry, and the crowd cries it back. "Wassail!" "Wassail!"

All the way we go, around the market and off to the Subscription Rooms, where we call for ale. And the mayor, he totters out in his robe and chains, and chases the Broad for sport and the bride for kisses while we children whoop and snigger behind our dirty paws.

Then we're off again, back up through the town to the Golden Fleece, where we make a horseshoe outside the door and sing for ale, even us little 'uns:

"Wassail, wassail all over the town,
Our bread it is white our ale it is brown.
Our bowl it is made from some maplin tree,
With my wassailing bowl I drink to thee…"

Never in all the long winters or idle summers of the five valleys, did I nor Frank nor Thicket expect to see Willets and Crumps leave the Golden Fleece together. But that they do, the wedding breakfast supped. And with our lips still sticky from plum cake we're off to go a-wassailing. From the doorway of the inn, Gareth Powell, the landlord, shakes his head and hollers, "Was Hail!" – 'Of Good Health' – and we all chorus "Drink Hail" – 'Drink Healthily' – back through the quiet streets.

Night closes around us and our torches burn bright as the Stroud Scarlet cloth on the backs of England's armies. On we go, to our orchard, where Aunt Alice holds up her hand to call a halt and Ma hobbles to the front with her carpet bag.

"Who brings the Wassail Bowl?" Ma cries.

"I do!" Will answers.

"Who's got the barrel?"

"I do!" Flora's got it tucked up under her arm like a fat piglet.

"Who's ready to scare away 'em ghouls and sing in the apple blossom?"

"Aye!" cry the Willetts – and we look to the Crumps.

There's a moment when the Crumps say nothing. But they've ale in their bellies, beef and plum cake too, and maybe us Willets and our country ways don't seem so strange after all.

"Aye!" cry the Crumps – and there and then it's as if the winter spell between our warring clans is broken.

The torches crackle, the night turns velvet, and Ma, she opens the carpet bag and starts pulling out pots and pans and wooden spoons and ladles, and Pa puts his pipe to his mouth as she hands out the noise makers.

Up we go through the orchard in our giddy glad-rags, whipping up a hullabaloo on our pots and pans and pipes. Will and Flora dance around the oldest tree, and Aunt Alice and Will's sisters string its gnarly branches with old bits of ribbon and flowers stitched from buttons, and us boys get to scrub in the dirt and sing the spooks from the shadows.

Our torches spatter and blaze, and we fill the orchard with cider-coloured light. And the funny thing is – the strange wild magick of it all – is that Crumps and Willets kick up their heels and slurp cider from a bowl and hoot and howl with all the mad hare wilfulness of life in our five valleys – and never's there been such a night as the Wassailers' Wedding, when the old springs anew.

~*~

I am fascinated by pagan traditions and the families linked to them. While "Field of the Dead" features Mummers and their ancient plays, "The Wassailers Wedding" is my exploration of another band of raggy-clothed high-jinxers. The term 'wassail' goes back to Anglo-Saxon times and is a toast. A rousing cry of "Waes Hael" means 'Be of good health', to which the company reply, "Drinc hael" – 'Drink healthily.' Close to 12th Night, wassailers go door-to-door or around the pubs, carrying a wassail bowl and singing to wish everyone a prosperous year. At the time of writing, I was living in Stroud in the Cotswolds and loved to watch the Wassailers parade their way to the cider orchard to scare away the dark winter nights and usher in the spring.

Divinity

Centre stage is a bar counter, optics behind and empty stools in front. The bar is lit by a wide spotlight. The remainder of the stage is dark.

ULBRECHT cleans glasses behind the counter. He is wearing a striped shirt. The soundscape is reminiscent of a nightclub from Berlin's Weimar era.

ENTER GRIM. He looks around, takes a seat at the bar. The soundscape fades into the background.

GRIM: Bourbon.

ULBRECHT: *(pours)* Ice?

GRIM: No ice.

ULBRECHT: Some prefer it with ginger. A brighter taste.

GRIM: I like a thing to have personality, but I'll stick to what I know.

ULBRECHT: *(waves away GRIM's attempt to pay)* First drink is on the house.

GRIM:(*extends hand for a handshake.*) I'm Grim.

ULBRECHT: (*shakes hand*) Ulbrecht Schaults. Proprietor, Bartender, Showman, Jew. Not necessarily in that order." (*He looks out into the audience as if surveying the 'crowd', examines the optics and mixes drinks as he talks.)* "I haven't seen you in here before. Where have you been all of my life?

Grim: You making eyes at me, Ulbrecht Schaults?

ULBRECHT: *(nods offstage)* With a table full of Brownshirts nearby to keep the likes of me in check…? Not likely. *(Leans in)* Few minutes back, my compere, Mishka, dragged two of their number up on stage to crawl around on the floor grunting like pigs while she sang 'Politicians are magicians who make swindles disappear.' Antics like that are more than enough to get this venue on one of the Brownshirts' *lists*! Luckily, I got a whiff of their ire in time and took care of it. *(He gestures to the drinks he is lining up. He shrugs)* What do you do, though? Brownshirts hate free speech. My fellow artists and I hate to hold our tongues.

GRIM: I've heard there is a bartender in Berlin who is far more than his profession. I've heard there is a bartender who mixes magic and presents it in a frosted glass. Like a wizard. Or a god. *(gestures to the optics)* Potent brews – to excite, to soothe, to inspire, and to chymically alter.

ULBRECHT: *(smiling)* I could tell you a tall tale about a young man who found he had a gift. One day and quite out the blue, the young man discovered the ability to change people with his masterful cocktail mixes. Not just intoxicate but change a person permanently. And here is the kick! The young man could psychically read the dry parts of a human soul, those that needed quenching. Or drowning.

GRIM: Is that so? *(offers up his empty glass)* And could that man read me?

ULBRECHT: *(fills GRIM's glass)* Some people are more complex than others, more guarded. Hardly surprising in this day and age when neighbour suspects neighbour, and Adolf Hitler is moulding our children into golems who can suffer pain and do his bidding! People come in here and they are scared, angry, perverse, jingoistic. The Nazi Party has stirred everyone up, not just the Communists, and it's a bitter brew. But here in the Showboat, I do my best to soothe the discontent. But, you, Grim, are difficult to read.

GRIM: I like to think I am an enigma. (smiles) So, indulge me. I am fascinated. You *fix* people?

ULBRECHT: If they need fixing. I don't do things by halves. I go for the jugular. The 'sin' in the sinner. The 'bloodlust' in the killer. The 'hate' in the fascist. This city is a whirling dervish of colour and cabaret and Lights! Camera! Action! It's the traffic tower in the heart of Potsdamer Platz, it's the hullaballoo of wild beasts in the zoo at Tiergarten. But it is also a political boiling pot, Grim. A man like you knows this.

GRIM: A man like me?

ULBRECHT: Emotionally reserved. I've met a few others like you out on the streets, religious men mostly, incapable of independent thought. Like babes absorbed back into the womb.

GRIM: You do not approve of faith?

ULBRECHT: *(snorts)* Faith! What is that, except a need to know the unknowable, to see the unseeable? I, at least, address those needs for my patrons. I offer libations…

GRIM: *(interrupts)* Libations? (*as if quoting from a book)* 'Drink poured out as a sacrificial offer to a deity.' (*He holds up his hands.*) I confess I have a soft spot for linguistics and theology. Who, then, do you pour your drinks for, Ulbrecht?

ULBRECHT: Who is my god? (*He slides the drinks out of view and speaks to an unseen figure.)* Thank you, Lucy. Table 9. (*Back to GRIM*) Isn't that life's fundamental question? Hitler, Mussolini, who do you think they raise a drink to? As for me, I believe categorically in heaven and hell, in right and wrong, and that is why I use my gift. Here, I have a story for you. I am on the tram to Wilmersdorf. Opposite, a mother is juggling two small children in the seats to either side. The tram stops and five teenagers get on, smart prigs, wearing their Youth Army armbands like the iron crosses they are so desperate to earn in war. (*shakes head*) We are on our way again when I hear the rumble. Not so much words as knives that carve up skin. "Jewish bitch and her suckling pigs." "Why are they allowed on trams?" "The stench ruins the journey for the rest of us." The mother, she stares at the floor while, oblivious to the insults, her children continue to fuss and make faces. "Little pigs belong in a pen, eating garbage and bathing in their shit," says the loudest boy. And now, at last, the children stop. Even at their tender age they understand the threat and the light goes from their eyes. The next moment, two girls from the group pipe up, "I want to sit down," and "I want to sit down too." Me? I am watching it all like one of the American movies we watch in the picture house. The mother has sense to gather her children up onto her knee, and the girls sit either side of her and they burst out laughing. One catches my eye. "Heil Hitler!" she cries, arm shooting up in salute. And they look at me, an old Jew fag. The mother, she reminds me of my own, and right then, in that moment, I feel pain and rage and humiliation, and I want to stab every one of those children in the eye. But instead, I lift my arm. "Heil Hitler!" I say, and that makes them laugh again.

GRIM: So you lose faith in prayer, in divinity. You take matters into your own hands.

ULBRECHT: (*pours a new order of drinks, considering the labels of the bottles as he goes*) I don't expect you to believe me, but I have tried my best to limit the violence in the minds of my patrons. Berlin is mouldering at the edges, but I do my bit to buff away the dirt. *(nods to one side of the stage)* The man in the beret and spats? He looks like a bohemian, born and bred, but there is betrayal in his heart. He is a spy for the Brownshirts, told to report in on his elderly companion. His own father. So I adapted his Old Fashioned; a dash of Backbone, a few drops of Loyalty.

GRIM: You changed his recipe in other words.

ULBRECHT: *(amused)* You could say that. (*nods to the opposite side of the stage*) The couple sitting by the stage? A lawyer's clerk and a bank teller. Both have seen their parents scrimp and save against this nation's crippling debt after the Great War. Both were set on travelling to Munich to hear Hitler give a speech. Or less a speech than a call to arms, a battle cry to strike through the word Victory and replace it with Fight!

GRIM: And so you took away that option?

ULBRECHT: I thought both would benefit from a glass of Champagne on the house. With a small blush of Compassion, disguised as cherry liqueur.

GRIM: And how long do you think you can keep this up? How long until there are too many broken hearts in Berlin, too many sour souls in Germany, and you can't pour fast enough? *(His tone darkens)* How long until free will overflows?

ULBRECHT*:* *(uncomfortable)* It's not a matter of free will. It's a matter of painting over the cracks.

GRIM: But you do change people by your own admission.

ULBRECHT: I tame the hate and rage for the greater good.

GRIM: At the expense of democracy.

ULBRECHT: *(pauses)* My father fought loyally in the German army during the Great War. No matter. My mother is still called a pig in the street. Her head was split open by a rock thrown by a boy with an armband and a pocket of liquorice.

GRIM: *(nods)* So you wash away the terror. It is understandable, friend. It is all too understandable. But beware the serpent, Ulbrecht Schaults. Man is, and ever will be, fallible.

ULBRECHT: So you would let the killers kill, the sinners sin?

GRIM: …and the lovers love and the open-hearted heal? I put it to you, Ulbrecht, that peace, drought, plentifulness, war… they are all poured from the same mix. And I put something else to you. (*taps fingers against the bar and the background noise cuts out.)* Let me make you a drink. It seems only fair since you have been serving the rest of us for so long now.

ULBRECHT: You want to mix me a cocktail? (*amused yet nervous*) Erm, I don't know if I should. It pays to keep a clear head around here. You never know when trouble might break out.

GRIM: *(goes behind the counter and busies himself mixing a drink)* Oh, don't you worry about that. We have time yet. It is thirsty making business, all this weighing of worth. It is enough to make you want to step aside and let someone else do the thinking. *(offers the cocktail, which ULBRECHT takes but is reluctant to drink.)* Now, you just try a mouthful of that. It's not too sweet, not too sour. In fact, I would go so far as to say that it is perfectly balanced. (*pushes the drink to ULBRECHT's lips. ULBRECHT takes a sip, pauses, and downs the full glass.)*

Silence.

ULBRECHT: (hand to his heart and speaking slowly) What have you done?

GRIM: What you did to others, all too often, for quite some time now. I changed you.

ULBRECHT: How..? Why..? *(tearful)* I only ever tried to make people better! Why would you take away my gift?

GRIM: Because you are a man and not a god. And because it was too tempting not to. (*He comes back out from behind the bar and pushes in the stool he was sitting on.)* I'll be seeing you, Ulbrecht Schaults. *(He puts a bank note on the bar)* Thanks for the drink.

GRIM walks casually offstage. As he does so, his shadow appears on the backwall, either with the addition of wings ***or*** *a pair of horns.*

Crossfade to a light shining from one side of the stage, with ULBRECHT its sole focus. He pins a pink triangle to his lapel, dons a striped hat and comes shuffling out from behind the bar to reveal that he is wearing striped pyjamas. The sidelight becomes a fiery glow and there is the noise of a roaring furnace. A Nazi soldier shouts, "Vorwärts!" ULBRECHT *puts a hand to his face to shield against the blaze and shuffles towards the light.*

Blackout.

~*~

"Divinity" is a short play which was performed at the 2018 Stroud Theatre Festival. At the time, I was researching the history of Berlin during the war years and the Nazi dictatorship for my dystopian science fiction novel, *Rise*. While the book itself is set in the far future, I felt the drive to write something more historically accurate. Although, of course, supernatural elements still slipped in.

Like *Rise*, "Divinity" focuses on the complex nature of good and evil. Religion often plays a part in my stories. In this case I wanted to write a dialogue between two characters with oscillating viewpoints on morality, prejudice, and right and wrong. A frustrated playwright, I loved the opportunity to have my play enacted before an audience and see my characters brought to life on the stage.

Goblin

The engine fan buffeted overhead, its huge silver fins slicing the air just a metre above his head. It was difficult to focus – concussion? Had to be a definite yes after the speed of the impact. Was that blood on the blades? His blood? Lieutenant Whates went through a mental checklist. His fingers moved, all ten. Toes too. There was an issue with his right leg; the pain was pretty acute. And he'd a weird numbness on the right side of his head. He felt around with his opposite hand. The blood had already begun to crust at the open wound where his ear should have been. A hollow wind blew on the right side of his brain, switching timbre from high to low as he shuffled around in the debris. Light filtered through the revolving blades – too white, too harsh. Whates cringed against its insistence, sheltered his eyes and turned his attention to his leg. A hunk of fuselage material had sliced into his skin like a knife into a birthday cake.

"Shit, Whates. You stupid bastard." His words echoed back to him in the dusty remains of the hull. The bodies of Lulan and Cheddar George hung lank in their harnesses. On re-entry, the corporals had been exposed to the worst of the radiation from the hole in the hull. Whates had no time to save them; in the seconds between life and death, he'd tucked in behind the panel separating the hull from the engine – a sheet of depleted uranium. Speeding towards Arcadia's surface, he'd listened to the screams of the others and soaked his pants in anticipation of impact.

"I let Saul pilot, despite his lack of experience," he admonished himself, and got lost in supercilious regrets – 'I never got to go with a Rubanese girl,' 'I'll never see El Terine, or the southern star-beds twinkle over Du Ham beach,' and 'I didn't get home after all.'

But here he was, sliced into and debilitated but very much alive next to the two bodies of his men hanging in their harnesses. "Come on, Whates. Get with it," he said aloud, his cadet training kicking in all these years later. *Talk to stay alive.*

"Now, what are you going to do about this fucker?" He crooked his damaged leg, resting his ankle on the opposite knee. The shrapnel stuck out of his shin like a fragment of exoskeleton. "You've got two choices here. Move with it in or risk pulling it out." Whates snorted. "No kind of choice." Gritting his teeth, he got hold of the shard. "Ah, you bastard!" He yanked, felt a pure rip of pain and hurried to tourniquet the wound with his belt.

Arcadia's rabid sun was already heating up the hold. Whates knew he hadn't long before he was baked alive in that tin can. Struggling to his feet, he ricocheted off the upturned cargo and thumbed the print pad alongside the suit locker.

"Good, good." The locker door slid aside; he stepped in and bonded himself into the 4400 factor weft, making it extra snug at the right shin to hold his flesh together in place of the belt. Tearing a square of duct wadding, he forced it tight against the clot spot where his ear used to be. The helmet was slipskin; it bonded directly onto his face, turning his brown skin black.

The lagoon was very still and very dark. Way overhead, the rock canopy was speckled with icy blue stars. Except, these stars crawled on thread-fine legs and it was their abdomens which pulsed with cobalt light. The fatter spiders lived up in the crevices; smash them and their innards burnt a hole in the floor. Scar had learnt to live with them instead. "Don't bother me none," she'd told Scratch after a while. Because it was true, and because the real threat lay in the womb of the water. She'd glimpsed the fin once or twice, just occupying its bit of surface. Scratch sniffed the water's edge on occasion. Mostly though, he stayed back while she filled the canteen, which was a battered old thing with her mother's initials on it. Her Daddy Uncle hated her venturing so far down into the cave system, but Scar couldn't help it. There was something that affected her down there amongst the gloaming. She could have sworn she heard its heartbeat. A slow tug and ebb of blood through dense muscle meat.

"I hear you," she would whisper to the creature in the water. "I hear the boom of your wickedness." Listening in, she'd press one hand to her chest and the other to Scratch's bowed ribs. "Hear that,

Scratch?" she'd say, and the dog would eye her mournfully and turn away his muzzle.

Today there was another heartbeat though. Scratch sniffed it out too and pricked up his raggedy ears.

"Yep. What's that, huh?" Scar mussed the backwards forwards fur on the dog's back. Scratch stared out into the gloom and bared his fangs. "No need, boy. No need," she soothed.

The heartbeat was a stutter. It reminded her of Old Sire Wan and his velveteen drum. Wan's crusted fingers would puck, puck, puck against the drum, and sometimes Newlean, the inn keeper, would take down her pipes from the nail in the wall and make her lips buzz with eerie notes.

But today's beat was unaccompanied.

"Come on, Scratch," she said to the mutt. "Our monster ain't going anywhere." With a swift glance back at the still black water, girl and dog set off into the labyrinthine cave system.

Even inside his suit, Whates pumped out sweat. Arcadia's salt flats were white as angel wings. The heat baked at the edges of his view. Smoke billowed overhead; it surprised him to see the hull relatively intact except for the hole in one side where the asteroid had struck.

"Bastard Saul," he whispered – and then regretted it. The pilot deck had caved in on impact. Whates didn't care to inspect the exposed guts of the deck; he suspected Saul would be spread pretty thinly over what was left of the console. But he did need to take action. The skin suit would hold out for a few hours but he was losing blood, added to which no one was coming to rescue him. Neither he nor the crew had wanted to trigger the ship's Retrieval Beacon. Bad enough they had been sent to overhaul the theonite cells in the weapons' rig. "No fucker wants that job," he'd told Saul when the allocation came through. But who were they to question orders? Just a gear squad who kept things greased.

He was on his own, then, and bleeding out inside a skin suit. Arcadia swelled around him. A gulp of water had subdued his thirst. Now the question was how far to the nearest burrow and could he reach it before the Bethzine arrived and put a chisel to his skin to make a senseless golem of him? Either that or brew up his meat and make trinkets from his bones. Regardless, out on the salt skim, he was a commodity. His only hope was to get out of the sun.

"Remember Mother Em," he told himself, forcing one foot in front of the other. "'No matter what trouble you find yourself in, keep your eye on the horizon and swim into that blue.'" It had been a favourite saying of hers and he repeated it over now she was dust in the wind and him not long to follow.

"Swim into the blue. Swim into the blue." He tried to keep the horizon in view, his eyes gone weepy against the glare. Salt left its layer on him. It was a taste of death in that whited out world.

"Swim out into the blue. Swim out into the blue." Mother Em's mantra and common sense kept him stepping on. Sooner or later, he would come across the bunker hatch leading down into one of the inhabited burrows under Arcadia. He hadn't cause previously to attempt entry to the dark zones below.

"Never wanted to step foot on this rancid crust." He said it aloud because he wanted to voice his complaint. It was a lousy lieutenant who would lose his squad, worse still one who couldn't guide a new pilot through Arcadia's predatory stratosphere. And all this to fix the weapons' rig supposed to pick up on and destroy the very space debris which had brought his craft down.

"Very fucking poetic," he told the universe, sensing it home in like a carnivore scenting blood.

"Now, Scratch, ain't that always the way of things? Just a short time earlier and we'd have got to him first," whispered Scar from their hidey hole at the entrance to the burrow. She'd chosen one of the camouflaged exits as opposed to the larger, more obvious bunker hatches so she could observe the man a while. But she was too late. There was blood on him – she could smell that on the air. So too had the Bethzine. They swarmed around him while riding on the backs of giant scorpios. The man didn't like that.

"Don't like it one bit, hmm, Scratch. See how he fights them? Got a good hook on him. Wearing a skin suit too. You think he's naked under there?" Scar's Father Uncle had recently explained about the making of people, and while Scar knew she was made a little differently, it didn't stop her marvelling at the crude biology of it all.

It made her sorry to see how they baited him, these Bethzine with their hair so long and silvery, and their bodies fine as whipwood and decorated in beads and chakra oil and scorpio carapaces. To the rear, the elderly and the youngsters went about setting up camp. Poles were righted up and knotted tight to one another, great swathes of woven stuff thrown over to make tents and carpets unrolled on the ground. All this while the sun sank overhead and the man fought tooth and nail. At last, though, the stutter heart hurt his chest and she watched him collapse.

"The poor soldier. He can't take them all," she told the tatty dog nuzzling her leg. "What's he coming down here for anyways? No business for a soldier man like that. And what would he have the Bethzine do? Ride on by? Offer him a tug on a water bladder? Not likely. Not when he's half dead already." Her nose wrinkled and she sighed crossly. The stupid soldier had brought her up to the surface when she was far happier sloshing around in the dark of the burrows. And what was she to do now that he was pinned under the weight of a Bethzine chieftain, his hands forced behind his back and trussed to his ankles? The Bethzine hoisted him up and moved him near the latrine which one boy had dug and parted his buttocks over. Tying him to a peg, they pawed over the skin suit, trying to work their way under – or check their prey for belongings. Empty handed, they abandoned him for the shade of the newly erected tents. Soon smoke rose from a camp fire. The scent of burning was weak out in the open, Scar being used to the throat-catching billowing off the fire pits lit below. Her stomach rumbled.

"Yep, it's getting near Eatings. You know it too, Scratch."

The dog snapped at the air a couple of times, as if there was sustenance to be had. Scar crossed her arms and tucked her hands up under her armpits. She frowned, puckering the stitch line down her forehead. It didn't exactly make sense to her but she didn't want to leave the soldier tied to that peg – and not because the Bethzine would treat him like any other wounded livestock. She just liked the flutter of his heartbeat, if that's what she was hearing. That, and now she had seen him, there was something so beautiful about the texture of his synthetic skin. Black as the ink water of the lagoon and so very smooth and solid looking over his bones.

But what was to be done? The Bethzine would never give the soldier to her and she had nothing to trade as currency. With their ornate costume and bone-white faces, they had always unsettled Scar. On the rare occasions the Bethzine ventured down the burrows, silence would fall like a shadow. They would move between the caverns, tall as night, white as salt, making their purchases from the underground market before slipping back out into the light. 'Ghosts' her Daddy Uncle called them.

"I can't leave the soldier man though. He'll end up stew or scorpio feed."

Scratch eyed her ruefully and chased an itch behind an ear with a back paw.

"Yeah, I don't know why I'm wasting time here either." Scar pulled at the root stock of her floppy, leather hair. "We'll sneak over when the light goes out. Unpluck that chain from its anchor and hurry the soldier man back below with us." She squinted at the horizon where the huge white sun was making its descent. In a very short space of time, the glare of sunlight would give way to the absolute darkness of night. She just hoped the soldier's life didn't get snuffed out first.

"Stop being a lazy bastard!" Mother Em had told him all that time ago. "Get up out of bed and be something." And so he had, signing up to the Terra Guard back when he still had baby fat and no notion of ending up marooned on the bur star, Arcadia.

"I have no eyes," he said softly, because it seemed to be true. Everywhere was blue-black where once it had been blinding. But then he became aware of the sack over his head and, shifting his limbs, heard the chink of a chain. Pain gnawed at his leg and the side of his head where an ear was missing. There had been Bethzine, which appeared in the hot distance of the day like coral grown up from the salt flats. With nowhere to run to, he'd tried to fight them off with his fists. But the scorpios – hell, how he hated those creepy-crawlies, all slobber-tailed and chittery – had guaranteed his surrender.

"Now what, Whates?" he said into the bag. "Is this the ending for you? Is this how you go out?" He liked the idea of being clever enough to get loose and evade his slaughter. But then it occurred to him that he had neither the energy nor the survival skills to escape the tribesfolk. He could run all he liked; they'd just mount up and chase his scent.

"I'm not lazy. I'm dying, Mother Em," he told the nagging voice in his head. Blinking in the pitch black, he thought he glimpsed hundreds of tiny dots of effervescent colour – luminous, like the fish shoals back on SanAd. He wanted to swim with them, far out beyond the sweet dark of pain, into the drift of nothingness. So convinced was he by the light flow that he snarled instinctually as his hood was tugged off.

"Still now, soldier man. You'll bring the Bethzine running out their tents otherwise and then we'll all be done in – you and Scratch as fodder, me as an Unthinky." The voice belonged to a young girl. Whates struggled to process what was happening. The vivid day had given way to night. A short distance away, the tents of the Bethzine were lit from within.

A second creature was alongside the girl. Whates heard it snuffling at his head wound. He could see very little but he had an impression of four legs and a muzzle. Like the girl, the creature – was it a dog? She had called it Scratch – smelt strongly of brine. He thought it might be the scent of a UV balm; skin suits were expensive, the reserve of military personnel and business funded scientists.

"Help me," he croaked.

"One who likes to state the obvious, huh?" She fiddled with the chain; he was surprised to feel it slack as, ever so slowly, she eased it free. "Going to have to walk some on that leg you got torn up. Yeah, I saw you hopping about on it. But maybe your second skin will keep you put together long enough. We only got to get as far as my Daddy Uncle and he can fix you up. Good as he fixed me."

She hesitated a moment, her silhouette picked out against the light from the tents. Then she reached down and fed an arm though his, tugging like the child she was. "Come on now, soldier man. Don't want me to set Scratch biting at your heels now."

He managed to get to his knees and, despite the agonising pulse at his shin, to his feet. Only then did he notice how small she was – just a bitty thing who pulled on his arm, leading him away from the tents into the blackness.

"I can hardly see a thing." He put his hands out in front, cutting a breaststroke through the denseness.

"Don't worry. I can see enough for both of us." The girl was staring up at him; Whates understood that much from the opalescent eyes that shone. He stumbled back a moment, but she led him on, muttering quietly about the gift of sight in the burrows and how her Daddy Uncle as she referred to someone had enabled her to peer through the gloom. "Scratch'll help lead you too," she added.

Whates was glad not to see a second pair of eerie eyes just floating in the dark. Then again, knowing the dog was there and not being able to see it was unsettling in itself. He was willing to trade death at the hands of the Bethzine for a walk in the wilderness with the girl and her dog, though, no matter how strangely they might have evolved.

"Who are you?" he whispered. But before the girl could answer, a figure reared up in the blackness ahead. Whates clutched his sides instinctively, feeling for a weapon which wasn't there. The girl and her dog went to ground; he saw her eyes shining out and something new. Burnished white fangs, lots of them, all crowded into a child's mouth.

The Gollum staggered towards them, a great lolloping thing that had once been a man but was now mindless other than in serving the needs of its masters.

"Ol ark! Ol ark!" it cried as it ran. A Bethzine cry apparently, designed to bring the camp to life. In the distance, Whates saw the flaps on the tents going back and the tribesfolk emerging, torches in hand or buckling on sword belts. Already the scorpios were being brought around from their sandnest and harnessed in readiness.

"Oh, Father Uncle will curse my ashes for this one!" The girl tugged on Whates's arm and rolled her fingers into a fist. "Smack the golem down, soldier man, or it'll never stop yelping."

Whates was used to acting on orders. He'd stood no chance against the Bethzine and their scorpios, but the Gollum was bred for servitude not violence. The shape of it suggested a large man-once-was, reduced by a knock from a chisel into a sluggish lump made for carrying, animal husbandry and emergency meat. Whates pushed against the pain and crushed his fist into the gollum's jaw. A second time and a third, he drove his fist into the thing. Crumpling over, it howled with a cloudy misunderstanding of its suffering. At his side, the girl tugged on him again and the dog started snarling.

"Enough, soldier man. This way, this way."

He followed after, fighting against the sensation of weightlessness in the dark. At their back, the Bethzine offered up yowls to the night and rode out in all directions.

Whates felt a huge tug of hopelessness. There was nowhere to go in the darkness of the desert.

Except then the girl must have dropped to ground; certainly he couldn't sense her next to him. "Where are you?" he hissed. But then he felt the dog weave between his legs and a hand grabbed his.

"Down now, soldier man. Into the burrows." Stepping towards the girl's voice, he found a dip in the ground which gave way to a sudden slope and rocky descent. The night cut out overhead and he was bathed in silence.

Scar's heart beat very fast. Two anterior chambers drove the blood around the cartilage bonded to her skeleton, keeping the muscles lively. She'd done it. The soldier man was safe in the burrow and neither she nor Scratch any worse the wear for helping him. She pictured the Bethzine running in zigzags back out on top, trying to locate their lost quarry, and she smiled at the thought. It didn't please her to deprive the tribesfolk of a meal, but the soldier man had sent his weak pulse out into the world and her skin had prickled.

"No doubt Daddy Uncle will say why I had to find you like I did. He's a knower, about all sorts of things and situations." Scar got hold of the man's wrist and pulled him after her as they descended. She liked the texture of his skin suit – smooth in one direction, faintly barbed if she ran her hand the other way. "There'll be light up ahead. There now. You see it?"

She let go, pointing at the subtle glow off the marsh lamps in the next corridor. "You can see the tide marks here where Arcadia's water left the surface and went underground all those years back. My Daddy Uncle, he says water brought with it all the creatures of the deep, all the sea vegetables too, and the moss slime we use as fuel. And that's gotta be true about the creatures because here they all are, slopping about in the rivers below us."

She saw the soldier squinting. He hobbled after her, but kept his distance. Scar had a feeling it came of him seeing her and Scratch in the light, and she felt a little sorry and a little angry. It wasn't her fault that she'd been stitched so, just as it wasn't her Daddy Uncle's fault that he'd been forced to save her with the materials to hand.

"Where are we going?" said the soldier. He was panting heavily. Blood was coming fresh at his leg wound again; Scar smelt its ripeness in the air. She understood why it excited her – there was a time she'd been bleeding too and felt so lousy with sickness that she longed for the Nothingness. But then Daddy Uncle worked his magic on her and raised her up, close enough as from the dead. Scratch had come next, when he got smashed under a boulder. Difference was her Daddy Uncle used his best supplies for her while Scratch got the scraps.

"He did you all right though, didn't he, boy?" she said, explaining her history to the soldier man. "My Daddy Uncle, he's an apothecary. A fine one, too. Works out of his store in the catacombs. Oh, don't look on so. It's just a name for a part of the burrows. Ain't no soul buried there. If there had been we'd have used those old bones for some practical purpose by now."

"So you are made up mostly of fish?" Sarcasm poured off the soldier and he scrubbed a finger under his nostrils as he walked. "Of course you are." He shook his head. "Fucking Arcadia."

Down among the spiders, she would sit at the edge of the lagoon and try to catch a glimpse of her kin. No one knew about the lagoon. In their twilight existence, there were more than enough tales of monsters without tracking down the real ones.

"Stay in the light and the suckers can't get you," Old San Wan would say, putting down his drum a while and puffing on his moss pipe.

But Scar liked the dark. She'd the eyes to see with and skin peppered with pulse receptors. To her, motion had a taste as distinctive as the smell of blood; it tickled her nostrils and agitated her gills.

"I'm thinking a soldier man like you is new to the burrows," she said, leading him through the entrance tunnels to the market. The man nodded. She wasn't sure he really heard her, though. Every so often his eyes would roll back into his head and he'd stumble. She'd grab his arm and do her best to support him.

"Well, so you know, here's a place to live like any other. Air's pumped from above." She pointed out the fat leather hosing that was buckled to the rock face. "We grow the crops that like the least light and we trade, amongst ourselves and the survivors up top." She stabbed a finger towards the craggy ceiling.

"My name is Whates," the man muttered as she pushed him on. "Lieutenant Whates."

"I'm Scar. And this is Scratch." She nodded at the cavern that opened up in front of them, lit with thousands of moss torches and echoing the noise of industry and voices. "And this is the marketplace."

She had rather hoped to show the place off, but the soldier – this Lieutenant Whates – was all but crawling on his knees now. The fibrillating heartbeat was slowing and it was all she could do to get him to move between the stalls, which were set into the rock and packed with wares. Smells of metalworking, tanneries, spice sacks, moss mulching and steamy stew crocks imprinted her nose like a map. She negotiated the pathways without needing to take in her surroundings. Instead, she concentrated on the soldier while Scratch ran on ahead and barked a warning to others to clear the way.

He came to as a cup of salty froth was pressed to his lips.

"What's that?" he managed, choking against the fluid as his head swam.

"Drink now, Lieutenant Whates," said the old man stooped over him. The cup came back and Whates did as instructed, didn't have the capacity to do otherwise.

He struggled to focus. "The child calls you Daddy Uncle?" The old man had a grey face, whiskers, and his breath smelt of herbals. A scar of stitches ran down one cheek. "You are a doctor?"

"An apothecary. I know the uses for the stuff we can grow here and the minerals we can mine." He tutted. "The skin suit has held the leg together well but now what, Scar? Would you have me slice it open when I have no means to clot the blood?"

"In this whole store, Daddy Uncle? Gotta be something. Gua-gum? Limepaste?"

"Only thing that'll guarantee the knit is the same cartilage I stitched into you. The radiation has set against his bones. You can tell so by the yellow in his eyes." The old man lent back, dabbing some potent plant stuff on Whates' brow. "Same as you when your daddy's ship crashed."

"Use that then."

"There ain't no way. The last of it is gone." There was a clattering of pots and an unscrewing of jars. "Best I can do is patch up his head and wait for the fever to take it." Quieter, like it was meant for the girl's ears alone. "Why'd you bring him down, Scar? Haven't I given you company enough with Scratch here?"

Whates heard the girl give a snort and say "I liked the sound of him!", the shadows of her arms thrashing about.

"The sound?" The old man didn't understand any more than Whates did in his state of sickness.

"The beat of him. Bo-boom." She mimicked his heartbeat softly, a hand against her chest. "Bo-boom. Bo-boom."

"His heartbeat? Well, okay. I can't question it, Scar. We both know you are much altered since I had to remake you. Maybe you did hear him – liked what you heard too. Doesn't alter the fact I can't mend him. Not without the shark fin. The cartilage is regenerative. I've nothing else like it."

"Inside this whole stinking place?"

Whates heard the girl's anger. He swung his head to one side and tried to process the view of shelves stacked high with witch jars and little spice sacks, vases filled with blousy cotton flowers and all manner of dried animal parts strung about.

"Got to be something to draw the fever out," he mumbled, and tasted salt on his lips and the sour broth in his mouth.

"Got to be, Daddy Uncle. Got to be."

A sigh of exasperation came from the old man's lips. "Scar. Do you have any idea how much shark fin is worth? Even the smallest piece of it? A small fortune, that's what. Got another value too in the way it adapts to our cells. There's not many were taught the right way to administer it. Folk have been known to sell a body part to buy a sliver but it won't do nada without the knowhow. Now…" Again with the clatter of jars and rustle of leaf matter. "Are you going to let me make your soldier man as comfortable as I can or keep yacking at me about a lack of medicine I can't fix?"

It was a short time after Eatings that Scar made up her mind. Tearing the last hunk of black bread in two, and feeding half to Scratch, she got a wobble in her belly and knew she had to do it. Daddy Uncle ministered to the soldier man in-between weighing out goods and offering his sage advice to customers. Every now and then he'd tense his shoulders up around his ears and give a hefty sigh; nothing hurt Daddy Uncle more than failing to save a soul. Scar knew as much from bitter experience the day he pulled her and her daddy out from the wreckage of their craft and only managed to save one. Radiation had turned her daddy's skin a filthy yellow shade and crisped his eyes. The apothecary couldn't save him, only the daughter with the broken spine.

Now it was Scar's turn to play rescuer. "I'm going out a while," she told Daddy Uncle, who grunted and carried on cutting up a scorpio tail, fat as one of the stalactites in the lower caves. Leaning in by the soldier's one good ear, she whispered, "I go get your medicine now. Don't you die, or I'll have gone swimming with that monster for nothing."

She'd an idea that Lieutenant Whates didn't like the sound of her place. He moaned incoherently, locked between consciousness and death – an ugly dream state she remembered from her own crash landing on Arcadia. It was a savage sort of world where folk scraped out a living and tried to avoid being baked alive. But it was better to have a chance to keep on living and she was grateful for her Daddy Uncle's intervention. She meant to offer the soldier man the same hope.

With Scratch gambolling ahead, nosing the dank air and stopping regularly to cock a leg, she headed off into the market. She waved to those who knew her and shouted out. Stopping for a drink from the well, she strode out of the cavern and into the warren of tunnels, moving from the newer, inhabited sections to the narrower routes which were the first to be cut all that time ago. Some of the walls were daubed with red crosses, indicating a tunnel in danger of collapse. Scar took no notice, just climbed deep down, ducking under the scaffolding carved from sun-hardened mosscake.

"I guess there's only one way I'm going to get to keep the soldier man, hmm, Scratch? I've got to go after the monster."

Scratch might have understood, but it seemed unlikely. Instead he was focused on the salt lick on the briny walls as they came closer to where the waterways ran. Running his tongue along the slick surface, he gave a tight sneeze and looked surprised by it.

They came at last into the great hole with the spider-lit canopy. Ahead lay the lagoon. So very still and melancholy in its blackness. Somewhere inside lived her monster – or, as her Daddy Uncle would have called such a thing, goblin. He had told his stories – and Old San Wan and Newlean sang their stories – about the creatures that made it underground when the water sank. Among the fairy-tales and folklore were the Tall Truths – stories which had a grain of reality to them. Talk of goblins was popular – terrible creatures with mottled, rubbery skin and a great, curved jaw full of spiky teeth. Luckily the goblins kept to their realm, deep down below where the water was lightless.

But Scar knew where the monsters lived.

"You stay on the shore now, Scratch." She pulled something out of her pocket – a paring blade that reflected prettily under the blue insect glow.

It might have been nice if Scratch could have turned to her and said, 'Okay'. She missed having friends. The other children in the burrows stared at her seams and kept clear. So it was just her and her dumb, beloved dog. He panted at her, eyes expectant, and she gave his head a pat. "Stay here," she said sternly and that he understood, sniffing at the floor and lying down.

"I'm telling you now, Scratch. I'm not awful keen to wade out there. But what's the use in rescuing the soldier man if I'm just going to let him choke out on Daddy Uncle's bed? No." She dragged a hand back through her floppy leather hair and pursed her lips. "This has got to be the way of it." Glancing down at her rag-dog, she gave him a crooked smile. "See ya later."

Kicking off her sandals, she edged her toes into the water. It was just as she had expected, searingly cold – at least until she waded in past her knees and up to her waist. Either she adapted to the chill or warmer currents ran beneath the still surface.

A few steps more and she lost her balance, the rock beneath her feet disappearing suddenly. Fighting a tremendous crush of panic in her chest, she flailed her arms and regained her footing.

"Come on, stupid. There's no use stopping now when the monster already knows you're here." Suppressing the instinctual fear she felt at the idea of so much open space beneath her, she stepped off the drop.

Overhead, the spiders swam in their own black element, weaving and clambering and twinkling bluely. Using the breaststroke she remembered from her childhood, Scar pressed on through the water, knife in hand. Back on shore, Scratch began to bark. 'Yes, I sense the monster too,' she wanted to shout back, and also to shush the dog before he spooked the fish. But then she saw the fin rise up in the distant water and slide towards her like a hand parting salt.

So here comes my monster, she thought, and sank down under the water. Blinking, the gloom cleared in front of her as she got used to it. Plankton danced, millions of them, in tiny, jerky zigzags of movement. She got a sense of so much hidden life out there in the lagoon and, beyond it, the seas at the core of Arcadia. Her lungs tugged at her, needing to draw fresh breath. She regretted that she hadn't sprouted gills which functioned fully, only the abilities to home in on sound – like the soldier's heartbeat – and being agitated by coagulating wounds. Her monthly spill of blood had begun recently; that had agitated her too, forcing the child in her to start evolving into a new and uncommon shape.

Ahead, the dark shape of the shark flick-flacked side to side, coming towards her. She fought the ache in her lungs while treading water and gripping the knife. The monster swam hard, aiming its great snout at her – only to veer off to one side and around her. Slowing, the creature circled her.

The eyes were small and dull, almost lifeless. It was indeed monstrous, head squashed horizontally, the 'nose' protruding grotesquely. The body was long, sleek and muscular with small fins and the thin slits of gills.

Scar struggled to stay submerged as the goblin continued to circle. The filarial sensors on shark and girl picked up on one another and rebounded. She found herself questioning the knife in her hand. Was she better suited to a life beneath the water? Would her throat sprout functioning gills if she just stayed below long enough? And what use was a soldier man in a skin suit next to the magnificent predator making its lazy circuits around her?

'Maybe I'll let my knife go and just watch it fall away into the darkness,' she thought.

If Scar had doubted her extraordinary metamorphosis in any way before, she was forced to acknowledge her swift reaction when the shark attacked. Drifting just an arm's length from Scar, the shark's response was both grotesque and extraordinary. The whole of its lower jaw unhinged and extended, its new mouth parts reforming. Stretching unfeasibly wide to expose many curved and needle-like teeth, the creature drove towards her head.

Scarlet reacted in kind. The burning in her lungs evaporated. Her jaw unlatched and craned wide – wider – disjointing and extending out from her face. The curves of her teeth bore down on the shark and the two open jaws smashed into one another. Girl and shark ricocheted back. The shark drove in again, its lantern jaw slicing through water and plankton. The creature snared Scar's shoulder; Scar kicked out against the bite, forcing the shark to surface with her. She wheezed, dredging air deep into her lungs as she and the shark thrashed about, sending great licks of froth across the glassy surface. Back on the shore, Scratch barked incessantly.

The fish broke free of her and Scar saw the foam turn red.

"You have a piece of me. Now it's my turn." In seconds, the whip of the goblin jaw broke through the water again; Scar countered with her own distended snarl. At the same time, she slammed her hand around to grip the top fin, cupped the tip and sliced it clean away. A second wave of blood joined the first. Diving down again, she drove her foot against the wound. The shark skimmed past her shoulder and wove away into the sequinned black of deeper water.

When Scar emerged onto the rocky shore, Scratch was on her in an instant. His yapping demanded to know where she had been, what had caused all the noise and why Scar was hurt. She sat down on the ground, sending spiders scuttling. He sniffed at her shoulder as she picked the teeth out.

"Monster's real," she told him, gasping for breath and holding up the glistening hunk of fin.

The old man had propped him up with a number of hard pillows. The pain shots into one of his arms had helped the fever to temporarily abate. Whates took sips from the salty tea when it was offered and tried to be thankful that he was destined to die in that twilit underworld and not in some stock pot or hanging from a harness. "Well, Mother Em. Guess I did get off my ass after all," he murmured, and braced his teeth as a tight wire of pain passed up his leg. The pain subsided and he relaxed his jaw.

"I'm sorry not to be more use to you," said the old man. "I never would have thought it possible to reengineer a living thing, but sometimes what I do here is less method than experiment. Scar and that yapper of hers worked out the best." He tugged on his beard and stared up at the hock wreaths and body parts. "Others, not so well."

It occurred to Whates that he might yet end up in a stock pot and he wasn't entirely sorry. Wasn't it better to go ahead and be useful in death than tucked away in a brown box in the ground? Like Mother Em back on SanAd, where the shoals of fish swam and the southern star beds twinkled.

"On Du Ham beach." Whates snorted. So he was back there again so soon, reminiscing over the sights he had never seen and the women he would never know! Life, death… it was all gravy on Arcadia.

"Hang in there, Lieutenant. At least until Scar gets back from wherever she's sulking. She's done her best by you, headstrong little savage that she is!" The old man smiled and chuckled to himself.

It was the shadows appearing in the doorway which stripped the apothecary of his humour. "Oh, Scar," was all he managed, reaching for the long thin knife he had been using to cut soap blocks and staying behind his stone counter.

Propped upright, Whates saw the Bethzine warriors fill the doorway. Two of their number stepped inside – the chieftain who had brought him down on the salt flats and a woman with white hair in a braid down her back and many obsidian rings extending her neck.

"The skin snake. We have come for it. We want it back," said the woman. She spoke very well, like someone who has studied a language and taken pride in perfecting the accent.

"By skin snake, I take it you mean me." Whates choked against the back of a hand. It took too much breath to speak. His vision grew red and he had to fight to stay conscious.

"The skin snake is a man, a soldier." The old man kept his knife raised and his voice steady. "Lieutenant Whates he says his name is. Sent here to repair the weapons rig out at Far Point. It ain't like we got military personnel clamouring to come down here to this white rock and help us out any. Besides –" He nodded his head in the direction of the bed. "Man's dying anyway from the radiation. Can't we give him rest as he goes into the Nothingness?"

The woman translated all of this into the toc-tongued language of the Bethzine, the chieftain listening patiently as she spoke. The tribesfolk in the doorway were more vocal; they clanked the tips of their swords off the rock floor and gestured expressively towards the old man and to Whates.

When the chieftain spoke, he did so in a whisper of a voice. His skin shone fantastically white against his beaded clothing and the gloom below ground.

"The girl is known to you?" the woman translated.

"She is. But she's not here. Just a young 'un too. Doesn't mean no harm." Knife in hand, the old man was ready to defend his point.

"She watches us sometimes. Peeps out from the hollows with her demon eyes. But there is a difference between watching and stealing."

"Can you steal a man you do not own?" Whates got the words out between strangled breaths.

"We own everything that crawls in the white world," said the translator, focusing on him with a look of elegant contempt.

"And when the sky goes black?" Whates remembered the density of Arcadian night. Surely the girl with her spectral eyes owned that aspect?

"Then we tell our tales of demons," said the woman without waiting on the chieftain's word. "And we take our swords to every beast and goblin."

"Guess me and the soldier man got lucky then." Scar squeezed between the tall Bethzine crowding the doorway. She looked up as she passed them, a child tempted to stick out her tongue. Scratch came tip-toeing after.

The chieftain patted the girl's head as she went by. He smiled and said something to his fellow Bethzine that made them laugh.

"Your daughter is a lively spirit. She will make someone a fine wife." The translator nodded towards the tribesfolk in explanation of the joke.

Scar was less amused. "What's the people eaters doing down here?" she said, glaring at her Daddy Uncle.

"They smelt you out." Resting his knife against the counter, the old man took a seat on a stool. He scratched his neck. "So, now what? I take it you want to take the lieutenant with you?" He stared over at the bed, sorry if resigned to the way things had panned out.

"We must recover what is ours." The translator listened while the chieftain spoke. She looked at Scar. "And the girl must be punished for stealing."

"Wait up there! We don't need to be so reactive." The old man was worried now and holding out his hands to his wares. "All this has done is speed up your next trip down to the market. Surely we can make a trade – you leave things be and I provide goods you find of use." He waited expectantly.

Scar slapped the wet hunk of fin down on the counter

Daddy Uncle was immediately on his feet and backing away. "A fin? How'd you find a fin, girl?" He looked back and forth between Whates and Scar. "Where'd she get such a thing?"

"From my monster." Scar reached for the old man's knife. She drew the blade cleanly through the centre of the fin and held one half out to the chieftain. "I'm sorry I stole the soldier man but I had to have him. And now my Daddy Uncle is going to make him better with this. It is shark fin. Very precious. Very expensive." She emphasised this last word and the translator followed suit when relaying the information to the chieftain.

"Only half, mind. I need the rest to heal the soldier man." Scar glared at Whates, who saw the peculiar light in her eyes and felt a weird, undulating shift between hope and mistrust of the girl and her strange biology.

The first time the blood came was a shock. No one to ask except Daddy Uncle, who looked her straight in the eye and said, "It's straightforward enough and messy at the same time." He explained her cycle and the messiness of sex. She'd wrinkled her nose and the stitches had stood out on her forehead as if dividing her thoughts about the whole thing.

But that was some time ago and she was grown enough to face the chieftain head on. Scar held up the half of fin; although she was the one who had taken it, now she was back amongst civilisation she felt a wave of nausea. There was something too familiar about the shine of the shark fin. She thrust it towards the Bethzine.

"It is very valuable, for medicine or for trade," said Daddy Uncle, standing behind her.

The chieftain let his translator finish. He peered past Scar at the bed where the soldier sweated. Opinions were offered from the doorway. He raised a hand and the voices fell silent.

Approaching the counter, he took the piece of fin from Scar. He went to turn away, stopped, stared at the girl hard and ran the bloody flesh down her cheek. He smiled, gently still, and walked away.

Passing the fin to one of the warriors by the door, he cleared his throat and spoke quietly to the woman. Without reaction she said, "The soldier is yours. The girl is sharp and is to be allowed to keep her demon eyes. But there must be punishment."

Before Scar could scream or her soldier draw ragged breath, a Bethzine warrior put his sword to Scratch's throat and tugged. The dog fell off to one side, legs jerking as the blood spilt. In his final agonies, Scratch looked to Scar with such miscomprehension and need for reassurance that she wanted to tear off her own skin.

Scar opened her mouth to speak but what came out was a guttural roar – rage so absolute that her mind went black. The new and secret part of her unleashed. Gasps went around the room. She saw fresh miscomprehension and fear on the faces of the Bethzine.

Her large and powerful jaw unhinged and she snapped at the air. The Bethzine gabbled in alarm.

"Scar. What have I made you?" said Daddy Uncle at her back, his voice regretful and wavering.

Scar had no comprehension. She craned her disjointed jaw wide, wide open. Scratch's killer was striding away; she flew at him, leapt on his back and sunk her angled teeth into his neck. The blood beneath her lips made her eyes glisten and she gulped at it, clenching down even as the man bucked and slammed his back against the cave wall. She was surrounded by noise, all those voices raised in horror at the predator she had become. Scar kept biting down, forcing the flesh between her teeth as the warrior slumped and finally collapsed.

Releasing him, she leapt aside and squatted beside his body. His juices clung to her chin. She wiped them away with a forearm as her jaw locked back in and the Bethzine deserted their dead and fled back to the surface.

The fever folded back over Whates, thick and white. Where the pulse had once been restricted to the wound in his leg, now it spread through all of his nerve fibres. He wanted to sweat it all out – the radiation poisoning, as well as the guilt for bad decisions which had cost his men their lives. Most of all, he wanted to lose the memory of a strange little girl made monster.

He'd a sense of the old man's movements at the counter – stitching the girl's wounded shoulder then slicing and heating the shark fin, rubbing it into a shot cylinder and tapping out the bubbles. The girl cleared away the dog's carcass. He'd seen her shoulders heave with the effort. When she returned, she seemed unburdened. Her eyes shone even in the light.

'What are you going to do to me?" he wanted to ask the old man. 'What kind of horror will you make me?' But his words evaporated in the heat of his fever.

"Would it not be kinder to let him die?" said the old man.

The girl peered in at Whates from his inner darkness. "I need a new friend," she said, and then, "And soon I will need a mate."

The old man approached, blocking out the light.

"Okay then," he said, and to Whates, "Grit your teeth now, fella."

The shot cylinder punched in at the Lieutenant's spine.

~*~

When writer and editor Jonathan Green asked me to write a story for an anthology called *Sharkpunk!*, how could I refuse? My research soon focused on the goblin shark. This magnificently grotesque creature has a lantern jaw which distends to reveal nail-like teeth. A 'living fossil', the otherwise named 'elfin shark' has a lineage some 125 million years old.

Further research led me to the treatment of severe burns using a thick underlayer made of pure collagen (protein) from cows and a substance called glycosaminoglycan derived from shark cartilage. Collagen and glycosaminoglycan are natural components of our skin, and this got me thinking about how biomatter might affect our biology. In the character of Scar, I found my own goblin shark to inhabit the murky depths.

Asenath

Tucked between the medina to the east and the rundown residential blocks to the north was the area of Santa Spišské known as the Crease. A two by fifteen kilometre slice of the city, the Crease was home to the 'Izobani' – Jeridian outcasts who counted among their number the mentally feeble, physically weak, sexually deviant and the criminal. Jeridia's strict caste system and increasingly orthodox morality meant many everyday folk were also forced into the ghetto. Lump houses piled on top of one another like clothhod droppings. Heat got trapped in their folds. Abandoned municipal buildings housed families and freaks in rotting rooms. The air stank of sweat and tannin.

Megumi had worked in the Crease for fifteen years, but she still felt uneasy on those narrow streets at night. She would have made the journey by day if not for the risk of being followed. Her only hope was that as much as the darkness hid those who would do her harm, it might keep her out of sight too.

The heat was stifling; it pressed in from all directions. Sweat ran down her throat and stained the underarm holes of her dress. But it wasn't just the temperature that made her feverish. Never before had she appreciated so fully that her life was in danger. It felt utterly surreal to be in the Crease at this hour, fluttering about like a moth that's lost the light.

At last she arrived at a pair of rusty gates. 'Casa Caca' had been daubed on a sheet of corrugated iron in neon yellow paint. The sign rested against the wall of a long building with a curved, tiled roof.

Megumi walked up the path, taking care to avoid any upended tiles or broken stone edging. She tried one of the large double doors at the entrance; it resisted her efforts and she had to jam a shoulder against the wood to force it. Folding her lace skirt close about her legs, she stepped inside.

The hall was thick with dust motes. Paint sloughed off the walls like snakeskin. A dirty white marble staircase led up. Megumi crossed the hall, listening out for a rush of feet or the click of a gun being cocked. The heat resonated – an eternal buzzing in her ears.

She started up the stairs, taking pains to make as little noise as possible. Her boots left imprints. The intensity of the heat and quantity of steps took their toll. She panted slightly as she climbed.

Arriving at the fifth landing, she leant against the wall to catch her breath. The upper reaches of Casa Caca were hot as a bread oven. She heard the scratchy warble of a gramophone record. Behind locked doors, a baby cried.

Megumi made her way down the corridor. She counted off the graffitied doors but needn't have bothered. The last was reinforced with wooden batons and corrugated iron – she'd arrived at the right address.

She knocked sharply. The sound echoed across the landing.

A panel slid back near the top of the door. Red-rimmed eyes appeared at the slot. A Pinkie.

"Kaj Želiš?" *What do you want?*

"I want to speak to Asenath."

"Who says Asenath wants to speak to you?"

Megumi reached into her pocket. She held up a roll of notes.

The eyes narrowed. "What's the job?"

"To bodyguard one of my patients." She pocketed the roll again and held out a business card. Fingers reached for it and withdrew. "Megumi Midori," the Pinkie read out loud. "General Practitioner. 251, Marlow Avenue, Santa Spišské." No caste definition, for which Megumi was grateful. Unlike Jeridians, Showmaniese didn't compartmentalise men according to their social status. Instead, her people believed in hard graft and self-made opportunities. It was just a pity about their disregard for human life – a trait that distanced Megumi from her own.

The Pinkie thrust the card back at her and slid the panel shut. Megumi heard the sound of bolts being drawn aside and chains jangling. The door opened. Before she had a chance to complain, the Pinkie's arm reached out and yanked her inside. The man patted her down roughly. When his hands lingered at her breasts, she kicked out. The Pinkie laughed and bolted the door behind them.

"Only weapon this broad's got are two fat titties," the man announced. "Wouldn't mind her firing those on me!"

"Maybe you try your luck later, ya, Ragorne? For now we hear more from our potential employer." A figure got up from a seat at one end of a long table. Megumi blinked; the room was lit by kerosene lamps and it took her eyes a moment to adjust from the moonlit corridor. Her first impression was of a tall, slim male with burnished red skin and hair greased into a Mohawk. But the voice was a woman's.

The Pinkie sniffed and backed off, leaving Megumi to study the speaker's face. Hard, high cheekbones, tigerish eyes, full brown lips. A ladder of piercings ran down the woman's throat.

Megumi's throat grew tight. This had to be Asenath – Jeridian warrior and leader of the Tai Mowa, a gang of rebels who refused to be drafted into either the government's Blue Coats or the People's Artillery Army. She understood their logic. Jeridia was tiny; it didn't deserve to be embroiled in political wrangling or bloody civil war. Unfortunately the country's economy was dependent on its giant neighbour known as West. Jeridia had also suffered the same lethal fallout from the insecticide, Soul Food, that blighted the rest of Sore Earth.

Steeling herself, Megumi said, "I have a proposition."

"Save the propositions for later." The gang leader smiled with her cats' eyes.

Megumi pressed on. "My name is Megumi Midori. I am a doctor. My practice is behind the Scarlet Cup brothel on Aziel Street."

"There are no doctors on Aziel Street or anywhere near the Crease," shot a gruff voice.

Megumi had been doing her best to ignore the other gang members at the back of the room but now she was forced to acknowledge them – three men, Jeridian braves going by their pierced necks and Mohawks, and two hard-faced Western women dressed like harlots.

She lifted her chin. "I'm the only one."

"Why would a doc work in the Crease? Not like Izobani have the dollars to pay for your services," said one of the women – a blonde in a tan leather waist cincher, bloomers and a tattered chemise.

"The outcast needs medical care as much as any man. I provide that."

"In exchange for what?" asked the gruff voice. It belonged to the largest brave who sat smoking a hookah pipe.

"Good question," said Asenath.

Megumi held the gang leader's stare. "In exchange for favours owed."

"She's a shitting debt collector!" spat the Pinkie, Ragorne, at her back. "Know what that is, Lizzie-Anne, Arlene? Newbies to Santa Spišské like yourselves ain't had cause to encounter scum like debt collectors. They work for a boss, often as not one of the Showmaniese overlords. This bitch treats the poor and, in exchange, they owe her boss a debt which he is free to call in anytime."

"It's the work of grubs feasting on the rotten end of the city," said another of the men. Jackogin bottle in hand. Wearing the red calico tunic of his warrior caste.

The gang stirred. Hands reached for the handles of scimitars.

"Wait! How dare a bunch of thugs for hire judge *me*? I debt collect because it's the only way to guarantee my personal safety and continue my surgery. Wherever possible I fail to record the debt, but I can only continue treating those in need under these circumstances." Megumi was breathing heavily again. The room was unbelievably oppressive.

"Pour Miss Midori a drink, Arlene," Asenath told the second woman – a redhead with spidery lashes and a scar down one cheek. "Leave off the door, Ragorne. The doctor has stated her case clearly enough."

Motioning to a high backed chair at the opposite end of the table, the gang leader said, "Sit, Doctor. We have business to discuss."

Jackogin. Colour of worn leather. Like smoke on the tongue. Megumi didn't look the sort to like it. Asenath wondered if the doctor was too bloody-minded to let on. Most Showmaniese had a palette more disposed to tropical flavours and sweetness.

The gang had joined them at the table. Her fellow braves – Ebo, Lisimba and Hondo – plus Hondo's half-brother Ragorne and the newcomers, Lizzie-Anne and Arlene. Asenath had tested each and every one in terms of integrity, combat skills, and worth. Their loyalty was impeccable.

So far, the doctor had told a pretty tale about volunteering in Santa Spišské's deepest, darkest crevices. She had alluded to bodyguarding but the criteria had not been defined. Instead, Lizzie-Anne was torturing the woman with a description of her latest kill – a pimp with a taste for underagers and dealing in Dazzle Dust.

"…so I tear off his balls and feed them to him…"

"What is the exact nature of the job?" Asenath interrupted. The question was an important one and Lizzie-Anne had the sense to shut up.

Megumi knitted her fingers. Asenath noticed the gold wedding band, the neatly filed nails.

"Blood Worms are taking my patients."

Asenath nodded. The others were more vocal.

"Flesh dealing scum!" spat Arlene.

"You can't be surprised, Doctor. Trade in the sick and dying like you do and sooner or later, Blood Worms will come sniffing." Hondo knocked a fist off Ebo's.

"I had never heard of the practice of stealing the living and selling them onto surgeons before I moved here. The fact that so many of my countrymen engage in the fact is abhorrent to me." Megumi's soft brown eyes glistened. Black hair fell to her shoulders; its shine reminded Asenath of the obsidian buttons on her Commodore's uniform at the Warrior Akademja in Lazarocruz.

"How do you know Blood Worms are responsible for your patients disappearing?" Asenath asked. "Folk come and go all the time in this city."

"Because the bastards came by to introduce themselves. Said they wanted to thank me for bringing the vulnerable out of the woodwork. Said I was doing the city and the Jeridian race a favour by weeding out the weak."

"Many of my countrymen would agree with that sentiment." Asenath took a smoke stick and a match from a wooden box on the table. She dragged the match across a sulphur strip on the box lid. "I believe folk have the right to life if they do not harm others and they respect Mama Sunstar." She lit the smoke stick, shook out the match, and exhaled, the air before her misting.

Megumi's confusion must have registered on her face because Asenath nodded and said, "You are surprised I keep with the old religion, ya? The same one that made me a pariah and cast me out." She put her elbows on the table and lent through the smoke. "It wasn't Mama Sunstar who wrote down the words in the Black Book, or mixed – and diluted – her teachings with those of West's Saints. Far as I can tell, the castes are manmade, as are the morals on which those castes are built. Only the voodoo endures, and the rule 'Honour those slain by your hand else they haunt your dreams'." Asenath jabbed the smoke stick in the doctor's direction. "Keep the devils off her land also. Although in this regard we are failing because the Blood Worms have come a-knocking."

Megumi lent across the table. Asenath noticed the woman's tongue skim her lips and the soft brown eyes which seemed to absorb as much as reflect.

"I cannot offer much in the way of financial reward but a debt collector can offer promises of their own. I am a doctor. You and your friends may have use of me now or in the future."

"Which reminds me," interrupted Lisimba. He passed the hookah mouth piece to the redhead, Arlene. "If these Blood Worms are picking off your patients, doesn't that affect your employment as a debt collector and, by proxy, your employer? A Showmaniese overlord will have more than enough manpower to deal with the problem."

"The Blood Worms pay my boss a percentage of their earnings." Megumi got up and started to pace. Asenath noticed her shoes – black, heeled, and tied with thin black ribbons.

"I guess the return is better on the flesh trade than favours owed." Megumi dragged a hand over the top of her head. Her agitation was contagious. Ebo drummed the table with his fingers. Lizzie-Anne got flinty-eyed.

"And who exactly is it you work for?" asked Hondo.

Wisest of her gang, thought Asenath. She nodded slowly. "Ya, some say there are as many Showmaniese overlords in Santa Spišské as there are roo rats in the open sewers."

The doctor stopped pacing. She put her hands on her hips. "His name is Akihiro Jun."

Hatred ripped through Asenath like an iron bolt. Akihiro had sent more of her fellow Jeridians to the grave than any other overlord. Among those deaths for which he was responsible was her commandant.

Asenath shook her head. "Of course it is."

"Of course?"

"Only in that Mama Sunstar does nothing accidentally."

"So you have heard of Akihiro Jun?" Megumi looked nervous. Maybe she wanted the transaction between them to go smoothly and Asenath had appeared to reveal a personal vendetta against her employee.

Asenath reeled in her emotions. "He has a reputation. But we are not interested in your employer, only the Blood Worms." *A lie.*

"We're doing it, then?" Hondo interrogated her with his stare.

"On two conditions. One, our good doctor here provides medical care for me and my friends as and when we need it. As you say, given our line of work your offer has value." Asenath smiled wryly. "Secondly, you agree to have dinner with me, Megumi Midori."

The gang snorted.

Megumi let her arms hang loose. She appeared to consider the offer.

"Okay."

"Lucky bitch," shot Ebo under his breath.

Asenath heard Arlene whisper, "Which one?"

The Hog Pen was just heating up when they arrived. Asenath gestured to one of the tables arranged around the fight cage.

"Sit."

The doctor did as she was told. Asenath signalled a waitress.

"Hello handsome." The young woman popped out a hip. She eyed Megumi and lost a little of her sparkle. "What can I get you?"

"Jackogin. Make it a bottle. And for you?"

Megumi faltered. One thing was obvious, Asenath decided the doctor might work in the Crease but she wasn't used to its darker crevices.

"You want Kislo Mieko?" asked the waitress sourly. *Buttermilk.*

"Rakija," said Megumi.

Asenath raised an eyebrow. The fruit brandy was pricey enough to suit the doctor's breeding, but it was also very much a drinker's drink.

"Shot?"

"Half jug."

The waitress looked to Asenath, who nodded and added, "Shot for yourself." It was enough to send the waitress away to the bar.

"I can pay for my own liquor," said Megumi, apparently aware of her upmarket tastes.

"You can, I am sure of that. But I asked to take you to dinner and that means settling the bill."

"Dinner?" Megumi let her eyes roam over their surroundings. The Hog Pen was an appropriately named grime bar complete with back room whoring and nightly cage fights. It wasn't somewhere most people would bring a date.

"Despite appearances, they serve the best Ful Medames and baklava in the district. Also, I can earn our supper." Asenath pushed back her chair and stood up.

Megumi looked confused. But she was quick to understand. Her beautiful, almond-shaped eyes went to the fight cage.

"I'd ask if you were serious but I suspect that would insult your warrior heritage not to mention your profession."

The waitress put their drinks down on the table. Megumi poured herself a generous measure of the fruit brandy.

Glancing up, she looked surprised. "What are you waiting for? I doubt it's my permission."

Asenath showed her teeth. She strode away.

The Hog Pit's fight cage was one of the few places that Asenath Sekula felt at home. She had been born into one of Jeridia's ruling Brah families, circumstances which delivered her from the abject poverty of the Izobani and the incessant labouring of the Veez majority. Instead, she was presented with four respected paths in life – priestess, teacher, judge, or warrior. Her brother, Solomon, inherited their father's cerebral nature and studied to be a teacher. Asenath had no such patience. Her skills were maniacally physical: the need to burn up vast amounts of excess energy like a match put to a source of natural gas, a love of victory over weaker opponents, and the desire to master weaponry and fight methods until she was deadly. Her years at the Warrior Akademja in Lazarocruz were inevitable. As was her banishment from the caste on account of another aspect of her nature. Loss of all she had been born to hardened her. In recent years, Asenath had considered herself more machine than muscle.

Time stretched. She paced inside the cage, waiting for her opponent. The game saw volunteers pit themselves against whatever champion the Hog Pit had in store that evening. Asenath's past conquests included a five tonne Grizzleclaw brought all the way from neighbouring Sirin's fossilised forest. Mostly though, she went up against street fighters.

The crowd pressed against the mesh of the cage, murmuring expectantly. Asenath eased her shoulders up and back. She wondered if Megumi was watching or still seated. Perhaps she was the sort to enjoy the spectacle of the fight and the spill of sweat and blood.

In the centre of the cage, the referee announced, "Today's challenger is Lady Killer!"

A cheer went up from those who recognised Asenath's moniker.

"This is Lady Killer's 12th bout and she is undefeated – a record which causes our most excellent hosts to groan every time on account of the damage done to their coinage. Tonight, though, we at the Hog Pit are excited to introduce a very special champion."

Asenath saw the crowd part. A figure strode towards the cage door. Male, judging by the hefty stride. Shorter than Asenath but broad.

The champion stepped inside the ring. Asenath felt a stab of anticipation. The man was a Sirinese gangster with some of the most extensive bodmods she had ever seen. Where the majority of his breed made do with a neck cuff or a brow bolt plate, this brute had concertinaed metal arms and a toolset instead of fingers.

Part of Asenath felt admiration for her opponent – the only true champion the Hog Pit had ever presented. Her training had taught her to use adrenaline as a fuel, dread as the hunger to win.

Both fighters pressed their hands into prayer and bowed. The referee laid out the rules of honourable combat: no biting, no fish-hooking, no eye gauging. Asenath just had chance to wonder if the gangster – introduced as Zero – was the honourable sort before the referee drew up his hand sharply between them, signalling the start of the bout.

Storming forward, Zero launched a flying kick at Asenath's skull. She sidestepped the manoeuvre and stabbed a heel into Zero's shin. The man hissed and spun around, driving a metal fist at her face. Asenath bent back at a severe angle to avoid the punch. The revolving hand skimmed millimetres from her face.

Flipping 360 degrees, Asenath landed in a crouch and slammed out with the heel of her right hand. She connected with the Sirienese's left knee and felt it give. Zero let out a grunt but continued his attack. Asenath heard the whir of deadly, bio-morphed hands, the snick-snick of mechanised knives descending. She was quick, but not quick enough. Pain ripped across her right shoulder.

Asenath bounced off the cage wall and the crowd roared as they got the first blood they'd been thirsting for. A metal mass launched towards her face again. She dove left and got in two jabs to Zero's ribs. The man gasped. Asenath rocked back onto her heels and, shutting off the pain in her shoulder, launched a series of volleys against the Sirinese.

Her advantage didn't last. She was an infinitely superior fighter but Zero had hardware. He blocked Asenath and drove a steel-jointed elbow into her collarbone. The blow tore into her flesh again. Asenath sucked air between her teeth and stumbled backwards.

Watching her with seeming impassion, Zero eased back his shoulders. Holding his arms out slightly from his sides, he separated his fingers; the tools glinted under the spotlight. At the opposite side of the cage, Asenath showed her teeth. The thrill of the fight was more intoxicating than any hit of Dazzle Dust. She focused through the carnage of noise and reminded herself that every opponent had their weakness. The secret was to avoid those deadly rotating hands and concentrate on Zero's flesh parts.

Again, he came for her. This time, Asenath crouched to avoid the blows, drove out a leg and whacked the front of one foot into the reflex spot on the man's left ankle. She somersaulted aside just as Zero collapsed to his knees, momentarily floored. Asenath was on him straight away, driving multiple punches into his kidneys. Zero bucked but gravity was on her side. At this juncture, Asenath would have usually drawn her scimitar across her opponent's throat. But this bout was friendly if bloody.

Apparently content to let her exhaust herself, Zero stayed tucked in. Asenath cursed internally. Her only options were to stay and pummel the man to little effect, or back off.

The decision was made for her when the bell sounded and the referee forced them to break apart. Zero stalked off to the opposite side of the ring, apparently nursing bruised ribs. Asenath shook the sweat from her hair, squatted on her haunches and pressed her hands to her forehead. While the Sirinese was sucking down water and taking a rest from his gum shield, Asenath slowed her breath and focused entirely on one goal – to emerge as victor. In her mind's eye she mapped the vulnerable spots on the Sirinese's body – genitalia, kneecaps, windpipe, nose.

The respite was short lived. The bell rang for the second round. Zero strode back across the ring, neck bunched, jaw tense.

Height, agility, flexibility, and years of training… Asenath ticked off her list of advantages against the Siriense. He came at her hard, arms revolving in their greased sockets; she found her moment and launched an uppercut at his chin. As the man staggered, she landed a sidekick, her foot connecting with his groin.

Zero roared in agony. She kept up the assault, driving multiple kicks into his soft belly and chest. He reeled backwards, the metal limbs making him top-heavy.

Asenath locked into the rhythm of her attack, raining down blows until Zero hit the floor. He lashed out, forcing her to arch back and weave to avoid the slicing hands. She might have been battling her shadow.

The champion hit home twice. Asenath clenched her jaw, feeling the hot spill of blood at a forearm, the back of a wrist. For a spilt second, she understood fear again – that emotion she had trained so hard to conquer. Then she saw Megumi's face amongst the sea of strangers outside the cage – and she was struck suddenly by a tremendous wave of boredom. The fight had satisfied the crowd's need for gore and violence. Time to wrap things up.

Zero staggered to his feet. His bare chest was already blackening with bruises. Asenath suspected that a good few ribs had suffered hairline fractures. But one thing was certain – the entertainment was not complete until she put Zero's specialist biomods out of action.

A phrase occurred to her. *Uporaba človeka moč proti njemu.* 'Use a man's strength against him.' Her Commodore's favourite mantra.

Charging at the cage wall, Asenath leapt up and kicked off the mesh. Momentum carried her into a somersault. Her right foot connected with Zero's skull, her left with his chest. He lost his balance and stumbled back. Asenath landed, feet firmly grounded, reached for the man's shoulders and propelled him hard into the cage wall. The whirring digits ripped into the mesh and knitted with it. Zero bucked again and again in a desperate effort to get free.

The referee stepped up.

"Yield?"

Zero craned his head to look back over a shoulder. Asenath flexed her fingers, bunched them into fists and started to walk over.

"Yield," said the Sirinese through bloody teeth,

The referee held up Asenath's arm and the crowd erupted.

Megumi laid her knife and fork down on the empty plate.

"You were right. The fava beans were excellent."

Asenath soaked up the slops with a piece of pita bread which she wolfed it down. Nothing stimulated her appetite quite like a fight.

"How is your shoulder?"

"It is fine. The waitress bandaged it for me."

She became aware of the other woman watching her and said, "What do you want to know?"

"Excuse me?"

"The way you are staring suggests you have questions." Asenath put her elbows on the table. "What do you want to know?"

Megumi cocked her head. "You are Brah: Warrior caste…"

"*Was* Brah." Asenath swigged from her cup of Jackogin. "I was expelled. Now I'm Izobani. Why else would I live in the Crease? And your next question, no doubt, is why was I expelled?"

"Yes."

Asenath shook her head, amused. The doctor wasn't shy about asking personal questions.

"I do not lie with men," she answered just as bluntly.

"You are celibate?"

"No, I do not lie with men."

"Ah." The revelation didn't seem to cause waves. But her ostracism did. "Is it really as simple as that in your culture? And how did they know, those in authority I mean?"

Something about the way Megumi asked her questions – bare-faced and apparently without prejudice – made Asenath more truthful than usual.

"I fell in love with my Commodore." She pictured Commodore Nefer. Skin like a sunrise. Stretched out naked on the bed in her private quarters. "We had a brief relationship. It ended when Nefer decided her religion mattered more." Asenath knew she sounded sour, and she was. Nefer had renounced her act of transgression as a momentary lapse in moral fibre – an admission which won her the right to stay on as Commodore and Brah.

"Mama Sunstar does not condemn. Hers is the old religion, though. Too often this country has been influenced by West, never more damagingly than in its adoption of the Saints and their sanitised ways. Commodore Nefer said sorry for her so-called sin and was welcomed back into the fold. I chose to dance on with Mama Sunstar and the creed which teaches all consensual love is sacrosanct. It was a choice which lost me friends, wealth and status."

"And your family?"

Asenath threw back the remainder of her drink. She poured a fresh shot. "My family might be Brah, but they are good people.

They live in Zan City now. My father thought it prudent to leave Jeridia – or as he calls it, 'the dying plain'."

Megumi nodded. "Every day I wait for news from my family. They promised to send for me once they found a place where the grass still grows. This poverty." She held out her hands to the tumbledown bar. "It's all consuming."

She looked sad suddenly and Asenath held up her cup. "A toast. To beauty in expected places."

Megumi smiled as they clinked glasses.

Casa Caca wasn't the kind of place Megumi expected to visit once let alone twice in the same day. As a medic, she had often visited the bedridden in the Crease. But she hadn't knowingly entered the domain of criminal Izobani before. Now, though, Asenath's whiskey-soaked voice and sparring skills had sunk hooks into her. She was not so much invited back to the tenement as dragged by her fascination with the woman.

The Jeridian brave gestured inside the now empty apartment. She closed the door. Megumi was aware of her wedding band. The heat of evening pressurised in.

It was Asenath who strode over, grasped the back of Megumi's head and kissed her. Not a loving kiss. A sharpness of teeth and a tongue forced between her lips. The brave's strong hands were already moulding her breasts, the swiftness of it promoting Megumi to gasp and kiss back deeper.

When Asenath pulled away, Megumi felt a wave of disappointment. But the brave was shedding her clothes – the skin-tight vest to reveal a taut stomach and small, pectoral-like breasts, the moleskin boots, and suede jeans peeled off and discarded. Moonlight blazed through the large windows. Asenath's legs were long and muscular; they shone like polished redwood. Her hips were narrow and she was shaved where her legs met.

"You like to look?"

Caught out, Megumi redirected her gaze to the Jeridian's face.

"No." Asenath took hold of Megumi's chin. "Look."

Megumi endured the tight grip a few agonising seconds. She pulled away and started to undo her dress.

Asenath smacked her hands aside. "I do it, ya."

The Jeridian leant in and soaked up the heat from Megumi's lips. Megumi felt a fresh burst of desire as Asenath broke free. The strong hands were busy with the buttons of her dress. Megumi stumbled under Asenath's pressure and rested against the edge of the long table.

"Arch," commanded Asenath, dragging Megumi's dress down off her shoulders. Megumi floundered, not understanding the instruction.

"Arch your back." Asenath fed a hand around to the base of her spine. The brave lowered her head and Megumi arched, feeling the spill of breath across her collarbones, the wet heat at her nipples. Asenath's free hand slid down her stomach and in at her underwear. The brave's fingers splayed and quested, and finally dug in. Megumi bucked, her legs automatically rising, her heels gripping the other woman's hips.

Asenath forced her to stay arched, the soft brown mouth feasting at her breasts while a tight bud of fingers took her deeply and relentlessly. Megumi wanted to run her hands over the brave's bandaged shoulder, share in the intimacy of touch. But apparently Asenath had no need for it. As demonstrated by her behaviour in the cage fight, she was built to conquer, Megumi realised while struggling to brace herself against the table. The knowledge that she was helpless against the warrior terrified and intoxicated her. She wanted to break free. Her arms were cramping while the lace of her underwear cut in at her hips. At the same time, she couldn't help soaking up the pleasure enforced on her. Pressing harder against Asenath's flanks, experiencing the confusion of tongue, lips and mouth passing from one breast to another, she reached the tipping point then fell away from it as if her body was teasing her.

"Please." The word escaped her lips before she could even process why. But Asenath understood, switching the thrust into a steady swirling motion. Megumi came in a sugared rush, gulping down air and shivering deliciously. Asenath slowed her hand and finally stepped away. She allowed Megumi a few moments to quiet her heartbeat. The oppressive heat settled in between them again.

Later, when the Jeridian had used her twice more and taken whatever pleasure she wanted in return, Megumi slipped back into her dress and hunted out a cramped bathroom. She scooped up mouthfuls of metallic brown water from the faucet.

Returning to the main room, she found Asenath lounging on a worn couch. The warrior had put her jeans back on but was otherwise naked.

Megumi drummed the fingers of one hand on the table. She felt the woman's gaze on her. "I'd best go." When Asenath didn't reply, she started for the door.

"Who are you protecting really?"

The question came out of nowhere. Megumi's breath caught in her throat.

"Excuse me?"

Asenath was on her feet and across the room in seconds. Megumi panicked as the strong hands which had touched her so intimately went to her throat.

"This great concern for your patients which led you to my door? I do not think it is the whole truth. This neighbourhood is too dangerous for a little rich girl, because that is what you are. Ya, you enjoy the thrill of a backstreet bar, a cage fight, casual sex. But I see your loathing to step out of this room and into the arms of the night. The Crease is not your neighbourhood, even if you do help its poor in daylight. Those silk underthings beneath your pretty dress cost more than any Izobani earns in a month. You say your family are travelling and they will send for you, but something keeps you here, something precious, something the Blood Worms want and you must protect." Asenath brought her face close. Megumi felt her breath on her lips. "Or should I say someone?"

The sun was up by the time Asenath awoke. She rubbed a thumb and forefinger across her eyelids – just as a loud rap sounded on the front door. Had she sensed the visitor's approach?

"Enough noise. I come now!" Asenath peeled herself off the saggy couch. Her scimitar lay on the table; she picked it up and used the tip to slide open the spy panel in the door.

A rheumy eye stared in at her.

"Late night, was it?"

Asenath closed the panel. Laying down her blade, she unbolted the door. Tadinanefer hobbled inside, the colourful robes of her order at odds with her gnarled face. Asenath had no idea how old Tadinanefer was; the priestess looked not so much alive as pickled. Her forehead was decorated with a crude depiction of the evil eye, drawn in the traditional paste of crushed Blue Glow beetles and designed to ward off spirits. She walked with a twisted cane and stank of incense.

"Got any brew?" The priestess eyed the table.

"I'll steep some." Asenath walked over to the kitchenette. Five minutes later, the leaf mulch was brewed. She poured out two cups of dank, tannin liquid.

"What's her name?" called the old woman.

"Who?" Asenath put a measure of Jackogin in Tadinanefer's cup, just the way the priestess liked it. She carried over the brew.

Tadinanefer was by the table, nostrils twitching.

"Who? Oh Asenath, you at least got her name? The girl you fumbled a few short hours ago." The priestess thumbed her nose. "I sniffed out the pair of you."

Asenath grinned. "I got bored, ya."

"Bored!" Tadinanefer shook her head. Joints cracking, she settled onto one of the high backed chairs. "Horny more like."

"Maybe." Asenath took a gulp from the steaming cup. The brew wide-eyed her. "Her name is Megumi Midori. She's a doctor. Works out back of a whorehouse on Aziel Street."

"Never heard of her. Then again, I ain't one for conventional medicine." Tadinanefer tapped her stick against the carpetbag beside her; she carried it everywhere and Asenath knew it contained the tools of the old woman's trade: elixirs, herbs, mineral pastes, and a surgeon's toolkit."

"What *have* you heard? I presume Lizzie-Anne asked you to put the word out."

"Yes, yes, the little strumpet came knocking last night. Said you were mindful of Blood Worms. None in sight, I told her. But she says look again and would you know it? There's a gang holed up at Stick Row. Got themselves attached to an abattoir over there."

Tadinanefer sucked her gums. "I'm not imagining the horrors they get up to there."

"Any visiting surgeons in town?" Asenath asked. Blood Worms stole people but it was the surgeons who paid for living flesh and experimented on it.

"There's talk of a surgeon holed up in Zan City. Lots of dollars. Into the unique."

"Unique?"

"Unique, you know. Odd skin tone, higher-than-average intellect, athletes, anomalies and so forth. Surgeons will always pay more for unusual specimens over your common Izobani." The old woman slurped from her brew cup. "Blood Worms pick on us because Jeridians heal faster. Makes us better subjects for the bio-morph implants. Pinkies sell well on the black market too, while a Showmaniese or Siriense anomaly with proven healing ability will attract a mighty price."

"Megumi has employed us as bodyguard to one of her patients. She eventually let on that our charge is a six year old boy. A Twists survivor. Blood Worms have already tried to snatch him twice."

Tadinanefer snorted into her cup. "Ah, it makes sense now. Lots of rumblings among certain parties in the Crease about a hunt for a boy. Talk of bounties, hefty ones too." The rheumy eyes pinched. "Sure you want to get involved in all this, Asenath? You and your friends have a nice little earner in protection, but there's something whiffy about this situation. Has to be more to the kid than this Megumi is letting on. Surgeons don't offer sums like those being bandied around without hoping to acquire something special. Something *unique*."

Asenath sat down, put her elbows on the table and steepled her fingers. A child was being pursued by Blood Worms and Megumi was doing everything in her power to protect that child. Asenath thought about the soft burn of Megumi's tongue, the unusualness of a woman who treated Izobani and drank Rakija, but who seemed at odds with the Crease.

The truth of the situation struck Asenath like a blow to the jaw.

"A mother would go to dangerous extremes to protect her son. The boy is a Twists survivor and Showmaniese, which would make him one of these rare commodities you mentioned. It would certainly explain the bounties on his head."

"The kid is Megumi's son? Why didn't she just say so?"

"I do not know." Asenath lent back in her chair, arms stretching, legs going out under the table. She knitted her hands behind her head. "When will the Blood Worms come for him again?"

"Blood Worms won't wait about." Leaning down, Tadinanefer rooted around in her carpetbag and produced a small black velvet pouch. Unfastening the neck, she shook out five tiny bones onto the table, spread them about and clucked her tongue. "They will strike tonight. So where is the boy now?" The priestess sniffed. "Is he here?"

"With his mother, I presume." Asenath picked up her scimitar and ran a finger along its shining blade. "Thank you, Tadinanefer. Let's hope I will be in need of your other services before the day is out."

251 Marlow Avenue was a featureless block hewn from the same grey bedrock on which the city was built. Once upon a time the building's harsh edges would have been softened by fauna and flora. But the same lethal insecticide which had created West's dustbowl had leeched Jeridia's formerly green and pleasant land, neighbouring Siria too. Asenath had no doubt that the residence was exclusive – it was on the right side of town and among other utilitarian but well preserved homes.

She rapped her knuckles against the large front door. At her back, the rest of the Tai Mowa gang assessed their surroundings.

"Ask me, these richies haven't got it much better than us," said Ragorne. "Sure, they've more space and no open sewers, but these buildings look like tombs."

"We came to Jeridia to escape West's dustbowl. Recently it seems we've just exchanged dust for rock," shot Lizzie-Anne while Arlene chipped in, "No wonder Blood Worms are picking us off. We've nowhere to hide in this hellhole."

The door was opened by Megumi in a black kimono, her dark glossy hair swept back. Behind her was a bright hallway. Marble floor, wide staircase, red papered walls and a monstrous chandelier hanging from the ornate plaster ceiling. The interior of the house was a world away from its stark exterior.

Asenath glanced over a shoulder. "Apparently some of us know how to hide very well." She found Megumi staring at her, almost accusingly.

"Come in." The doctor stepped aside. Asenath and her gang filed into the hall. Megumi closed the door and bolted it.

"You live here?" Hondo tightened his eyes.

"Yes."

"And you chose to work in the Crease?"

A pause.

"Yes."

"Wow! You must have one big heart to go with them big titties." Ragorne knocked elbows with Hondo. The wiser brother shook his head in bemusement. Both looked uncomfortable when Megumi looked over at one of the doorways leading off the hall and said, "Come in and meet my friends, Chi."

The boy let go of the doorjamb he was hugging and came into the hall. He had a slight limp. The arm which hugged a knitted roo rat was disfigured by the familiar ropey flesh of a Twists' sufferer. Unlike most, he had fought off the disease. He was one of the lucky ones.

"Hey there, little 'un." Ebo squatted down, the sheathed scimitar at his back knocking against the floor.

"Hey." The kid tried a wave. Ebo waved back.

Megumi stroked the boy's hair. She cleared her throat and stood upright.

"I must tell you that Chi is my son. I was afraid you wouldn't come if you thought I was just some rich bitch looking out for her son."

"We know that already." Asenath considered the boy. "What we don't know is why you spun us some yarn about a doctor's surgery out back of a whorehouse." Her gaze flicked to Megumi, who was biting her bottom lip. "Why'd you think a sob story about your patients being picked off by Blood Worms would appeal to our tastes more than the truth?"

Megumi shook her head vehemently. "The doctor part was true, at least until I got married. Then things changed. Chi became my priority, especially when I realised my husband was not even close to the man I had thought him to be. When Chi became a prize to be fought over, I knew I had to get out of my marriage." She held out her hands. "This was my parents' house. I brought Chi here with his loyal Nana. My patients from the Crease helped me track down your Tai Mowa gang. They said you could be hired to act as our protectors."

Asenath wasn't letting up. "But why lie?"

A housemaid wearing a plain apron and a careworn face appeared at the doorway. Megumi gave her son a hug. "Go with Nana now. She will fix you some yogurt and ruby fruit."

The boy looked pleased. He hobbled back through the door presumably leading to a kitchen.

With the Nana and Chi out of sight and earshot, Megumi dropped the act. She paced up and down the hall.

"I didn't think you would help, not if you knew the extent of my situation. Why would anyone help? It's tantamount to suicide."

Asenath sensed the gang getting edgy.

"What shit is this?" Ragorne slung his rock rifle down off his shoulder. His lips curled back from his teeth. "I'm not liking this situation one iota." Ebo rubbed his chin. Lisimba glared off into the corners of the hallway.

Asenath shut them up with a hiss. "It's not so different from the tale she told yesterday." She eyed the doctor. "These old patients who told you where to find us, you still treat them?"

Megumi nodded.

"You treat all of them?"

"When I can. It hasn't been easy for me to escape unnoticed."

"Of course. The controlling husband you mentioned. And do you still debt collect for the overlord you mentioned?"

"No."

"So you treat these paupers for free, all the while flouting your husband's rules and doing your old employee out of debt revenue?" Asenath managed a sour smile. She fed a hand behind Megumi's neck and squeezed, offering comfort or asserting authority. "Our doctor here is not such a bad sort. But she does have one vivid imagination." Asenath felt Megumi tense. She tightened her grip. "Friends, I'd like to introduce Megumi Midori, only her real name is Megumi Jun – wife of Akihiro, Showmaniese overlord and cold blooded killer."

"Shit, Asenath. Shit!" Ebo looked like he might just rip Megumi's throat out in the spot.

"Akihiro's wife? Good Souls almighty." Lizzie-Anne aimed her rock rifle at Megumi's head. "Shall I shoot her now or once she's guaranteed us safe passage outta here?"

"Put the rifle down," said Asenath. "Now!"

Lizzie-Anne did as told, but the gang looked primed to take Megumi apart. Asenath didn't blame them. The woman in her grip had woven a complex web of half truths and deceit.

"So who are we protecting Chi from really? Blood Worms or his father?"

Tears streaked Megumi's face. She trembled under Asenath's touch.

"I didn't trust Akihiro not to sell Chi to them, to the Blood Worms. Chi is Shomaniese with AB negative blood type. He survived the Twists, which makes him a phenomenally rare commodity."

In the pause that followed Asenath assessed the situation. She had Akihiro's wife and son – worth a fortune in ransom money alone. But Megumi had paid her dues in the dangerous if close-knit community in the Crease. Plus, Megumi's son had already survived the horrors of the Twists; Asenath was damned if she was going to hand him over to his father or Blood Worms. In her mind's eye, she saw Chi strapped to a mortician's slab, a surgeon teasing out the boy's innards and feeding in steel bones and wires. Asenath knew she had lost too many friends and family members to that bloody trade.

But she was being presented with access to Akihiro and that was invaluable.

Apparently the others understood as much. She announced, "Let them come. We bodyguard the boy. The mother fends for herself. You agree, ya?" and the rest held up their weapons and nodded.

"Thank you…"

Megumi would have said more but Asenath held up her hand. "Do not speak. We've had our fill of lies. Just show us the layout of the rooms and let us do the job you employed us to."

No one joined the Tai Mowa gang without expecting to make enemies; Akihiro Jun was one of the most powerful. His business interests spanned dealing in narcotics to whoring to extortion via a network of debt collectors. Asenath understood how Megumi as a young, impressionable doctor could have encountered the sharp-suited overlord and fallen for his good guy impersonation. How long had it taken Megumi to wonder where her husband's money came from or why his employees acted like bodyguards? She suspected the doctor had married Akihiro in ignorance and gone on to bare his child under the same illusion. When had Megumi seen the edge behind Akihiro's sharp suits and charm?

Watching Megumi now, standing in front of one of the large, white-washed windows in the drawing room, arms folded against the dark, Asenath couldn't help feeling slightly sorry for her. She liked the way Megumi operated in the divide between wealth and poverty,

But the bitch had lied – and lied repeatedly. Now the Tai Mowa gang were in danger. Yes, they had chosen to stay, every one wanting a shot at one of the big bad overlords who left such stains on their lives. But had they known the truth of the situation ahead of time, they could have offered up peace prayers, chosen their weapons with more care, even opted out if the spirit wasn't willing. There would have been no judgement; each member of the Tai Mowa shared the same philosophy – that each chose their own path.

But now Megumi had chosen for them and time had run out. Asenath heard the sound of a heavy implement strike the front door. Megumi turned sharply, the softness gone from her eyes. She had sense to stay quiet, even when the Nana came bustling in.

"What now, Miss? Chi is sleeping. Do I bring him downstairs?"

"You go back up and watch over him," Asenath cut in. She looked at Megumi. "You too. Stay with the boy. You employed us to do a job. Let us do it."

Megumi went to leave. Asenath gripped her arm.

"What of your husband?"
Megumi's eyes tightened.
"Kill him."

The door splintered and swung open to reveal a broad Showmaniese with a smoke stick between his lips and a steel ramrod in hand. The man stepped back. Akihiro strode into the hallway, shouldered by gangsters. Asenath was standing on the first step of the staircase, arms at her sides, scimitar in hand.

"Good evening, Akihiro."

Akihiro smiled. His small black eyes were bright as a bird's.

"I know you. Lady Killer, am I right? You like to brawl in the Hog Pit's fight cage." He glanced at his men. "You recognise her too, right? She's good." Undoing his jacket button, he slid his hands into his pants' pockets. "So, what's the score Lady Killer? Megumi pay you to play bodyguard?"

"That's exactly the score." She gestured to the doorways leading off the hallway. Each was occupied by one of her fellow Jeridian braves. Shoulders broad as rhinohorns. Mohawks spiked with green reed sap. Neck piercings glinting. Asenath held out her scimitar and pointed up. "Got a few nursemaids installed upstairs too."

Akihiro looked down his nose at her, exposing the black 'V' tattoo etched across his throat. "Is it inconceivable I should want to see my son? Or that I am entitled to object to my wife running away and taking Chi with her? You have met her – it is not out of the question that everything she has told you about me is a lie."

Not remotely out of the question, thought Asenath. In fact, Megumi had proven herself an adept liar over the past 24 hours. Then again, if Akihiro thought he could rewrite his malignant personality in her eyes, he was equally delusional.

"I have been employed to keep Chi safe from Blood Worms and from you."

"There are no Blood Worms after my son!" Akihiro rocked back on his heels, chuckling. "Megumi has woven you a pretty tale no doubt, about how special Chi is – which he is, but I say that as a biased father – and about how I am willing to sacrifice my son for financial gain. I ask you, Lady Killer, do I strike you as that sort of a man?" Akihiro smiled again, revealing nothing except a gold-capped incisor.

Asenath stared at the overlord. "Do you remember Commodore Nefer?" Akihiro looked blank and she continued, "I trained under her command. When I knew her, she was a strong brave. Later she was reduced to poverty when the Twists struck her. The disease could not be cured. Instead Nefer was reduced to debt collecting for a Shomaniese overlord. When she became too sick to work, the overlord ran her through with his sword. This I leant of after the fact." She showed her teeth. "I not only believe but I *know* you are the kind of man to sell out your son to Blood Worms. Throw your wayward wife into the bargain too, ya?"

Akihiro's smile stiffened. "Now that's a shame, Lady Killer. I hoped you had brains as well as brawn. I am not a kindly enemy. Why antagonise me?" He took his hands out of his pockets and crossed his arms. "I take it your friends have their own motives for taking against me?"

Each Jeridian knocked the flat of a hand against their throats; a traditional insult and one which stressed revenge.

Akihiro nodded. "Okay then." He glanced to either side. "Karera o korsu!" he told his men.

Asenath didn't speak Showmaniese but she understood the command to kill. She glanced up in praise of Mama Sunstar and requesting the deity's protection. Ebo, Lisamba and Hondo offered their own prayers. Lowering her eyes, she saw them draw their scimitars from back holsters. Asenath gripped the handle of her own.

Akihiro's men split into four units. She made a swift assessment of the slim, suited gangsters with lemony skin, high cheekbones and the traditional 'V' tattoo at their throats. Street fighters without code or honour – which meant, in spite of the odds, she and her fellow braves stood a chance.

Her fight instinct kicked in. The five gangsters allocated to her charged at the steps. She drew her scimitar around and up in a blur of silver. Two men produced rock pistols. Three wielded tanto short swords. Akihiro really did believe in the 'look' of his men being as important as their abilities; Asenath hoped to use that to her advantage.

A shot from one of the rock pistols skimmed her ear, burrowing itself into the wood of the stairs. Asenath took the opportunity to dip down alongside the shooter before he could reload. There was no room for maiming in this game; she dragged her blade across his tattooed throat and was already dodging shots from the second shooter before the first hit the ground. Rock amo was crude, the pistols and rifles prone to violent kickback and miscalibration. Firing at short range increased the accuracy. Fortunately Asenath had three swordfighters between her and the second shooter, making aim difficult.

Maintaining her higher ground on the staircase, she wove her blade back and forth in front of her, daring the swordsmen to strike. They took it in turns to confront her. The first used his tanto like a staff, blocking Asenath's slices but unable to land a blow. He exhausted himself and started to back off when the shooter missed Asenath but made a mess of the swordsman's ear. The man yelped and clutched his bleeding head.

Asenath was distracted by the second swordsman who proved nimble on his feet, matching her for grace as he arched back to avoid her blade. Their blows were strong and multiple. The chimes of swordplay came at her from all directions. Her braves were performing their own violent choreography. The air stank of sweat and spark powder.

If the gangster matched Asenath's grace, he couldn't match her relentlessness. The scimitar sliced across his shoulder. Blood welled where his suit tore and he backed off quickly, face contorted.

The third opponent powered forward, tanto in hand, just as Asenath felt a rip of pain at her outer thigh – rock shot. She cursed, skidded under the swordsman's arm and dragged her blade across the shooter's chest. The pistol fell from the man's grip; she caught it in her free hand and turned sharply. The third swordsman received a short range blast to the throat. Flesh jettisoned at the impact. The man slumped to the floor, gagging on his own blood.

The victory was short lived. Asenath heard a roar from one of her own – Ebo. Her gaze whipped over to the doorway he'd been guarding. The brave had fallen onto a gangster's blade. He fought on though, teeth stained red, the blade's hilt jutting from his ribs.

Asenath threw back her head and sang an eerie, warbling note which cut through the crush of blades and grunts of men. Whirling around in a tight 360, she tore open the throats of the two injured gangsters who'd backed away. She charged to Ebo's side. Too late to save him – his opponents had cut him too many times. But he would see them destroyed before Mama Sunstar took his spirit. In the heat of rage, Asenath's scimitar became as much of an extension of her bones and muscle as Zero's biomods were in the fight cage the previous evening. She tore into the gangsters, severing a carotid artery, a jugular, the ligaments at the back of a third's knees.

"Moj nagradu!" she cried, beheading each. *My prize.*

Lungs screaming for air, the noise of the battle at her back, she met Ebo's gaze. He blinked in acknowledgement. His chin rested forward on his chest. Asenath offered up a second war cry.

Turning to the fray, her instinct was to help Lisamba and Hondo. But then she noticed Akihiro and several gangsters at the top of the stairs. Her chest felt sawn in two – her fellow braves were outnumbered but Akihiro was moving closer to the boy she had sworn to protect.

When Hondo shouted at her – "Go for Akihiro!" – she forced her feet to move. The choice was inevitable; unless a brave was at death's door, it was insulting to take on their battle. She offered up a prayer for the braves locked behind walls of swords. The other thing she did was to slit the throats of two shooters positioned near the front door. Now the battlefield was even, she reasoned, taking the stairs three at a time.

She could hear gunfire – Akihiro's men attempting to clear a path through Ragorne, Lizzie-Anne and Arlene, who would be firing back. Her people had the advantage, though, having built a blockade from a wardrobe and a strip of corrugated iron which had covered a wood chute outside. Asenath heard the pings of rock salt bouncing off the sheet metal.

Reaching the top of the stairs, she brought herself up sharply and peered around the corner to see a number of figures on the landing, all dressed in sharp suits and cream fedoras. It was impossible to distinguish Akihiro from that angle. No matter. She would work her way through the gangsters until he was the last one standing.

Her thoughts were interrupted by the sound of wood splintering and a scream. Asenath recognised the voice as Lizzie-Anne's. Judging by the strength of the cry, the girl had received a serious wound. The barricade would not survive much longer.

Asenath stepped out onto the landing, the blade of her scimitar bowing out from her side like a claw. She ran forward and sliced the throats of four gangsters as easily as if she had been threshing grass. The last managed a strangled cry as he died, alerting the rest to her presence. She saw Akihiro direct a couple of fighters and a shooter her way then give his attention back to having the barricade cleared.

The gunman peeled off a couple of shots. Asenath snaked her body to avoid the blasts. Her mouth tensed. She hated shooters – no elegant combat, no skill, just point and click. How was she meant to concentrate on swordplay with those stinging rocks careering her way? She charged at the two fighters, dropped to her knees and slid between them, her blade cracking off one man's ribs. Before the other could react, she was on to her next kill. The shooter aimed his rifle at her face. His finger never pressed the trigger; the scimitar sank deep into his stomach and was twisted free.

Back on her feet, Asenath just had time to launch a strong right hook at a gangster who was beating Lizzie-Anne across the collapsed barricade before turning back around. Both swordsmen came at her. The one with the broken ribs wore a rabid look. Their short swords were slick with blood; whose, Asenath wasn't sure, but she didn't like it one bit. The combatants came up either side of her.

"This what you are looking for, bitch?" The wounded man still managed to leer at her while brandishing his tanto blade.

The second grabbed his crotch, sneering, "Bet you'd like to suck on this first!"

Asenath actually considered ignoring the men. They were so unworthy of death at her hands. Theirs should be an agonising demise from the Twists or dysentery.

She put aside personal sentiment and told them calmly, "Come and get me, gentlemen." In seconds, blows were raining down from either side. Using her training from the Warrior Akademja, Asenath imagined herself a reed weathering a storm. The men's blades sliced and stabbed; she deflected each manoeuvre until she saw the moment to strike. The man with the hurt ribs stretched and exposed them. Asenath delivered a right hook to the tender spot. The man 'oophed' and doubled over. She knocked him out cold with the handle of her scimitar.

Sensing the second man raise his sword to finish her, she tossed her weapon up into the air, caught the handle so that the blade pointed down and drove it beneath her underarm. The blade slid into the man's soft guts.

She forgot him instantly. The barricade was dismantled. Lizzie-Anne, Arlene and Ragorne were engaged in an ongoing scuffle at the door to Megumi's bedroom. Asenath wondered how the boy felt hearing his father battle to reach him? And what about the Nana and Megumi? She pictured the first in hysterics, the second a picture of cold resignation. And her fellow braves, Lisamba and Hondo? They should have worked their way through Akihiro's grunts by now.

There was no time to wait for them. Lizzie-Anne tucked behind a low divan, spraying out rock shot from her rifle, face distorted with pain. Ragorne had disarmed Akihiro's shooters with his ranch whip and was cracking it off any skull in reach. Arlene had a look of grim determination, like a woman who'd lived a sour life and learnt to fight back against it. Rifle butted against one shoulder, she peeled off shots whenever a Showmaniese gangster made a dash at them.

But all that fighting spirit meant nothing against a mine cone. Asenath was running towards the gangsters when she spotted the device in one man's hand. The pin was already pulled, the cone turning liquid silver. Asenath pulled up sharply. There was no time to stop it.

"Grenade!" she cried over the noise of gunfire.

The mine cone soared clear of Akihiro and his men, the conical design protecting those behind from the sonic pulse which visibly arched out, vibrating off the walls and furnishings, and incapacitating her gang.

Asenath felt a tug of dread in her stomach – she was hopelessly outnumbered. The panic switched to a tremendous rush of relief as Hondo and Lisimba arrived on the landing beside her.

"Mine cone," she mouthed, registering their disbelief. The weapon was costly technology, usually restricted to government warfare. Akihiro had to have friends in high places, or at least be lining the pockets of a corrupt official.

"Protect the others until they recover and don't let the bastards release another grenade," she told the Jeridian braves while watching a figure break off from the other Showmaniese, try the bedroom door handle then produce a key. "Akihiro," she muttered under her breath. Leaving Hondo and Lisimba to make their presence known, she sidled up to the bedroom door and slipped noiselessly inside.

She absorbed the scene. Chi lay on the bed. Megumi was brushing his hair back off his face and whispering soothingly. The Nana stood at the foot of the bed, rock pistol held in a quivering hand. Akihiro had paused halfway across the room.

"You stay there, Lady Killer," said Akihiro softly. He knocked the pistol out of the Nan's grip with the flat of his short sword and pointed the tip at the woman's chest. He spoke over a shoulder. "I have the right to appeal to my wife to come back to me. I have the right to say hello to my son."

Asenath wasn't so sure but knew it wouldn't pay to sacrifice the Nan's life needlessly. She shut the door, dulling the noise of the fight outside.

Akihiro nodded. He gave his attention to Megumi.

"How is a husband meant to fix problems in his marriage if his wife won't talk? Come now. Let's work this out."

Megumi rolled the boy behind her and slashed at Akihiro's outstretched hand with a kitchen knife. Akihiro roared as blood dripped from the wound onto the carpet. He rammed his sword home into the Nana's chest while Chi hid his head in the folds of his mother's kimono. In spite of the Nana's terrible wheezing, the child stayed silent. Perhaps he was accustomed to violence in his father's company, thought Asenath. Or perhaps he sensed the inevitability that he too would be put to the sword.

"So that is the way of it?" Akihiro stared at his hand.

"Leave us alone, Akihiro." Megumi's eyes crystallised. Her face twitched with fear as she looked past her husband. "Asenath?"

"Lady Killer knows her place when it comes to relations between a husband and a wife, don't you, Lady Killer?"

Asenath heard the sneer in the overlord's voice.

"I fucked your wife," she said simply.

Later, Asenath would question her decision to distract Akihiro and have him spin around to face her. She would wonder if her method had been too crude, if she had made Megumi distrust her bodyguard and take action. With the full knowledge of how it would end, she saw Megumi take her knife and drive it into Akihiro's shoulder. As the overlord's features pulled in on each other and set hard, Asenath raced across the room, arms pumping. Inside she knew it was too late. Akihiro turned and slid his sword between Megumi's ribs while Chi kicked backwards and worked his way up the bed, breath coming fast like a panting desert dog.

Megumi stared past Akihiro's shoulder at Asenath. Her eyes softened and became incredibly sad. "Chi," she mouthed.

Asenath didn't pay attention after that. Akihiro dragged his blade free of his wife's chest in time to block the scimitar's descent. Asenath circled the blade in repeating figures of eight. The Shomaniese blocked her every time, his face slick with sweat. He risked wiping a hand down his face to keep the salt water from his eyes; Asenath saw the opportunity and nipped the tip of her blade across the wrist of his hurt hand.

"Red bitch!" The overlord tore into her in return, raw pain giving him a desperate energy. Asenath imagined her feet lighter than air and her sword arm a shield. From somewhere she heard Megumi's last rasping breaths. There was no time to reminiscence or regret. As her Commodore always instructed, she had to focus on the now.

A child was crying. A blur of voices and violence resonated from beyond the door. Amid the relentless smash and fall of blades, Asenath knew that she had to use her opponent's strength against him. Akihiro – Showmaniese overlord, husband, father, collector of paupers' debts… Her mind backtracked. *Father*. Whether Megumi had been truthful about Akihiro's intent towards his son or not, Chi was still a precious commodity.

The thought cost her. Akihiro broke through her defences to slice into her collarbone. Asenath hissed, more out of indignation than agony. With no time to process the depth of the wound, she used the glee on Akihiro's face to fuel her reactions. Tucking beneath his arm, she ran up alongside the bed and directed her scimitar towards the crying child.

"No!" Akihiro's hands went out in front of him.

Gaze flicking between the two, Asenath saw crushing fear in the young boy's eyes and the oval shape of his father's mouth. Within the second, she called Akihiro's bluff and sent her scimitar flick-flacking through the air. It struck the overlord in the chest – the same lethal wound he had inflicted on Megumi.

Asenath forgot the overlord and looked down at the boy. Chi appeared to have fainted. "Poor child." She laid a hand on his head. The kindest thing would be to end his life too – now while he was unconscious and protected from the reality that, within the space of minutes, he had become an orphan. The moral part of her knew she would not do it. Instead, she waited for him to come to.

As she did so, she homed in on the silence. Had Akihiro's men taken victory? Had her gang destroyed the threat and retired downstairs, knowing better than to interrupt her in one-on-one combat?

"Sleep," she told the boy and crossed the room to Akihiro's body. Putting both hands on the hilt of her blade, she pulled it free and froze. Footsteps sounded out on the landing. She watched the door handle turn. The door opened to reveal five rock pistols trained on her. One shooter might miss. Five guaranteed a strike.

She straightened up as a man strode into the room. Western, tall, and dressed in a government Blues' uniform.

The man put his chin near his shoulder. "Fetch the boy."

Two Showmaniese filed inside. They approached her with caution.

"Don't mind the woman. She knows there are too many guns pointed her way to object." The man's accent had a rough edge. He was a dogsbody as opposed to someone of higher rank, Asenath concluded.

The men walked either side, still edgy. She heard the sound of bedsprings and a grunt of exertion. The men walked back past her. One held Chi in his arms. They disappeared through the door.

Asenath reached over her shoulder and slid her scimitar into the sheath at her back. There was no action to be taken. Her fellow gang members were either held at gunpoint or dead already. The Akademja had taught her to know when she was outnumbered.

"How much will you make on him, Blood Worm?" she muttered.

The government man lit a smoke stick. He exhaled a stream of smoke. "Enough to risk going up against Akihiro. But you've only gone and saved me the bother, Lady Killer." He knocked the flat of a hand against his brow in mock salute.

Turning his back, the man walked away. The last gunmen shut the door after him, leaving Asenath alone in the room except for the dead.

Moonlight streamed in at the large windows. Asenath had extinguished the lamps. The priestess had brought her own candles, six wads of brown tallow, each fat as a man's arm. The tools of her trade lay on the table: hacksaw, thread, curved needles, scoops, paring knives, skewers, and similar apparatus. The carpet bag sat open on a chair; every so often Tadinanefer dug around in it for some new herb.

"Had a sticky feeling about that bodyguard job. Gave me cramps in my belly just thinking about it. But sometimes it ain't up to an old hag like me to interfere. Sometimes the young have to do what they will, even if it kills them." Tadinanefer paused in her ministrations, holding the severed head by its hair. A sigh escaped her papery lips. "Ebo was a good 'un. I didn't care for that Lizzie-Anne much, but it's not like she deserved to get belly-sliced." She scooped out the head as she talked. "And you say Ragorne bore the worst of it too? Bruiser like him'll pull through. I got the knowledge in my bones."

"And what about the kid, Chi? Do you have knowledge in your bones about his whereabouts?" muttered Asenath from the couch. She took a long drag off a smoke stick. Her shoulder and collarbone ached where Tadinanefer had stitched up wounds.

"Yes, I have that too, but what do you need it for, hmm?" Hobbling off to the back of the room, the old woman lowered the head into a pot of boiling water on the stove. She didn't bother to rinse her bloody hands, just returned to the table and bent over to retrieve a fresh head from the sack, bones crackling as she moved.

Asenath exhaled heavily. "I failed in my duties as bodyguard. If the boy is still alive, I will make good on the grounds of my employment."

"Employment? Paah! Little need for honour code when your employee is dead, the poor bitch." Tadinanefer touched the evil eye symbol at her forehead.

Asenath took a fresh drag and let the smoke sit in her lungs, feeling the weight of it. "I am tired," she said quietly. Smoke bled from her lips.

"Of course you are." Tadinanefer put the head on the table. It was Akihiro. The overlord had died with the expression of overwhelming hate he wore so well.

"The others have the sense to lay up a while. Ragorne is letting Arlene tend to him." Tadinanefer winked. "There'll be a babe born from that arrangement, mark my words."

Asenath watched the priestess take a scalpel to Akihiro's eyes, plop them out of the sockets like ruby fruit from the pod. "I need to honour the dead before I rest," said the warrior. She nodded towards the head.

"Of course you do! But it's a few hours since the killing. These heads could have gone another day or so."

"No, they couldn't. There's no let up in the heat these nights. No ice to store them, either." She ground the nub of the smoke stick into a cup by her feet. "I need to make my peace with these spirits so I can focus on the living – by which I mean, find Chi."

"And what if you do find him? Do you play happy families? You killed the boy's father in front of him!" Tadinanefer started to muddle the brains with a skewer poked through an eye socket. "No mama, no papa. Maybe the boy is better off dying on a surgeon's table."

The words were harsh, but Asenath heard the sadness that underpinned them. "I just need to know where to look for him," she murmured. Rising from the couch, she walked over to the table and stood, hands on hips, watching the priestess pack the eyelids with seeds. Candles flickered. Shadows played over the walls.

A few moments later, the old woman sighed. She shook her head. “So you won’t let it rest, hmm? Well, I can only tell you what I’ve heard. The boy is being transported to Zan City. Some high and mighty surgeon is willing to pay a hefty price for his creed and blood type.” She brushed her hands off one another, scattering seeds over the gored table. “That’s the lot. I know no more.”

Asenath narrowed her eyes. “My family live in Zan City.”

“There you are! Ha! Kill two birds with one stone.” The priestess chuckled to herself. The laughter tailed off and she stared across the table at Asenath. “That enough for you?”

Asenath nodded stiffly. Zan City was an island of stone in a solar strip. A city with a wriggling underbelly of Blood Worms, so she had heard. A place to get lost in. It was over 3000 miles away in the vast dry country of West. On the one hand, that kind of distance gave her the chance to catch up with the Blood Worms. On the other, there was no single route to the city; her best bet would be to reach Zan City ahead of them.

“Know how I can get there quickly?”

Tadinanefer snorted. “The hell if I know! Jump aboard one of them wagon trains shifting dust. Join a circus!” She threw up her wrinkled hands and hobbled off to the boiling pot. Akihiro’s head was set bubbling alongside the others.

Asenath crossed her arms. The Tai Mowa gang were loyal but weakening. Life had calcified their bones. It was time to leave her colleagues to their own devices in Santa Spišské and set out on a new adventure.

Tadinanefer rooted around in the sack again. Asenath knew it contained one last head. Megumi’s long black hair gave the old woman something to grip onto; it flowed around the bloodstained face like thickened shadows. The doctor’s enticing eyes were closed, the finality of death the more acute for her beheading.

“Wait.” Asenath put a hand out as if to protect Megumi from the priestess’s butchering.

Tadinanefer squinted across the table.

"I did not kill this one. I took the head to keep her safe from Blood Worms and their flesh dealing." Asenath faltered and then added, "She meant something."

It was difficult to sum up what, if anything, she had felt for the doctor in the short time they had known each other. Physical longing, yes, and a sense of liking. Emotion enough for a Jeridian warrior to want to honour a lover in death. What she did know was that she owed Megumi a debt.

She picked up a paring knife. "This one I do. And then I rest." Her mouth tightened. "I set off for Zan City first light." A pause. "You coming?"

~*~

Sometimes a character resonates for the author beyond the pages of a book. In *Cyber Circus*, Jeridian warrior Asenath took her place amongst the strange and colourful inhabitants of a biomorphed circus tent. When I was asked to contribute a story to the brilliantly titled 'Fight Like A Girl' anthology, my mind went straight to Asenath and a desire to explore her backstory in a standalone novella. If the conclusion remains open-ended, it is because Asenath lives on in *Cyber Circus*. To me, she epitomises my idea of what it means to fight like a girl – with passion, resilience, fierce sensuality, and free of gender stereotypes.

The Harvest

Ridgeway School squatted in its nest of run-off chalk and clay. Gas light shone from tall windows fitted with slats of pig iron. Shadows moved behind lime-washed glass, small and flitting. Shadows of children. Young voices filtered out, dissolving on the misty air.

High up on one side of the bell tower, the steam clock struck nine. The bell stayed silent, long rusted to its hinges. Instead, a hand bell rung out through the vaulted classrooms, narrow corridors and echoing hall. When the clanging ceased, the school answered back with a low moan – wind beating at the rafters – the dry thwump-thwump of the furnace bellows in the boiler room, and the rattles of the radiators as they gave off their filmy heat.

Inside the small reception office, Bluze Christchurch was generating a letter to the parents on her typewriter ball. The concave keyboard didn't allow for a view of the printout, but Bluze attacked the keys with confidence. She gave the last letter a decisive punch. Sliding the typewriter away on its thin metal tracks, she held up the page. The reconstituted paper was the same off-white as Ridgeway School's exterior.

She read aloud: "…Need volunteers to patch the library roof, apply lime-wash sealant and re-bracket with spare pig iron."

"Spare pig iron?" The woman who appeared at the doorway snorted. Tucked up in rolls of her own fat, May Moon was chief dinner lady and pig slaughterer. She kept blood in the creases at her elbows. Her hat was a ward matron's – crisp, white and authoritarian.

"Never know unless you ask." Bluze took a fresh sheet off the stack between the wood pulping hand-mixer and the twin metal plates of a paper-making press. Unscrewing the typewriter's ink feed cap, she reached for a large stoneware bottle that was stained bluish-black. She uncorked the bottle and topped up the ink reservoir.

May watched from the doorway. "Want to put on gloves before you mess with that poison. You never know what it's made from.

Could be Devil's Rain, could be effluence." She spread out the vowels of this last word, pleased with her use of it.

"I make it myself. Every morning I mix two solutions, iron salts and tannic acids." Bluze stabbed the cork back into the bottle. "Nails and vinegar, and an extraction of oak galls." She glanced up and smiled. "Don't want to develop a case of Sticky Skin, do I? We've enough mayhem dealing with eighty kids, let alone inviting the sickness in."

The other woman stared back. Her lip curled. "Got to go scrub up… with filtered water." Retreating to the hallway, she continued to stare in. "We got need for eggs. Hens have gone grey at the legs and are only good for eating. I told Mr Gower, leave birds wallowing like pigs in their own mire and they're gonna go grey legged."

It didn't surprise Bluze to hear the headmaster was uninterested in May's drenched farmyard. Ridgeway's inner courtyard might produce the meat for meals and the dung cakes to fuel the boiler. But it was also responsible for the underlying stench of mildewed feathers and animal shit that permeated the school.

Not that Bluze had any interest in stoking the feud between the two factions. She nodded. "I'll add a request for eggs."

May eyed the typewriter with suspicion. "Uh-huh." She slumped off down the corridor.

Out on the Ridgeway, the wind punished the last of the beech trees and broadleaves, branches straining against its bite. The rain soaked down from a roiling sky. Either side of the ancient path, the hills were beaten back to a chalk under-crust. A wash of white swept down and out across the plains.

It started thirty years earlier. 2009, a fifteen million waste treatment plant opened in Westbury. The site was dedicated to the transfer, bulking up, acid neutralisation and solidification of waste. The stewing pot included pharmaceutical, photographic, printing, painting, laboratory chemicals, acids, alkalis, solvents, chlorinated hydrocarbons, cyanide compounds and elemental chemical waste. The resultant fly ash was intended for controlled disposal in Bishop's Cleeve and Stoke Orchard, Gloucestershire. The railcar incident at 20.18BMT on 22nd February saw an unseasonable north-easterly wind carry 40 tonnes of fly ash into the atmosphere over south-east England, though it drifted.

For a country ravaged by political divide, the fall of acid rain – or Devil's Rain as it became known colloquially – was just another environmental issue to wrangle over. For the families affected by its fall and a resultant sickness called Sticky Skin, the incident proved devastating. Wiltshire became the 'Whited Out' county. Home to ghosts, ancient burials, and the Harvesters.

They were men, or had been before the sickness curdled their looks and minds and they took to mixing mechanical bolt-ons with the living flesh they stole from others. Over their shoulders they carried giant keep nets. In the folds of long leather kilts, they kept weapons – serrated blades and keratin-shelled Sone guns. Warrior-like in their black armour, they moved noiselessly over the pale land.

Pig iron furnaces littered the hills like demon eyes. In-between, the housing pods were scattered. Slathered with a plaster of lime-kiln dust mixed with clay from the north-west hills, the barrows resisted the rain. But they were vulnerable as snails' shells to the footfall of the Harvesters.

Except, the dry leathered bodies of the old and the furnace workers were not to the invaders' taste. Their eyes were on closer quarry – the large lime-choked building with a bell tower.

The boy pressed his face into the monitor mask located alongside the meshed hatch. Words filtered out into the passage, the voice tinny and distorted.

"Thank you, Sam. I'm pressing the buzzer to let you in."

He pulled away from the chilled metal. Weak daylight flooded his corneas. The thin rasp of the buzzer sounded. He grasped the handle of the heavy dividing door – reinforced with wavy sheets of pig iron and thick wooden buttresses on the inside – and entered the main lobby of the school.

"Late again, Sam?" The secretary, Ms Christchurch, put her head around the door of her office. Ms Christchurch had a wide smile that showed her gums, bright red hair that fell lankly around her shoulders, and a tendency to seem smaller than the rest of the teachers and staff at Ridgeway.

He nodded. "My mother got a frickentickle in her throat. Couldn't walk me here and I'd already missed the Sledge."

Ms Christchurch smiled. Her eyes flitted between the boy and the handgun she was polishing. "Never known you catch the school bus, Sam. As for your mother, you ought to get her some elm syrup. Has she ever seen you to school?"

Sam scratched his hairline, chasing a louse. "Sometime maybe." He undid the heavy layers of blanket and sealskin that had sealed him away from the acid rain and shook them off like a dog. Then he slumped off down the corridor in the direction of his classroom, dragging the heavy layers of outerwear behind him.

The room was silent but for the knocks and sighs of steaming water in the radiators. Each child sat spine-straight and alert. Overhead, a large gas lamp gave off its insubstantial glow. Rain attacked the high windows like tiny beating fists.

"Burrow down. Lock up. Don't make a sound," repeated the class in unison.

"Again," said the headmaster, Mr Gower. A dry scab of a man.

"Burrow down. Lock up…"

"Sam Devises!" Mr Gower looked over his half-moon glasses.

The children broke off.

Sam stared down the barrel of a blackboard eraser.

"I suppose you have no need to fear the Harvesters," Mr Gower reared. "I suppose they won't have use for your skin, your fat, your organs."

Sam stared back. The headmaster sucked his cheeks. He retracted the eraser and presented the boy with a folder.

"Since you were last to class and so clearly well versed in what to do should the bastards break in, you can take the register to Ms Christchurch."

The front door to Ridgeway School softly un-clicked. Wind swept into the passage like a biblical flood, scooping up all that lay in its path: dried mud, skeletal leaves, the odour of not-quite-clean. The door drew to.

Bluze did not trust the sound. This was how they came, too quietly, where the children and parents brrr'd against the cold or coughed or squabbled.

The mesh at the hatch was woven on a slant which enabled her to see out but prevented those outside from looking in. She depressed a slim iron lever to one side of her desk. A set of kick steps smoothly unfolded. She climbed them and stood on the desk, feet ledged between the paper-stack and the large irons of the press. Her fingers moved as lightly over the munitions rig as they had over the typewriter ball. She selected a pair of ear defenders: tiny, tight-fitting shells secured by a thin black harness that fed across the forehead and lopped in tight around the back of the head. The pockets of the utility vest she wore were already packed with cartridges and spark dust. She snatched up a couple of sawn-offs, slid in the fat magazines, crossed her arms behind her head and packed them down into her back harness. The hand gun she'd polished earlier went into a hip holster. A bowie knife slotted in at the side seam of the utility vest. A brace of thin black sparklers clicked into the sprung brackets to form an 'X' over her chest.

Pinning up her knee-length skirt at either hip in a well-practised series of folds and garter snaps, she kicked on steel toecaps around her blue, buckled biker boots and leapt off the table in a backwards somersault.

She yanked out the voice funnel alongside the window hatch.

"Face to the mask," she barked.

Ten seconds later there had been no response from the other side of the mesh. A Harvester would trigger the mask's magnetism, the quantity of metal additives to their flesh signalling them as the flesh-warriors they were.

Bluze checked the grip of her ear defenders. They were snug. Blood roared inside her head like a hurricane. She eased up to the grid and peeped through. At first she saw nothing but the empty corridor. Then a huge shadow blocked the greater part of her view. She got an impression of other figures, but before she could focus, she felt a sharp tug on her arm.

She spun around and brought her handgun up under the chin of the boy, Sam. The kid didn't blink, just offered his class register. Bluze put a finger to her lips. Placing the folder in its correct tray on the desk, she slid open a drawer and retrieved a spare pair of ear defenders.

"Put these on," she mouthed. The Harvesters were clearly opting to save their Sone weapons until they were closer to their prey, else the boy would be twitching on the ground, mouth frothing.

Sam put the ear defenders on. He'd the look of a kid who had lived so long with fear he developed a thick skin against it.

She pointed at a large red dial on the wall.

The kid nodded and she lifted him up by the waist. She watched him struggle to unhook the wind handle, felt the soft expulsion of air from his chest as he grunted and revolved the alarm dial. Bluze knew it would filter out silently through the building while triggering a stopcock on the gas feed to each lamp to plunge the school into semi-darkness. Valves in the radiators would open, releasing a steady blast of hot steam to fill each classroom with its own early morning mist. Harvesters were used to the acid rainfall outside, but the sickness cramped their joints in the steamy heat.

As for the children, they would be donning their ear plugs, crawling into the individual panic rooms of their lock-ups, and bolting the door to each metre sized cube on the inside. Then silence would fall and the waiting would begin.

She didn't have time to get the boy safely back to class. He'd have to take his chance in the tiny reception office.

"Harvesters," she mouthed and pointed to the mesh. The kid followed her finger. "You stay here." She mimed the request with absurd emphasis.

No reaction appeared to mean agreement as far as the seven year old was concerned. Bluze peered through the mesh again – just as a Harvester brought his face to the magnetic mask and broke it in two with a head-butt. Seconds later, shockwaves off a crushed semtex strip knocked Bluze sideways. She clutched the boy to her; he felt stiff in her embrace. She thrust him away.

"Stay here," she mouthed.

Bluze slid up to the door and opened it. The corridor was dusty from the blast, and empty. No doubt, the Harvesters had retreated as far away as possible while the blast punched in the dividing door. She ducked out into the dust, pulling the door to behind her.

Reaching over her shoulders, she drew the sawn-offs, pressed her back against the wall and glanced left then right. Her stoppered ears threatened to play havoc with her balance. But better to deal with that potential disability than fall victim to the Sone gun and end up on her back.

She saw the shapes of the Harvesters forming through the dust cloud. Running down the corridor to where it hooked a sharp right, she leapt onto a broken chair and up on top of a locker cabinet. Biker boots planted firmly on the sheet steel, she swung the automatic 12 gauge sawn-offs up in unison.

The Harvesters materialised. Seven of them, she determined, making a quick head count. Half living-scarecrow, half reanimated, the men pressed towards her. She peeled off a dozen shots, striking an arm, a shoulder blade, a cheekbone. The red flashes as the AA shot landed told her that she had hit metal mostly. But one brute took a canon-punch to the face; the patched flesh tore back, revealing bone and welded metal. Bluze fired another couple of shots in the direction of that one. The head ricocheted back at a distorted neck angle.

But the others were on her now. Six devils who'd cut the flesh from others to re-patch their acid-scorched skulls and upper backs. They were broad, made so by the metal grafted under and on top of their human bones. Their height was just as sinister; they rose up and retracted on long, spindle limbs like human spiders.

Two drew their serrated blades and lunged for her. Bluze raced to the end of the lockers, thrusting off with one foot at the last second. She propelled herself up. A ceiling tile popped as she slammed a fist into it. Grasping the iron framework either side, she levered up inside the false ceiling.

Her breath came in tight, agonising bursts. A blade shot up into the ceiling space; she bucked backwards, only to roll sideways when a second point sliced up and swiftly withdrew.

Their interest in her was short-lived. Bluze knew the Harvesters had come for the children, lured by the possibility of those young bodies with their fresh living cells and bone growth. Adults were an irritant, best ignored or despatched with no more care than a child tearing off a butterfly's wings.

The Harvesters headed for the first classroom. Bluze knew she would need to get closer yet retain her higher ground in order to take them out.

Sam stood in the office. He slipped off the ear protectors. They were uncomfortable, plus they reminded him of dark crevices where a child might sleep unnoticed. He discarded them.

Standing in the room, he noticed mist seeping under the door. There was a small window in the door which had escaped the lime-wash. Through it, he saw an atmosphere of steam and dust. It reminded him of fog out on the hills and the spill of rain.

He considered trying to reach the handle of the alarm again. It had been fun to turn the dial around and around. He'd pictured the children scrabbling past their desks like mice desperate to escape a flooding drain, and how the teachers had donned ear protectors and run away to the staff room, leaving the young boxed up and alone. It was new to experience a harvest free of the constraints of his own one metre cube.

He gripped the door handle and stepped out into the corridor. Either side of the narrow passageway, radiators piped a continual flow of steam. They fizzed slightly under the effort, water knock-knocking inside their tin ribs.

Sam turned and walked down the corridor towards the first classroom. His view was obscured by the false mist and he drew up sharply. A Harvester occupied the space ahead, pinned steel craning out from beneath a long leather kilt. The not-quite-man reeled in; Sam felt the space between them growing smaller.

Now he saw there was no head to the thing, only flopping neck threads and arms that clawed just short of him.

Sam crouched down and lay flat on the floor. Drops of burning water splashed down on him from the ceiling. Condensing steam.

He inched slowly forward, beneath the reach of the swaying headless carcass.

Bluze moved across the framework of the false ceiling in a crab-like motion. The classrooms had the original vaulted ceilings, her only option being to scoop out the two tiles directly next to the doorway, hook her legs over the metal bars and propel her body down. She prayed to all that was holy that she survived to swing back up.

Stowing the sawn-offs at her back, she uncrossed the two black sparklers from their harness at her chest. Tucking them into one palm, she slid the opposite hand into a pocket of her utility vest and nipped out two precious packets. Spark dust was expensive but effective, possessing the same magnetic signifiers as the monitor mask. She fed the packets into the batons, used two fingers to press in the load springs and flipped the ignition switch. A tiny spark appeared at the tip of each baton. She held them carefully away from her body, took a deep breath and dropped.

Legs hooked over the frame, she swung upside-down at the open doorway and fired the sparklers with a splatter-gun approach. Harvesters recoiled from their efforts to un-prise the boltholes where the children hid. Hands clutched at their Frankenstein faces. Spark dust. A cloud-mass of nanites that grouped together to form centimetre long metal grubs that attached themselves to the Harvesters' metal nips and tucks, then found the soft connecting flesh and began to burrow in. If they were swift, the Harvesters could peel the grubs off and squash them underfoot like swollen leeches.

Two of the invaders drove through the pain to attack her. The first bled from one eye. She saw grubs inching in at a plate stitched beneath the eye socket. The pain the man endured was a match to the thrust of his blade to her shoulder, not to mention its dragging retrieval. Bluze gasped, lost her leg hold and crashed down onto the floor.

She flipped back onto her hands, spine bowing, and landed, hopping back a couple of steps. The two Harvesters bucked against the agonies of the spark dust, but carried on coming. The slash of their blades had brute strength but lacked skill. She ducked, drew her bowie knife out the seam of her utility vest and volleyed. Tucking in tight under the first brute's underarm, she scored the blade along the tender flesh. Immediately, she faced the second monster. Again, she utilised the knife. The spark dust grubs acted as a dye, indicating the weak spots. She bowed back to avoid the tremendous swing of the Harvester's blade, stood up straight and slid her knife in quickly at the neck sinews. The grubs crept in at the open flesh. She abandoned the two Harvesters to those drilling mites. They were walking dead men.

Through the steam, she saw one of the monsters work his serrated blade into the door seal of the first of the miniature panic rooms. The spark dust must have disintegrated; it was a temporal weapon that dissolved two minutes after impact. She considered loading her two remaining packets into the sparklers. Better to save them and take the creature out by hand, she decided. She started to stride towards him, bowie knife dancing like a silver fish in that sea of half-light. Her breath caught as a colossus stepped across her path.

The Harvester was a witch's poppet stitched from different shades of skin. Leather strips crisscrossed up the length of each arm, mummifying them. In place of hair, long black feathers were grafted to his skull. Half of the face had melted back to the bone. Small riveted steel sheets covered the remainder of the face, like scales.

He had a Sone Gun trained on her. She looked down. Tiny red dots danced over her chest.

Bluze felt a crush of nausea as the sonic waves hit. She fell off to the side, her hands clawing until she found and collapsed against the wall. The sound blast was repelled by her ear protectors, but the noise still managed to assault her at a cellular level. Her head swam. Shapes loomed.

Get back up, Bluze demanded of herself. *Make your legs carry you before the monsters use their blades.* She felt them closing in. Flesh warriors with minds like ice. She had to get control back. She had to fight to save herself.

Bluze strained to see past the billowing white. The shapes were gone. Her mind quietened. Steam drifted.

She pressed her palms against the moist wall and stood up. It terrified her to think of the Harvesters having moved on to the classroom belonging to Ridgeway's five to seven year olds. She remembered Sam. A strange child. Stiff as an armful of frozen washing when she'd lifted him up. She hoped he endured back in her office.

The bulky figure that materialised through the mist had Bluze reach over her shoulders for the sawn-offs. She froze mid-act as the figure took on the vaguely feminine aspect of the dinner lady, Mrs Moon. The woman carried a meat cleaver in one hand, a Harvester's head suspended by the hair in the other. Bluze was used to seeing the woman waddling through school, some decapitated animal clutched to her breast like a ragdoll. The sight of Mrs Moon in possession of a human head seemed perversely acceptable.

The woman performed a grand mime of taking off a pair of imaginary ear protectors. Bluze caught on. Begrudgingly she held one headphone out from an ear.

"Mrs Moon?"

"Bastard Harvester tried to muck in with my beasts," said the woman with bright-eyed excitement. "Maybe he fancied plucking himself a new pair of eyebrows or cooking up stew. Either way, he's dead now." Mrs Moon grinned ghoulishly. Shaking the head at Bluze, she added, "You can take them ear plates off. The nasties and their Sone guns are out of range. Saw the lot shuffle off to Mr Gower's classroom."

Despite the dinner lady's reassurance, Bluze desperately wanted to keep her ear defenders in place. But closing off her hearing was resulting in an increasing sense of claustrophobia. Plus, it was easier to stalk the enemy when she was in possession of all five senses.

"I've got to catch them up," she said.

Mrs Moon tossed the Harvester's head off into the cloudy atmosphere. She placed a hand on Bluze's undamaged shoulder, fingers gripping in.

"Funny how it's left to a bit like you to save the babies. We ain't about to see Mr Gower risking his neck out here." She released Bluze and scrubbed her hand around her fleshy chin. "Our headmaster's too scared the Harvesters will tear his pretty face.

Truth of it, as you and I have witnessed, is the nasties'll let grown ups alone if there's young 'uns to be had." She leant in conspiratorially. Her breath stank of straw and vinegar. "But you and I, we ain't going to let it unravel like that."

The boy walked through the steam and approached the staffroom door. He held up a fist and knocked. The door opened a crack, a great many safety chains pulled taut.

Mr Gower peered out. His eyes were nervous as a cat's, switching every which way. They settled on Sam and tightened.

"Sam Radley. Why are you out of your lock up? The alarm to give the all clear hasn't sounded yet."

"Harvesters are here," said the kid plainly.

"I'd gathered." The headmaster's mouth queered.

Sam kept on staring up at the man. "Ms Christchurch is fighting them on her own, Mr Gower."

"As is her job as secretary and school security." The headmaster's voice matched Sam's for inexpressiveness.

A second face peered over the headmaster's shoulder. Miss Keggle, the school nurse. Her face melted into a mask of fear.

"Shut the child out, Robert!" she exclaimed. "We don't want Harvesters blundering near here by accident."

"I suggest you tuck yourself away somewhere, Sam, if you don't want to end up in a Harvester's keep net."

The door to the staffroom closed, leaving Sam alone in the dark corridor.

Bluze eased in alongside the door to the classroom housing Ridgeway's youngest. Mrs Moon shuffled in behind her. With her ear defenders back in place, Bluze couldn't tell what was occurring inside the room. Mrs Moon, though, had refused to wear the standard ear plugs provided for all staff and pupils. "Just let those bastards try to put me down with a bit o' noise," she'd told Bluze minutes earlier. Folding her arms over her chest, breasts bundled up like egg sacks, she'd added, "Reckon I can holler louder than any of them flesh freaks or their Sone guns." Bluze hadn't seen the point in arguing with the woman. Instead she stood alongside her outside the classroom and prayed Mrs Moon would prove more help than hindrance.

She felt a rap to her bleeding shoulder. Glancing back, she saw the dinner lady pretend to rub her eyes with her fists, a mock crying motion.

The children! Bluze fought against her natural terror, balled the emotion in the pit of her stomach and used it to fuel her attack. Tucking her last spark dust packets into the twin batons, she stepped across the doorway, raised her arms and fired. The powder sprayed into the mist with the quick release of a puffball fungus.

Throwing the emptied batons aside, Bluze strode into the room. Several of the children's' lockups had been prised open and the Sone guns fired to render the youngsters passive. They twitched as one nervous system inside the large keep net. If they cried or whimpered, Bluze was glad she could not hear it.

While the largest marauder continued his vile harvest, the others beat off the spark dust grubs to redirect their attention to the newcomers. Bluze stood her ground and let the first two come for her. Mrs Moon was keener to get into it and charged head-on at a third, meat cleaver raised. The dinner lady fought with a slice and dicing motion, powering into the Harvester with bullish grit. Bluze, meanwhile, had drawn her sawn-offs. She wondered why the Harvesters facing her down didn't draw their Sone guns. Then she noticed the fitting children held in each brute's grasp.

Bluze tried to aim. The combination of children as a shield and the steaming environment meant she couldn't get a clear shot. At least not instantaneously. While the Harvesters staggered towards her, dragging the children as easily as sacks of feathers, Bluze made a quick assessment of the lockups, teacher's desk, small tables and two dozen wooden chairs. Her gaze lifted to the unlit gas lamp overhead, a huge bowl of dank green glass.

She rammed the sawn-offs into the back harness and ran between the two Harvesters. Both launched their serrated blades out at her in unison. She dodged the blows; the blades clashed off one another, steel sparking. The wooden chairs became stepping stones; she skipped across them and onto the desk, where her footfall sent papers flying. She kicked off and up onto the first set of lockups –

and couldn't help imagining the children cooped up inside. The Harvesters were on her tail, their human shields mauled inside the crook of one arm, leaving the other free to wield a serrated blade. The sharp steel sliced into the lockups as she dodged, flashes lighting up the darkness. She propelled herself off the far edge of the lockup cabinet, hands grasping for the silhouetted shape overhead. She got a grip with one hand, the other clutching wildly at thin air. A brief instant of floundering then her hand found its grip on the gas light. Bluze pulled herself up, each breath a painful squeeze and tug. The huge bowl threatened to tip under her weight; its fastening held tight and she fought her way up to stand, legs straddling the curve of heavy opaque glass.

She retrieved the sawn-offs. Below, the Harvesters mauled their young hostages across their organ-rich bodies. But Bluze had her clear shots now. She aimed in-between the plated metal at the vulnerable skulls and fired. The guns kicked back. She sucked in air against the pain from her stabbed shoulder. The Harvesters also felt the blaze of pain, if only for an instant as their skulls burst. The hostages broke free from the slackened grip. The Harvesters' bodies slumped.

Across the room, Bluze made out a clash of Titans, Mrs Moon versus her opponent. The dinner lady had the upper hand as she brought her meat cleaver down twice in quick succession, taking off a hunk of the creature's forearm then a slice of face. But just as it seemed Mrs Moon would win herself another head, the Harvester delivered a lethal stab with his serrated blade. Mrs Moon took the length of it through the chest. Bluze was glad of the distance between them. She was spared the old maid's look of shock at the death blow, how the eyes would fix wide, drained of excitement and horribly pitiful, how the mouth would pop-pop for air and at last be still.

She could offer Mrs Moon one consolation. Bluze took out the Harvester with a single shot to the throat.

Sam walked back from the staffroom, trailing a hand along the steam-soaked wall. He didn't understand why the teachers canned themselves away in the staffroom. Adults had bodies which could achieve so much. Then again, they were just as easily broken, he concluded, turning into his classroom to be met with the sight of slain Harvesters and the crumpled body of Mrs Moon.

He focused on Ms Christchurch, standing on top of the vast gas lamp that was suspended from the ceiling.

"Hello," he said.

Opposite was a huge bird man of a Harvester. The man stared at the child and put down his keep net, already half full of children. Producing his Sone Gun, the Harvester trained it on the boy while Ms Christchurch worked hard to perforate the brute's armour with shots from her sawn-offs.

The Harvester fired the Sone gun. Ms Christchurch reeled and toppled off the gas lamp, landing on the desk in a mess of limbs. Immediately, she was fighting to stand again.

Sam winced. He stayed upright though and pointed a finger at the crenulated Sone gun. "They don't work properly on me."

The Harvester discarded the gun and produced a pair of colossal serrated blades. He whipped them in front of his body like a silver Catherine Wheel.

"Goodbye," said Sam, and he turned and ran out of the classroom.

Behind him, the Harvester forgot his existing catch and focused on the live mouse of a boy who'd darted away. Tucking the blades in tight to his elbows, he ran out the doorway on steel-pined limbs.

What did the kid think he was doing optioning himself as live bait? Bluze threw aside her emptied sawn-offs and strode determinedly out of the classroom.

The Harvester had discarded his Sone gun. She removed her ear protectors and broke into a jog. Hearing the steel clug of metalmorphasised limbs further along the corridor, she sped up, running past a blur of lockers, water fountains and stairwells.

She stopped suddenly. A wheeze of sprung steel alerted her to the opening of the heavy boiler room door. Her heart got tight. She approached the door, inched it open and slid through the crack.

Inside, the pyramids of dung bricks had been demolished where the child had presumably scrabbled over while the Harvester's twin blades gorged out hunks of the stuff. Ahead, the huge algoid water tank was running dangerously low; the school's steamy atmosphere was beginning to dissipate, which would allow the Harvester to move even more easily. The tank was hooked up to the furnace and colossal bellows by a great many pipes. Rigged with levers, hose, and a stitched skin of bolt plates, the furnace exuded a rich red glow.

The boy stood silhouetted before a large glass window in the furnace door. Meanwhile, the Harvester became less human than arachnid. He craned up on two fat limbs of scaffolded metal. Each limb split into four. Squatting over the centre of the room, limbs craning out in all directions, the invader wove the serrated blades above his head, an action that reminded Bluze of silk being spun from spinnerets. The blades were brought down to bear over the child like huge fangs.

Bluze chose to take to higher ground. She charged into the room's bloody glow. Suppressing her instinctual revulsion at contact with the thing, she clamped her hands around the nearest metal limb and climbed. The Harvester bucked in an effort to shake her off. But she continued to climb, slicing her palms on the sharp, bolted rods.

Sam stood below, a small morsel with ever-staring eyes. The Harvester clattered forward, the folds and feathers in his skin scraping up against the hot boiler. Bluze gasped as her own thigh made contact with the roasting plate. She drew her handgun, positioned it against the soft meat beneath the intruder's chin and fired.

The Sledge drew up to the main entrance, a ravaged hole of dust and brick after the grenade blast. Children began to climb aboard the idling school bus, a mechanical warthog with spines of pig iron sticking out at every angle and fat bull bars.

Bluze had got to work on the punctured door, retooling the lock mechanism. She waved off the children, a monkey wrench in one hand, a fistful of fresh bolts in the other. "See you tomorrow, Lloyd," she called, and "Walk don't run, Meg." Wincing, she put a hand to her shoulder where she had stitched her skin. The burn at her thigh pulsed angrily. "Don't forget to hand the letter to your parents," she called after the rabble, adding, "And ask for any spare eggs!"

"Ms Christchurch." Mr Gower appeared alongside her, blocking out the weak afternoon sun.

"Afternoon, headmaster."

"Congratulations on fending off the raid." The man sniffed and pushed his half-moon glasses up the bridge of his nose. "With Mrs Moon departed, we'll need someone else to tend the farmyard. The teachers voted and allocated you the job. We have our hands full looking after the children."

Bluze would have responded, perhaps with a brief nod, a generous smile or a monkey wrench smashed into the headmaster's ungracious face. But the man had already stalked back inside.

The Sledge pulled away, honking goodbye. Bluze watched the bus recede into the misty landscape.

She became aware of the boy at her side.

"Did you teach yourself to lip-read, Sam?" she asked, staring down.

He nodded.

Bluze nodded too. The boy was deaf. It explained why the Sone gun had barely registered with him.

"What happened to your parents?"

"They got the Sticky Skin. I ran away."

"And you've been living…?"

"In the woods behind the school." The boy wrinkled his nose. For the first time, Bluze saw a hint of real human emotion. "It's frightening at night-time," he said.

Bluze put the wrench down on the floor just inside the blast hole. She eased up the folds of oil skin and cloth around her face. It was beginning to drizzle.

Reaching down, she adjusted the boy's outerwear to protect him. He peeped at her from inside his hood. Bluze tried not to think about the hours the child had endured out in the freezing woods, or how the Devil's Rain may have already started to eat its way into his skin.

She extended a hand and the boy took it.

"You'd best come home with me," she said.

They walked down the chalk path, away from Ridgeway School.

~*~

Raised on a diet of horror movies thanks to two older brothers, I was 8 or 9 years old when I watched John Carpenter's *The Fog*. Two things resonated with me – the sense of monstrous silhouettes in the form of the ghostly mariners, and how mist's all-encompassing impenetrability makes everything scarier.

Plotting the story, I asked myself: "What is the most terrifying thing I can think of?" With my daughter very young, I thought about how it was frightening enough just sending her to school every day, to an environment where I had to put my trust in other adults to keep her safe. "The Harvest" grew out of those fears alongside an appreciation for the chalky wilds of Wiltshire and the desire to bring one kick-ass secretary to life. I was deaf as a child, so shared that sense of being cut off from reality with my character, Sam. I was terrified of monsters creeping up on me unheard. Sam faces them head on.

Wanderlust

Perched on the rug in the middle of the tent, Old Gholi toked on his coil pipe and told *The Tale of a Boy Who Captured the Moon.* But Jal, son of Mach, wasn't listening. He stood with his younger brother Sukab at the opening to the tent, wondering if he was about to die.

"...the boy went to give the moon back. But he rolled it too hard, cutting a groove in the sky. And so, forever more, our moon is chased by the sun and our sun is chased by the moon. As for the boy, his skin was eternally silvered by tears and every other living creature blinked in fear and shunned him forevermore."

Like the boy who stole the moon, Jal knew how it felt to be a pariah. Ever since the sheik's daughter had made him her bedfellow, he'd laboured under the weight of the clade's judgement. And now, as the sun slept below and the moon rolled above, he was counting down the seconds to see if Sheik Alhaj would embrace him as a son, or execute him as a sinner!

"The lesson is, do not steal what is not yours. At least, not without permission." Old Gholi winked at the children gathered at his feet. Shaking out the greying mantle of polyp strings that ran over his skull and hung down his back, he struggled to his feet and took himself off to the back of the tent.

Watching the storyteller hunker down, produce a rind fruit out a pocket and set to peeling it with a small knife, Jal envied Old Gholi. *How nice it must be to enthral the clade rather than disappoint!*

"Jal, son of Mach!"

The sheik's voice swelled through the tent.

'Keep your answers brief,' Jal's father had advised him earlier that evening while his mother fussed at the state of his mantle, combing its strings with her fingers as she had when he was a child. Now his father sat with the rest of the men, smoking and sipping pungent kahwa. His mother chewed a strip of leather with the other makers and watched him anxiously.

Jal planted his feet on the rug, in the spot Old Gholi had recently vacated. He cleared his throat. "May the moon whet your blade and the sun light your path, Sheik Alhaj."

Reclining in a cornucopia of cushions and leer-cats, the sheik grimaced. His mantle threads were braided over the crown of his head, as was the signature of the royal family. His blade, passed down through ten generations of Herisian sheiks, rested on the ground in front of him.

"That they do," he said, more softly. He eyed Jal and spoke up again, inviting the entire clade to overhear. "So, you visited the bed of my daughter. Am I to believe it was at her invitation?"

Jal fondled the ankh strung at his neck. He kept his answer respectful and yet neutral. "I am beholden to your daughter, as I am to you and your judgement in this matter, sheik."

"My judgement?" The sheik adjusted the great belt of coins where it dug in beneath his belly. He had gone to seed in his dotage, but there was power in his birth rite – and the great blade nearby. "Mine is not the only judgement that counts here." He craned his head over a shoulder. "What is your will in this matter, daughter?"

The sheik's daughter sat straight-backed on a low stool nearby, her aspect hidden behind a veil. Her gaze, though – Jal felt that intensely.

"I say he is an eldest son of this clade and of good breeding stock."

The sheik gave a snort and shook his belly, coins clattering and sending leer-cats scattering. His humour didn't last. Rounding back on Jal, he squeezed up his eyes and settled his chin into the fat of his neck. "There is protocol. It's not like I go about adopting son-in-laws at my daughter's behest. There is worth to be proven, gold to be proffered…"

He jangled his coin belt. "So here is my quest for you, Jal, son of Mach." He leant forward and stroked the glinting surface of his blade. "That I might see her face reflected in this surface., you will take my daughter to meet the moon."

The clade fell silent. Jal heard a great rush of blood in his ears while the sheik's daughter leapt to her feet and flared her mantel, scarlet threads sticking out on end. She charged her father – only to be stopped short by the tip of his blade at her throat.

"The other clades will kill us!" she screamed in his face. "A sheik's daughter and a Herisian warrior? We'll be flayed alive!"

The sheik chuckled. "Most likely. Most likely. But I haven't finished with my demands." He indicated with his blade that his daughter should stand alongside Jal.

His brow folds deepened. "In addition, you will bring me a new piece of sun gold."

"*Sun gold?*" Jal pulled the solar grips from the camel's charge pack and threw them through the open flap at the rear of the craft. Hoisting in water bladders, oil urns and a satchel of flatbread, he couldn't shake his anger. "How in the name of all the ghosts of the ancestors are we meant to barter in the gold mines? Then we're meant to just go driving into the canyons to hunt down the moon? It's suicide!"

He was thinking of the clade wars which had raged over centuries. The current peace was reliant on no cladesperson stepping out of line – which really meant sticking to their clade territory. Herisians kept to the desert in the basin, Miners, the ore-rich interior to the east and west, and Tidesfolk, the moon and sun troughs above and beneath.

"Cladesfolk won't stand for a Hersian princess nosing outside of her territories," he muttered to no one in particular, but in the hearing of the sheik's daughter.

The young woman's mantle bristled. "You have a big mouth. If you hadn't a fine thrust, I'd bite off your cock and give you something to really moan about." Passing close on her way to the hump of the cab, she ran a hand down the small of his back and squeezed his left buttock. "I'll drive first. See what this shit-heap can do."

She beat him to the driver's cradle. Jal strapped into the passenger cradle alongside. "This shit-heap has seen me outstrip every other competitor in the last five sand races…"

"I noticed." The sheik's daughter unhooked her veil. It was the first time Jal had seen what she looked like, a bitter joke since he knew what lay beneath her skirts intimately. But now she had on leather work pants to match his own, and her strong, hard face was bare.

He slid up the grill shield, allowing them to see out but without taking a face full of sand spray. "You've been watching me a while then. I suppose I should be flattered."

"You should be grateful." With a jab of her hand, the sheik's daughter hit the drive stick and sent the camel sledging forward on its sand skies. The cab ricocheted around them, the hoists of the cradles absorbing the shock.

"We're going to win our freedom!" the sheik's daughter cried over the noise. "Freedom from my father, freedom from clade law. We're going to see the wonders of our world and then we're going to buy our way out."

"Out?"

"Out." Her eyes reflected the sunlight off the sand dunes. "I am Rasa Dru, Jal, Son of Mach. Together, we will take on all this rock has to throw at us and we will emerge victorious." She showed her sharp teeth. "Else I've made a poor choice of mate and I'll have my father behead you."

As the camel rattled through the midday blaze of the desert, Jal tried to decide what scared him more – prising a nugget of sun gold from the hand of a Miner or returning home empty handed and bending his neck to the sheik's great blade? At his side, Rasa was whooping every time they crested a dune and came crashing down the other side.

"We might get there faster if you kept to a straight course," he ventured. It was their third day of travel and there was a shift in the air which agitated his mantle. The black polyp threads at his head twitched and nosed one another suspiciously.

"You sense it too," said Rasa, ignoring his jibe as her own mantle stirred. "The air is growing stale." Glancing out the filter grill, she peered up at the white sky. Jal looked too. The sun was locked in a high grove overhead. Its motion was invisible to the naked eye. It was moving, though, in small increments through the channels carved in Clade's bedrock.

"Take your last look at the heavens." Rasa exhaled noisily.

Jal nodded. "I'm going to have to insist I take a turn at driving. How'd it look if a Herisian princess arrived without her veil, let alone piloting a camel?"

Rasa hissed at him, polyp threads flaring out from her head like the legs of a whip spider on the defensive. "On the contrary, I insist we forgo all formalities once we're blinkered from the sunlight." She glanced across, face livid with excitement. "If my studies of Miner etiquette are correct, I know just how to charm that gold right out of their hands."

It was Jal's turn to hiss. "You reckon?"

The mines appeared at the desert's edge like some unholy mirage. Driving the camel under the rocky canopy at the entrance, Rasa gave a low whistle. "My father made sure I was schooled in war lore and solar engineering, but I've never left the confines of the desert. This –" She nodded beyond the grill shield. "– is exactly as Old Gholi described it!"

Jal tried to make sense of the ore-speckled twilight; there was whole mountains of shale and clinker, vast fiery lakes, colossal stalactites and stalagmites, and, everywhere, Miners.

He was distracted by the stench. "The storyteller knew what he was talking about, especially the smell of the air. What do you make of that? It's like the breath of death itself."

Rasa was distracted. "Despite the fairy tales, I still expected them to look like us," she said softly.

Likewise, Jal couldn't tear his eyes away from the sight of the beetle-backed Miners. Where Herisians had their mantles to bat away sand flies and lash out with poison, Miners boasted thick skin ridges across their backs to assist with carrying heavy loads and protect them from rock falls.

"There!" Jal pointed to where the road forked, one path winding up a shimmering mountain pass, the other side leading into a narrow tunnel. Carved over the entrance was a picture of Clade's sun – an orb spitting out wildfire.

"A gold mine," said Rasa, showing her sharp teeth.

Jal's heart contracted.

*

Old Gholi's stories were full of goblins infesting Clade's underbelly. Laying eyes on Miners up close, it was easy to see how they could be mistaken for monsters. Within moments of Jal and Rasa driving inside the mine's entrance and stepping outside of their camel, they were nose-to-axe with twenty or so of the hunchbacked cladesfolk.

"What's Hesians doing in the arse end of my gold mine?" One Miner, a heavily bearded devil, lumbered forward of the rest.

"We're here to trade…" began Jal.

Rasa, though, had other ideas. "You're a fat fuck!" she snarled and swaggered. "Got a beard on you like a leer-cat's minge. I'm here to take away three nuggets of your precious sun gold and you are not just going to give it to me, you are going to beg me to take it!"

Insults plus three times the amount of gold the sheik had requested! Jal's shock was physical; he clutched a hand to his chest and inhaled sharply. *Why didn't Rasa just kill him herself rather than antagonise the chief Miner and have him do her dirty work?*

The rest of the miners, too, were silent a moment. Shoulders brooding. Picks and axes, ripe for swinging. Rasa stood, arms folded, mantle threads haloing her head like snakes with their tongues out.

"I want to marry you," said the chief Miner. He smiled soppily.

"In your dreams." Rasa held out her hand.

Oh, that it was so simple to separate a chief Miner from his gold! In reality, it took an oil urn, a sack of softened leather, one of the camel's head mirrors, ten days of hard labour from Jal (for which he earned fists full of calluses and a new respect for light), and several bouts of verbally abusive foreplay on Rasa's behalf to earn their golden nuggets.

Cheered on by foulest of insults from the Miners and their chief, they finally returned to the camel and Rasa let him saddle up in the driver's cradle.

She held up one of the nuggets then swiftly pocketed it. "Let's hope Tidesfolk still have their appetite for sun gold." With a yawn, she settled back into the passenger cradle. "I suspect they are less hungry for insults." She smiled wickedly. "Shame."

*

It was Jal's turn to dream. In his mind's eye, he saw the great rock of Clade tumbling through galaxies. He saw its inhabitants; some crawled through the bore tunnels like beetles, others basked in the sand like rare desert flowers, and others still had silver skin and huge black eyes that sent him swimming back out into the universe. There, the moon rolled in its groove and the sun razored down – transforming itself into a scarlet mantle which haloed Rasa's face.

He awoke with a jolt as the cab ricocheted around him.

"We've hit stone again." Rasa glared across from the driver seat. "It won't be long before the Tidesfolk know we are here."

Jal shrugged off the drowsiness. He took a few gulps from a water bladder before tucking it back into the pocket under his cradle. "It's night already?" They had travelled for six days straight in the direction of the canyons.

"There's a chance we might pass through without notice," he said, more through hope than judgement. "Most Herisians know better than to trespass here, especially since we don't have the biology to endure close contact with the sun."

"We have other gifts." Rasa's mantle threads interlaced themselves over her skull. Jal felt a familiar prickle as his own mantle battened down – an unconscious response at cellular level.

"They're coming," said Rasa.

Old Gholi had always compared the canyons of Clade to the wooden maze games Herisians carved for their children. While the aim of the game was to tip the board and guide the marbles home, the trajectory of Clade dictated the paths taken by its sun and moon. Centuries before, the ancestors of the Tidesfolk had stepped in to artificially readjust the route of those celestial bodies – and had stuck with the task ever since. Jal could not begin to imagine what would cause a people to infest Clade's pocked walls, but he also allowed that Tidesfolk might think the same of Herisians choosing to keep to the desert. One thing Jal knew with absolute certainty was Old Gholi had undersold the strange appearance of Tidesfolk – and their ferocious response to interlopers! Within moments of the camel sledging down into the rocky base of a canyon, the noise began. Hundreds of voices raised in a click-clacking war cry.

Rasa hissed. "All my study of war lore and diplomacy is useless if we're to be butchered inside this camel. I need for us to be granted amnesty – just long enough to bring the gold to light."

Thumbing the release catch on his harness, Jal swung up to stand precariously in the passenger cradle.

"What in the name of the ancestors are you doing, Jal, son of Mach?" Rasa tried steering the camel while reaching to drag him back down.

Jal had already punched through the grid mesh in the roof. He hauled up through the hole, felt the bite of steaming wind against his skin, and tucked in behind the camel's twin flood lights.

"Drive dead on through the heart of the swarm!" he called down.

"Why not?" Rasa cried back. "We're dead anyway!"

Jal peered over the top of the flood lights – and felt his mantle spasm. Arcing either side of their craft was a great flood of Tidesfolk. Spears raised, they charged around the camel, forcing Rasa to reduce speed while Jal tried to make sense of a sea of black eyes, silver skin and wide shrieking mouths.

'If you must go up against a Tide, make sure you match his ferocity,' Jal's father had advised him on his last morning in camp. In that moment, Jal let all the mutterings of his clade come crashing in around his ears. He'd been gossiped about, flaunted by his mother as Rasa's beloved, humiliated by Sheik Alhaj… Nobody took Jal, son of Mach, seriously.

Likewise, the Tidesfolk had them pinned as easy prey.

Determined to shake their expectations, Jal launched himself off the back of the camel. He hit the hard rock, muscles tensed against the knocks and bruises of impact. As Rasa swung the camel around and to a halt, dust billowing off the sleds, Jal scrabbled to his feet.

Throwing his arms wide, he barrelled his chest and opened the gills at the back of his throat. Air streamed in and through to the fleshy threads of his mantle, forcing them to stream out from his head. The noise as their tips rattled and hissed and spat was like the sun itself exploding. War cry of the Hersian.

Where his poison fell on bare flesh, the Tidesfolk collapsed in agony. A shower of spears flew towards Jal; his mantle threads snarled around the weapons or stiffened to deflect them. Over and over, the spears came until Jal and his mantle were a balletic flow of motion. He was a Herisian warrior where he had been a man shamed into boyish behaviour! As the Tidesfolk came in for hand-to-hand combat, he sent out slops of poison or drove his fists into their spindly bodies.

"Enough!" cried a voice from the heavens.

"Enough!" echoed a voice from the camel's roof.

Rasa was standing on the top of the craft, feet planted firmly apart. Jal followed her gaze, raising his eyes to see the long, telescopic limbs and cab of a Tide boat – those craft which enabled the clade to live and work in the canyons and which inspired Old Gholi's tales of star spiders.

Rasa spoke up again. "I am first born of Sheik Alhaj of the Herisians, and I am here to trade not warmonger."

"Without sending emissaries as per war lore protocol?" The voice from overhead was an older female's.

"My apologies," Rasa replied. "There was neither time nor opportunity."

"Which doesn't explain why your bodyguard here has seen fit to maim a number of my people." As the Tide woman spoke, her boat sank low on its front limbs, the giant spear at its helm moving closer.

"Your welcome didn't give me much choice!" spat Jal.

"But it is not our desire to antagonise," Rasa interrupted, continuing her efforts at diplomacy. "For most, the pain will lessen as the poison dries. For those who got too close, the prognosis is not so good."

"And you will make amends how?" The Tide boat rose back up a notch.

"With freshly mined sun gold."

Jal caught the glint as Rasa held up one nugget – and, here, Old Gholi's claim that Tidesfolks were beloved of sun gold proved true. The swarm held up their hands in worship – thumb to thumb, forefinger to forefinger, the better to frame the sacred treasure.

The boy who stole the moon did not ask first. That had been the moral at the heart of Old Gholi's tale. Jal had always wondered why or how the boy was meant to have sought permission. But now he and Rasa were proffering sun gold in exchange for an audience with that very same moon. Admiral Biyela of the Tide Nation grated the tiniest slivers off the nugget of sun gold. She dusted her tongue with the shavings, made a swilling noise and swallowed. Then she smiled, revealing newly golden teeth which only served to exaggerate the silver of her skin and the dark pools of her eyes.

"Yah, we take you," she said, quite simply. "Herisians do not fare well near the sun, that much I observed during the war of forty four forty when prisoners were shown its heat." Her smile became a little nasty. But then she shrugged. "Our moon may prove a kinder mistress."

With that, she leaned over the side of the hull, waved away her warriors, and then instructed her crew to set sail. In seconds, they were rising up and around, as the legs spidered through the canyons, the cab pendulum-swinging at their centre to stay horizontal.

It might have been Jal's imagination, but he thought he caught Rasa looking at him differently since his battle with the Tidesfolk. Like the charged gold of their sun, she made him feel repelled and attracted simultaneously. It was a strange, disconcerting feeling.

"Are you ready for this?" he asked as she stared.

Rasa swung her chin up around. "I am ready to take a bite of the moon and spit it at my father's feet! Metaphorically speaking," she added when the Admiral reached for her spear.

"And you absolve my Clade of any responsibility if your biology rebels?" The Admiral eyed their mantles, Rasa's in the crown style of her royal lineage, Jal's hanging straight and loose down his back. The Tide guard jabbed their spears against the floor of the boat in warning.

Rasa looked to Jal and he nodded.

"We absolve you," she said.

Millenia before, asteroid Miners had released a river of liquid gold which flowed around the walls of Clade to form the caverns. In an effort to preserve life, the Miners worked quickly to ionise the gold and form a magnetised ball of light, heat, and neurotoxins. Only Tidesfolk had the biological neutrality to survive close proximity to the sun – and to guide it over and under their world, turning night into day. By way of contrast, the moon was a quart crystal dipped in silver, a construct designed to light the night.

These things Old Gholi's tales had taught them. "We should be grateful my father requires us to visit the moon and not the sun." Rasa grimaced.

At that moment, the whole cab swung down to hang beneath the canyon.

"We're on Clade's ceiling," Jal whispered in awe.

Their conversation halted as the vast quartz crystal of Clade's moon came rolling towards them, the pendulum design of the Tide boat meaning they were able to observe the movement of the moon above.

"It's magnificent!" said Rasa, the silver glow reflected in her eyes. "I didn't expect it to be so… luminous." She stayed fixated, her entire face lighting up.

Jal felt it too. A sense of being utterly immersed in vibrations as the grand crystal rolled above them at speed. "What's happening?" He held out his hand; the atmosphere itself was alive with a mass of squirming silver particles. Like sand fleas, they skipped over his skin, biting in.

"It's colloidal silver, spraying back off the moon's surface as it turns," announced the admiral with fierce pride. "You are part of the tide now." She titled her face and bathed in the shine.

"Jal. Your mantle?" Rasa's eyes were wide and mirroring. "It's changing!"

Jal put his hands to his head. His mantle felt stiff, almost stone-like.

The transformation echoed in Rasa's threaded crown. Witnessing the princess's mantle shift and harden, Jal also saw a dramatic change in the rest of her biology. The starlit eyes became pools of black. Her brown skin silvered.

"What is this?" he cried, the moon's spray settling over every part of him. "How do I scrape it off?"

The brilliance of the Admiral's skin reflected his own. "You are moon struck, my friend. You both are. You cannot undo the gift she has bestowed."

Jal was incandescent with fear and horror. Rasa, though, began to laugh. "My father is clever. He has made sure we can never usurp him. The Clade will shun us. But –" She rounded on him, her mantle a new crown of glassy spikes. "We will carve ourselves a new kingdom."

"Where? There isn't a speck of Clade which isn't already titled to some sheik or admiral or princess!"

"My betrothed, the entire surface of this rock is yet to be colonised. Until now, the clades have been restricted to the interior. We, though, have no such restrictions." She showed her sharp teeth, a match of Jal's own, and shook out her mantle. As she did so, the fine glassy polyps swam before her face, intermeshing to form a hood. When Jal followed suit, he was surprised to find the hood acted as a breathing filter. The moonstruck quality of his silver skin felt pressurised and strangely weighted.

The feeling eased off again as he deflated his mantle.

"What are we?" he asked Rasa, a tremble of emotion in his voice.

"We are the wanderers," said Rasa, huge black unfathomable eyes burning out from behind her mantle hood.

They left the admiral and her Tidesfolk behind and turned the camel back the way of the sands. Rasa said they needed to show their faces to the Herisians one last time. Jal was nervous. Whether Sheik Alhaj had intended for them to fall foul of Miners or Tidesfolk, or simply turn to stone when faced with the moon, one thing was clear: he did not care if Rasa made it home again; in her pursuance of a mate, she had betrayed her father's supreme right to dictate All Things. It was simply a matter of power; Jal understood that much as he watched Rasa steer the camel across the sands, the sun beating down in its own bid to devour them.

"I am glad you chose me," he said finally. The camel rattled around them.

"I chose you a long time ago, Jal, son of Mach. I watched you win your first sand race. The grit you displayed alongside a lack of care for your peers or elders convinced me. If anyone could help me escape a life of mundane privilege, it was you." Rasa kept her new black eyes on the grit-shield and grimaced. "And now there's no going back for either of us."

When the kited tents of the Herisians came into view, the sun was on fire at the horizon, the sky, a vast, canyoned stretch of star-flecked gold. Familiar smells drifted in on the wind – spices, rind fruit, and drying leather, alongside the pungent stench of animals and smoke and meat roasting over coals.

It was not long before a welcoming party rode out to meet them. The warriors gaped and blinked at the sight of them. One raised the shofar to her lips with uncertainty and blew, signalling the return of kin.

Pulling into camp, they exited their craft. A woman ran towards them, arms outstretched – only to falter and fall to her knees.

"Mother!" Jal smiled broadly. "We have returned safely…"

"By the souls of the ancestors, I did not expect you so changed!" His mother set to wailing while his father strode out with purpose, only to likewise lose his momentum and stand, clutching the ankh at his neck and muttering prayers.

"Shall we?" Rasa jerked her head towards the grandest tent.

Jal grimaced. "Let's get this over with."

Sheik Alhaj nestled amongst his leer cats and cushions, the great belt of coins chinking as he rolled towards his visitors and blinked sleepily.

"There you are, daughter!" He showed his sharp teeth. "I don't need to ask if Jal succeeded in taking you to meet the moon. That shade of silver skin is most becoming!"

"And so you would condemn me to life as an outcast, Father." Rasa showed her teeth in return. "How considerate! Anyone would think you feared I would usurp you with a strong young warrior for my husband." She nodded at Jal, who stood, arms folded, the glassy folds of his mantle shifting and resettling as plated armour.

The sheik brushed off his daughter's claims with a flick of a plump hand. "You always were prone to extravagant tales, Rasa. Maybe you should have chosen Old Gholi as a mate! Although, I doubt if even that dried up maggot would have you now the moon has left her spit on you." His round eyes hardened. "Now, where is my gold?"

Jal's mantle splintered into his own crown of silver shards. "Gold that was hard won? I would rather feed it to the sun myself than hand it over. But the princess has insisted we pay a final homage…" His mouth twisted. "Before you cast us out for good."

"How changed you are, Jal, son of Mach!" The sheik moved to sit cross-legged in his nest. He ran a hand along the handle of the great blade at his feet. "Where you would have fallen on this sword if I had commanded it before you left, now you return with fight and spirit and a gilded sense of self-entitlement. How very royal of you! How fitting for my daughter's betrothed. And you have me to thank."

Jal was not convinced. Wasn't it Rasa who had singled him out, who took him with her to the dark mines and the blinding moon, and who had helped him to understand that their world was far greater than a clutch of Herisian tents in a sand box?

"Throw my father his gold, Jal." Rasa knelt before the sheik and bowed her head.

Surprised to see her offer deference, Jal held out the second nugget of sun god and tossed it over. Sheik Alhaj snatched the treasure from the air, triumphant and far too sluggish to stop Rasa reaching for the royal blade. Spears showered down. Rasa, though, was glowing silver, her whole body shielded by the moon's own armour. Likewise, Jal stood tall, face luminous with animosity and pride.

"The royal blade belongs to me now!" cried Rasa, circling on the spot, blade held high and mirroring her fierce expression.

"Give it back to me, you shrew! You harlot!" The sheik wobbled to his feet, shaking his fist and foaming at the lips.

Rasa gently brought the tip of the giant blade down to touch the sheik's nose. "Father, you have your gold. Be content. Jal and I are leaving. Our people do not recognise us as kin, thanks in no small part to you, but we are content to be wanderers. The royal blade, though. That belongs to me."

She swung the blade up to rest over her shoulder while Jal stared off into the shadows of the tent where his mother shrank in on herself and his father hid. For the briefest moment, he mourned the loss of childhood. Only his younger brother, Sukab, braved a wave.

Shrugging off his parents' weakness, and the weight and judgement of the clade, he joined Rasa in backing up to the exit.

There, Old Gholi waited, toking on his coil pipe. The grey threads of his mantle nosed the air, shrank in and rattled. "And so the boy was eternally silvered by tears and every other living creature blinked in fear and shunned him forevermore." Repeating the end to his favourite story, he exposed his black gums.

Jal leant in. "But this boy captured the moon and he did not give it back," he said, placing a hand in Rasa's.

Together, they stepped out of the tent and walked away into the night.

"What now?" Jal asked, once they had climbed back aboard the camel and set the engine running.

Rasa held up the final nugget of sand gold, its glow adding to her radiance. "Now we find a way to Clade's surface and live ever after amongst the stars."

~*~

"Wanderlust" is a middle-eastern tale in the vein of *Aladdin's Wonderful Lamp, Ali Barber and the 40 Thieves,* and *The Seven Voyages of Sinbad the Sailor.* Writer and editor Dave Gullen approached me to write a futuristic fairy-tale for *Once Upon A Parsec,* a British Fantasy Award shortlisted anthology. Fairy-tales are by their very nature didactic, often cruel, and quest-like. In Jal, I wanted to tell the story of a young man divided by what constitutes loyalty to his tribe. In Rasa Dru, I embraced the agency of heroines in modern fairy-tale retellings. It is Rasa who commands her prince charming, challenges a familial patriarch, and avoids warmongering with diplomacy.

Before Hope

The light rack flicked from green to red. Lu De Lun felt a small judder as the lock rods sealed against the tank of the Eighteen Wheeler, pinioning the craft inside the parking bay. He punched the six engine stabiliser buttons into neutral, unharnessed himself from the driver seat and stood up.

Stretching his legs, he felt his knees crack and his ankles pop as he brought back the circulation. Even inside the K01-961 planetary system, the satellites and 18 planets were thousands of kilometres apart. A driver had to enjoy a life behind the wheel. Which was why the long haul business only suited loners and fugitives. Although, as Lu knew from his 21 years as a trucker, the latter never lasted long given that the Fuel Prospectors they did business with liked to supplement their income with the fat bounties offered by the People's Armed Police. But Lu was happiest riding out among the stardust, the red dwarf that sustained the solar system an ever present reminder of Something Bigger. Bigger than him. Bigger than the PAP with their guns and Absolute Law. Bigger than the Fuel Prospectors and their corrupt management of the decaying planet he'd just landed on.

Right that instant though, Lu was less concerned with the rights and wrongs of life outside the hanger as filling his stomach and getting some fresh air.

Of course, the notion of 'fresh' air was a misnomer on K01-461-12. Having stripped down to a mandarin vest and gone with light weight combats, Lu was still unprepared for the searing temperature inside the domed market of Man Fu. He was instantly soaked in sweat and badly in need of a drink.

"How much?" he asked a passing Kool-Aid vendor.

The man stopped and lifted the top container off a haphazard stack on board the cart.

"Five yen."

Lu dug around in a side pocket of his combats and handed over the coins. The man picked up one of the metal beakers that hung off the sides of the cart and filled it with garish yellow liquid. Lu drained the cup.

"Labour Hall open today?"

"Yes, sah. I can take you there. Fifteen yen. Good price." The vendor peeled back his lips to show one good tooth.

"No thanks. I know the way."

Leaving the Kool-Aid vendor to wheel away, Lu set off through the market. The outermost circumference of the dome was given over to food stalls – those pockets of death for a multitude of live vermin stacked high in cages. The cat meat stall had an array of flambéed carcasses on display. Old women in folk tunics and headscarves sat behind tiny mountains of spices. It always amazed Lu that, despite the great girdered structure overhead, the ground inside Man Fu was still a sodden mess. A cockroach burst beneath his boot. The sticky air clung to his lungs.

Stepping over a pool of slurry, Lu found a sync screen thrust in front of his face.

"Credentials," barked the officer holding the tablet. The regulation PAP visor made the man more cyborg than human. Lu knew that was by design.

A second officer kept a hand on the gun strapped across his body, a black keratin-shelled automatic. Standard issue.

"Lu De Lun. AfroAsian male. Age 43. Employment: Fuel Transportation." He reeled off his own data while inputting his signature code to the sync screen and scanning the birth bar at his wrist.

"Specialist or independent?"

A Specialist transported one type of geofuel and was likely in the pockets of the corresponding Fuel Prospector. Often as not, they acted as middle men between the PAP and the Prospectors, adding another layer of corruption to K01-461-12's feudal monopoly. Independents, on the other hand, paid fealty to no one Prospector or crop type.

Begrudgingly, Lu admitted, "Independent." *Now came the wack bureaucracy and timewasting.*

"We're going to need some more details," said the sync screen waver.

"All the necessary licences are there, linked to my signature code." Lu flashed a sour smile.

"Of course," said the officer tightly. His partner stroked the automatic. "But there are still the quotas. There's plenty of chicken waste to load. I'd strongly recommend you make your way to the slurry vats."

"Of course," Lu mimicked. Stinking chicken waste, worth half the value of other loads like pokeberry, potato or citrus peel. He knew that he needed to get shot of the officers before they forced him to preregister for a chicken waste load via the sync screen.

"I don't suppose you gentlemen could direct me to the magistrate's quarters." He took a clip of dollar notes out of his back pocket and held it up. "I need to make a deposit of fifty US dollars."

While unable to see the officers' expressions, he knew they understood the bribe well enough.

The first officer plucked the clip from his hand. "We will see the magistrate gets your deposit."

Lu waited. The men had accepted his bribe, but they could still opt to harass him anyway.

In the end, it was the Robot Arena which came to his rescue. Standing fifty metres or so outside its wire perimeter, Lu could see the upper halves of the crop giants over the heads of the crowd. Most were the usual models – 9Z4s, P99Ps, couple of borers. The huge steel mechanisms were designed to withstand the ravages of K01-461-12's theogermic landscape. But some lucky vendor had a new model on display. A Titan SLS. The crowd thickened around it. Apparently the two officers were also keen to take a closer look.

"Go on now." The officer pocketed the money clip. With a swipe of a hand, the sync screen went blank. Both men moved off, their visors turned towards the Titan.

Taking care to keep his distance, Lu joined the crowd at the opposite side of the arena. The older models of crop giants oozed smoke from the seals of their feed hatches. The stench was incredible; Lu was all too aware that the faeces of Prospectors and itinerant workers alike went into fuelling the things. The design of a crop giant was fundamentally basic. Lu knew how to repair one and how to take it apart. Colossal shears moved on pinioned arms. Bucket jaws delivered into thresher spools. Balls of revolving caterpillar tracks gave the robots their arachnoid motion. Mothers frightened naughty children with tales of crop giants abandoning the fields and acquiring a taste for blood.

Lu had never seen a robot like the Titan. The head was black and gridded like a compound eye; Lu suspected the design was precisely that – a grid of stereoscopic cameras delivering 3D images of an entire field of crops. If the older robots were spiders, the Titan was a king crab, its kin dangling from hooks at chop bars or hissing inside stock pots. Six huge harvesting arms were multi-axis and reticulating, doubling up as legs. Sonar booms served as antennae. A central jaw sat in a cradle of synthetic sinew. Traction engines were bolted beneath, alongside a complex bowel system of cabling. The entire system was powered by a Cyclops 84 chip – so declared the neon data screen above the robot. 'Titan is the first crop giant with surveillance mapping and a PAP sanctioned weapons system.' Lu noted the gas guns at the pivoting midpoint of each arm.

"That will put the noses of the Yellow Scarves out of joint," remarked a man standing next to him.

"I'm yet to meet a machine the rebels couldn't destroy," he replied, thinking of the men and women who fought back against their overlords. Too poor to leave K01-461-12, many families found themselves entirely dependent on the dire wages offered by the Fuel Prospectors. Thanks to the increasing utilisation of crop giants, the workers were being deprived of even that small source of revenue. The Yellow Scarves fought for survival, and Lu understood why. But could they really take down the likes of the Titan?

The man didn't share his faith in the rebels. "If those Yellow Scarves don't take a shot to the belly from those guns, I reckon it can keep a grip on them until the PAP arrive." He smacked his heat-dried lips. "Then it'll be off to the Heat Zone for those they catch. Poor bastards." Rolling his rheumy eyes, he seemed to squat down inside the sorrow of the thought.

Lu moved on.

Labour Hall was packed with workers putting themselves up for sale. Lu squeezed past men, women and children, aware of their bony limbs, leathered skin, and the stench of desperation. He made his way up the sweaty iron stairs to the hiring platform. Taking a numbered bat from a nearby table, he joined the twenty or so foremen on the platform. Each held the fates of those below in their grasp; raise a baton to indicate a job offer, keep it lowered to opt out.

Lu scanned the crowd. He saw scores of faces and skins of every shade. China might have originally colonised K01-461-12 fifty years earlier, but rubber stamped work visas and the promise of good wages had attracted a 10% US contingent. Finding the planet's geothermal activity too unstable, China had pulled out. That was 23 years ago. Now the Fuel Prospectors lorded over their volcanic real estate and the workers were forced into the Labour Hall.

A ramp led up to the hiring platform and another led down. The workers took turns to file past the foremen. The hour was allotted to 'Unskilled Labour'; a neon sign tickertaping around the circumference of the hall declared as much.

Poverty was the true equaliser, Lu concluded, watching the procession with his arms folded and a knot between his eyebrows. The younger men and women had the advantage when it came to attracting a foreman's eye. Those who were elderly or in any way disabled did not attract a bid.

When the tickertape switched to 'Apprentices', the age of those in line dropped considerably. So did the number of potential employers. Lu joined four other men on the viewing step. He wasn't entirely welcome in their company.

"Surely you don't need to train a kid to join the long haul," spat one out the side of his mouth.

"Maybe he needs an apprentice to clean the ship's toilet? Is that it, driver?" said a second.

"That's it." Lu concentrated on the children filing past. He needed a strong one. Own teeth wouldn't hurt either. And then there were the eyes. His father had once remarked on the inner grit contained within a man's eyes. "Look for the soul beyond the sadness," he told him. "Those are the ones we can trust with our secrets."

"Come on, come on," he muttered.

"Eager to be on your way again, huh? I don't blame you," said the man to his right. Guy in his fifties, Lu guessed. Big old boots that belonged on a soldier. Neatly darned tunic to his knees.

"No one should have to live out their days in this stink hole, least of all the young." He nodded at the girls and boys so desperate to find a trade. "Me? I can only help one of them today." He raised his baton as a boy of twelve or so stepped forward. None of the foremen challenged his bid, not with so many youngsters to go around.

"I'm offering a three yearer in chicken waste," announced the man.

"Oh shit," said one of the mouthy foremen. The others shook their heads and laughed.

The kid didn't laugh. Instead he got the hopeless look of someone who'd hoped for the best and heard the worst. But Lu knew the kid was in no position to argue or negotiate. The new apprentice and the man moved aside.

For the next half hour Lu watched the children come and go. Some were taken on as apple pickers, mulch grain sifters, gas pump operators or kitchen staff. The majority went home wanting.

A small boy stepped forward, the sort with bones still soft enough to allow him to root around the engine of the Eighteen Wheeler. Lu was about to hold up his baton when he spotted the girl up next. She had long black hair in a braid, crooked teeth in an over-wide mouth, and long, slim eyes. He put her at 15 – the maximum age for an apprentice.

When she took the boy's place, Lu raised his baton. The remaining foremen knocked elbows and he heard one whisper, "A girl on board a fuel ship?" and another, "If it's a whore he wanted, there's cheaper to be had at Pig Town."

If the girl was afraid of him, she didn't show it. Instead she met his gaze and held it.

"Two yearer hauling gas." Lu would have tried to sell the proposition if he thought she had any choice in the matter. As it stood, he didn't bother.

She nodded, even flashed her crooked smile. "Yes, sir."

Lu followed the girl over to the PAP officer busy registering new vocations against workers' employment sheets on his sync screen. At his back, the foremen offered a few crude comments then forgot about them.

The officer scanned the birth code at the girl's wrist.

"Pay rate?"

"Bed and board."

Lu looked at the girl for a reaction. Surely she'd expect some kind of wage. Her expression didn't change, though. Inside minutes, she signed away the next two years of her life for an apprenticeship on board the Eighteen Wheeler. Lu led the way back down the stairs and through the crowd, praying he'd made the right choice.

The girl's name was Hope Turner. She thought she was 15, but couldn't be sure having lost her mother and siblings to cholera several years earlier and with a father too busy lugging potato sacks at the local farm to count birthdays. Lu didn't care. He just wanted someone to grease the engine of the Eighteen Wheeler, hook up the hoses for liquid fuel, scrub the dry bay to keep it clear of fungus, and otherwise stay out of his business. At least to start with.

So far Hope was turning out to be a good choice of apprentice. Her reaction on seeing the Eighteen Wheeler up close in the hanger was genuine awe.

"She's a dark horse, but there's value in that," he explained. "Keeps nosy children and parts pirates at bay. Fast too. We can make the trip between here and K01-461-13 in a week."

The girl had nodded, the huge craft reflecting in her pupils.

They'd left Man Fu that afternoon, flying over beet farms and vast golden stretches of wheat. The vegetation was hardy fuel stock, tough as a sun-dried rat's carcass and able to withstand the harsh conditions. Hope had sat alongside him in the co-driver seat, absorbing everything.

"I've never seen the farms from up here," she told him in a strong provincial accent. "The world looks alive."

"Not rotting to pieces." Hands steady on the wheel, he glanced over at her. "The farms are no different to embroidering a rotten bandage. Sooner or later the fabric will tear and the crud will pour out."

They arrived in Pig Town early that evening. K01-461, the Scarlet Star, pulsed at the horizon. The Heat Zone was just visible to the west – five hundred kilometres of the planet's most active geothermics. The area was home to geysers, boiling springs, mud flats and fumaroles. With magma flowing so close to the surface and subject to colossal pressures, the water achieved a boiling point of 300°c, meaning the zone was perfect for cultivating algae – another source of fuel. It was also where convicts laboured in the carbon dioxide rich atmosphere and treacherous working conditions.

"I can't believe I'm back in Pig Town again." Hope nodded towards the open sewer running the length of the main street. "Thought I'd escaped that stench."

"You walked to Man Fu?"

The girl shrugged. "Walked some, hitched a lift with a market truck couple of times." She pointed at her bare feet. "My father says I have my mother's feet. Small enough to attract a husband. Broad enough to carry life's woes."

Lu surveyed the shanty huts and makeshift chop bars, the chicken-shit peppered paths in-between. "I've got business here. You can stay with me or pay your father a visit. Your choice."

Hope jutted her chin. "My father would be ashamed to see me home so soon. I'd prefer to stay and start to learn my trade. That, after all, is the reason you took me on."

She showed her crooked teeth. Lu grunted.

"Come on then. You can help me choose a present for someone."

In Man Fu, the very visible presence of the PAP kept any reminders of the resistance at a minimum. But out among the villages, people were braver. Every so often he'd spot graffiti on the dung brick walls – the tag of the resistance or 'Death to the Dark Greens' – a reference to the PAP's olive coloured uniforms.

It took guts to go up against the authorities in such a direct way. Those who were caught earned a one way ticket to the Heat Zone. But that didn't stop people – some whispered their support for the rebels, some daubed walls with graffiti, and some took action.

"What kind of a present are you looking for?" asked Hope, fingering the strings of beads that hung off a hook to one end of the stall. "My mother always said to give the gift of colour. Red for good fortune, yellow for freedom from life's cares, green for health and harmony. Never white – the mourning shade."

"You like the beads, huh?" Lu examined some boxes of paired chopsticks. They were crudely made, no doubt deliberately to appeal to the pockets of Pig Town's inhabitants.

"I do," Hope murmured. "The red and gold remind me of my mother's hair. It was the colour of corn oil."

Lu thought about his own mother. Strong as an ox. Spine soldier straight so that she looked the world head on.

"I want something bigger," he told Hope. "The farm we're going to visit is extremely large. Mister Gun Mao Rong is a powerful man."

"A Prospector?" Hope's upper lip curled.

"Yes, a Prospector." Lu picked up a cigarette case made of monkey wood. A silhouette of the Scarlet Star was carved into the lid.

Hope spat onto the ground. Lu ignored her and looked for the stall's owner. He found him round the back, crouched on a low stool between bundles of low grade reflector cloth. The man was old as the soot hills judging by his appearance. Face, a thousand wrinkles. Eyes turned milky by cataracts. He sat on his stool, smacking his lips as he whittled a new set of chopsticks.

"Hello, Father Time."

The man grunted at the colloquial greeting.

"Hello, Buckrabbit."

"I need to buy a present for an important man. What can you recommend?"

The man picked up the walking cane resting against the fabric bales. He poked the end of it at a wooden box towards the back of the stall.

"Every man likes a music box. Rich are no different to the poor. I spent six months carving the thing. It's made of blackwood. Open it." He redirected his cane to Hope. "Go on now. Open it."

The girl did as instructed. With the lid raised, music started to play. Tinny yet pretty, it was a classic melody Lu had heard many times from the plucked strings of a qin.

"Bring it here, Hope." The man bared his gums.

She carried the box over, its tune mingling with the sounds of street children playing nearby and the wail of a baby coming from one of the tin shacks.

"You know my name?" Her brow knitted.

"Pig Town's not so big."

Hope handed the box to Lu. He could see that it was well made with elegant wooden hinges and an interior lined with preserved moss. Weighty too.

"Price?"

"500 yen."

Hope took a sharp intake of breath. The cost was astronomical compared to the sums she was used to in Pig Town.

Her eyes widened further when Lu said, "For this? 900 is closer to the value."

"That is too much," said the man quietly. "Too much."

"Yes, 900." Lu produced a money clip from a side pocket. It was bigger than the one he had given the officers in Man Fu. He peeled off the notes and pressed them into the man's hands.

"It's not worth that much," Hope tried to argue. Lu raised his hand sharply and she fell silent.

The man fed the notes into the top of his tunic. Lu turned to leave when the man said, "No news for me, Buckrabbit?"

Lu put his hands on his hips and sighed. "Man Fu is as ugly as ever. The crop failures around Pig Town haven't garnered much sympathy from the law makers. For now, there is not enough fuel to be loaded around here for an Independent to make a living."

"So you will be heading for pastures new for the time being." The man nodded a little sadly. Lu kept his chin high.

As he strode away with the girl in tow, the old man called after them, "Take the girl to see the blooms growing out at the cemetery. Maybe the last chance you have."

The cemetery was carpeted with safflowers, token survivors of one of the first oil crops artificially seeded across K01-461-12. Having originally thrived in the arid conditions, the crop had become infected by a rogue fungal disease brought in with a shipment of rapeseed. As the sight of the spiky yellow flower heads became rarer, so the workers came to see them as a symbol of their personal fight for survival. The wilted heads were steeped in water and distilled into a lemony pigment – the dye favoured by the rebels. Safflowers had also been his mother's favourite.

The girl was at the far end of the field, praying at her family's graves. Lu surveyed the rows of tombstones – small markers carved with individuals' signature codes. He turned his back on the grand sweep of the dead.

In front of him was an area fenced off from the rest with barbed wire. The safflowers were the only obvious inhabitants of the area. In accordance with Absolute Law, there were no carved markers, no shrines and no gifts left for the spirits.

Lu knelt down besides the barbed wire. He plucked one of the flower heads and crushed it inside his palm. He prayed for worlds, for Hope, and for his ancestors.

"You have a relative among the Unmarked?"

Lu got to his feet, brushing the remains of the flower off his hands. Hope stood a respectful distance behind him. She'd been crying; he recognised the tell-tale gloss in her eyes.

"My mother," he told her, a break in his voice.

She bowed her head. "I'm sorry. The way PAP treat the people sentenced to work in the Heat Zone is awful. Everyone has a right to a headstone."

"Even convicts?"

She hugged the music box she carried and sucked her bottom lip. "Depends on the crime."

"Indeed." *They'd both loved and lost*, thought Lu. The true crime on K01-461-12 was that of a nation trapped in servitude. "You and me are the fortunate ones," he told his apprentice. "We have the means to fly away."

They ate dim sum at a chop bar then retired to the Eighteen Wheeler for the night. Lu slept on the bunk to the rear of the cabin. Hope reclined the co-driver seat and curled in on herself. The next morning, Lu used a small gas stove to brew tea and cook up a sharing bowl of wheat noodles layered with pig fat. The addition of spices came from his Jamaican ancestry.

By 11.00am, they had flown the 2000 kilometres to the area known as the Money Fields. Below were great expanses of rapeseed, field penny-cress, flax, and soybean, as well as sprawling orchards of apple and citrus fruit trees. The grand estate belonged to Mister Gun Mao Rong, a man with enough power to have Titan SLS prototypes already at work in his fields.

"Look at those things!" Hope had her face pressed to the windscreen. Her breath misted the glass. "What if they go wrong and don't see the difference between harvesting plants and humans?" she asked in a child-like way which made Lu smile in spite of himself.

Hope wasn't smiling though. "What if the jaws never stop eating and before we know it, the planet is deserted except for two of those machines charging head on at each other?"

"Then technological advancement will eat itself and we, its creators, will be dust on the wind." Lu winked at his apprentice. "Now buckle up. I'm taking us down."

They left the Eighteen Wheeler parked in an immaculately maintained hanger alongside a number of work vehicles – one man crop sprayers known as 'dragonflies' and churners with their giant revolving cylinders that processed plant fibre on the move. High end transportation craft lined one whole side of the hanger. One had recently docked and Lu and the girl watched the side door curve aside and a silver walkway unfold. Staff emerged, the women dressed in figure hugging, red silk cheongsams, the men in black tunic suits. The last was a woman, terribly and deliberately thin. Her clothing was tailored, her glossy black hair scraped back. Lu noticed Hope's expression was a mix of anger and awe.

"There'll come a day when one of the Titans mistakes her for a blade of grass." He pressed his hands together and mimicked the snapping motion of the robot's jaw until Hope showed her crooked teeth.

Lu had worked many long years to establish himself as one of the fastest, most reliable fuel transporters to work the circuit. Consequently, he didn't deal with foremen. He took his business dealings direct to the Fuel Prospectors. Despite his wealth, Gun Mao Rong was no exception.

Hope appeared resistant to follow him into the glittering mausoleum where Gun Mao Rong lived with his achingly thin wife and children.

"If you are going to get to grips with this trade, you have to learn to ignore all this." By which he meant the opulent entrance hall with its silver grid-work underfoot and corridors and grand staircase leading off to numerable rooms.

The girl absorbed the idea, tough little hands folding over themselves. "I follow where you go."

They removed their shoes and Lu led her down one of the corridors on the ground floor. The temperature controlled air was as welcome as it was disquieting. Staff materialised, as if from the walls. As his side, the girl took three steps to his every one. Lu could have sworn he heard her heartbeat.

At the end of the corridor, they came out into a beautiful circular room. As Lu had discovered when he first visited the Prospector twenty years before, a man like Gun did not sit behind closed doors. He perched on a low bamboo stool, legs folded up under him. His hands were busy scrolling through projected data screens. He wore a v-neck white t-shirt and a sarong skirt, and possessed the casual good looks associated with considerable wealth.

Lu bowed. Hope followed his example. From his perch, Gun returned the courtesy.

"Lu De Lun. It is a pleasure to see you."

"The pleasure is mine, Gun." Lu knew the girl would be surprised by his use of the Prospector's first name; if she was to succeed in the fuel game, she would have to achieve the same level of connection.

He gestured to the box Hope carried. "Please do me the very great honour of accepting this gift."

Hope tiptoed forward. Lu was relieved when she presented Gun with the music box using both hands. Despite her rustic upbringing, she knew rudimentary etiquette.

Gun considered the box, nodding appreciatively. "It is exquisite, Lu. But I cannot accept."

"My apprentice selected it. Her first task and one in which she took great pride."

"I can see that." Gun smiled at Hope. "But such a beautiful gift is too much."

"It was carved with you in mind. There can be no explanation for such splendour."

"I really must refuse."

"No, you really must accept."

There the game ended. Gun had refused three times and Lu had persisted. The Prospector put the box on his lap and opened the lid.

"Wonderful!" he cried as the tinkling melody filled the room. "Oh indeed, a gift I shall cherish." Taking in the girl's appearance – her coarse clothing and staring eyes – he cocked his head and said gently, "The kitchen is at the opposite end of the house. My man, Francis, will show you the way. You will find him directly outside this room. Ask the cook to give you a glass of soda." He switched focus to Lu. "I have a shipment of bioethanol that needs to be in K01-461-15 inside the month. Shall we talk terms?"

Lu had hoped the girl might be allowed to stay. She needed to experience the art of fuel negotiation. But he was not about to offend Gun by disagreeing.

"Go along now, Hope," he said.

"Hope?" Gun stuck out a hand. Again the girl proved aware of social niceties and used both hands to clasp Gun's. "A good name," he told her. "I look forward to conducting business with you, Hope."

"And I you," Hope replied, voice strong, back very straight.

Lu watched her leave the room, her soft tread at odds with the steel he had just witnessed.

The wheel vibrated under his hands. Lu felt the g-force hit him as the Eighteen Wheeler lifted off. His spine moulded into the driver seat. It took considerable effort to keep his chin up. He worked his way through the gears with the stick shift. The craft levelled out and the pressure eased.

At his side, the girl released her grip on the co-pilot seat harness. She wasn't used to take off yet, he saw that. But she would be soon.

"He was nice," Hope said, interrupting his thoughts.

"Who?"

"Mister Gun Mao Rong."

"Did you expect a monster?"

"I guess." The girl's forehead wrinkled. "It's just that there he is in that big house with all that money while the rest of us struggle even to breathe. And then he's just so *nice*."

Lu gave a tight smile. "A dilemma, isn't it?" Through the windscreen he saw Titans at work in the fields of blue, green and yellow below. From that height, they looked like dung beetles.

"That's why the box was so beautifully carved. It was a genuine gift. But my father still hid an HPM unit in the base of the box and I still brought it from him." He sensed the confusion washing over Hope and wondered if he should have trusted her with the facts sooner. "My father and I cannot communicate openly. I have had to distance myself from the great unclean of Pig Town in order to be taken seriously as a Fuel Transporter. But I still try to help when I can." He glanced across at Hope. "You were right. 900 yen was too much for the box. But I wasn't really paying for the box. I was giving my father money to live off."

"What are you telling me, Mister Lu?" She bit her bottom lip while Lu really hoped he hadn't made a mistake in his choice of apprentice. He needed someone who had become as jaded with the system as he was. He needed a fellow soldier.

"What's an HPM unit?" she asked suddenly.

Lu liked that question. His lies were less important to her than the details of that deception.

"High-powered microwave weapon. The unit inside the music box emits bursts of electromagnetic energy. Harmless to humans but capable of burning out the circuitry of all crop giants within a 200 kilometre radius. To avoid detection, the transmission stops working after 24 hours. Enough time to do a farmstead damage but not long enough to arouse suspicion."

Hope stared out the windshield. They were still flying over Gun's vast estate. It was difficult to tell from that altitude, but the Titans would already be grinding to a halt, their insides seizing. The build up of biogas in the algae-fed boilers would do the real damage. A design flaw would be cited as the cause of the problems, putting a dent in the seemingly impenetrable armour of the Titan SLS crop giant model.

"But what's the point? They'll only fix them or buy more," said Hope, voicing the same frustration in the pointlessness of it all that he had felt so often over the years.

"The point is quiet rebellion," he said carefully, as much to remind himself as explain to Hope. "We remind a Fuel Prospector like Gun that the machines taking the place of the human workers can go wrong and are nowhere near as cost effective. Just as importantly, we remind the PAP that we have a voice and their law is not absolute."

"You're a Yellow Scarf." Hope said it simply, without fanfare and apparently without fear.

"As my mother before me."

It was enough. As he had hoped all along, he saw a look of complex pain and anger on the girl's face. Same one he'd seen reflected in the mirror every day since his mother paid for her commitment to freedom in the Heat Zone. Hope had lost her mother and siblings to poverty. Her father hadn't the strength to fight back. But she did.

"Quiet rebellion?" She appeared to mull over the idea. "A war without bloodshed."

"For now." Lu held her gaze.

The strength he'd witnessed in front of Gun returned. Hope sat up straight in the co-driver seat and titled her chin to meet the glow of the Scarlet Star.

"Then that is one trade I am eager to learn," she said firmly.

Lu nodded, aware of the burden of bringing Hope to the rebels. Suddenly he needed to be free of K01-461-12 and its poisoned atmosphere. He wanted to be cocooned in the black velvet of outer space.

"Let me show you what you'll be fighting for," he told the girl, adding, "Now hold on."

Lu pulled the wheel towards him and drove the Eighteen Wheeler into a steep vertical trajectory.

Just occasionally, I want to leave all the bells and whistles of action adventure and combat behind and focus in on the details of a world and its inhabitants. In "Before Hope", I set out to write a hard SF story with Asian influences and exploring one of the subjects I am most passionate about – protecting our environment and acknowledging the damage we do to it every day with pesticides and over-farming. The idea of a 'quiet rebellion' reflects my belief that activism can take a subtle form while providing hope for our future and the world(s) we inhabit.

The Killing Fields

The 1974 Triumph Stag V8 prowled the country roads, oiled black angles flickering against the night like a mirage. Regan gripped the leather steering wheel and glanced behind her. Curled up on the back seat under a worn blanket, the kid slept, her head awkwardly positioned on the makeshift pillow of an AK-47 assault rifle. She was snoring.

They hadn't hit a road block for the last fifty miles. Just as well since they'd run out of currency as far back as Birmingham, Regan mused, downshifting the gears and easing off the accelerator to coast into a hairpin bend. But while she doubted any self-respecting road hog would bed down in such a desolate spot, it never paid to be complacent. Not when thy neighbour would sooner sell your ass to the highest bidder as help you out, particularly if it guaranteed a dozen extra food stamps or a tankful of bioethanol. Not when the 2020 civil war had seen every major city in England shorn back to its seedy underbelly, like stains on an otherwise green and pleasant land. Not when they were navigating a land of single-track roads, tangled hedgerows and night-shrouded middle distance, and Regan's foremost thought was *too much silence.*

"Are we there yet?"

Regan stared at the melancholy girl reflected in the rear-view mirror. "We're definitely *somewhere.*"

All raisin eyes and bed-head, the kid slung the gun aside and poured herself over the handbrake into the front seat. "Got anything to eat?"

Reaching sideways, Regan punched the glove box. She located a scrunched up brown paper bag and handed it over. "Couple of boiled eggs you filched off that farmer's wife this morning."

The kid grabbed the bag. Rooting around inside, she retrieved an egg, tapped it on the dash and started prising off the shell. "Nice lady," she said a minute later, her voice thickened by a mouthful of egg.

"Who?" shot Regan. She reined in the Stag as they approached a signpost.

"Mrs Jacobs. She pinched my cheeks." The kid rubbed at her face as if shining up the memory.

Another half a mile. Regan kept the vehicle at a sedate pace as the road turned into a dirt track. "Guess she thought you were just a kid."

"I *am* just a kid."

"Might look like one, but you've as much in common with the average eleven year old as I have with a primary school teacher," said Regan flatly. "Pinched your cheeks." She shook her head, bemused by the kid's idealised version of events and keeping stum about the truth, which was that while Mrs Jacobs had acted mother hen, her husband had followed Regan to the tithe barn where the Stag was garaged.

Bolting the door, Mr Jacobs had fixed her with rheumy, thread-veined eyes. "Wife says sorry but we can't let you leave without some dispensation."

Regan raised the bonnet of the Stag, leant into the engine and drew out the dipstick. She swiped the rod with a rag. "We traded a day's labour for provisions," she reminded him without emotion. "It was your wife who suggested we kip in the hayloft. I'll just load up the goods we rightfully purchased then me and the kid'll hit the road."

"Except I can't let you do that. It's the wife, see. Says the car's worth eight gallons of bioethanol on the open market. So I'm going to have to *insist.*"

Regan glanced back over a shoulder to see the man reach for a pitch-fork. She replaced the rod, unhooked the arm of the bonnet rest and let the hood fall. "You're not getting my car."

The farmer moved towards her. He tried out a nasty smile. "What if I let you keep the car and you pay me in kind for my wife's hospitality. Nice girl like you has got to know a trick or two."

"I sure do," she drawled and eased back against the bonnet. Mr Jacobs passed the back of a hand across his lips. Bending at the waist, she reached between her legs and ripped two CZ-75 handguns from their tape holsters under the Stag's front bumper. She tossed the guns up into the air, snatched at each with the opposite hand, cocked the clips and aimed twin barrels at the man's forehead. "I can juggle," she said dryly.

Later, when the farmer was duck-taped to the rusty, cobwebbed tines of an old ripper, trousers round his ankles, and Regan had refastened the handguns under the bumper, slung back the bolt and eased open both sides of the creaking barn door, she leant in by his ear. "And I'm not a nice girl." The pitchfork pierced the dirt an inch short of his groin.

"These are *bloody* tasty."

Regan became aware of the half-devoured boiled egg being wafted under her nose and forced her mind back to the present.

She cut her eye at the girl. "Don't swear." Turning in between part-hinged, dilapidated gates, she took it steady on a minefield of earth clods and potholes.

"I can fire guns but I can't swear?" The kid crammed the remnants of egg into her mouth.

The red haze of the beet farm's first warning lamp bled into the Stag's headlights. Regan felt a familiar sense of foreboding. "You don't have to swear to stay alive," she muttered.

Two types of farm existed post-civil war. There was the conventional sort devoted to agriculture and raising livestock, with produce quotas pooled and reassigned by the government, and which remained a relatively tranquil way to make a living. And then there was the beet farm, its acreage seeded with the raw plant stuff used to make bioethanol, and as such, reduced to a rabid war zone by gang violence, mafia-owned cartels, and vigilantism. Given its rural location in the Shropshire Hills, the welsh-stone farmhouse could have been mistaken for the former, were it not for the bullet-pocked sheet steel coating the front door or the iron mesh at the gable windows either side of the porch. A sense that visitors were anything but welcome was reinforced by the hostile blaze of motion-triggered halogen bulbs and the warning bursts from a pair of wall-mounted flame throwers.

"Who's there?" demanded a voice sandpapered free of sentiment.

"The Scarecrow." Arms draping the open, driver-side door of the Stag, Regan tossed back her head, gulped to activate the resonator chip embedded in her throat then rapidly exhaled. The sound that issued from her lips was a reverberating caw, just bearable to the ear and synthetic. She closed her mouth suddenly. The noise cut off.

Regan waited as bolts shifted back, chains rippled, and in a series of halting jars the door worked open. A figure filled the doorway, chest panelled like a mutant armadillo, legs elephantine in voluminous canvas combats, feet encased in twenty hole bovver boots, and hair that stretched beyond the waist.

"Chase the red dragon out of my arse, if it ain't the original Scarecrow. Malkin as we'd call you in these parts, but who's splitting hairs?" Harrison stepped into the light, piggy eyes blinking. He stuck out a hand. Regan swung the car door to and strode over. Their hands sealed.

"Regan. I'd say thanks for dropping by, but we both know it was the scent of money got you hooked."

Regan cocked her head at the dark fields. "Grapevine says you've got yourself some rats."

"A proper pest problem this year. They're holed up at old man Robinson's o'er the hill. He pegged it last June."

"What breed?"

"Pirates."

"Shit." Regan raked a fist over her shaved head. If there was ever a breed of raiders guaranteed to kick up a stink, it was pirates. While their peers were employed by a handful of the world's elite crime syndicates – south-east Asian triads, Russian Bratva, a clan of the Naples' Camorra, and a few significant others – pirates were gang-led, targeting a different beet farm every harvest and with zero scope for negotiation.

"Numbers?" Her mind raced ahead, checking off hardware and small firearms stored under a false lining in the boot of the Stag.

"Crew of about eight or nine. Haven't had a run-in yet but I've seen the freaks cruising out by Claw Pond. Couple of choppers, a quad, dune buggy, dirt bikes, a Baja bug. Stilt walkers too."

"Just your common old garden variety of crop pirates then."

"Reckon so, except…" Harrison indicated Regan's bee stung mouth – or as she interpreted it, the lethal voice box stitched inside her throat. "This crowd have got themselves a bona fide Captain Hook."

Regan dragged the back of a hand across her lips as if she'd been slugged in the mouth. Captain Hook was slang for a bandit touting the hardware to deflect a Scarecrow's infrasonic scream. She spat into the dirt. "Harvest starts…"

"First light tomorrow. I pulled the specimen beet on Thursday. Got the thumbs up from the lab today for sugar content."

"I'd best get an early night then. Half my money up front." She put out a hand.

The farmer rooted around beneath his breast plate. He drew out an envelope. Regan reached for the cash, but he held onto the envelope a second. "Where's that pretty little girl of yours?" His piggy eyes interrogated the Stag's backseat. "You've never gone and hid her in the boot again?"

"Not mine." Regan ripped the envelope from his fingers and stashed it inside her cropped leather. Stalking over to the car, she popped the boot and slung up the lid. The kid rolled out in a tangle of assault rife, daisy-shaped sunglasses and skinny limbs. She landed crouched with her gun trained on Harrison's breastbone. "Not pretty," Regan added darkly.

Mist ghosted the soft panorama of patchwork fields and drystone walls. Astride the icy metal gate, Regan swiped her stun baton to and fro like a homicidal majorette. She put her lips together and blew. A reedy whistle echoed off her cold surroundings. It was a human sound, but Regan recognised the nuances in the crackle of static on her tongue, and the small rush of air through very fine, steel vocal chords.

"Warming up?"

Regan stared up at a colourless sky. "I told you to stay back at the farm."

The girl scooted up alongside Regan, the gate clanging noisily with the extra vibrations. "Didn't want to. That farmer gives me the willies."

“Harrison? He’s a harmless old coot.”

“Folk said the same about Pol Pot.”

Regan stared at the youngster.

“What? I went to school once. Once,” repeated the girl, hiding her face to chase an itch at her ankle. Then she froze.

“Yeah, I hear it.” Regan jerked her head left then right. She sniffed. The strange sweet smell of burning bioethanol filled her nostrils. “Coming in from the south. Stack of them. Going to scoot now?”

The gate reverberated. The girl had gone.

Regan waited with an even throb of a heartbeat, aware of the silverware in her throat. She cooed devilishly.

Claw Pond was an excellent spot to pick a fight. Less of a pond than a dip in the ground, it was a dust bowl in the summer, glacier in winter, and a mud track all the weeks in-between. In its present frosted state, it was also the spot to house a nine row, self-propelled Beet Harvester. The pirates had raided more than the farmhouse at old man Robinson’s, Regan concluded, pressing her mouth to the lock. The vibrations which emanated from her throat worked the pins and released the lock. Opening the door, she swung up inside and crouched – it would pay her to observe the gang. To know a man was to kill him.

Inside the minute, the grid beneath her feet shook with the noise of them. In great scooping waves of sound, they descended. Regan gauged the gang from behind the cover of grimed glass. Harrison was right in his estimation. Nine pirates, sand sharks judging by their weathered leathers and sun-dirtied skin. It was unusual for sand sharks to desert the beaches of the south west and Wales, and their hijacking of anything the sea cared to deliver up: pleasure craft, fishing trawlers, air ambulances, and the solitary swimmer. But the beet farms were rich pickings. Regan’s upper lip curled. Every other piece of scum in the UK believed himself man enough to have a go.

“Saddle her up.” The command came from a man who looked as if he had been torn out of the earth and left to mulch down amongst his own bones. His hair was a tangled yellow mane. His leathers were dirty brown, and cracked or patched at the joints. He was short and muscular, and his dirt bike pep-pepped under him.

"You sure the Scarecrow ain't here already, Samson?" This from a large man in the bug, a pirate who was over-fleshed at the throat so that his head seemed to float above his shoulders.

"Not sure of anything when it comes to the Scarecrow, but we've got ourselves a Hook. Only question is, are any of you pussies man enough to stick it in her?"

Regan patted herself reflexively, feeling for the bone handle of the buffalo skinner poking out of its smooth leather sheaf on one hip, the checkered grip of the holstered P-32 semi-automatic on the other. She could see the Hook, or at least its harpoon cannon mounted between the handlebars of the yellow maned rider's dirt bike. If discharged, the canon fired a miniature magnetised disc designed to home in on her throat, slice flesh and disable her sonic scream.

So the man in brown was its Captain. Regan felt the ghost of something like revulsion. She'd keep him in her sights; it'd be good to see him die. All she had to do was get the rest of the pirates within a ten metre radius then start screaming.

"I'll do the first shift on the harvester." The voice was young, a boy not yet comfortable in his adult skin. A second dirt bike was silenced. She heard footsteps and the scrabble of rubber sole on metal. Vehicles idled in the background. The voices of walking dead men melded. To Regan, the cab of the harvester was hot as hell and airless suddenly. *Now it starts.*

Opening the cab door, he saw her, startlement etched on his face as she slid in the knife… she'd learnt the rough way in the past that it did not pay to negotiate with pirates. He died in her arms like the child he had longed to be. Regan shook the body off.

It took a few minutes for the dead pirate to be missed. Regan knew she had the Captain spooked when he sent his next weakest soldier, a thin girl, all hips and lips with a shock of lemon-coloured hair. She rode in on her quad, a wide-axeled black wasp. Dismounting, she sidled up onto the Harvester and reached for the cab door; Regan kicked it out into her face.

The girl ricocheted back. She fell badly. Regan heard bone snap. Staring up at her, the female pirate's features shrunk in upon themselves. "Scarecrow!" she hollered before swallowing a bullet.

Regan launched herself out of the harvester, tucked in her elbows and sprinted.

First to react were the stilt walkers, gangly and muscular on their clanking, pneumatic metal limbs. They moved towards her in enrapture, like insects siphoning off her juices.

It was the crackle of electricity which made her risk a glance backwards. The stiltwalkers reached for her with long rubber batons tipped with coiled metal. Regan felt the flush of extra adrenalin. Her taser was a toy next to those mothers.

"Run Scarecrow run," teased the tall boys in their hoodies and graffitied board shorts. Regan sprinted harder. Her flight had been intended as a rouse to lure all of the pirates into pursuit. Now the stakes had been upped. On impulse, she slid down as she ran, drew the P-32, used the propulsion to roll onto her back and peeled off a couple of shots. One stiltwalker crumpled, his baton falling onto the earth, rolling, and completing a 360 degree radial before shocking its owner. The other daddy long legs plunged his coil against her arm.

A tight rip of pain shot through her. Regan fought the need to gag. Air flooded between her parted lips, lit up the antechamber of her throat with its chords, flesh and resonator, and she sang then, a string of metal notes designed to ground her. The pain vanished. The stiltwalker stabbed her again with the cry of "Shoot her now, Samson, while she's out!" Her song had also drained his baton of its charge; the stiltwalker used it as a battering ram while kicking out at her with his mechanical legs.

Steam released in great wet bursts. Pistons shunted hard against her face. Amongst the blur of flesh and metal, Regan made out a face. She smashed out with a fist and felt the pull of skin beneath her knuckles. The stiltwalker buckled back. Regan threw aside the now useless P-32; she had needed to return the handgun to its memofibre holster to shield the weapon against her song. Ripping her taser from a sheath inside her leather, she jacked back up onto her feet and lunged at the stiltwalker's face. Spasming, he collapsed to one side as the roar of what Regan knew had to be the choppers dirtied up the morning air.

Her game was off. Only three dead and she was way out in the open. With the rest of the pirates outside of the ten metre radius that she required to unleash the full, lethal capacity of her sonic scream, she was a sitting duck.

Regan squinted at the Captain sitting astride his dirt bike and resting forward, his elbows on the handlebars. Her skin prickled. He was playing with her. But she was on fire with the thrill of the fight. She could deflect their bullets and knives; all she had to do was give a little whistle. Meanwhile, they'd got the Hook, which meant that she would just have to have eyes in the back of her head.

With the choppers circling her like tremendous metal dragonflies, Regan tore her gaze left and right. The men astride the hogs wore tight black leathers, mirrored aviators and tie-dye bandanas, their features indistinguishable. Identical twins, she realised, pondering the best route to take them out. A couple of metres away, her opponents were at too close range to draw, aim and fire the borrowed AK-47 assault rifle from the sling at her back. The P-32 handgun abandoned, Regan wielded the stun baton in one hand, the buffalo skinner in the other. If the hogs' riders tried to take a pop at her, she'd lock up their guns' mechanisms with a single note.

But these riders touted a Sai sword a piece. They also seemed less concerned with bringing her down as baiting her.

"Hey, girlie. Bet she doesn't get many takers with that throat full of metal."

"Going by appearances, I'd say she's a man hater. What do you reckon, Billy? Think the dyke's gonna cry?"

Regan was kneeling down. Utilising the blade as a mirror, she kept the Captain in view. The twin pirates struck her as innately stupid; if she could just sprint past their blades and head for the Captain, she was pretty sure they'd follow, and then she would have the full crew inside the crucial radius.

"I thought Scarecrows were meant to be tough, Billy."

"That's what I heard too, Brad. Whereas this girlie seems sloppy."

"Things aren't always what they seem." Kicking off an icy tree stump that she'd crouched down to disguise, Regan spun herself into a high round house kick, the boot of one foot ricocheting off the left cheekbone of one of the twins. The rider skidded, just managing to right the chopper before he collided with a massive oak. Regan landed, feet splayed, fists tight to her sides, and still clenching her weapons.

The second twin whipped open the throttle of his hog and charged for her. *Beautifully stupid.* Regan took to her heels and ran. With the subterranean pulse of the pursuing choppers at her back, she zigzagged in and out of the branches and brambles at the field's edges. And she could run, Regan reminded herself, feeling the air thick as syrup in her lungs. She'd been running all of her life and she was damn good at it.

Heading for the Harvester and its fresh dead, Regan ducked as one twin drove his Sai at her neck. She didn't want to unseat him, but draw both men back to the killing ground. The incessant swish and stab of the blade was distracting, however; she clucked on a mouthful of air, pursed her lips and threw a slicing note at the pirate's hand. He dropped the Sai as if the double-pronged handle was liquid metal.

She stared hard ahead – the Captain hadn't changed position. Neither had his men. The Baja bug idled. Throaty rumbles spattered from the dune buggy's exhaust. And while the chopper rider who had pursued her closest slowed to a crawl as they returned to the basin of Claw Pond, it was the other twin who was most noticeable by his absence.

Regan glanced over a shoulder. No sign. Then she felt the blade plunge in. In seconds, the hot wetness of her own blood greased the inside of her jacket. An inch to the left and the Sai would have punctured a lung; Regan knew her own physiology like a studied map. She tore her shoulder aside before the pirate had a chance to rip out the sword and retry for her heart. *How'd he got up so close?* She risked a sideways glance. He'd abandoned his chopper for her first victim's dirt bike, its sound a more subtle wheeze of noise that had been lost to the revs of the nearing vehicles.

Too late Regan realised that she had taken her eye off the Captain. She heard a cicada-like whirl of sound before feeling a pure, clean bite of pain as the Hook sliced in. Blood ran from her throat, draining between her breasts, becoming cold at her stomach… Regan faltered as she ran. Through a blur, she saw the Captain unfold from the sight of the harpoon at the rear of his dirt bike. She was just aware of a great gust of noise tumbling towards her, the war cry of human voices and engines.

"Shot you down, Scarecrow! Now let's really hear you scream," she heard the Captain demand.

Regan tried for the rifle at her back, but couldn't rip it from its holster. Craning her jaw in a futile bid to drink in the vital air to sound her scream, Regan tried to rip the Hook out. The disc was slippery with blood; she cut her fingers on its razor edge. Through a film of pale, fading consciousness, she saw the pirates closing in, led by their Captain and with their swords and guns drawn. *Get up and fight,* she screamed internally.

Sound pummelled in her ears like fast flowing water. She reeled. The pulse grew stronger, deep, reverberative and lushly mechanical… Regan's eyes shot wide. A dragon in gleaming black body armour smashed through the metal gate to the right of Claw Pond. Regan felt the transfiguring glow of victory as the Stag crashed head on into the soft meat of the Captain's body and carried him high on its bumper before he ricocheted off and was flayed beneath the wheels. The Stag ripped a path through the beets; Regan fastened her grip hard on the Hook and disgorged it from her throat. She discarded the disc carelessly, like a handful of soil returned to the land, and looked up.

The remaining crop pirates had frozen in mid-stride, their mouths slack, eyes greased and reflecting the figure of the resurrected Scarecrow.

Regan stretched out her arms. Had the girl driven the Stag out of range; Regan imagined that she would have had to crash it, having very little control over the beast of a vehicle and straining to reach the pedals. Her pause was brief. Letting her head fall gently back, feeling the wound at her throat weep, Regan made her voice heard.

Harrison had cleared a good part of the first field by noon. She'd helped him clear away the bodies. The girl she'd found inside the shadowed ribs of one of Harrison's unused hay barns. Having ripped clean through the barn door, the Stag had come to rest against a wall of aged hay bales. The girl was alive, forehead blooded at impact. The Stag was intact bar some new scars to the paintwork.

Having patched up her throat, Regan pocketed the remainder of her payment, refuelled the Stag with a full, complementary tank of bioethanol, and pilfered enough of Harrison's larder to last them to the Scottish border. She paused then, resting a foot against a back wheel of the Stag, arms crossed, and surveyed the beet fields, the hardy leaf set in rows and unobtrusive on the landscape. A subtle ache pulsed in her throat.

Where was the girl? How long did it take to clean up a bruised forehead?

Regan eased away from the Stag. She crossed the yard, stepped up onto the porch of the farmhouse and reached for the pocked steel door when the kid came crashing out.

"Filthy bastard!" snapped the girl. She glanced back at the doorway and the figure of the farmer now filling it. Harrison was nursing a stained cheek where the girl's fist had connected. He breathed in gulps, eyes wary as they settled on Regan.

Stepping backwards, the Scarecrow drew slowly off the porch.

"I told you not to swear. Get in the car."

She listened for the slam of the passenger-seat door.

"It'll be your turn again in five years, Harrison." Her gaze was steady. "Girl will be all grown up then. Her aim gets better all of the time. Time comes we're knocking at your door again, I'd suggest you watch your ass."

She left the farmer behind, his piggy eyes at her back as she slid into the driver seat of the Stag, told the girl to buckle up, revved the engine and pulled off down the dirt track.

~*~

All writers have favourite characters. Regan, the Scarecrow, is one of mine. She was born out of a love for those icon female warriors – Sarah Connor, Ripley, Katniss, Buffy, Lagatha, and their ilk. When writing science fiction, I like to fuse real-life cutting edge technologies with medical innovation. Biomodifications play a huge role in my books and short stories, and Regan was one of the first to lend me her synthesised voice. "The Killing Fields" touches on the repurposing of land in a desolate environment – a theme which permeates my writing. And it features a Triumph Stag!

About the Author

A dark fantasy and science fiction author, Kim Lakin (formerly Lakin-Smith) has a love for all things other, mechanical and macabre. Her novel, *Cyber Circus*, was shortlisted for the British Fantasy Award and the British Science Fiction Association Best Novel Award. Kim's other novels, *Tourniquet* and *Rise*, reflect her horror leanings, with the young adult novel, Autodrome, steeped in steampunk and futurism.

This collection is drawn from the short stories Kim has published in numerous anthologies and magazines over many years, and reflects the author's preference to inhabit that edge between science and the fantastical.

Kim currently lives on a farm in Derbyshire with her cat, Diablo, who mainly ignores her, and two extremely vocal donkeys, who do not.

ALSO FROM NEWCON PRESS

The Wild Hunt – Garry Kilworth

When Gods meddle in the affairs of mortals, it never ends well… for the mortals, at any rate. Steeped in ancient law, history and imagination, Garry Kilworth serves up an epic Anglo-Saxon saga of swordplay, witches, giants, dwarfs, elves and more, as a young warrior wrongly accused of patricide sets out to clear his name and regain his birthright.

The Chinese Time Machine – Ian Watson

A new collection from one of science fictions most inventive writers; a volume released to celebrate the author's 80th birthday. Features ten stories published over the past five years in *Asimov's, Analog*, and elsewhere, plus a new 34,000 word novella that is original to this collection. Ian Watson at his entertaining best.

The Double-Edged Sword – Ian Whates

A disgraced swordsman leaves town one step ahead of justice. His past, however, soon catches up with him in the form of Julia, a notorious thief and sometimes assassin. Thrust into an impossible situation, he embarks on what will surely prove to be a suicide mission. "A cheerfully brutal story of betrayal and skulduggery, vicious fun." – *Adrian Tchaikovsky*

Queen of Clouds – Neil Williamson

Wooden automata, sentient weather, talking cats, compellant inks and a host of vividly realised characters provide the backdrop to this rich dark fantasy. Stranger in the city Billy Braid becomes embroiled in Machiavellian politics and deadly intrigue, as the weather insists on misbehaving, putting the Weathermakers Guild in an untenable position…

How Grim Was My Valley – John Llewellyn Probert

After waking up on the Welsh side of the Severn Bridge with no memory of who he is, a man embarks on an odyssey through Wales, bearing witness to the stories both the people and the land itself feel moved to tell him, all the while getting closer to the truth about himself.

Ingram Content Group UK Ltd.
Milton Keynes UK
UKHW012234150323
418605UK00004B/81